TH

Quinn thought he had taking over the Organ. cake for such a smart guy. But what he didn't figure was that boss Ryder would stuff him in a large crate with enough water and food to sustain him—and ship him around the world. When the freighter ports at the North African town of Okar, the captain of the boat decides its time to unload the box. It's starting to make noises, and it smells bad. What emerges from this wooden coffin looks barely human. But once Quinn recovers, he starts to look around. Is this a new chance at life, or an opportunity to cash in on another racket, halfway around the world?

JOURNEY INTO TERROR

There was a robbery that went bad and a girl was accidentally shot dead. Just an accident. But to John Bunting, it was the end of all his hopes. The girl was his fiancé. What could he do? The cops weren't looking. He had to find the killers himself. And that's when he ran into Linda. She had lost her husband, had stopped caring. But she knew the men responsible for the killing. She could get Bunting close to them while he figured out who fired the actual shot. They were two wounded souls, one filled with hate, the other trying to find a reason to live. It's funny how much they needed each other...

PETER RABE BIBLIOGRAPHY

From Here to Maternity (1955)
Stop This Man! (1955)
Benny Muscles In (1955)
A Shroud for Jesso (1955)
A House in Naples (1956)
Kill the Boss Goodbye (1956)
Dig My Grave Deep (1956)
The Out is Death (1957)*
Agreement to Kill (1957)
It's My Funeral (1957)*
Journey Into Terror (1957)
Mission for Vengeance (1958)
Blood on the Desert (1958)
The Cut of the Whip (1958)*
Bring Me Another Corpse (1959)*
Time Enough to Die (1959)*
Anatomy of a Killer (1960)
My Lovely Executioner (1960)
Murder Me for Nickels (1960)
The Box (1962)
His Neighbor's Wife (1962)

Girl in a Big Brass Bed (1965)**
The Spy Who Was Three Feet Tall
  (1966)**
Code Name Gadget (1967)**
Tobruk (1967)
War of the Dons (1972)
Black Mafia (1974)

As by "Marco Malaponte"
New Man in the House (1963)
Her High-School Lover (1963)

As by "J. T. MacCargo"
Mannix #2:
  A Fine Day for Dying (1975)
Mannix #4: Round Trip to
  Nowhere (1975)

*Daniel Port series
**Manny deWitt series

THE BOX

JOURNEY INTO TERROR

Peter Rabe

Stark House Press • Eureka California

THE BOX / JOURNEY INTO TERROR

Published by Stark House Press
1945 P Street
Eureka, CA 95501, USA
griffins@northcoast.com

Text set in Adobe Garamond. Heads set in Dogma.
Cover design and layout by Mark Shepard, http://shepdesign.home.comcast.net/
Cover art by Campbell Shepard

*The publishers would like to thank Max Gartenberg, Ed Gorman, George Tuttle, Bill Crider,
Donald Westlake and Bill Pronzini for all their help and assistance in bringing this book to life.*

First Stark House Press Edition: December 2003

0 9 8 7 6 5 4 3

Table of Contents

INTRODUCTION
By Ed Gorman and Bill Crider

A number of people, writers and critics alike, feel that Peter Rabe was the best writer produced by the Gold Medal line of paperback books. I'm not sure what "best" means. Most innovative? Most stylish? Most perceptive? If he was the "best," he sure had some mean competition in John D. MacDonald, Charles Williams and Vin Packer, to name just a few.

He told the truest gangster stories, no doubt about that. He knew how the mob worked and how mob people thought. He saw it as one more American success story--albeit a perverse one--the dons, capos and killers not all that much different from their equivalents on Wall Street and Madison Avenue. Profit was everything. Ruthlessness was the order of the day.

Journey Into Terror touches on the edges of all this. It is typical in the desperation of its people--Rabe's people, even his protagonists, suffer constant headaches, upset stomachs, nightmares. What separates them from the creeps is that we usually meet them when they are trying to start new lives for themselves.

The book is atypical of Rabe because it deals less with the externals of life in the mob than with the internals of people who are being ground up daily by its stresses, humiliation and terror. Rabe wrote a number of fine mob books about Daniel Port, a man trying to escape the mob. This is the opposite. Here a man from the outside seeks vengeance from those on the inside. It is the mob that must escape.

Peter's books were just starting to come back into print when he was diagnosed with cancer. He knew he was dying. He sent me three complete unpublished manuscripts, which now reside with my own collection of materials in the Coe College library in Cedar Rapids, Iowa along with other material of Peter's.

At the time of his death, Bill Crider and I wrote farewells in Mystery Scene, which I'm including here.

–Ed Gorman

In the spring, he would come to Cedar Rapids on a train from California. He would stay for three or four days and then he'd head east.

I'm not sure how long we planned this trip. Two years maybe. He talked about it long before he got sick; and with a certain sad desperation once he knew he had lung cancer.

Peter Rabe is not much remembered now, not in America anyway. In Europe he's still regarded as one of the seminal crime writers of his generation, and deservedly so. Along with John D. MacDonald and Charles Williams, he was one of Gold Medal's Holy Trinity. When he was rolling, crime fiction just didn't get much better.

He was equally good as a friend, shy, wry and always just a bit mysterious. I didn't know much about his background until after he died—Russian Jewish father; German mother; raised in both Europe and the United States—or even about his publishing history. He was that most remarkable of creatures, a good listener. He took pains to understand what you were talking about—the nuances, the implications—and then he would give you his somewhat halting but always considered (and considerate) opinion. He almost never laughed but when he did, you felt as if you'd just won over the toughest room you'd ever played.

The night he got copies of his Black Lizard reprints, he called me. He took an almost child-like pride in seeing three of his best books in print once more, even though he spent most of his time telling you how much he wished he could rewrite them. At one point that evening, I told him how much he meant to my generation of crime writers and for the first time ever, I heard tears in his voice.

He died quickly. I hadn't spoken to him for a month and suddenly I learned that he was in the hospital; and then, American doctors giving up on him, he was on his way to a Laetrile clinic in Mexico. We talked several times; he was optimistic; and in fact Mexico seemed to cheer him up. He sounded much better.

But not many days later, I phoned the California hospital where he now resided, and a nurse hesitated when I asked about his condition and said I'd have to speak to another department, and when she said, "Are you a relative of Mr. Rabe's?" I knew, of course, he was dead.

Goodbye, my friend. Your books stand as testimony to the sad and rueful way you saw life, and yet—like you—they shine with hard humor and forgiveness.

I drove pass the train depot the other night and imagined you stepping off an Amtrak at midnight, ghostly in the darkness.

I wish it could have been, Peter. I really do.

–Ed Gorman

Peter Rabe is dead. I suspect that the majority of readers are asking themselves right now, "Who's Peter Rabe?" That's too bad.

Peter Rabe was a damned fine writer of paperback original fiction who began his career in the 1950's. He wrote mostly for Gold Medal, but he didn't have the success of a John D. MacDonald, whose books continue to sell in the millions, or even an Edward S. Aarons, whose Sam Durrell series was so popular that it was continued by another writer after his death. He never even achieved the sort of cult following attained by Jim Thompson. And that's a shame, because many of Rabe's novels rank with the best paperback originals ever published, back in the days when writers like MacDonald and Thompson and Charles Williams were all doing books better and more daring than anything the hardback houses were publishing then. Or now. This isn't to imply that Rabe was "like" any of those other writers. He was no more like them than they are like each other. He was an original.

Rabe wasn't a mystery writer, for the most part. He wrote crime stories that were tough, bitter, real, and powerful. What's more, he wrote them with economy, understatement, and cool precision. Anthony Boucher recognized Rabe's talent early and reviewed many of his books favorably in his "Criminals at Large" column. Gold Medal, publisher of most of Rabe's work, gave him a big push at the beginning and plugged his books hard. Yet with all these things going for them, Rabe's books never really took off. By the mid-sixties he was down to doing a spy-spoof series that ran for three books; in the early seventies, he did a couple of mafia books when GM was trying to capitalize on the success of *The Godfather* in any way that it could. Hardly anyone cared about or remembered the fine books that Rabe had been doing only ten years before, books like *The Box, Kill the Boss Good-by, Benny Muscles In,* or the books in the Daniel Port series.

When he was at his best, Rabe brought to his books an intensity that you could feel in your gut as you read, and he wrote stories that were unlike anything else on the racks. In *Kill the Boss Good-by,* for example, Fell, a crime boss is under treatment for a manic psychosis. He leaves the sanitarium in order to fight off a threat to his organization, and in the course of the book he degenerates into genuine madness—while retaining the sympathy of the reader. It's an incredible book. Pick it up, read the first couple of chapters, and then put it down. Just try. The ending is a kick in the kidneys. Power? Intensity? Rabe's got it all going here. Or read *The Box*. Hell, you won't be able to put this one down after the first page or two. It's the north African town of Okar, and a box is unloaded from a ship. The box stinks, and there are funny noises inside. Let the blurb writer take from there: "Out of the box comes Quinn, a screaming, filthy madman who'd been packed alive in his coffin as punishment for losing out in a gangland feud halfway around the world in New York." What happens after that? Read it and see.

Rabe could be funny, too. In fact, some of his toughest books have moments of off-the-wall humor that are doubly amusing because they're so unexpected. And *Murder Me for Nickels* is a crazy-funny mystery with a first-person narrator, so different from *The Box* that you'd think a different man wrote it, but it's equally fine in its own way.

Peter Rabe's writing career ended twenty-five years ago, though the sad fact is that it was effectively over ten or twelve years before that. The fact that for thirty-five years now Rabe's work has been shamefully neglected by readers and students of crime fiction is sadder still. And Peter Rabe's death in 1990 is a tremendous loss to all of us who cared about the man and his work and to those readers who will come to know that work in the future.

–Bill Crider

Noir and Gestalt: the Life of Peter Rabe

By George Tuttle

G old Medal Books discovered many talented novelists who could write hardboiled fiction, but in 1955, the editors felt that they had found its biggest discovery, Peter Rabe. On the cover of Peter's second novel *Benny Muscles In* (1955), their opinion is expressed: "Not since Dashiell Hammett and Raymond Chandler, who—under the guidance of that great editor, Joe Shaw—established the school of hardboiled fiction, has a writer and a style come to the front with such brilliance and power as Peter Rabe. The editors of Gold Medal can remember nothing like it in the last quarter of a century."

Gold Medal Editor-in-Chief Richard Carroll believed that Peter could be a new giant in the mystery field, a status eventually obtained by fellow Gold Medal writer John D. MacDonald. But unlike MacDonald, Peter never reached that exalted level. Though he had a successful career throughout the 1950's and received high praise from the likes of New York Times critic Anthony Boucher, his success did not carry on into the 1960's. This article will try to explain what happened to Peter Rabe; why one of the most promising writers of the 1950's fell short of fame.

Peter Rabe died on May 20, 1990, of lung cancer, fifteen years after his last novel. In 1967, he felt forced to walk away from professional writing to become an Associate Professor at California Polytechnic State University at San Luis Obispo. Five years later, while still a professor, he returned to Gold Medal with *War of the Dons* (1972), and then after one more book under his own name and two under a pseudonym, he stopped writing crime fiction for publication. Peter loved writing and continued to write for his own amusement, but he quit attempting to sell his fiction.

The novels of Peter Rabe will give you little insight into the man. Unlike some writers whose stories are filled with personal feelings and experiences, Peter always keeps a certain distance from the characters he created, and the stories he told. His thrillers are almost all written in the third person and are not attempts to live vicariously. Instead, these novels are truly the theater of his imagination, and though Peter directs the action, he is not a participant.

An example of the distance that he maintained is revealed in the set-tings he used. He rarely set his novels in places where he lived, at the time, but instead, he preferred to use settings from his past and often used places that he had only known briefly. In *A Shroud for Jesso* (1955) and *A House in Naples* (1956), there is the Europe experienced as a child, updated to contemporary times. In *Stop this Man!* (1955) and *It's My Funeral* (1957), there are scenes from L.A., where he lived for a short time, during the early 1950's, while attempting to establish a career as a practicing psychologist.

Peter's early novels (probably just his first two) were written while liv-ing in Maine. Later, Peter lived in Cleveland and in the scenic town of Provincetown, Massachusetts. By the late 1950's, Peter had moved to Europe. *Bring Me Another Corpse* (1959) was set in Cleveland, but by the time it was written, Peter was probably in Germany receiving treatment for a misdiagnosed terminal illness.

Peter grew up in the Germany of the 1920's and 1930's. His father Michael Rabinovich (Rabinowitsch, the German spelling) was a Russian Jew, who had immigrated into Germany so that he could study medicine. After attending the University of Strasburgh and being interned as an enemy alien during World War I, Michael moved to Halle where he enrolled in the Martin Luther University. There he met a secretary who worked in one of the departments, Elisabeth Margarete Beer. They were married in Halle in January of 1921. Peter was born November 3, 1921. A few months later, they moved to Hanover, in Northern Germany, where Michael set up a practice as a physician and surgeon. Two more sons, Valentin and Andreas, would follow about a decade later.

As a child, Peter learned to live with intolerance, even though he was only Jewish on his father's side (his mother's family was Lutheran.) One memory he shared, years later, with his daughter Jennifer was an outing in which he participated with a group of boys. At one point, during their hike through the countryside, they had to ask a local property owner for permission to cross his field. In response to their request, the man looked at the crowd of boys, pointed his finger at Peter, and said, "All of you can cross but him. Not the Jew."

As the Nazi movement grew, it became apparent to Peter's father, Michael, that it was no longer safe for his family to stay in Germany. One day, he was ordered to appear at the Gestapo office and was confronted with a huge file of transcripts of conversations he had had in his office with patients on politics. It wasn't long after this that, in October 1938, Michael and Peter, who was nearly the age for military service (or possible internment) immigrated to the United States, first settling in Detroit. Michael's brother, Robert Rubin, sponsored them. Peter and Michael stayed with the Rubin family while Michael took a course in obstetrics in Chicago and got his license to practice medicine. He later located a village named New Bremen that was settled by Germans and needed a doctor to replace a retiring one. Michael bought his office and telegraphed Peter's mother to come to America. Peter's uncle, Robert Rubin, who had changed his family name, recommended to Michael that he do the same. The family name was changed from Rabinovich to Rabe ("RA" from Rabinowitsch and "BE" from Margarete's maiden name); hence Peter Rabinowitsch became Peter Rabe.

Peter, who could speak English before he came to the United States, adjusted quickly and soon enrolled into Ohio State University and received his bachelor's degree. After a stint in the Army, he attended Western Reserve in Cleveland, where he got his Masters and Ph.D. in psychology and worked as an instructor. It was while he was at Western Reserve that he met and fell in love with Claire Frederickson. She was five years younger than Peter, but like him, she was also a psychology major and she and her family had fled Europe to escape the Nazis.

An important fact about Claire is that she had a passionate interest in literature. She would sit in on the meetings that the graduate English majors held in the University's cafeteria. It was during these sessions that Claire became friends with Max Gartenberg. Claire introduced Peter to Max, a man who would later become a fundamental part of Peter's writing career.

Peter and Claire's relationship led to marriage, and after they'd finished their studies at Western Reserve, the couple moved to Bar Harbor, Maine, where Peter had received a post graduate grant from the National Institute of Mental Health and worked for Claire's brother, Emil Frederickson, at the Jackson Memorial Laboratory. Peter admired Emil and felt that Claire's brother was brilliant.

Despite his respect for Emil, he grew to dislike the work, which consisted of psychological experiments on animals. These experiments went against Peter's love of nature and respect for animal life. The research resulted in two papers: "Experimental Demonstration of the Cumulative Frustration Effect in C3H Mice"(The Journal of Genetic Psychology, 1951, 79, p163-172) and "The Cumulative Frustration Effect in the Audio-Genic Seizure Syndrome of DBA Mice"(The Journal of Genetic Psychology, 1952, 81, p3-17).

When the project was finished Peter and Claire traveled to Los Angeles where Peter set up a practice as a therapist. He quickly discovered that the market for therapist in Los Angeles was sewed up by those receiving referrals from established psychiatrists. By August 1952, the Rabes returned to Cleveland, Ohio, where Peter eventual found work at a factory, but was soon elevated from a blue-collar job to writing copy, doing layouts and illustrating for ads. Around this time, Claire became pregnant. She gave birth to their first child, Jonathan, on April 5, 1953. This experience was the basis of Peter's first book, a book totally unlike the novels to come. This work was a humorous narrative, illustrated by Peter, about the trials and tribulations of childbirth.

Peter submitted the manuscript to an agent, who tried unsuccessfully to sell it, telling Peter it was not marketable. Peter was still unwilling to give up on the story, and since the agent had tried only book publishers, Peter decided to submit it to McCall's magazine. After waiting two months, he called McCall's and was told that they were enchanted with the story and planned to publish it.

The story appeared under the title "Who's Having This Baby?" in the September 1954 issue. After its appearance, Peter was contacted by Vanguard Press, who wanted to publish it as a book. To work out the contract, Vanguard recommended that he get an agent. So he contacted the agent he had used previously, the one who couldn't sell it, originally. The story was finally published in book form by Vanguard, in 1955, under the new title *From Here to Maternity*.

As all of this is happening, Peter happened to have a completed novel called *The Ticker*. It is the story of Tony Catell who steals a radioactive ingot of gold and is unaware of the deadly nature of his actions. Tony travels to sell the ingot and starts a cross-country manhunt. Of all of Peter's books, this one is more of a traditional thriller, rather than noir. The story has a hero, Jack Herron, and a clear, distinct resolution. It isn't an anti-hero story like many of his later works.

He showed the manuscript to his agent, who told him that she didn't handle those types of books, what the publishing trade called "blood 'n' guts" stories. So once again, Peter was on his own. He submitted the book to Gold Medal.

Meanwhile, Claire had heard that her old friend Max Gartenberg had formed his own literary agency. Since Peter would eventually need representation, she went to New York to see Max and ask him if he'd be interested in checking on the status of *The Ticker* and handling Peter's next book, *The Hook*. Max said, "Yes."

Max happened to have a friend at Gold Medal, an editor named Hal Cantor. He contacted Hal and was informed that Gold Medal was delighted with *The Ticker* and wanted to do more books by Peter. So Max offered them *The Hook*. Peter's career was off with a bang.

Gold Medal's excitement over Peter's work led Gold Medal's Editor-in-Chief Richard Carroll to look for a way to give this new author a big send-off. Carroll decided on getting an endorsement from Erskine Caldwell, one of the biggest selling authors in the history of publishing, and sent the galleys, with an endorsement fee to Caldwell's agent. But since Caldwell didn't have time to read the book and the agent didn't want to turn down the fee, his agent endorsed the book for Caldwell, with the words' "I couldn't put this book down!"

The Ticker was released August 1955, under the title *Stop this Man!* When Peter visited the offices of Fawcett after the publication, he asked Carroll if he could have Caldwell's address so he could thank the famed author. In response, Carroll said, after a long pause, "Peter, do you know why Erskine Caldwell said,'I couldn't put this book down?' It's because he never picked it up."

The humor of the situation wasn't lost on Peter, who took the incident in stride. Endorsements were all part of how paperback originals were marketed. Peter accepted this and didn't resent Gold Medal for doing what it felt necessary to promote a book. Likewise, he took it in stride when Gold Medal changed the titles of his novels -- when *The Ticker* became *Stop This Man!*, and when his next novel *The Hook* became *Benny Muscles In.*

Title changes were a standard operating procedure for Gold Medal. They saw a book's cover as the chief means of advertising a paperback and reserved in the contract the right to change the title to something more marketable. All of Peter's early novels had their titles changed. The only exceptions were *A House in Naples* and *The Box* (1962), though in the case of *A House in Naples*, the title was actually suggested by Max Gartenberg, Peter's agent.

Even though he didn't care much for the titles chosen (most were too crass for his tastes), he didn't let this color the fact that he liked writing for Gold Medal. He was intrigued with the type of situations dealt with in crime fiction. He liked the directness in which the characters reacted to one another and how the situations unfolded. These stories came easily to him and were well received by Editor-in-Chief Richard Carroll, who was very enthusiastic about Peter's work.

To write a novel, Peter would start with an outline. Using a clipboard and unlined yellow paper, he would write down the basic events that made up the plot. Once the outline was finished, he would work at the type-writer with the clipboard next to him, creating the story as he typed. He typed quickly and would only occasionally pause to light a cigarette, take a drag, and place it in the ashtray where it was usually allowed to burn out. He composed his novels directly on the typewriter, typing quickly and rarely rereading what he wrote.

During the mid-1950's, Peter's life changed for the better. His writing career took off, and he bought a summer cottage on Commercial Street in Provincetown, Massachusetts, a scenic town on the tip of Cape Cod. His family grew. A second child, Julia, was born on March 6, 1955, and later, another daughter, Jennifer(November 22, 1957).

In 1958, the success in publishing continued, but a complication developed. Peter started having health problems due to a stomach tumor. By July 1958, he received a report from a specialist in Boston recommending a gastric resection. After the procedure, a suspicious spot was biopsied and diagnosed as cancerous, and he was told that his condition was terminal.

As a result of the surgery, Peter lost weight and looked close to death. Peter's father made arrangements with the Ringberg Clinic, which specialized in alternative treatments for cancer. The clinic sits along Lake Tegernsee in Bavaria, Germany, and was run by Dr. Josef Issels. Peter moved his family to Taormina, Sicily, while he relocated to Germany. (Claire had no desire to revisit memories of Nazi Germany.) So Peter and Claire separated. While his family stayed in Sicily, Peter received treatment in Germany, hoping for the best, but preparing himself for the worst.

Soon after this happened, a second event occurred that would severely damage the writing career. Richard Carroll stepped down as Editor-in-Chief at Gold Medal Books, due to his own health problems. He eventually died on March 11, 1959. Carroll was one of Rabe's biggest fans. He thought Rabe could become a major writer of hardboiled thrillers, and Rabe might have if Carroll had lived. It's rare that a writer can find an editor who is truly willing to work with him. Carroll was that type of editor. He would let Peter know precisely how he felt about a novel. If a story had a weakness, Carroll would let Peter know where it fell short. In a 1991 interview (published Paperback Parade, issue 25) Peter described Carroll as "a very incisive and swift person, but he was open to dialogue. There was nothing particularly dictatorial about him. He was very explicit about what he didn't like, so I liked working with him."

Peter's health had no immediate effect on his writing. Carroll's departure did. Knox Burger, who had been in charge of Dell's First Edition line, eventually replaced Carroll at Gold Medal. Since Knox had no previous ties to Gold Medal, he tended to favor writers he knew while working at Dell, authors like Donald Hamilton and James Atlee Phillips. This made things tougher for most of the old regulars, Peter included. Though Rabe sold several novels to Gold Medal while Burger was in charge, he didn't have the close relationship with Burger that he had with Carroll. Burger did think highly of Peter. Peter was one of the few writers from the Carroll era that Burger respected. He later describes Rabe, in a 1992 interview for Mystery Scene (appearing in issue 34) as one of "two or three very good writers I thought had been sort of mishandled by the previous regime." Burger seemed to think that all the writers under the previous regime were either hacks or mishandled. Burger's attitude did not mellow, over the years, particularly when paperback collectors and fans would ask him questions about David Goodis, Wade Miller, Lionel White, Bruno Fischer, and other writer associated with the Carroll years and would neglect to ask questions about Burger's pet writers.

Meanwhile in Europe, Peter's health improved. The reason for the improvement was uncovered when his father Michael double-checked Peter's test results and found a major blunder. The results of Peter's biopsy had been switched with that of another patient. Peter's biopsy was cancer free. Michael telegraphed, Peter the news. Soon after receiving the telegram, Peter left Germany, in July 1959, and returned to Sicily.

The separation and the emotional strain of this whole episode had severely damaged Peter and Claire's marriage. The whole series of events that brought them to Europe were not easy for either to handle. The fact that much that had happened was needless didn't help the situation.

In an attempt to salvage the marriage, Peter and Claire left Sicily and moved the family to Torremolinos, Spain, in the hope that the change in environment would help. It didn't. After about six months, Peter left for the United States, while Claire and the children stayed in Spain. Some time later, after attempts at reconciliation failed, they divorced.

Peter returned to America a different man. Many things had happened to change his outlook on life. First there was the illness that had been diagnosed as fatal, then the discovery that it was all a mistake, and finally, the split in his marriage and separation from his family. The man who returned to America in the early 1960's was not the same man who left, and it showed in his writing. In the sixties, Peter's style became less direct and more ambiguous. His sentences no longer had the crisp, simple clarity of his early writing. Peter explained the change in the 1991 Paperback Parade interview, stating that he had gone through "some very deep disturbances. Out of those disturbances emerged a man who no longer felt like writing that sort of thing."

As his writing style changed, so did the book publishing market, and unfortunately, it didn't change in his direction. The bottom dropped out of the paperback original market and a number of companies died or cut back on originals. Though Gold Medal stayed prosperous with a number of successful series like Shell Scott, Matt Helm, and Travis McGee, it found itself less interested in noir fiction. From 1961 to 1964, Gold Medal published only one new Peter Rabe novel unlike the previous four years when it published ten.

That one novel, *The Box* (1962) is a story about a man who crosses a crime boss and is punished by being packed alive in a box and shipped around the world. Max Gartenberg, who had heard of a similar incident from his cousin, a lawyer, gave the idea to Peter. It was one of his finest novels, clear evidence that his talent had not died.

In an attempt to weather this lean period, Peter started selling to Beacon, a paperback house that specialized in sexually suggestive literature. Beacon's trademark was a lighthouse and probably the greatest example of the use of a sexually subliminal image to market a product. Many paperback original writers who fell on tough times during the sixties, sold to Beacon, Harry Whittington, Ovid Demaris, Michael Avallone, and Robert Turner to name some. It wasn't a high paying market like Gold Medal, but it was a paying market. At the time, Peter needed money.

The first book Peter wrote for Beacon was *His Neighbor's Wife* (1962). It's a good work of noir in the tradition of some of his best Gold Medal work, but it is unlikely that Beacon was completely happy with it. The problem with the book from Beacon's point of view is that it's centered on a criminal conflict, not a sexual conflict. Since they specialized in sexual-oriented fiction, it's doubtful they would have been happy with this novel. The book focuses on a hit-and-run accident and the psychological effects of the accident on the driver Martin Trevor and the passengers, his wife and another couple. Though the book has its share of sex, the sex is only a sub-plot, and hardly transforms the novel into the wife-swapping romp that the cover blurb promises. *His Neighbor's Wife* is a good book, but it's wasted on a publisher not interested in a psychological crime thriller.

Peter's next two novels for Beacon were more tailored to their need. *Her High-School Lover* (1963) and *New Man in the House* (1963) are the type of erotic thrillers Beacon is associated with, but not the type of book that Peter had interest in writing. Though not a prude, he had no desire to write novels based solely on sex. Peter was not proud of these efforts, and published them under the penname Marco Malaponte.

As Peter was trying to get his writing career back in order, he also tried to piece together his personal life. He met and fell in love with a blond Scandinavian beauty named Kristen, nicknamed Kiki, and they married. But the marriage lasted about as long as Peter's relationship with Beacon. They lived awhile in Spain, where Peter could be close to his children, and then moved to California where Peter and Kiki divorced. Little came of the brief relationship, though while Peter was in Spain, he developed a friendship with writer Lorenzo Semple, Jr., who would later join Peter in California, where they both tried to find work writing for television.

Television seemed to be the logical next step, since the paperback original market was suffering due to television. And though there was initial optimism, the optimism was quickly crushed. By June 1962, Peter writes in a letter from L.A. that out of ten TV script outlines he's sent out, only one has been rejected. The rest were all still under consideration including one for Hitchcock they'd asked he write based on one of his books. He also had a script accepted by the producer of the "Alcoa Hour." But later, both, the Hitchcock and Alcoa projects, were rejected by the sponsors. Interest followed by rejection characterizes Peter's career in television.

Around this time, Claire Rabe wrote a book called *Sicily Enough* (1963). The book was published in Paris, by Olympia Press. This short novel was later anthologized in The Best of Olympia (1966) and became a minor classic, receiving praise from authors Henry Miller and Thomas Sanchez. It was later reprinted with a collection of short stories by Claire, under the title *Sicily Enough and More* (1989). Claire is a totally different type of writer from Peter. While Peter preferred to maintain a distance from his creations, Claire's fiction has an autobiographical quality. The feelings and experience of the protagonists are intertwined with the author's, to the point that it's difficult to separate them. *Sicily Enough*, which is about a woman stranded in Taormina, Sicily, with her three children, mirrors many of Claire's experiences during her time in Taormina. It is interesting how Peter and Claire, who were so close, wrote fiction that is so radically different.

Throughout the Sixties, Peter continued to struggle. He roomed together for a short period with Lorenzo Semple, Jr. It was Semple who got the first big break when he landed the job of head writer on the *Bat-*

man TV series. As a result of this break, Semple was able to send work in Peter's direction and Peter penned the episodes: "The Joker's Last Laugh" and "The Joker's Epitaph." Peter did other writing for *Batman*, but it was not used because of a format change in the series, the addition of Batgirl to the cast. Though Peter did other television work, the *Batman* episodes were the extent of his screen credits.

Peter moved regularly during this time, living in Anaheim, Hollywood, and Laguna Beach. He would occasionally take trips away from the West Coast. One trip was to Provincetown, and showed in an ironic way, that his readers had not been forgotten him. Peter's old home had sold, and he had come east to remove his things, and transport the bigger items, temporarily, to a friend's home, outside New York City. Unbeknownst to Peter, there had been a string of robberies of summer places on the Cape, and the police had a description of the car, a model that resembled Peter's. Peter finished what he had to do late on a weekend night, packed the back seat full of paintings, lamps, and other furnishings, and started out for New York. On the way, he was pulled over by a small town cop, who spotted the suspicious car full of what looked like loot, and Peter ended up in jail. Peter tried to reason with the officer, but the cop, who was also the jailer, kept stating that nothing could be done until the Justice appeared Monday morning. Eventually, the cop realized that he had read several of Peter's books and asked him to autograph one of them -- but still the law was the law, and the officer had to keep Peter in the tank until Monday.

While Peter was trying to break into television, he continued to write novels. He created the Manny deWitt series for Gold Medal and wrote a novelization for the movie "Tobruk." To make ends meet, he also delivered newspapers, drove a taxi and did other odd jobs.

In 1967, Peter married Barbara Renard, whom he had known back at Western Reserve University and had met again while in Hollywood. As a result of Barbara's insistence and the need for a steady income, he quit professional writing and reluctantly returned to the field of psychology. He obtained a teaching job at

California Polytechnic State University at San Luis Obispo. They eventually bought a home in nearby Atascadero, California. Had it not been for Barbara, Peter might have stayed in writing and maybe roughed it out through the Sixties. As it was, teaching gave him financial security and a chance to be a father to his three children.

In the late 1960's, a little remembered actor/director, Peter Savage, bought the rights to *A House in Naples* and with producer Joe Justman, made a movie. The movie "A House in Naples" starred Pete Savage and his friend, boxer Jake LaMotta and was filmed in Italy. It had a limited release in 1969. Peter's agent Max Gartenberg, who saw the movie at a special screening, described it as awful, and said, "The negative is probably in somebody's warehouse, rotting away, which is the fate it deserves." At the time, the movie must have seemed like a disappointing final note to a once promising career.

Peter grew to love his work as a teacher. He renewed his interest in psychology and established a reputation as a respected Gestalt psychotherapist. But then his marriage with Barbara fell apart, and he gave writing another shot. The opportunity to be published presented itself when Knox Burger left Gold Medal and Walter Fultz took over. Walter provide a friendlier atmosphere for the old Gold Medal regulars of the 1950's and published Lionel White, Robert Colby, and others who had been frozen out when Burger took the helm. The result of this effort was entitled *War of the Dons* (1972) and became one of Peter's biggest sellers. It capitalized on the interest created by Mario Puzo's *The Godfather*. Rabe followed with another organized crime novel, *Black Mafia* (1974), a book in the tradition of his early gangster novels, like *Benny Muscles In*. In *Black Mafia*, an individual operator, a black man named Cutter, attempts to challenge the authority of the crime bosses. It's very much like the noir novels that first established Peter's reputation and was a fitting end to his relationship with Gold Medal, an end that was foreshadowed by the death of Walter Fultz and the hiring of a new editor.

Peter's last mass-market project was for the paperback house Belmont Tower. He wrote two novelizations based on scripts from the TV series *Mannix*. Both were published in 1975, under the penname J.T. MacCargo. Then Peter left professional writing, this time willingly. Things had changed in twenty years. There was still no one to replace Gold Medal's Richard Carroll, a man whose enthusiasm was an added incentive to stay in the business. Also, teaching was a much more stable profession than writing and a job where there were no concerns about changing markets or adapting to the individual taste of a particular editor, nor writing novelizations while waiting for markets to open up. Though he still wrote fiction throughout the Seventies and Eighties, he just no longer concerned himself with publication. He wrote for his own amusement.

As Peter made the transition from noir to gestalt, his life became more settled. As a professor of psychology, he had a greater control over his destiny. In 1971, he met Chris Neilson, a psychology student. Once again he fell in love, but this time he didn't jinx the relationship with marriage. Chris moved into his Atascadero home where they lived together until his death.

Still noir didn't abandon him. The dark images of Tom Fell (*Kill the Boss Good-By*), Daniel Port (*Dig My Grave Deep*), Jack St. Louis (*Murder Me for Nickels*) and anti-heroes of the earlier Rabe returned. During the late Seventies and throughout the Eighties, a following grew in both Europe and America for the old Gold Medal crime fiction and for Peter Rabe. In 1988, Black Lizard Books started reprinting Peter's books. He was surprised and flattered by this interest and deeply touched that he hadn't been forgotten as a novelist.

Peter career in noir was short. It started in 1955, soaring, only to crash and burn in the Sixties and then briefly resurrect itself in the early Seventies. When asked in the 1991 Paperback Parade interview, "Do you think if Carroll had lived longer that you would have stayed in the writing profession?"

Rabe answered: "I feel very sure that I would have become a better writer, a more consequential storyteller and may well have stayed in longer."

Possibly, if Carroll had lived into the next decade, Rabe would have made the transition from noir to a fiction style more marketable during the 1960's. Maybe, Daniel Port wouldn't have retired in Mexico or Rabe might have developed a series based *Blood on the Desert* instead of creating the character of Manny deWitt. As it was, Peter Rabe did have a good life with Chris Neilson in Atascadero.

The Box

BY PETER RABE

Chapter 1

This is a pink and gray town which sits very small on the North edge of Africa. The coast is bone white and the sirocco comes through any time it wants to blow through. The town is dry with heat and sand.

The sirocco changes its character later, once it has crossed the Mediterranean, so that in Sicily, for example, the wind is much slower, much more moist and depressing. But over Okar it is still a very sharp wind. It does not blow all the time but it is always expected, fierce with heat and very gritty. The sand bites and the heat bites, and on one side the desert stops the town and on the other the sea shines like metal.

None of this harshness has made the inhabitants fierce. Some things you don't fight. There are the Arabs there and there are the French. Once, briefly, there were the Germans, the Italians and the English, and a few of these remained. The people move slowly or quietly, sometimes moving only their eyes. This looks like a cautious, subdued way of living, and it is. Anything else would be waste.

There were not so long ago five in Okar who moved differently, perhaps because they forgot where they were, or maybe they could not help what happened; none of them is there any more. They were Remal, the mayor, who also did other things, and Bea, who did nothing much because she was waiting, and Whitfield, who was done waiting for anything, and Turk, who was so greedy he couldn't possibly have made it. And Quinn, of course. Put simply, he came and went. But that's leaving out almost everything....

"You got me out of my bath, you know," said the clerk.

"Mister Whitfield," said the captain, "this is your pier."

"Because of this bleedin' box you got me out of my bath."

"Mister Whitfield. I'm tied up at your company's pier, and in order to lower the box I need your permission."

"If Okar isn't the destination, why lower your box? And during siesta," the clerk sighed.

"I'm sorry I interrupted your sleep."

"I take a bath during siesta," said the clerk. He did not seem angry or irritated, but he was interested in making his point. It reminded him of the bath and he smiled at the captain, or rather, he smiled just past his left ear.

The captain thought that the clerk did look very clean—Englishman-clean—and he thought that he smelled of gin. Take an Englishman and give him a job where the sun is very hot and he soon begins to smell of gin. Perhaps this one, for siesta, bathes in gin.

The captain squinted up at his ship which showed big and black against the sun, much bigger than the tramper actually was, because the pier was so low.

"The winch man dropped a crate on the box down in the hold," said the captain, "and something cracked."

"I can understand that," said the clerk because he felt he should say something.

He looked at the captain and how the man sweated. How he sweats. Why doesn't he shave off that beard? Siesta time and I must worry about his cracked box. Such a beard in this heat. Perhaps a Viking complex or something.

"So the crew in the hold," said the captain, "two of the crew down there, they went and took a look and next they came out running and scream-ing. Uh—about something bad," said the captain and looked the length of the empty pier.

The empty pier was white in the sun and much easier to look at for the moment than anything else, such as the clerk, for example, and his patient face. And why doesn't he sweat—?

"Eh?" said the clerk.

"And they described a smell. A bad smell."

The captain looked back at the clerk and went rasp, rasp in his throat, a sound to go with the beard.

"Now, you understand, don't you, Whitfield, I can't have something like that down there in my hold."

"You're Swedish," said the clerk.

This sounds like nonsense, thought the captain, all of this, including Whitfield's unconnected remark, because of the heat. Otherwise, every-thing would make sense. He made his throat rumble again, out through the beard, and thought a Swedish curse.

"Is your crew Swedish, too?" asked the clerk.

"Those two from the hold, they are Congolese."

"And they described a strange smell. And perhaps a strange glow? You know, something wavering with a glow in the dark, eh?"

"Goddamn this heat," said the captain. "Don't talk nonsense, Whitfield."

"I?"

"Whitfield..."

"Captain. You know how ghost-ridden they are, those Congolese. Very superstitious, actually."

"Whitfield," said the captain. "I understand you want to get back to sleep. I understand..."

"I take a bath during siesta."

"I also understand about that, Whitfield, and that this is an annoyance to you, to come out here and sweat on the pier."

"I'm not sweating," said the clerk. His blond hair was dry, his light skin was dry, and the gin smile on his face made him look like an elderly boy. "However," he said, "I wish you would take your box to destination. It would save us so much paperwork." Then he thought of something else. "And I'm sure the smell doesn't reach topside and nobody lives in the hold anyway."

The captain looked way up at the sky, though the brightness up there hurt his eyes. Then he jerked his face at the clerk and started yelling with both eyes closed.

"I must look at the box and repair the box! I can't repair on deck because of the freight lashed down there! All I request..."

"Heavens," said the clerk, "how big is this box?"

"Like a telephone booth. No. Bigger. Like two."

"Jet engine," said the clerk. "I've seen those crates when the company had me in Egypt."

"They—don't—stink!" yelled the captain.

"Of course. Or glow in the dark."

But the clerk saw now how the siesta was being wasted. With the gin wearing off on him under the heavy sun he got a feeling of waste and uselessness, always there when the gin wore off; when this happened he would take the other way he knew for combating these feelings, these really cosmic ones, in his experience, and he became indifferent.

"Very well," he said. "Lower away, if you wish. Gently," and with the last word he again and for a moment found his own dreaminess back. He smiled at nothing past the captain's left ear, and then up at the ship where a box would soon be swinging over. For a moment, inconsequentially, he thought of a childhood time in a London mews; it was so clear and still, and he saw himself walking there, eyes up and watching his green balloon. How it floated.

All this went by when the captain roared suddenly, giving the clerk a start of fright and alertness. Someone roared back from the high deck of the tramper and then the winch started screeching.

"What was it this time?" said the clerk.

"The papers," said the captain. "We need a bill of lading and so forth. Someone will bring them."

"Ah," said the clerk. "I should think so."

The winch started up again but because of the strain on it the sound was now different. It mostly hummed. From the pier they could see the black line of the gunwale above, and the boom over the hold, the boom holding very still while the humming went on. The clerk, for no reason at all, felt suddenly hot.

"I'll be glad," said the captain, "to weigh anchor tonight."

"Of course."

"Load, unload, go. Nothing else here."

"In Okar?" said the clerk, feeling absent-minded.

"What else is here?"

"I don't know," said the clerk. "I don't even know what is here."

It's the heat, thought the captain, which makes everything sound like nonsense, and when a seaman came off the ship, bringing a clipboard with papers, the captain grabbed for it as he might for the coattails of fleeing sanity.

"Where did you load this thing?" asked the clerk.

"New York." The captain kept flipping papers. "And your route?"

"Tel Aviv, Alexandria, Madagascar, New York."

"Find the destination of your thing yet?" The clerk looked up at the sky where the boom was, swaying a little now and all stiff and black against the white sky. Then the box showed.

"Just a minute," said the captain and licked his finger. The box also looked black, because of the white sky. It was very large, and swayed.

"Where to?" the clerk asked again.

"New York. Un—"

The boom swung around now and the black load hung over the pier.

"New York is port of origin," said the clerk. "You mentioned that earlier."

"Just a minute—"

When the box was lowered the winch made a different sound once again, a give and then hold sound, a give then hold, a sagging feeling inside the intestines, thought the clerk as he watched the box come down. It grew bigger.

"New York," said the captain.

"My dear captain. All I've asked..."

"Destination New York!" said the captain. "Here. Look at it!"

The clerk looked and said, "Queer, isn't it. Port of origin, New York. Destination, New York."

They both looked up at the box which swung very slowly.

"What's in it?" asked the clerk.

"What's in it. One moment now. Ah: PERISHABLES. NOTE: IMPERATIVE, KEEP VENTILATED."

The clerk made a sound in his throat, somewhat like the captain's rumble, though it did not rumble when the clerk made the sound but was more like a polite knock on a private door.

"That's a very queer entry, captain. They do have regulations over there, you know, about proper entries."

The captain did not answer and kept riffling the papers. The box was low now and really big. It no longer looked black, being away from the sky, but quite stained.

"And you know something else?" said the captain and suddenly slapped his hand on the clipboard. "There's no customs notation here anywhere!"

Now the winchman above kept watching the seaman who stood on the pier. The seaman made slow signals with wrists and hands to show when the box would set down. He is an artist, thought the clerk, watching the seaman. Sometimes he only uses his fingers.

There were also two dark-looking Arabs who stood on the pier and waited. One held a crowbar, resting the thing like a lance. The other one had an axe.

The box touched, not too gently, but well enough. It just creaked once. A pine box, large and sturdy, with legends on the outside to show which side should be up. The side panels, close to the top, had slits. The top panel was crashed down at one end.

"It does smell, doesn't it?" said the clerk.

"Christus—" said the captain.

The seaman by the box undid the hook from the lashing, fumbling with haste because he was holding his breath. When the hook swung free the seaman ran away from the box.

"Look at those Arabs," said the clerk. "Standing there and not moving a muscle."

"And in the lee of that thing yet," said the captain.

Then the hook went up and the winch made its high sound. No one really wanted to move. The clerk felt the heat very much and the bareness of everything; he thought that the box looked very ugly. Siesta gone for that ugly box. It doesn't even belong here. That thing belongs nowhere. Like the winch sound, the screech of it, which doesn't belong in siesta silence.

Both Arabs, at that moment, gave a start.

"What?" said the captain.

The winch stopped because the hook was all the way up. The boom swung back but that made no sound.

"What?" said the captain again. He sounded angry. "What was that?"

But the Arabs did not answer. They looked at each other and then they shrugged. One of them grinned and rubbed his hand up and down on the crowbar.

"Goddamn this heat," said the captain.

"Sirocco coming," said the clerk.

They stood a moment longer while the captain said again that he had to be out of here by this night, but mostly there was the silence of heat everywhere on the pier. And whatever spoiled in the box there, spoiled a little bit more.

"Open it!" said the captain.

Chapter 2

Some of the crew did not care one way or the other, but a lot of them were on the bridge of the tramper, because from the port end of the bridge they had the best view of the pier. They could almost look straight down into the box, once it would be open.

The captain stayed where he was and the clerk stayed with him, away from the box. Just the two Arabs went near it now because they were to open it and did not seem to mind anything. The seaman who had thrown the lashings off the hook was now back by the warehouse wall where he smoked a cigarette with sharp little drags.

"They're ruining it, including the good parts of the box," said the captain.

"You wanted it open," said the clerk.

The Arabs had to cut the bands first, which they did with the axe. Then they used the axe and the crowbar to pry up the top, which took time.

"Well—" said the captain.

"Let it air out a moment," said the clerk.

They waited and watched the two Arabs drop the lid to the ground and then watched them looking into the box. They just looked and when they straightened up they looked at each other. One of them shrugged and the other one giggled.

Up on the bridge the men leaned but said nothing. Perhaps they could not see well enough or perhaps they could not understand.

"All right," said the captain and he and the clerk walked to the box.

I am probably, thought the clerk, the least interested of all. Why am I walking to somebody else's box? I am less interested than the Arabs, even, because they get paid for this. I get no more whether I look or don't look, which is the source of all disinterest, he considered, because nothing comes of it.

He and the captain looked into the box at the same time, seeing well enough, saying nothing, because they did not understand anything there.

"Shoes?" said the clerk after a moment. "You see the shoes?" as if nothing on earth could be more puzzling.

"Why shoes on?" said the captain, sounding stupid. What was spoiling there spoiled for one moment more, shrunk together in all that rottenness, and then must have hit bottom.

The box shook with the scramble inside, with the cramp muscled pain, with the white sun like steel hitting into the eyes there so they screwed up like sphincters, and then the man inside screamed himself out of his box.

He leaped up blind, hands out or claws out, he leaped up in a foam of stink and screams, no matter what next but up—

It happened he touched the clerk first. The clerk was slow with disinterest. And when the man touched he found a great deal of final strength and with his hands clamped around the clerk's neck got dragged out of the box because the clerk was dragging and the captain tried to help drag the clerk free. Before this man from the box let go they had to hit him twice on the back of the head with the wooden axe handle.

"I need a bath," said the clerk.

"Do you have any gin at home?" asked the captain. "I thought perhaps if you had any gin at home..."

"Yes, yes," said the clerk, "come along. You have the gin while I have the bath." They walked down the main street of Okar which was simply called *la rue*, because the official Arab name was impossible for most of the Europeans and the European names of the street had changed much too often.

"That isn't much of a hospital you have there," said the captain.

"The Italians built it. For the ministry of colonial archives."

"They were hardly here long enough."

"Look at the hotel," said the clerk.

They looked at the hotel while they kept walking along the middle of the main street. They could not use the sidewalk which was sometimes no more than a curb. When it was not just a curb there would be chairs and tables which belonged to a coffee house, or stalls with fly-black meat where the butcher was, or perhaps lumber because a carpenter worked on the ground floor. It was that kind of a main street, not very long, and the hotel was the biggest building and even had thin little trees in front.

"It reminds me of Greece," said the captain. "I don't mean really Greek, but I can't think of anything closer."

"The Germans built it, and they were here less time than the Italians."

"In America," said the captain, "it would be a bank."

"It was *a Kaserne*. You know, garrison quarters, or something like that."

They talked like that until they came to Whitfield's house, because they did not quite know what to say about the other matter. The clerk showed the way up a side street, through an arch in a house where a breeze was blowing, across the courtyard in back, and to the house behind that.

"The French built it," he said. "They were here the longest."

"The Arabs didn't build anything?"

"There are native quarters," said Whitfield, with his tone just a little bit as if these were still Empire days.

His two rooms were on the second floor and there was even a balcony. The captain looked at the balcony while the clerk yelled down the stairs for his Arab to bring two buckets of water and some lemon juice. There was no view, the captain saw, just rooftops and heat waves above that. And the balcony was not usable because it was full of cartons.

"You do have gin," said the captain.

"Those are empty."

The clerk turned the ceiling fans on, one in each room, and then went to the landing again to yell for the Arab. He came back, taking off his clothes.

"I don't think he'll come," he said and threw his jacket on a horsehair couch. The couch was not usable because it was full of books.

"Who, the mayor?"

"No, Remal will come. He said so in the hospital."

"I don't understand why he wanted to see you and me."

"That's because he didn't say."

The clerk kept walking all this time and dropping his clothes. When he got to the second room he was quite naked.

There was a brass bed in this room, a dresser, and a tin tub with handles.

"I'll just have to use the same water again," said the clerk, and stepped into his tub.

"Did you say you had gin, Whitfield?"

The clerk sighed when he sat down in the water, reached down to the bottom of the tub, and brought up a bottle. The label was floating off.

"This way it keeps a degree of coolness," he said. "There is ice only at the hotel. You see the glasses?"

The captain saw the glasses on the dresser and then was told to fetch also the clay jug from the window sill. The gray earthenware was sweating small, shiny water pearls which trembled, rolled over the belly of the jug and became stains shaped like amoebae.

"It's a sour wine," said the clerk. "Very safe," and he uncorked the gin bottle.

They mixed gin and sour wine and the glasses felt fairly cool in their hands.

"*Min skoal din skoal,*" said the clerk for politeness.

The captain didn't recognize the pronunciation and said nothing. He made himself another glass while the clerk watched from the bathtub. There was a deep cushiony valley where the captain sat on the bed and the clerk thought, He looks like an egg sitting up, beard notwithstanding. I am drinking too fast—

"What a sight," said the captain. "That creature we found there."

The clerk stretched one leg out and put it on the rim of the tub. He looked at his toe, at the big one in particular, and thought how anonymous the toe looks. No face at all.

"I can't remember what he looked like, do you know that?" said the captain. "All that hair and filth."

"When he came to," said the clerk, "the way he kept curling up." He said it low, and to nobody, and when he thought of the man on the hospital bed he did with his toes what he had seen on the hospital bed. "God," he mumbled, "the way he kept curling up—"

They said little else until the mayor came and they did not hear him because of the soft, native shoes he was wearing. Or because of the way he walked. Remal came straight into the bedroom, a very big man but walking as if he were small and light. Small steps which did not make him bounce or dip, but they gave an impression as if Remal could float.

"Good afternoon, gentlemen," he said in English, and this also confused the impression he made. Remal looked as native as a tourist might wish. He had an immobile terra cotta face, with black female eyes and a thin male mouth. He wore a stitched skullcap which the clerk had once called a *yamulke*, to which Remal had answered, "Please don't use the Jewish name for it again. Or I'll kill you." This politely, with a smile, but the clerk had felt sure that Remal meant it.

"I'll fix you one of these," said the captain, and looked around for another glass.

"Don't," said the clerk. He put his leg back into the tub and curled up in the water. "He's Mohammedan, you know, but he won't kill you because he's also polite."

"Please," said Remal. He made a very French gesture of self-deprecation and smiled. "I'll have something else. Where is your man?"

"Couldn't find him. Disappeared. Captain, you might fix me a Christian-type cocktail."

Remal left the room and went out to the landing and then the two men in the bedroom could hear him roar. "What was that?" and the captain stopped mixing.

"It's a kind of Arabic which a European can never learn," said the clerk.

When Remal came back he brought a chair along from the other room, flounced the long skirt of the shirt-like thing he was wearing, doing this in the only way a long, shirt-like thing can be handled, and sat down.

"Ah, Whitfield," he said. "How relaxing to see you."

"Stop flattering me. I will not give you the bathtub."

An irreverent way, thought the captain, for a thin, naked man to talk to a big one like this mayor, but the light talk went on for a while longer while the captain sat in the valley of the bed and wondered what Remal wanted. Perhaps five minutes after the roar on the landing the clerk's Arab came running into the room with a tray. It held a pot and a cup and the tea smelled like flowers. After everything had been put on the dresser, the clerk's Arab ran out again very quickly because Remal had waved at him. Then Remal poured and everyone waited.

"That was a remarkable coffin," he said when he was ready. "I looked the entire thing over with interest."

"Custom-made," said the clerk.

"It would have to be," said Remal. "Few people would want such a thing."

"About the man," said the captain. "You wanted us to discuss..."

"Dear captain," said the clerk. "Our mayor is being polite by not coming to the point. You were saying, Remal?"

"Yes, yes. This coffin had everything."

"I don't think so," said the captain. "Not by the smell of it."

"Perhaps," said Remal, and drank tea. "But I was thinking, to lie in your own offal does have a Biblical significance, doesn't it?"

"And the box man is a Christian fanatic," said the clerk. "You better watch out, Remal."

"I am."

"This is ridiculous," said the captain. "I want..."

"You are interrupting Remal," said the clerk. "You were interrupting one of his silences."

In a way, thought the captain, this Arab is taking a lot from the clerk.

"There were remarkable arrangements for a long journey," said Remal. "A great number of water canisters strapped to the side of the coffin..."

"Can't you say box?"

"Of course, Whitfield. And a double wall filled with small packets of this food, this compressed food the American soldiers used to carry."

"You think he's an American?" asked the captain.

"Of course. Didn't you load him in New York?"

The captain put his glass down on the floor and when he sat up again he looked angry.

"I got papers which say so and I got a box which looks like it. That's all I know. The way it turns out, the damnable thing did not go through customs, my crew didn't see the damnable thing coming on..."

"Didn't they load it?"

"Crew doesn't load. Longshoremen do the loading."

"Ah. And port of origin and destination, I'm told, they are both the same. Americans do things like that, don't they, Whitfield?" asked the mayor. "Perhaps a stunt."

"A Christian-fanatic stunt," said the clerk. He took water into his hands and dribbled it over his head. "I name thee Whitfield," he murmured.

"As fanatics," said Remal, "we would be more consequential."

"Bathe in the blood of the lamb, not water."

"I beg your pardon?"

I'll get drunk too, thought the captain. That might be the best thing. But his glass was empty and he did not want to get up and squeak the bed.

"Yes," Remal continued. "In the coffin, there were also those pills, to make the fanaticism more bearable."

"The doctor analyzed them?"

"That will be a while," said Remal. "I gave one or two, I forget how many, to my servant, and he became extremely sleepy."

"Your scientific curiosity is almost Western," said the clerk. He waited for something polite from the mayor, something polite with bite in it, but the mayor ignored the remark and quite unexpectedly came to the point. It was so unexpected that the captain did not catch on for a while.

"This person," said the mayor and smoothed his shirt, "is your passenger, captain. I don't quite see the situation."

"Eh?" said the captain.

"I hardly see how he can stay."

"You don't see?" said the captain. He himself saw nothing at all. "Well, right now he's in the hospital," he said. It sounded like the first simple, sane thing to him in a long time.

"Yes. You put him there, captain."

"I know. Just exactly..."

"Why don't you take him out?"

"Take him out? But I'm leaving this evening."

"Take him with you."

"But he's sick!"

"He's alive. And your passenger."

The captain made an exasperated swing with both arms, which caused the bed to creak and the glass to fall over.

"Whitfield," he said, "what in hell—what—"

"He wants you to take the man from the box along with you," said the clerk. Then he took water into his mouth and made a stream come out, like a fountain.

"I will *not*!"

"Your passenger..."

"And stop calling him my passenger!" yelled the captain. "He's a stowaway and there's no law on land or sea which tells me, the captain, that I must transport a stowaway!"

Next came a silence, which was bad enough, but then the mayor put his teacup down and shrugged slightly. This made the captain feel gross and useless.

"Dear captain," said Remal and looked at his fingernails, "you are leaving tonight, you say?" Then he looked up. "I could hold your ship here for any number of reasons. Mayor in Okar, I think, means more than mayor in Oslo, for instance. You may find I combine several functions and powers under this one simple title."

"Just a minute!" His own voice shocked the captain, but then he didn't care any more. "I'm not taking him. I'm not even taking the time to show you the regulations. I'm not even taking the time to ask why in the damn hell you're so interested in getting the man out of here."

"My interest is very simple," said Remal. "I would like to avoid the official complications of having a man land in my town, a man without known origin, without papers, arriving here in an insane way."

"You are worried about something?" said the captain with venom.

Remal began a smile, a corner of his mouth curving. Then suddenly he turned to the clerk. "He landed on your company's pier, Whitfield. The responsibility..."

"It—is—not!"

"You interrupt, Whitfield."

"I know what comes next. I should persuade the captain to get the paperless lunatic out of the country."

Remal waited but this turned out to be of no help.

"Head office of my shipping firm is in London. I can't telegraph for instructions and get an answer before the captain leaves. I can't ask him to stay—his ship isn't a company vessel. My company leases both pier and depot from your state; it's a small shipping point only, which is why I am executive clerk on this station." The clerk sat up, feeling ridiculous with the pomp of his speech. He therefore put his arms on the rim of the tub, sat straight, and imagined he was sitting like this on a throne.

"Whitfield," said the mayor, "how can you refuse all responsibility for a sick man who lands on your pier?"

"Oh, that," and the clerk let himself slide back into the water. He looked up at the ceiling and said, "Of course I will visit him in the hospital."

There was more talk, polite talk guided by Remal, but it was clearly tapering-off talk. It showed how flexible Remal was. It showed, perhaps, that the mayor was thinking of another way.

"Perhaps it will all be very simple," he said and got up.

"Perhaps the man will die?"

"Of course not, Whitfield." Remal smoothed his tunic and took a deep breath. This showed how large his chest was. "He will wake up, talk, and explain everything." And Remal walked out.

The man from the box did not talk for several days.

Chapter 3

At first they thought that he was in a coma. He was extremely unresponsive, and of course there had been the blows on the head with the axe handle.

They washed him and shaved his face and put him to bed.

Then they thought of it as a deep sleep, due to extreme exhaustion. But for that diagnosis he slept too long. Catatonic stupor was suggested, but that did not fit either. When they sat him up he collapsed again.

They let him lie in bed and attached various tubes.

"Same?"

"Same."

They were French nurses and the older one was in his room because she had to switch glucose bottles. The younger one always came in a few times each day to see how the man was doing.

"Look at him," said the younger one. "How he looks."

"You look at him, Marie. I know how he looks."

"A baby—"

"Marie," said the older one, "he does not look like a baby. With that face."

"He's just thin."

"You talk about babies a great deal, Marie."

"Don't you think he looks gentle?"

"Well, he's asleep."

"I think he looks gentle. I think that he probably is."

They watched how he tried to turn in his sleep....

He tried to turn in his chair but the man behind him cut the heel of his hand into the side of Quinn's face, not hard, but mean nonetheless, and effective. I'm not going to make more of this than it is, Quinn thought, this is just meant to be one more of his talks. With trimming this time, but just a talk.

Quinn kept his head straight, as he was supposed to do, and looked at Ryder behind the leather-inlaid desk. How a fat bastard with a sloppy mouth can be so hard, thought Quinn. How? I've got to find out. I must find this out.

Ryder sat still in his chair on the other side of the desk and the window behind him showed a very well defined stretch of electrified skyline. That's why he looks so impressive, thought Quinn. That and the red silk bathrobe. And the desk, and the tough guy behind me.

"You got maybe a lot of education," said Ryder, "but you ain't smart, Quinn."

"Can't get over it, can you, that you never got past reform school?"

Ryder shook his head at the man behind Quinn's chair and said, "Don't hit him again. That's just smart-aleck talk."

"Smart-aleck lawyer talk," said the man behind Quinn. "They're all alike."

"No, they're not," said Ryder. He coughed with a wet sound in his throat. Then he lowered his head, which added another chin. And suddenly he yelled, with a high. fat man's voice. "This one ain't smart enough! You, Quinn! You were hired to be smart in this organization, not stupid, you shyster, not stupid enough to try and slice yourself in!"

Ryder closed his eyes and sat back in his chair. He wheezed a little, which was the only sound in the room.

Quinn said very quietly, "I'm not slicing myself in. I'm improving the organization."

"Hit him!" said Ryder without opening his eyes.

Quinn got a jolt on the side of the head, and when he tried to get up the man behind him cut the edge of his palm down on Quinn's shoulder.

Quinn exhaled with a sudden sound, like a cough almost, and bent over in the chair. He bent and stayed there. Of all the things he wanted to do— mostly violent and some quite insane—he did none of them. He held still with the pain in him and felt he could actually see it. A red wave with blue edges. Don't move, don't move, because that way, Ryder, that way I'll get you later for this.

"Those unions are mine," Ryder was saying, "and that sews up the waterfront. I think you're trying to undo that for me, Quinn."

"All I really did..."

"You're lying, Quinn. You reshuffled the North end docks so that I got less say-so and you got more. And clever too."

"Shyster clever," said the man behind the chair.

"No. Not crooked at all. That's where he got me. Never occurred to me to look for a straight way I could get robbed."

"Okay, Ryder," and Quinn sat up. "The set-up is still yours and the fact that you're making less money has to do with the racket squeeze and nothing with me."

"Then how come you're making more money, Quinn?"

"I'm not."

"You're lying."

"Should I hit him?" said the man behind the chair.

"Shut up. Quinn, you listen to me. You been working good the two years you've been over to my side, good like a real hustler. But do it for me, not for you."

Nothing else came and there was just the wheezing from Ryder, and then a clink. When Quinn looked up, he saw that Ryder had put his false uppers into the water glass. He was going to bed.

"You mean you're done?" said the man behind Quinn's chair. "He's walking out?"

"Sure," said Ryder. All the words made a flabby sound. "He's smarter now than he was." Ryder bunched his empty mouth, then let it hang again. "And he knows we got methods—"

My God, what a face, thought Quinn. And I wish I had hit him and his face looked like that because I had done it to him.

"Out," said the man behind the chair. "You got the message."

After that, on the street, Quinn just walked. But it wasn't enough moving for all the holding still he had done. He concentrated on a dream that came out ugly and strong, red, with blue edges— and then I go over, cool as cool, I don't listen any more. I am cool as cool, fire inside though, fire in fist now, and suddenly ram that into the executive pouch—poof! plate jumps out, face collapses, fat lips hanging down, and I step on the plate, a crunch of pure pleasure—

"No, Ryder, you shut up and you listen because *I* pulled *your* teeth. No, Ryder, why hustle for you? And why is it I can make more than you but hustle for you? And why is it I'm smarter than you but it makes no difference? Why try being like you and get pushed for it, not being like you? Answer me, Ryder. Don't flinch when I'm screaming. Just answer me. What's the big answer—Ah, forgot, you haven't got any teeth." And then cool with my rage inside me, I hand him his plate, pink and white stuff that's left of it, something like splintery gravel, and let it dribble into his water glass. And I leave and laugh. I want to laugh very hard, this is funny, I laugh harder, this could be so funny, why in hell can't this be funny....

"Same?"

"I don't know, Marie. Would you close the windows for me?"

"Look. He's sweating."

"I know. The first time. Close the windows for me, Marie, while I strap this."

"But the heat..."

"Sirocco coming. Doctor Mattieux put a note on the board."

"Ah. I hope this one is short."

"They are sometimes the strongest."

"How the last one screamed, you remember? How that sand can scream."

"You have pinched the curtain in the window."

"Oh. Why are you strapping him?"

"Mattieux's order. He has been too restless."

"Perhaps he wants to wake up?"

"In the meantime the straps, so he cannot cut himself on the needle."

"Why doesn't Mattieux wake him up? Perhaps just a little ammonia, perhaps no more and he would wake up."

"Doctor Mattieux said, perhaps he is in this coma because he needs to be."

"You know, Renee, he doesn't look gentle today. He looks very much as if he were suffering."

They watched how he tried to turn in his sleep....

He did not dream of the good times, the times when he had reached out and touched success; only the failures became important. He didn't dream how he had gone ahead and split the organization right down the middle, the sweet sight of the power running right out of Ryder's hands, the sweet sight of Ryder himself full of threatening talk, sweet silence from Ryder while he, Quinn, felt the better man, because he was worse than Ryder.

He dreamt how he tried to turn in his bed and couldn't.

"Who in hell..."

"Lie still."

"That's all right," said another voice from across the dark room. "Let him get up. So he'll know."

Quinn knew who it was even before he was out of the bed and before he could see well enough. He said, "Ryder, you son of a bitch! Ah, there's two more? The strong arm? You don't think..."

"I don't have to, Quinn, and as for you, it won't do you any good."

"You have those goons lay a hand on me, Ryder, and you think I don't have the set-up to make you float down the river by six in the morning?"

"Tut, tut, such violence. Show him, Jimmy."

There were, after all, two of them and they hadn't just woken up. They got him without a punch. A silent, panting affair. A wrestler. Not one punch but all wrestler, and the other one could murder me any place, any way, with his buddy's grip crippling me out of shape. And he's just standing there, doing what—

"Ryder, listen to me. I've got a call coming in, five in the morning, and if I don't answer..."

"I'm not interested, Quinn. Whyn't you watch what he's doing?"

What is he doing?—Ryder wiping his sloppy mouth, the gorilla behind me not moving a muscle and neither can I, and the other—knife? No. Fountain pen? I should sign them a document?

"I left standing orders, Ryder, I told you once, that should I get roughed up..."

"No violence, Quinn. Look."

Damn, this grip on my back, my arms like worms, and the waiting, the waiting, and why don't you hit—ah, the other one heard me think, coming over—

"Ryder, for God's sake—"

"Doesn't hurt, Quinn. Just a little sting."

And the man comes over and carries the syringe and a needle. A small, cold-looking thing like that and I've never been so scared in my life.

"Ryder, what in *hell*—"

"No violence, Quinn, nothing like it. But you'll end up a changed man."

"Where'll I put it?" said the one with the needle.

"Any place. What's the difference?"

"Come on already," said the one holding Quinn doubled over. "He's trying to struggle or something."

"Ryder! *What is it?*"

"Trip around the world for you, Quinn. In a coffin. Ever hear of the method?"

"My God, Ryder—"

"You'll be a changed man, Quinn. Maybe a better one. Give it to him, Jimmy."

Ryder, for heaven's sake—and I didn't even feel it, didn't feel anything at the start of such an important—Letting go of me now? You let go too soon. Watch what I mean by you let go too soon—too thick this air, too thick in the brain, but you, Ryder, I get you, don't float away, Ryder, oh my God please don't leave....

"How he sweats."

"But he's lying still now. Put the fan in the door, Marie."

"Mercy, how that sirocco screams."

"Not yet, really. It will get worse...."

Dead. Dead? Nonsense. I wouldn't ask if I were. But this nonsense of not knowing what's up or down. Drug in the head explains it, explains everything. Yes. Feeling fine. Feel fine with gray cotton inside of me and black cotton outside of me. Ah, not cotton at all but space to move. Black space to move. Closet? Of course, of course. Everything else is pure nonsense. For the moment I can only remember sheer *nonsense*. Everything will be all right—*all right!* There *must* be a door, *must*—I *must stop screaming*—

Fine now. At the bottom of panic it is very quiet. No, no. There is no need to move. Careful now, leisurely so as not to frighten. I am not frightened. I can say it. Say box. You see? Since box, by any other name, still makes no sense— Easy, please, please—

And I remember as a matter of fact that a Seventeenth-Century nobleman who had displeased his king was made to spend nine, was it nine? Was made to spend all those years in a cage, having fewer conveniences, fewer water cans. I am sure, no little cabinets full of provisions, no little pills. And for example once a child was found in a closet without light, the child moon-white and lemur-eyed, but it got out! Got Out! *Got to get out!*

—How dull inside my head. But better this way, much better and thank you, little pill. And though dull, I will check again, check the entire universe, all the cans, all the boxes in boxes what blessed certainty—

One, two, three, five... Watch it.

One two, two, three... No! I insist on the right count, left count, right, twoop, threep, foa, one twoop, rip, *rip* to pieces, I am ripping *apart!*

—And cannot stand the screaming any more, I can't any more, can't, though wish I were more tired. Dead tired. No! Don't go out! Please, little flame, don't go out! And please stay little inside your egg and then sometime when it cracks, little flame, you can leap more—Crack? Wait! Don't go out, little flame, jump a little—

Jump, little one, JUMP!

"Call Doctor Mattieux! Quick!"

"What is it?"

"He's violent! Call Mattieux!"

And then Renee, the older nurse, waited for the doctor. She had prepared the morphine injection, but when Doctor Mattieux finally arrived, he decided, no, I think this time we shall let him be awake.

Chapter 4

Three days after Quinn woke up, Whitfield came to see him in the hospital. Things had been a little unusual—the sirocco, for instance, and a great deal of dull time with no dock work possible—and therefore Whitfield walked carefully with a three-day hangover. He felt that he carried it very well and only hoped that Quinn would not be difficult.

"Is he ready?" he asked the nurse in the corridor.

She said he was ready and that his clothes would be brought into his room. Then Whitfield went to see Quinn.

Whitfield, of course, did not recognize him. Only Quinn's hair, which was thick and black, seemed familiar.

Quinn sat in his bed, doing nothing. He wore a night shirt which was split down the back and his hands looked bony and his arms were thin. Not really thin, thought Whitfield, but rather lean, because there are all those muscles.

Quinn crossed his legs and leaned on his knees. He watched Whitfield come in and said nothing.

Empty eyes, thought Whitfield, but then he changed his mind. I'll be damned if they don't look innocent.

"Eh, how do you do?" said Whitfield.

Quinn nodded.

"I'm Whitfield. We met, you know. You don't remember? We met at your—uh—resurrection."

"I couldn't see too well."

"Yes. A blinding day."

"You the one that hit me?"

"Oh no. I'm the one whom you choked."

"Oh."

When Quinn did not say anything else Whitfield, unexpectedly, felt embarrassed. He took care of that by thinking of Quinn as an idiot. The way he stares, he thought, and then of course that thick hair. All the idiots I've known have invariably had this very thick hair. All this while Whitfield smiled, but when Quinn did not smile back or say anything else, Whitfield went to the window as if to look out. He could not look out because of the sun shutters, so he looked at the window sill. There was some sand lying along the edge of the frame.

"Some blow we had there, wasn't it?" and he turned back to the bed.

As expected, Quinn was looking at him. Talk of the weather, thought Whitfield, and now *I* feel like an idiot.

"Are you from the police?" Quinn asked.

"Police? Oh no, nothing of the sort. They have been here, haven't they?"

They had been by Quinn's bed several times, and only afterwards had it struck Quinn how docile he had felt towards them and that somehow cop hadn't meant cop to him, the way he had been used to it in the past. I'm still a little bit weak, he had explained to himself, not quite myself. And he had started to answer everything: name, James Quinn; occupation, lawyer; residence, New York.

Then, the matter with the box. At that point, Quinn had slowed down. His hands under the sheet had started to tremble a little, but it had not been the thought of the box so much as the thought of Ryder. So he had left Ryder out, and told them the box thing had been an act of revenge, something cruel dreamt up by a man who, however, was dead now. Quinn had wished this were true.

"How do you know this, Mister Quinn?"

"He was dead before, before I left."

"Who was he?"

"You wouldn't know him. Besides, there were several."

"Are you trying to confuse us, Mister Quinn?"

"I'm confused."

"Of course. Understandable. Tell us, Mister Quinn, is this type of— uh—punishment usual in your circles?"

"What circles?"

"You are a criminal, aren't you, Mister Quinn?"

"I have no record."

"Hm. A very good criminal then, eh?"

Quinn thought that with no record he was either a very good criminal or no criminal at all, and perhaps it came to the same thing. He had not been very much interested in deciding on this because other things meant more to him. Whether he had been smart or stupid, for example, and here the decision was simple. He had been very stupid with Ryder, but that, too, was a little bit dim, since he, Quinn, was here and Ryder was not. Maybe later, more on this later, but now first things first.

He sat up in bed and said, "I'm here without papers. Illegal entry and no identification, you told me. And that is all the business you have with me, isn't it?"

He wondered what had made them ask if he was a criminal.

"Did I talk in my sleep?" he asked.

"Yes."

"And?"

"We understood very little, except perhaps the word racket. We understood that."

"I told you I'm a lawyer."

They had just smiled and then one of them had said, "We've asked around, of course, and have learned about this box method. It even has a name, doesn't it, among criminals?"

Quinn had not answered, and not all the vagueness on his face had been faked. Only the simplest things did not make him feel vague.

"You must get papers, and then you must get out."

"Yes. And I need clothes."

They were pleased he was tractable, and then they had left.

Now Quinn looked up from his hands at Whitfield, who was the first stranger since the police had been there. I think he smells of gin, Quinn thought.

"Feel up to a little trip?" asked Whitfield.

Quinn thought for a moment and then he said, "I don't have any papers."

True enough, thought Whitfield, and for that matter you don't have any pants either, and so forth. And not much brains left, is my feeling, and I must say a sad shock you are to me and my cinema knowledge of an American gangster.

"You don't have any papers," he said, "which is why I am here. Ah, the clothes."

The nurse Marie brought a suit, shirt, and the other things and put them on the bed. She smiled at Quinn and held it a while, wishing that he would smile back. She has a sweet girlish face, thought Quinn, and a lot of old-fashioned hair. How does her little cap stay on? But he did not smile back at her.

"These are not the clothes in which you came," she said. "These are not cut like your own, but I hope you won't mind."

"I don't mind."

He was easier to look at when he was asleep, thought Marie, and when she left the room she wished he might stay a while longer and sleep here again.

Quinn got out of bed, took his nightshirt off, and started to dress. Whitfield said nothing. He is definitely not an official, thought Quinn, and he looks a little bit dreamy.

"Did you want something from me?" Quinn asked suddenly.

"Uh—want? Oh, no. Quite the opposite," and Whitfield giggled.

Quinn buttoned his pants which took him some time. He was used to a zipper.

"And you'll get me papers?"

"Well, it's like this. I'm going to drive you to the American consul so that you can start getting your papers. We'll drive to Tripoli."

"Why Tripoli?"

"Because Okar is too small for a consul."

"And you are with the consulate?"

At last, thought Whitfield. I myself would have asked that question first.

"No," he said. "It's like this. I run the pier—I'm with the company at whose pier—how to put this?—*where* you were unloaded." Whitfield smiled again, but Quinn was looking down. "This circumstance," said Whitfield who suddenly felt he could not stop talking, "this event, you see, gives me a sort of proprietary feeling about you, don't you know? I mean, if you'll picture the circumstance, you being delivered to me." Whitfield had to giggle again.

I have rarely felt so uncomfortable in my life, thought Whitfield with distraction, natural of course, with a man who has no sense of humor. Apt to happen, of course, when boxed. I will cultivate a note of compassion. But then this thought was startled right out of Whitfield when Quinn said the next thing. Quinn did not look up from buttoning his shirt when he talked and perhaps this helped startle Whitfield. For the first time it struck Whitfield that Quinn was talking to him without looking him straight in the face.

"Something stinks here," said Quinn.

"Uh—I beg your pardon?"

Quinn reached under the bed for his shoes, and when he straightened up again he sighed. Then he put his shoes on.

"Look," he said. "You run this boatyard, you are not a cop, you take me traveling from one town to another, and all this traveling with me having no papers. That stinks." Quinn straightened up and looked past Whitfield at the window. "I don't care," he said, "but I'm not stupid."

That you aren't, that you aren't, thought Whitfield, but how confusing. How can anyone with eyes open like that have a cunning brain? How confusing. And yet how uncunning to be so confusing. At which point Whitfield gave up, feeling that the thread of his thoughts was escaping him. He shrugged, because he, like Quinn, did not care too much either. What he explained next therefore turned out to be the truth.

"The mayor," he said, "is anxious to clear all this up. Let me say, he wants to expedite all this, so that you can get out. You do want to leave, don't you?"

"Oh yes," said Quinn, because everything that had been said to him since waking up had been about leaving.

"Now, the mayor, being also chief constable and a friend of mine, has asked me to take you, being his charge, on police business to Tripoli. And then I bring you back. Simple?"

"It sounds very simple," said Quinn.

But you don't sound simple, oh no you don't, thought Whitfield. He said, "Button up and off we go."

"I did already."

"You missed one."

Quinn buttoned up and then stood there, looking at Whitfield. He did that like a child, thought Whitfield. What to think of him? Whitfield smiled at Quinn but then looked away, so as not to see in case Quinn did not smile back.

"You know, Quinn—uh, how to put this?"

"How to put what?"

"Of course. That's the problem. What I mean, coming out of this thing—"

"Box?"

"Yes, that'll do it. Coming out, it's sort of like starting at the bottom. New chance and all that. You know, all new, everything. I mean, you look like that sometimes."

"Do I?" and Quinn did not know what else to say.

The two men walked out and Quinn remembered that Ryder had said it would make a new man out of him.

Chapter 5

The narrow main street looked pink and blue to Quinn, pink on the side where the sun hit and blue on the shadow side. There were not many people. There was an old woman who scraped camel dung into a basket. When Quinn passed he saw that the woman was a man. Three children looked at Quinn, because he was so pale, but one child looked with one eye only, because the other was covered with flies. And a man stared down from a balcony, watching the stranger walk. The balcony was birdcage thin and a little water dribbled down to the street. The man was holding a wet rag to the back of his head, and when Quinn passed the man closed his eyes again.

"Peaceful town, eh?" said Whitfield.

"I don't know. Just lying still doesn't mean peaceful."

Whitfield looked at Quinn for a moment but said nothing. Before driving out of here I'll have a gin fizz. With ice this time.

"We turn in here," he said.

Quinn saw the little trees on either side of the steps, and the big stone facade.

"The bank?"

"It's the hotel. Between ten and two our mayor is at the hotel."

"He owns the hotel, too?"

"Oh no. Owned by a Swiss couple. They always own hotels, you know."

"I didn't know."

I must stop making these little remarks, thought Whitfield.

There was a yellow dog on the bottom step, belly turned sunward. This was a thin, yellow dog, Quinn could see, and only his bare belly looked meaty. Quinn did not feel right about the dog.

"Thin enough to survive," said Whitfield.

"What?"

"They eat them, you know. When they're fat. You like dogs?"

"I've never eaten one."

Now I surely *must* stop, Whitfield thought.

They went from the dry heat into a hall which was tiled and cool, thin brass columns going up and up, past the second-floor balcony which ringed the hall. They turned through an arch into a large room which seemed filled with nothing but little round tables. Then Quinn saw a big

Arab get up in the dark corner. Somebody else sat there at the table with him.

"Ah," said Remal, and bowed. "Our strange traveler," and he offered his hand like a European.

When they got to the dark corner Whitfield said, "This is he, Beatrice, this is Quinn, and you'll probably be disappointed."

Quinn saw a fine-shaped woman who looked up and shrugged, but she smiled with it. "What he means," she said to Quinn, "is that he thinks I expected something non-human."

"I didn't mean anything of the sort," said Whitfield and sat down at the table. "You were *wishing* for something non-human. I think I'll have..."

"I know what you'll have," said Remal and clapped his hands. "And you, Mister Quinn?"

"Pardon?"

Still feeble-minded, thought Whitfield, and confused, thought Beatrice, and Remal reserved judgment while he kept smiling at Quinn. The smile meant, I'm watching you but you can't see me.

"What would you like to drink?" Remal asked.

"Scotch. And water."

"I don't suggest water," said Remal. "Try Vichy."

"All right," said Quinn. He did not care.

"Don't you want ice?" said Whitfield.

"Of course."

"Then you have to ask for it, Quinn."

"Maybe Mister Quinn hasn't traveled much," said Beatrice. "I mean, not counting your last trip."

"That trip didn't count, educationally," said Whitfield.

Quinn did not think of his trip, because to him there had been no trip. There had been the box. He thought of the box and had no idea if it counted or not. Altogether, his recollection was vague, or perhaps of no interest, the way a meal eaten, a cigarette smoked, an argument finished, an arrival completed, of no interest any more.

When the drinks came there were only two—one for Quinn and the other for Whitfield. The woman, Beatrice, still had her own, and Remal was no longer at the table. And then Whitfield took a long gulp from his gin, which was cloudy with lemon juice, got up and said that he would be right back.

"Are you staring, sleeping, or thinking?" said the woman to Quinn.

"Uh, I'm sorry. None of those things," and Quinn picked up his drink.

"But you were looking at me."

"Oh yes. I was looking. Just that."

She did not entirely understand that, but it was all Quinn had been doing. He saw that she was probably European: she had honey-colored hair, and she wore something short-sleeved and white, a cold white next to her skin which looked warm with tan. He looked down the row of little blue buttons on her front—how they ran down her round curve in front, tucked out of sight under her breasts, went straight down to her belt where the buttons ended.

"I feel touched," she said.

He did not know why and had nothing to answer.

"I meant by your look. By your looking just now."

"Oh. I wasn't thinking anything."

"I know you weren't."

She sipped her drink and looked beyond him. Quinn could see her neck, a nice round neck which showed a soft beat, a soft shadow which came and went to one side where her dress collar started. Then she sighed and looked back at him and smiled. Suddenly she seems very slow, thought Quinn. Like a cat in the sun.

"Mister Quinn," she said, "are you always speechless like this?"

"I'm not speechless. I can talk."

"Then talk to me a little."

"Are you with this Turk?"

"With what? You mean Rental? He's not a Turk," and she had to laugh.

"Are you with him?"

She smiled and looked at him, as if she did not mind being asked such a question, or answering it, though she did not answer it.

"I meant something else when I asked you to talk. I wanted to hear about you."

"You know about me."

"Do you mind talking about it? I'm very curious, I'm really curious about you inside that box."

"I don't mind talking about it but I don't know what to say."

He meant that, she thought, and picked up her glass to take a slow sip. Quinn said nothing else. He looked out of the window where he could see a small slice of sea between the walls of two houses. This is just about like starting up from the bottom, he thought. When nothing happens it doesn't matter, but sitting here it isn't so easy. He felt annoyed and suddenly the light outside the window hurt his eyes. He thought that was the reason why he was annoyed. He looked briefly at the arch behind his back and then humped over the table and looked at his hands.

"They'll be right back," she said.

"Oh." And then he said, "I asked you about you and—what's his name?"

"Remal, the Turk."

"I asked you about you and Remal before but I didn't mean do you go to bed with him."

"Oh? Why not?"

Then he knew why he felt annoyed. The two men's sudden departure felt like something secret. Something I can't deal with, he felt, something shut instead of open. And this was his first moment, since waking up in Okar, that he thought there must be some habits, old and dim right now, something to make all this newness less hard.

She saw that he had changed just a little, that he said just a little bit less than he thought.

"What I really wanted to know, I wanted to know why you're sitting here at this table."

"I wanted to see you."

"I'm no zoo."

"And I brought my car. You're going to use it going to Tripoli."

"Oh."

She waited a moment but Quinn said nothing else. He thought, Whitfield is a friend of this Remal, and she is a friend of this Remal. Everybody is a friend of this Remal. He has no enemies.

"Just a friendly gesture," she said. "Mine is the only good car in town, aside from Whitfield's two trucks. You wouldn't care to ride in one of those, on these roads. Quinn, you're staring again."

"I'm sorry."

She shrugged and smiled. "What did you see?"

"I like your tan."

She did not answer anything but closed her eyes for a moment and kept smiling. She sat still like that as if feeling her own skin all over. Now she also has a face like a cat, thought Quinn. I can see her lie in the sun like a cat, the way they lie and you want to touch them. And the cat face, very quiet and content, with cat distance.

"You know," she said, and opened her eyes, "I like to be looked at."

Quinn finished his Scotch, put the glass down, and felt light-headed.

"In that case," he said, "you, looking the way you do, should have a good time of it all day long."

She laughed, because a laugh was now expected. This is the first time, she thought, that I've heard him say something flip. Maybe that's how he used to be.

"Clever of you to say that," she told him, "but you're forgetting this is Okar."

"You must have picked it, and not because of being broke or anything like that."

"What made you say that?"

"You told me you got the only good car in town."

"Oh." She wondered whether he was being flip again. Then she said, "Yes. I've got enough. I've been married enough."

"Often enough or long enough?"

"Often enough."

Quinn looked the length of the hall again and wished he were leaving. He would have to leave anyway and Okar meant nothing to him.

"With your dough," he said, "why sit here? Why not Rome, Madrid, Paris? That kind of thing."

"Why here?" She had her hands on the table and looked at the backs of her hands and then turned them around and looked at her palms. "I don't know why. Confusion. I came the way you came. In a box. What do you know when you come in a box?"

"Nothing."

This stopped the conversation so abruptly that Beatrice felt she had to do something immediately.

"Anyway, what did you used to do, before nothing?"

"I was a lawyer. Which also means nothing. Right now I've got to know what to do next."

"You'll hang around. We all do."

"I have no papers. And no money."

"Money?" She looked at him as if she disliked him. "Well, there must be something you can do while you wait for papers. Don't you Americans always have something to sell?"

He shrugged and didn't answer.

"I used to be an American myself." She felt embarrassed and laughed. "And now?"

"All very confusing." She sipped from her drink without liking it.

"You are sort of confusing right now."

"I was born in Switzerland," and she sounded like a document, "but I'm not Swiss. Parents from the States but I lived there only like a visitor. My last name is Rutledge, because of the British husband. Also Fragonard, because of the French one." She took a breath and said, "I know. That's only two of them." But Quinn didn't answer her.

"I could sell my cans," he said.

"What was that?"

"The water cans I had in the box."

Quinn, sitting opposite her, was as surprised by his sudden thought about the water cans as was the woman who did not know him at all.

The mayor and the clerk came down the stairs in the main hall, and when they could see Quinn and the woman from the arch that led into the dining hall they stopped, or rather the mayor stopped, holding the clerk by one arm.

"You understand, Whitfield," he said, "the quicker the better."

Whitfield peered along one leg of the arch at the couple in back and then straightened up again.

"You're now worried she'll go to bed with him."

"Don't be trivial, Whitfield."

"All right," said Whitfield, feeling bored. "I shall pressure the government of the United States of America to expedite this stowaway's removal, because the mayor and so forth of Okar—I'll have to explain to them where Okar is—that the mayor feels a certain shakiness in his position and..."

"You ignore this," said Remal. "I am not shaky in my position and, besides, the outside officials are gone. But you ignore this. Our traveler was clearly part of a large organization. And they punished him. Or they tried. Once they find out, dear Whitfield, that he did not complete his tour, his tour of penitude..."

"I think you mean penitence."

"His punishment, Whitfield, then they will look to see where he is."

"And you would sooner have the officials hanging around than those American organization men."

"Officials I can buy."

"My fizz is getting warm, Remal."

"Go take care of him," said the mayor, "while he is still here."

"No problem. He's a lot like a child."

Remal did not answer and left after making his habitual bow.

Whitfield went back to the table and sat down. He saw that Beatrice had her chin in her hand and was smoking her cigarette too short. He found that his fizz was warm, and he saw that Quinn sat with his hands in his lap, quiet and patient.

"I want to sell my cans," said Quinn.

"I beg your pardon?"

"I want to sell my water cans, the ones I brought in the box."

A child, thought Whitfield. A child with the brain of an operator.

Chapter 6

They first walked to the house Beatrice had because the car was parked there. The car was a Giulietta, small and fast, and an Arab from Beatrice's house stood by the garden wall to see that nobody stole anything out of the car or took off the wheels. The garden wall was very solid and high and the house behind was not visible.

"Come in for a drink," said Beatrice. "You'll have a long drive."

"Which is why I don't want to come in," said Whitfield.

"I want to go down to the pier first," said Quinn.

"All *right*," said Whitfield.

"I think you could use the drink," said Beatrice.

"Never mind, never mind. Siesta going to be shot and everything if we don't get cracking."

"I can drive," said Quinn. "You can sleep in the car."

"I take a bath during siesta. I don't sleep."

Whitfield got behind the wheel in a fair state of irritation, and when Quinn had slammed his own door Whitfield got the car down to the main street in something like leaps and bounds, as if inventing a new way to shift gears.

"You're not turning towards the water," said Quinn.

"Eh?"

"I want to check on those cans."

"Preserve me, yes."

"But you're not turning..."

"Quinn, baby, listen. I must first stop by a store."

"For what?"

"A preservative." And then Whitfield shot down the main street until it petered out and stopped at the mouth of an alley where no car could enter.

"Native quarter," said Whitfield. "Note the native craft of whitewash, the rustic filth on steps and cobbles, the aboriginal screams of joy and of anger as they chat in the street. Wait here, I'm buying me a bottle of wine. *If* you please."

Quinn watched Whitfield go into a door. Or into a window, thought Quinn, because Whitfield had both to stoop down and step over a high stone sill all at the same time. Quinn got out and leaned by a stone wall and smelled the street and looked at the confusion of people. There were windows in the walls reminding one of gunslits, and a goat sat in the middle of the street looking at a butcher shop.

"Ah, the new one," said somebody next to Quinn. Quinn gave a start which was close to fright.

"You're Quinn, no?"

The Arab had a young face but an old-looking mouth because so many teeth were missing in the front. But he smiled just the same. He wore pants and an old army jacket.

"Now what?" said Quinn.

"I mean you just came, right?"

"You seem to know everything."

"If I know your name, wouldn't I know you are here?"

That sounds like an old Arab proverb, thought Quinn. And the guy looks like a cadaver which is still young. Quinn could think all this but he didn't know what to say.

"Call me Turk," said the Arab.

"That's a fine old Arab name."

"My good Arab name you couldn't pronounce."

"You want something?" asked Quinn. "You live here?"

Which he said to get just something or other straight.

"I live," said Turk and kept smiling.

"Where'd you learn so much English?"

"Like this," said Turk, and counted off on his fingers. "I once drove for the French. Then I went to France. There I soon moved to Paris. In Paris are Americans, and I learn to speak."

"How'd you know who I was? You a friend of the mayor's, too?"

"Who?"

"Remal."

"Oh no."

"That seems strange. All I ever meet..."

"He doesn't trust me. Not at all," and Turk laughed.

Quinn looked away to see if Whitfield was coming back yet.

"It always takes fifteen minutes," said Turk. "Because of the talking you do with the purchase."

"You sound like a guide," said Quinn.

"Oh I could. Would you like to see the streets?"

"The mayor and I *both* don't trust you," said Quinn.

Turk shrugged and leaned by the wall, next to Quinn.

"You have a cigarette?"

"I don't smoke," said Quinn.

"I meant for me, not you. Ah well," and he scratched himself. "Anyway," and now he looked earnest. "If you do want to see the native quarter, you know you should do it now."

Quinn waited because he did not follow the man.

"You know that Remal won't let you come here again."

"What's that?" said Quinn. He understood even less now. But somehow he felt he understood this Turk rather well, not the man perhaps, but the type. New arrival in town, little sucker play, a quick piaster or dinar or franc or whatever they use here, that type, and Quinn felt familiar with it. Not the pleasure of familiarity, just familiar—

"You don't know anything, do you?" said Turk. He folded his arms, looked at the doorway Whitfield had taken, then back at Quinn. "You are a stranger," said Turk, "and have upset him. Him, Remal."

Quinn frowned and looked at the doorway again, wishing that Whitfield would show up.

"Leave me alone," he said to the Arab. Quinn was almost mumbling.

Then Whitfield appeared, stepping through the doorway like a crane toe-testing the water. Quinn suddenly thought, What's keeping me from asking what in hell Turk is talking about?

Whitfield waved at Quinn to come along, and when he saw Turk he nodded at him and Turk smiled back.

"What's this about Remal?" said Quinn. "What's he got here that he's worried I might upset it?"

"What's he got here? Almost everything."

"Quee-hinn!" called Whitfield.

"Like everything what?" Quinn asked again, feeling rushed.

"He's coming back," said Turk and nodded towards Whitfield. "See you again, eh, Quinn?" And Turk moved away, smiling with his young face and the old gums where the teeth were missing. "You'll be here a while, anyway." Then Turk left.

Whitfield held a moist jug of wine by the neck, and when Quinn reached him he turned and walked back to the car.

"Fine friends you have," he said to Quinn. "Did he ask you for a cigarette?"

"Yes. Who is he?"

"Did you give him one?"

"No."

"Ah, saved," Whitfield said. "Will you drive, please?" And he stopped at the car.

"You don't think I followed any of this, do you?" said Quinn.

"You didn't? That's only because you don't know Turk." Whitfield opened the car door. "*If* you had given him the cigarette," and Whitfield interrupted himself to sniff at his jug, "then I would now ask you to look up your empty sleeve to determine if something at least were left in it. In short, he is not trustworthy." And Whitfield got into the back of the car.

Quinn got behind the wheel, slammed the door, and when he had the motor going he let it idle for a minute.

"How come he doesn't like Remal, that Turk?"

"What gave you that idea, Quinn? He loves Remal."

"Look, Whitfield, I just talked…"

"We all love Remal, dear Quinn, but some of us more, some less. But Turk loves him most of all, would love to be Remal altogether. He would steal Remal's teeth out of his head to have a smile like the mayor's; he would cut his heart out, I mean Remal's, to have a big heart like that. *But*—Swig of wine, Quinn?"

"No, thank you."

"But Remal does not like him. And I'm sure that's what Turk told you and no more. Drive, Quinn. We U-turn and go straight out of town."

Quinn shifted and drove back down the main street.

"Do we pass the place where you keep my cans?"

There was no answer from the back—just the hissing and gurgling which came from the jug.

"Did you hear me, Whitfield?"

A deep breath sounded from the back, as if Whitfield were surfacing, and when he talked he sounded exhausted.

"Quinn, baby, I realize you don't have any money, and if I can be of any assistance while you…"

"Are you stalling me for any reason?"

"Turn right, the next street," said Whitfield. "This wine gives me a headache. While you look at your bleeding cans I'll just dash into my office for a headache potion I keep there."

The side street ended on a cobblestone square of which one side was open to the long quay. There was just one warehouse and Quinn pulled up next to it. The two men got out, and on the water side of the building they walked along the white pier.

Quinn saw the place for the first time but it did not interest him. The cement threw the heat back as if the sun was below them. There was a small tramper tied up where the warehouse doors stood open, and a barge

lay at anchor a little way out. It had a single lanteen sail furled in some
messy fashion which made the yardarm look like a badly bandaged finger.

The box had been moved. It lay on its side at the far end of the pier and
the splintered edge of the top gave a ruined impression. A mouth with no
teeth, thought Whitfield. It gapes, after spitting out.

And somebody had cleaned the inside. There was not much smell,
which was also because of the sun. And all the cans were gone.

"Where are they?" said Quinn.

"Ah yes," said Whitfield. "Obviously gone. Quinn, look here. My company and I will reimburse you, all right? Theft is common around here,
you know, but in view of, ah, yes." He petered out that way and squinted
with the sun in his face. This is new, thought Whitfield. That look on his
face is no longer simple. Maybe this is how he used to be.

"All right, just a minute," said Whitfield, and then he turned around and
yelled something in Arabic.

Two Arabs were carting boxes from the tramper into the warehouse and
one of them put down his load and looked over at Whitfield. They yelled
at each other across the distance, Whitfield and the Arab, and since the
language was meaningless to Quinn, and since they had to yell at each
other because of the length of the pier, Quinn could not tell if there was
anger in all this, or even excitement. They stopped yelling and Whitfield
turned to Quinn.

"I have good news for you," Whitfield said, looking as if good news were
no news at all. "Your bleeding cans have not been stolen, he knows where
they are..."

"What's that?"

"Quinn, there's a storage hut which we own on the trackless wastes of
the North African coast. We can't drive there in this car, I won't buy the
cans from you till evening when we get back, and in the meantime they
will bring your cans to the warehouse, so you can count them, so we can
bicker about them, and so you can make your profit. *Please*, Quinn, does-
n't that sound nice?"

"Don't treat me like an idiot," said Quinn and put his hands into his
pockets.

But for the first time Whitfield thought that perhaps Quinn was an
idiot, in some ways.

Chapter 7

The bottle which Whitfield got from his office turned out to be gin. He sat in the back of the car while Quinn drove, holding the jug on one knee and the bottle on the other. Now and then Whitfield sighed, which was always at the end of having held his breath while drinking from one or the other of his two bottles. A practiced drinker, he was proud and content with his skill in handling the situation, and he neither sank into drunken befuddlement nor rose into painful clarity. I am a man of proportion. And highly adaptable. I don't even miss my bathtub.

"How long will all this take?" Quinn asked.

Whitfield, having been elsewhere, gave a small start. He didn't mind conversation, but he was in no mood for questions.

"What, for heaven's sake?"

"Till I can get out of here, with papers and all."

"I don't know, Quinn. Your State Department does move in mysterious ways, you know. Want a drink?"

"No. I'm driving."

"Your answer shows you don't know how to drink, Quinn. Done well, drinking can open your eyes or, if need be, close them. An advantage only available to the fearless, or the tippler."

Quinn hardly listened. Every so often he could see the Mediterranean when the gray rocks or the gray humps of dry ground fell away, and there would be the water with a sharp blaze like glass. But most of the time the road was a band of dust with no view.

"Take the goat, for example," Whitfield was saying. "Strange eyes, you know? I know their eyes by heart. Some wine?"

"No."

"Remember the goat sitting in front of the butcher shop? Watching his nanny's meat turn blue in the dry air. That would make anybody's eyes strange, wouldn't you say so?"

"You're drunk, Whitfield."

"I am not!" There was silence, then the sigh after the bottle was down. "Quinn," said Whitfield. "You have eyes like a goat, somewhat."

Quinn felt himself become tense, not liking the remark Whitfield had made. Nor did he like the image of the goat. Being all new, he thought, is not easy. It must have been easier, before. The thought was vague and the

memory was without interest. He thought of the Arab called Turk, and of
Remal.

"Whitfield."

"Yes?"

"The creep who talked to me by the quarter, he made some remark or
other about Remal. That he wouldn't allow me to walk around or something like that."

"Sounds very vague to me."

"That's why I'm asking you about it, goddamn it."

"*Please,* Quinn. Don't jab the accelerator like that. You made me spill and
I shall now smell of gin."

"God forbid," said Quinn. "And you haven't answered."

"But I told you, dear Quinn. Turk loves Remal and Remal does not love
him back. This causes tension, don't you see, this causes pauses—oh, for
heaven's sake—"

At this point, Whitfield realized that he had misjudged his siesta capac-
ity with the two bottles, which, as a matter of pride, distressed him a great
deal. Stands to reason, however, he thought to himself. Bathtub alters temperature exchange, rate of metabolism and so forth, and me here with all
the experimental controls shot to hell in the back of the car, so naturally.
He felt better but wished he were asleep.

Quinn asked nothing else. He drove and slowly became aware of the
muscles in his back. It was not a pleasant awareness and he had to think
of the shell of a turtle. Going nutty, like that Whitfield back there. And
without benefit of drink. He felt cramped and withdrawn.

This got worse during the hour or two he had to spend with the consul.
He withheld information, faked dates and invented places, which, all in
all, came surprisingly easy to him. But when he left and went out to the
car where Whitfield was waiting, he felt sullen and stiff.

"Ah!" called Whitfield. "How was it to be back at the bosom of mother
country?"

Quinn did not answer and walked around to the driver's side.

"I didn't mean to embarrass you with the question," said Whitfield. "All
I meant..."

"Stop talking a minute, will you?"

Whitfield had a headache. When it came to drinking, he felt a great deal
like an athlete in training, and a headache to him was tantamount to a dis-
qualification. And now Quinn, on top of all this, acting churlish and
sullen. He watched Quinn start the car and felt ignored.

"You're unhappy, I'm unhappy, and perhaps your friend the consul wasn't happy either. That's all I meant to say."

"One month," said Quinn. "He says it'll take one month for investigation and papers."

"I'd like to have a month of absolutely nothing," said Whitfield. He had an impulse to reach back for one of his bottles, but turning his head he felt a sickening sting go through his brain. He felt out of training.

"You've got a month of nothing every siesta time," said Quinn, but the joke did not interest him. The month ahead seemed like a vacuum to him, or like a view without focus.

Goat-eyes looking, thought Whitfield, and he turned his head straight, to look out through the windshield.

And all Quinn could think of, at first, was what he had been told, that he must get his papers and must get back to the States immediately.

The consul had said nothing about leaving. He had only said to comply with the local rules while awaiting his papers.

And why go back? Because the police had said so while he, Quinn, sat half dumb in the hospital bed?

There was a bend in the bare road and behind that bend came a small village. Quinn knew this but did not slow down. He leaned the car through the bend and pushed through the short village, leaving a big ball of yellow dust in the air.

Go back there for Ryder? The question seemed almost meaningless. As if long ago he had screamed all the rancor out of himself, struggled it out of himself, and had been left blank.

But what to do, what to do, staying a month in a truly foreign place, where no one meant anything to him, or everyone was somehow beyond him? How did I do it before, what did I do, filling the time and finding some tickle in it? A month of nothing— Quinn wiped his face.

"Listen, Whitfield, the boat that brought me, where is it now?"

"Oho!" and Whitfield folded his arms, closed his eyes. "That does worry you, then."

"How come you never answer the first time you're asked a question?"

"Because I'm a conversationalist, Quinn. Are you concerned, then, that whoever shipped you will want to finish the job once they find out where you are?"

It was put so crudely that it hardly fit, though Quinn himself could not have been more specific. But he knew he was sweating for more than the remote possibility that Ryder would send down a goon to pack him in a box again. He felt a bigger anxiety, which waved and wove about, obscuring the feeling of his helplessness, his worry that he had somewhere been wrong but did not know why. At the bottom, from somewhere, came the notion that he must always defend himself or he would sink away, and that would be fine with everybody.

He felt his back again, as once before, and how stiff his wrists were now.

"Quinn, you have a positively boxed-in look. Stop thinking. You don't seem to be used to it. Weren't you going to ask me something else?"

"You still haven't answered the first thing I asked."

"Yes. Where's the boat? I don't know. Ask someone else."

"Is it back in New York?"

"Out of the question. With the run she had, I'd say she'll be two months out yet."

"Two months," said Quinn.

"I follow you," said Whitfield, and then he felt he might say something witty to make this more like conversation, but Quinn didn't let him.

"Maybe you know about procedure in a case like this. What happens when a captain finds something irregular with his, let's say, with his cargo, and he's away from home port when he discovers the irregularity?"

"He dumps the mess as best he can, as he did you."

"I don't mean that. Does he report it to somebody?"

"Yes," said Whitfield, "he reports it."

Quinn said something which Whitfield did not catch, but it sounded vulgar.

"I want to know what he reports," said Quinn.

"In this case that's up to the captain. He's an independent. Otherwise there'd be a company policy, such as ours, where a stowaway matter, for instance, goes out by short wave to the closest office, and the office handles the red tape from there."

"You mean this captain who brought me has nobody to report to on this?"

"Yes, he does. Immigration, customs, that sort of thing."

"He didn't, by any chance, ask you to send out a report for him back to New York?"

"No. And he left the same day he came, you know."

"And for two months he won't be back in New York."

"He might report by letter," said Whitfield, "from his next port of call. Tel Aviv, I think he said."

Quinn asked no more questions. A report on him from the consulate would get to the States long before the captain would check in, but it wasn't at all likely that Ryder had an ear in the State Department. Only the captain, reporting to harbor authorities right in New York— He hung onto that thought for a moment but then shook his head, almost as if snapping a whip.

Farfetched, all of it. The captain was gone, glad to be rid of his troubles, New York four thousand miles away, and the Ryder thing was really over.

But why would Remal forbid me the streets? And who's trying to steal my cans? And why does everyone think that for one month I'll dry out in the sun in Okar, goat-eyed, watching myself turn dry and blue?

Must learn to think clearly again. He felt sly and secretive.

Until they slowed down in the square by the warehouse Whitfield did not look over at Quinn. Whitfield had a headache and felt he should leave well enough alone. They slowed in the square and rolled to a stop by the warehouse, and Whitfield looked at Quinn sitting still for a moment, holding the wheel.

He used to look like something dumped out of a box, thought Whitfield, but no more. Something wide-eyed, maybe a little surprised, but not any more.

Because this was the first time that Quinn no longer felt entirely new but had the help of some of his of habits.

Chapter 8

A late half light was over the town and in a very short time the sudden dusk would fall and then night. Quinn stretched when he got out of the car, slammed the door. He watched a dog run away. Run, he thought, or you'll get eaten—

Whitfield still sat in his seat. When Quinn bent down to look into the window, Whitfield had the wine jug on his lap where it was making a stain.

"Dear Quinn," said Whitfield, "this may surprise you, but in addition to everything else I am extremely hungry. Eat your headaches away, is what my sainted aunt used to say. You should have seen her. Which is to say, Quinn, can't this entire maddening transaction with the goddamn cans wait till morning?"

"We're here now."

"I'm just afraid you might haggle with me."

"Look," said Quinn. "None of this means a damn to you. To me it does. Suddenly, to me there is nothing as important as getting what is mine. Those cans are mine. And any more..."

"Please, please. You're quite right. None of this means anything to me," and Whitfield got out of the car.

It was still fairly light over the water, the sea black and yellow, zebra striped. Inside the warehouse the bulbs had been turned on, six hard lights in clear glass, like hard, shiny drops on black strings hanging from the high ceiling.

"Ah!" Whitfield said, and his sigh was strong and genuine with the relief he felt. "Here is your treasure."

The canisters, ten of then, lay in a corner. Whitfield sat down on one of them. Quinn stood and counted them, as he had often done before, though he couldn't remember this. Now they were completely his and worth money, and even if it was pennies only, the difference was big. He had back one of his habits, namely, to let nobody think they could take advantage of him.

"Well, now," said Whitfield, "I've heard about cases of this sort, of course, being a fascinated student of your country's folklore." He waved his arm and looked bright. "Here lies the start of it. The bent, bumped and humble beginnings of a great fortune, no less. And there you are, born in a box, raised in a gutter. Next he owns the gutter, next he owns everything that floats, crawls or swims in that gutter— Stop me, Quinn, something is making me feel ill."

Surprisingly, Quinn smiled. He had no quarrel with Whitfield. Most of all, he did not take him seriously. He looked at his canisters which were lying around in a puddle of water. How considerate that they should have washed the cans.

"Let's say a buck apiece," said Quinn.

He didn't look at Whitfield when he said this, but picked up a canister and turned it over. A little water ran out.

"My dear Quinn. A buck is a dollar. I understand, and in view of that fantastic price let me ask you what in the hell you think I'm going to do with all these cans."

"I don't know," said Quinn, "but I need the money."

He does sound simple again, thought Whitfield, but I no longer believe it. He watched Quinn pick up another can, lift it and hold it for a while with a look on his face which Whitfield thought was almost dreamy.

"Let's say I give you five dollars for the lot," said Whitfield, "which is a veritable fortune in Okar. And all because you were, so to speak, shipped to me and I feel responsible in a way, though don't ask me why. It would sound too sentimental. I do, however, feel responsible, as I might, for example, were a little bird to land on my window sill, exhausted from travel."

He liked that image and thought about it with his eyes closed. Then he heard Quinn laugh. But when he opened his eyes and looked at Quinn, he did not see a simple laugh, simple enjoyment of a tender comparison to a tired bird; in fact, the smile and the face were complicated. By God, thought Whitfield, if this simpleton isn't getting amazingly versatile with his features. He watched the smile fade off and Quinn put the can back down.

"Price just went up, I think," said Quinn.

"I beg your pardon?"

"Let me check first," said Quinn, and he picked up three more canisters at random, one after the other, and seemed to hook into the open tops. "Yes, yes," he said, "price went up."

Whitfield waited, being sure that there was an explanation for all this somewhere.

"You drink, don't you, Whitfield?" said Quinn and straightened up.

"Now Quinn, are you trying to reprimand me?"

Quinn smiled at Whitfield as if with affection. "I'm eight feet away from you, Whitfield, and you stink like a distillery."

"I *beg* your pardon."

"Of course. I take it back because I was mistaken and you don't smell like a distillery. Here, *catch.*" He reached for the can at his feet and made it sail in a slow arc toward Whitfield.

Whitfield caught the can because he did not want to get hit. He held the can in both hands and caught the damp wave of alcohol odor which came out of the hole in top. Goddamn those sloppy Arabs, he thought.

Quinn held out another can but Whitfield shook his head. Goddamn their disregard for the most elementary rules of cleanliness, such as to smell clean after cleaning.

"Explain this to me," said Quinn and leaned against the wall.

"Very well. As you know, Quinn, I am a drinker. As a matter of fact, I have been a trained drinker..."

"Not from five-gallon cans, Whitfield. Your supply comes in a bottle, capped and sealed, like the one you brought from the office. Besides," and Quinn nudged a can with his foot, "this smell here is alcohol, pure and simple, not gin."

"I mix my own. I am a trained..."

"Not trained well enough," said Quinn, "not enough to cover the racket I smell here."

"Your instinct for the illegal is uncanny," said Whitfield. "You must have been an excellent lawyer."

Quinn smiled again and enjoyed it.

"Small port on the North African coast," he said, looking up at the ceiling. "Dock clerk and Big Brother Remal are natural friends. Ten useless cans lie around and get filled with raw alcohol. I want my cans back, so they quick get washed out—almost washed out—so they're just cans again and not contraband carriers." Quinn looked down at Whitfield and said, "Right?"

A lot, Quinn thought, depends on Whitfield's answer. I have only conjectures, and they have holes. But Whitfield has a habit of not caring much—

"Uncanny," said Whitfield, and he hurried to his office.

He was sipping a little bit of straight gin from a teacup when Quinn found him. And now he'll crucify me with further questions, propositions and reprimands, Whitfield thought, making me feel like a schoolboy caught smoking for which I thank him not, the bully. Bottoms up.

Quinn watched Whitfield upend the cup and waited for him to catch his breath after the maneuver. He, by all accounts, is probably the weakest link in the chain, Quinn was thinking, and the nicest. I could like Whitfield a lot and don't care to know why. But I won't badger him any more. Besides, I might look elsewhere.

Old habits were stirring in him, rising like snakes uncoiling. Quinn felt relaxed, confident and no longer pressed. And if feeling friendly was not one of his old habits, it had always been an old wish. He let it show, not feeling worried about Whitfield.

God help me, thought Whitfield, he has either gone simple again or that smile is genuine.

"Back to business," said Whitfield, as if he were somebody else.

"Okay."

"You can sell me the bleedin' cans for eight dollars the lot, an outrageous price as I told you, a love price, Quinn. But then I don't love anyone anyway and so can afford it. Deal?"

"Deal."

"Preserve me. Let's go home." Whitfield turned on his heel and walked to the door.

First they drove to the garden wall of Beatrice's house, where the servant stood by the gate, waiting for the car. No, he told them, Missus Rutledge wasn't in, and Whitfield said they could say goodbye to chances for a normal dinner. Home then.

They walked away from Beatrice's house and smelled the night smell coming out of the garden. Between two houses, they took stone steps which went up to another street, and on that street they came to a corner where a strong odor of roasted coffee hung in the dark air, a warm smell lying there like a pool.

"It's always here," said Whitfield, "because of that roasting house at the corner."

Quinn saw no roasting house—only dark walls and the sky overhead, like a gray upside-down street.

"Which means," said Whitfield, "day or night, drunk or sober, I can always find my way home by the odor cloud at this corner. Doesn't that make you feel weird? Makes me feel like a dog, Quinn, going home by scent, and that does make me feel weird."

"I don't like to feel like a dog. They get eaten around here, you said."

"Well," said Whitfield. "Well! I thought *I* was being weird."

At Whitfield's apartment Quinn saw the two rooms, the two ceiling fans paddling around and around with an oily motion, and the tub in the room where the bed stood. There was water in the tub and in the water swam a label which said GIN. While Whitfield changed his shirt Quinn looked at the balcony through the French doors. Then he opened the doors and looked at all the cartons out there. He saw all the regulation gin bottles there, not cans, not odd bottles, and each of them the same brand. True, the labels of some were missing, but Quinn knew how that had come about. He closed the balcony doors again and thought, if there is no sweet racket here, smuggling this and that, then there sure as hell ought to be.

He sat down on top of the books on the couch and watched Whitfield come back with a handful of bills.

"I'll have to give you your money," said Whitfield, "in local currency. It's a pile, like I told you," and he put it on the table. "Now, watch this. Bottle of wine? A dollar to you, I should think. Here, fifteen cents. A meal. Dollar-fifty or more? Here, ten cents and up, to maybe fifty cents, figuring your kind of money. You follow?"

"Yes. Cheap spot here."

"There is an additional point: carry no more than one of these bills on you, which is about fifty cents. You don't need more to get through a day or so. This way it won't be too likely that you'll get robbed."

"All right," said Quinn and got up. He absently stuffed all the bills in his pocket and then he hitched his pants.

"You can sleep here tonight," said Whitfield. "I forgot to mention it."

"All right," said Quinn and walked to the door.

"I say, you do sound absent-minded, Quinn."

Quinn stopped at the door and opened it. He hadn't been listening.

"And I say, are you going out?"

"Yes. I'll be back in a while. Got to go out and think."

"But you mustn't!" and Whitfield ran to the door. He touched the door and then he took his hand away. He blinked at Quinn but did not quite understand the expression he saw on his face.

"And of course Remal will be over shortly. To find out how it went with the consul, to arrange for your accommodations..."

"And to tell me I'm confined to quarters after dark?"

Whitfield raised his hand once more to touch the door, but then he just dropped it. He said, "Oh, hell," and stepped back. What's happened to my baby from the box, he thought, and why the hell should I try to handle it—

Quinn walked out and down the stairs. He stood in the hall downstairs for a moment and wondered why he hadn't heard Whitfield close the door all this time, but he didn't dwell on it. He walked out, found the roasting odor, made his turn in the dark. He walked in the dark, except when crossing the main street. In the darkness again he occasionally watched the sky street overhead, and sometimes the blind walls of the houses. He felt alone and liked it. He felt he was growing up again, old habits, new habits, no matter what, and this feeling was like a tonic, the way recklessness can be.

At the end of a street was the long quay with the sky now very big overhead. The Mediterranean was black. It was here only a licking sound and a wet smell, but not an ocean.

The warehouse was dark and Quinn went there. At both ends of the building a fence closed off the company dock, a wire mesh fence, where Quinn hooked his fingers into the loops and stood looking. He saw a junk with a light swinging somewhere inside and he saw a motor yacht tied to the pier. Then the wire mesh moved under his hands, a give and a sway, making Quinn think of a net.

"Yes?" said the man.

Quinn saw that the man stood by the fence the same way he himself was doing it, hanging his hands there from hooked fingers. Big, white teeth showed in the man's very dark face and Quinn wondered if this was a smile.

"Yes? Yes?" said the man, always showing the smile.

"Yes what?" said Quinn.

"Yes, Yes?"

It's the only English he knows, thought Quinn, and he is a beggar.

"Yes?" said the man again and this time he laughed. He swayed the fence a little and laughed.

"I don't know what you want," said Quinn and turned away.

He looked through the fence and wished that the man, who might also be an idiot, would stop swaying the wire mesh. The mesh swayed more and suddenly gave a wild jerk, hitting Quinn in the face.

"Yes? Yes?"

The man laughed again even though Quinn turned with a sharp motion, full of anger.

"Yes!"

What to say. How talk to an idiot who knows one word and laughs all the time. And then Quinn saw that there was another man.

Then he realized why he had not heard either of them. One of them was barefooted and the other, the grinning one by the fence, had rags wound around his feet, giving them the shape of soft loaves.

The barefooted one came from the water side and the grinning one also came closer. Then the barefooted one leaped.

Quinn smelled a terrible stink from the man, and for that first moment Quinn struggled only because of that. But then the grinning one hurt him. He had his arms around Quinn's middle and his hands dug Quinn in the spine. For some strange reason, Quinn could suddenly hear nothing. The man let go, stepped back, hit Quinn in the face. Quinn felt confused and therefore weak. Even the slap in the face did not arouse him. He found no anger, no strength, no clear-cut emotion. He wanted to say "Why?", and he wanted to ask this for most of the time that he was still conscious.

It was a strange fight and it did not last very long. Quinn hit back and saw the man laugh. He could hear again in a moment and heard the dry skin sound of bare feet, the lick sound of the water, cough sound of the idiot laugh, twang sound of the fence, which gave like a net when the three men rolled against it. Quinn did not hurt much while they fought nor did he enjoy much what he was doing. Then he tasted blood and then his head jarred and he went out.

When he woke up he thought that he was on the junk with the light inside. He saw the light swaying and felt his insides turn over with nausea and thought, I'm seasick. But then he felt the stone floor under his hands and the hard weave of the fence pressing into his back. I've been out less than a minute, he thought. He knew this for certain because there was still the hard muscle pain in his stomach where he had been hit and the blood was fresh and warm on his lip. Also, his breathing was still going deep and heavy.

The other thing he knew for certain was why he had been jumped. He put one hand on his thigh, feeling the money wad still in his pocket. They hadn't been beggars and they hadn't been robbers, but Whitfield was in on this thing and the strong-arm business told him, Keep away from the pier. Here in Okar. Not back home, but here in Okar.

He looked at the lamp and saw how close it was and then he looked up and saw who was holding it.

"Are you all right, Mister Quinn?" said Remal.

Quinn set his teeth and did not answer. He heard footsteps running and saw Whitfield come around the side of the building. He was carrying a wet rag. He ran over to Quinn and crouched next to him and offered the rag to him. He tried to say something or other but nothing came out. He was also trying to smile and frown at the same time but was too upset for either.

"Put it on the back of your neck," said Remal. "It will clear you."

Clear enough, thought Quinn. Everything is very clear, except that the instinct has gone out of me and I sit here and feel so clear that I'm empty.

"Quinn? Uh, Quinn, I'm most terribly sorry..."

"Let Mister Quinn get up, if he wishes," said Remal.

Quinn got up. He did this carefully, hooking his fingers into the fence and working up that way like a slow-moving monkey. When he stood he took a deep breath and looked at the other two men. Whitfield looked nervous and even embarrassed. Remal smiled. Quinn felt that he did not know about Remal yet.

"Can you walk?" said Whitfield. "If you can't, just sit down again. Or come sit in my office."

"Why sit in your office?" said Quinn, and, "Why are you here?"

"Remal wanted to talk to you," said Whitfield. "You remember I told..."

"You had left when I came," said Remal, "so we went out to look for you."

"Here?" said Quinn.

Remal lifted the lantern he had in one hand and held it so the light shone on Quinn's face. Remal looked closely at him and squinted a little.

"Bad cut," he said. "Does not look very good," and he put his free hand out and poked at the cut with two fingers, causing a sharp pain. "Yes, yes," he said.

Quinn jerked his head back because of the pain and then wiped one eye, which had started to water. He felt confused again, and therefore weak. The instinct's gone out of me, he thought. Damn all of them, but I'll get it back—

Then they went around the long warehouse and into Whitfield's office. The walking was not so bad.

Remal held the lamp and Whitfield found the switch on the wall for the light. Remal put the lamp on the floor but did not blow it out.

The office was a place with chairs, files and a desk, but it was not an Okar place, thought Quinn. This is a lot like a picture I've seen, illustrating something by Dickens. The desk had a pigeonhole back and there were ledgers with red leather spines. The swivel chair, Quinn thought, will probably creak.

Remal sat down in the chair and made it creak. The big man flounced his long shirt, crossed his legs, and touched the stitched skullcap on his head. This spoiled the illustration of something by Dickens. The Arab did not belong in such an office, the office did not belong in Okar, and Quinn, inconsequentially, thought of the upside-down street which had followed him overhead on his way down. His left eye still watered. That's why I can't find a focus, he thought.

"Yes, well," said Remal, and looked at his hands. Then he folded them and looked at Quinn. "So it seems," he said, "that your own consul has, one might say, committed you to my care. Does it hurt?"

Quinn took his hand away from his face and looked at his fingers. There was a small stain of blood there and he felt it by rubbing his fingertips together.

"I didn't like it when you hurt me like that," he said. "It felt like on purpose."

"I apologize. Really, Mister Quinn."

"Was it on purpose?"

Whitfield felt as if the air was suddenly getting terribly heavy. Quinn hasn't moved and Remal hasn't moved, he thought, but something has. A mood in Quinn. Everything he hasn't done while he was getting his beating is now starting to move in him. Like a very slow waking up—

"Of course not," said Remal. He even smiled, but without looking at Quinn. Then he said, "What needs to happen now, Mister Quinn, is to take better care of you while you are still here."

"I don't need any..."

"Please. You just got beaten up. I also apologize for that."

"You didn't do it."

"I am the mayor. I do feel responsible."

Whitfield sighed and sat down on a chair. Remal was acting official, which somehow took the black mood out of the room. Or perhaps now the mood could be ignored, the way Remal seemed to be ignoring Quinn. He talked to Quinn as if about routine business.

"And feeling responsible, Mister Quinn, here is how we shall handle this."

Quinn leaned back in his chair, very slowly and cautiously it seemed to Whitfield. Then he saw Quinn stick out his tongue and touch the tip of it to the cut which ran down to his lip. Quinn did that very slowly too.

"As long as you have no papers," said Remal, "you must stay here in town. This you know. And as long as you stay in this town, Mister Quinn, you must observe a few rules of safety."

"Like don't go out after dark?" said Quinn.

"Why, yes," said Remal and smiled. Then the smile went again and he cleared his throat. "That is point number one. Point number two, please do not go into the Arab quarter. You are unfamiliar here, unfamiliar with ways and with people. They will find you strange and you will feel the same about them, which is always dangerous. It is best you have nothing to do with them."

There was a small silence and then Quinn said, "Was there a third point?"

A silence again and Whitfield fingered his chin. He wished he were some place else.

"Yes. Point number three: Do not go near the waterfront after dark. I don't think I need to explain why."

"No. That you don't."

"After all, you are still suffering the consequences."

Quinn got up from his chair and stretched himself carefully. He did this mostly to learn where he was hurting. Then he walked to the window which looked from the office into the warehouse, but it was dark on the other side and he saw only his own head reflected.

I don't know, I don't know, he thought. I give up Ryder and now I get this. Like a clear jinx riding me. Jinx in the box.

"And now that we understand each other..." Remal was saying, when Quinn turned around from the window.

"Have you got any idea why you don't like me?" he said to Remal.

When Quinn heard himself say this he was as startled as the other two men. He turned back to the window. Got to get out, out of here. Go see Turk, he thought. See what there's to see. I need more than my guesswork about cans smelling like booze—

"I really don't know what you mean, Mister Quinn, seeing that you and I hardly know each other."

We don't, we don't for a fact, but still I have this feeling—

"I have no feelings about you, Mister Quinn. Perhaps it is that which offends you."

And he may be right. He's the one who makes this vacuum around me, with no feelings one way or the other. I lost the instinct— Get a beating, get the runaround, get the law laid down to me. And nothing happens inside. I've lost the instinct—

"However," said Remal, "I have not finished. There is this fourth point. If you do not obey..."

"Obey?" said Quinn.

"Perhaps my English is inadequate." Remal shrugged.

"I think it is good," said Quinn. "I don't know what else to think of it but I think it is good."

Remal looked at Whitfield and frowned. Quinn's talk was confusing him. Perhaps, this Quinn person himself was confused, he thought, and he'd best put a halt to this quickly now.

"To finish," he said and got up, "as I gather from the police officials and by inference, you are familiar with the rules of disobedience. I have talked to you, Mister Quinn, and I wish you no harm. But I have talked to you about rules and I am now finished talking. Whitfield, take him home." Remal turned and walked out the door.

He left Quinn speechless and Whitfield worried. Whitfield did not think Quinn would stay speechless or dumfounded like this for very long.

Chapter 9

After the sirocco comes through and then disappears over the water, there is often a motion of slow, heavy air. Nobody feels it move in, but it is there, like a standing cloud, a mass of heat. This phenomenon, in a Western climate, might mean a thunderstorm and release. But not in Okar.

Quinn walked out into the street and felt it. He felt the still heat inside and out and how nothing moved. Something's got to happen, he felt, something—

He walked next to Whitfield, ignoring him, aware only of the heat which did not move.

"Quinn, not so fast. Please," said Whitfield. "The steps, you know," and Whitfield puffed a little, which he blamed on breaking training with the two bottles in the back of the car.

Quinn stopped a few steps ahead of him, where the street leveled out again, and touched the side of his face.

"Uh. Quinn."

"Yes."

"I wanted to tell you I am most awfully sorry about what happened to you tonight. Please believe me."

Nothing's happened yet, thought Quinn. He felt himself breathe and how hard it was. He almost began to count. Like a count-down, he thought, except I don't know how many numbers to go—

"Believe me, Quinn, I had no idea. What I mean is, I was most terribly shocked coming upon that scene there by the fence. Really, Quinn."

"I believe you," said Quinn. He was suddenly bored with Whitfield. "I really do, Whitfield," he said in order to make his point and stop talking. He wanted to get away. Whitfield would soon start meandering again and that had a dulling effect. Like getting drunk on Whitfield, Quinn thought. Got to get away now. Nothing holds as still as I've been holding still and I don't know how but it can't be much longer.

They crossed the main street and Quinn stopped under a light. "Whitfield, listen. I'm not going home yet. I'm nervous."

"Fine. We can go to the hotel, where they serve..."

"Not that kind of nervous. When you get home, leave the light on for me."

"What's that you said?"

The question was stupid because Whitfield had understood well enough. He stopped and watched Quinn walk off. Sighing, he watched Quinn's back lit by a lamp, then dark in shadow, then lit by a lamp, the footsteps getting fainter.

He's batty, thought Whitfield. Now he's going to the Arab quarter. But I'm going home. The last time I told Remal where Quinn might be, Remal had the poor thing beaten up. I feel shaken about it even now. I must plan something soothing at home—

The Arab quarter, Quinn discovered, was not very large. He walked the narrow streets slowly and twice ended up in open country where he could see no roads. The quarter was not large but it was complicated, and Quinn knew he was lost almost immediately. But that did not bother him. He knew with an uncomplicated certainty he would find his man. Or Turk would find him. It was also very simple in his mind why he had to see Turk. There is a rat here whom I can understand. And maybe I can use what he knows. Quinn had no clear notion what this last thought really meant, but he did not question it. Remal, of course, had pushed him around, but the fact was, he had not yet reacted to it.

Maybe it never rains here, he thought, and the heat just hangs, just stays this way— He broke out in a sudden sweat, as if frightened. The noise got to him just as suddenly as if there had been silence before, which was not true. Some Arabs were arguing, or perhaps they were just talking, but they yelled, and children yelled, and a dog howled. Even the light makes a noise, thought Quinn. The yellow light in the doorway wasn't still but jumped and gutted.

Quinn took a deep breath and smelled the warm oiliness of something cooking. All right, I'm hungry. That's what all this is about, and he walked through the doorway into a long, crowded room with long tables, short tables, and men sitting on benches. The men stared at him but kept eating or talking. They looked at him as if they knew who he was.

Quinn sat down next to a man who was slurping a stew. He was an old man who seemed to have only one tooth and his jaw churned wildly while he ate. When Quinn looked up, there was a boy standing next to him who said something in Arabic.

"You the waiter?" said Quinn. "Eat," and he showed what he meant by pointing at the stew the old man was eating.

"Don't order that stuff. It's not any good."

Quinn turned and saw Turk standing behind him. Turk smiled quickly, as if it were expected of him.

"Why? Is it dog?"

"Not the point, friend. That dish is very cheap. The price goes by how rotten the meat is." Then Turk said something to the boy, and when the boy had gone Turk sat down opposite Quinn. "I ordered for you. Okay?"

"Thank you."

"You were looking for me, huh?"

Quinn felt an unreasonable annoyance at the remark, but then he admitted, yes, he had been looking for Turk. He wanted to ask, how in hell did you know I was looking for you, but felt cramped with his anger and said nothing.

"He beats you up, he beats me up, so of course we meet," said Turk, and his smile made it sound like a stupid joke.

"You're talking about Remal," said Quinn.

"Of course. He who had them beat you up."

"You seem to know everything."

"Almost."

"Is that how you lost your teeth, he beat you up?"

"No. I was speaking in a manner of speaking," said Turk. "He beats me in some other way."

"What way?" said Quinn, but his stew came at that moment, and while the boy put the bowl down Turk did not answer.

"In what way?" Quinn asked again.

"How does a strong man beat a weak one?" said Turk. "He ignores the weak one. He beats me in that way."

That's got nothing to do with me, and the thought came to Quinn in a rush of anger. He took a spoonful of stew and burnt his mouth.

"I would do an errand for him here and there," Turk was saying, "and I would see how badly run all his business really is."

"The smuggling?"

"Yes. And I would make suggestions, try to advise him on how to do better, more money, more everything. Ek—" said Turk with a shrug and a face as if avoiding the touch of something disgusting, "and he would ignore me."

"You're a sensitive bastard, aren't you?" said Quinn, but though Turk answered something or other, Quinn did not hear him. The night's beating, the off-hand treatment by Remal—all that came back now as a clear, sharp offense, like a second beating, not of the body this time, but something worse.

Like I didn't exist, it struck Quinn. And this time, without moving a

muscle, a cold hate, which seemed very familiar, moved into Quinn, settled there and started to heat.

"He could be somebody to admire," Turk was saying, "but, well, ek—"
and he made his gesture again.

"You poor bastard," said Quinn with a lot of feeling. "You poor bastard,"
and he started to eat his stew.

"Oh?" and this time, with a smile, Turk laughed. "What about you, man
from the box?"

The stew was over-spiced and had some offensive flavors in it, but
Quinn didn't taste a thing. He swallowed without chewing very much and
stared at Turk.

"All I meant was," said Turk very quickly, "here you are now, here you
come innocent like a lamb..."

"Tell me something, Turk. Why do you hang around me?"

"Oh that? Well, you were new in town, I heard about you and..."

"Stop crapping me. What do you want?"

Turk shrugged and said, "Perhaps money. Perhaps company. Perhaps
nothing else to do."

"Money. That's the only thing that makes sense in your answer," and
Quinn thought, I can use this bastard. I can maybe use him—

"It is really simple and no mystery and no double-talk," Turk explained.
He felt he had better say something solid now and no more grinning and
crapping around, as the American had expressed it. "I have heard, of
course, about your background. Or at any rate, the talk that has been
about you, that you must have been somebody with the big-business criminals in your country.

"Go on."

"And, as you did find out this night, how Remal is perhaps worried
about you..."

"Why?"

"An unusual arrival draws unusual attention."

"I never did anything to him."

"Ah, that is Remal. He anticipates."

Quinn felt suddenly dangerous and important. He felt like an embarrassed boy about this, but the sense of drama remained.

"I felt," Turk went on, "that if you are pushed, you push back."

"You haven't told me yet what you want."

"Ek—" said Turk. "I would like to see how a man like you deals with a
person like Remal. That's all."

You left out the money, thought Quinn. And for that matter, so have I, so have I— A month or more in this burg with really nothing to do, and there's some kind of set-up here, no mistake about it, and maybe a thing to be made. But the thought did not really interest him.

Quinn touched the side of his face where he had been cut in the beating, and he touched there to feel the burn and the sting. He touched there to feel just how much he had been hurt.

And then, eating stew as if nothing else mattered, he got back more of the old habits. It happened that smoothly. The old habits of grab and kick, of anticipate, the sharp, quick decisions to be ahead of the game, any game, or somebody else would be playing it his own way which means, Quinn, you're out!

"The strangest thing," said Turk from across the table. "You look like a new man," and of course he grinned.

For a brief moment Quinn felt confused, and then lost and sad. But it was too fast and he knew nothing clearly. And of course neither he nor Turk understood that there was nothing new about Quinn now, that he was no longer new at all.

They left the place because Quinn couldn't stand the smell any more, after he was done eating.

"The hotel?" asked Turk, because he would have liked to go there.

"No. Some place here is fine. But I don't want to have to sit on the same bench with everybody."

"Ah. You have secrets."

"No. But I want to ask some."

They walked down the street, deeper into the quarter.

"I don't get this," said Quinn, "how a smart man like Remal will pull such a primitive stunt. He gets me beaten up right there where he doesn't want me to look around, and then when I wake up he's standing over me with a lantern."

"Why do more?" said Turk and shrugged. "He just wanted you beaten. If you should want to know about Remal and his business, you can always find out. He did not try to hide things from you, but he tried to tell you what happens if you interfere with him."

"He'll have to do better than that," said Quinn.

"He can," and Turk laughed. "However, at first, he is polite. We go in here."

They walked into a cafe, a small room with small tables, and this time there was no grease smell and food smell but heavy clouds of blue smoke and coffee odor. Through an arch they went into a second room which was much like a basement, with one slit of a window high up, and the walls bare stone. Not many people sat here. Each round table had only two chairs, which looked intimate.

"To keep their secrets just a little bit longer," said Turk, "merchants come here, and the traders from across this or that border."

They sat down and leaned their elbows on the table. The waiter appeared and nodded to Turk.

"You know," said Turk, "they have good little cakes here. Would you like some with a glass of liqueur?"

Quinn thought that sounded revolting and asked for a pot of tea.

"I'll have the liqueur, with permission," said Turk.

They ordered and then they sat, looking at each other. Obviously, thought Quinn, he and I want different things and we don't know how to get together. He wants to import a Made in USA gang-organizer, which is ridiculous, and I want to be left alone by the likes of this Remal, and that sounds ridiculous too. I want more.

Quinn stopped there, feeling sick of thinking. He sipped his tea and looked at the other tables. The faces were shut, the gestures were fast. The heads were close to one another over the tables so that the talk would not go very far. They hiss like snakes, thought Quinn.

"Does Remal come here?" he asked.

"Sometimes. But not tonight. Tonight he is elsewhere."

"And naturally you know where."

"It's no secret. He sleeps with the foreign woman sometimes. How is your tea?"

"Like hot perfume."

"Salut," said Turk, and tilted his little glass.

The liqueur was red and smelled like sugar and the tea was yellow and smelled like flowers. And I belong here, thought Quinn, like I belong in a box. Both don't fit. But he didn't think any of that through and asked something else.

"About Whitfield," he said. "Is he very important? I mean, when it comes to Remal and his business."

"I like Whitfield," said Turk, "but I don't like the other one."

"I didn't ask that."

"Salut," said Turk and finished his liqueur. "I admire Whitfield because he knows how to live with limitations. Remal does not, nor do I."

"I asked you if he is important."

"Whitfield is a dock, a very good company name, and he has a short-wave radio, all of which is important. Whitfield, however, is not. I like him," and Turk put down his glass.

Bad Mohammedan, thought Quinn. He drinks.

Bad Westerner, thought Turk. He sits and does nothing, like me, but he feels badly about it.

It was then Quinn got up. "All right," he said. "Show me the way out of here, Turk."

"You are going home?"

Quinn paid the old man who waited on tables, slapped Turk on the arm, and said, "I want you to show me the quarter."

"In Paris," said Turk, "that type of remark used to mean only one thing."

"I've never been in Paris. Come on."

There was a second door which led from the room and Turk went that way. After the door came a passage which smelled dry and spicy.

"They belong to Remal," said Turk, "some of these bundles."

The passage had hemp-wrapped bales all along one side and the bales were tied with fiber.

"Contraband?" said Quinn. "I didn't know spices were still smuggled."

"It isn't all spices. He smuggles everything."

"Everything what? Tobacco, silk, alcohol, drugs, what?"

"Everything. These things here go tonight. Come."

A wide-open set-up, thought Quinn. Remal, not being stupid, must he very powerful—

The passage led to the outside, but Turk stopped at a door between stacks of bundles. He opened it and went inside.

The room was for storage, Quinn thought, because of the barrels which were stacked by the walls. There was an oil lamp on top of a barrel and all the men standing around seemed to shift and move, though they stood quite still. The light dipped and bubbled and constantly changed the shadows. The men did not talk and only their clothes made small sounds. They were waiting.

Quinn sucked in his breath, trying not to feel shocked.

There was a small, low table and a very young girl lay on top of it. Quinn could tell that she was very young because her long robe was pushed all the way up. It was bunched up under her arms and under her chin where she held it with her hands. She had small, brown hands, like raccoon paws. One man stood at the end of the table where he held the girl by her hips.

"All of them?" said Quinn, and he heard himself whisper.

"It's all right," said Turk. "She goes on the boat."

"The what?"

"Tonight's boat. I told you that Remal trades in everything."

The man at the table wore a wide burnoose which covered all of him. When he leaned more and gripped the girl hard, his shadow suddenly flapped up the wall like a bat, up the wall and over the ceiling. Then it collapsed again and went away. The man stepped away and there was shifting and murmuring. The girl stayed on the table.

"You are a guest," said Turk. "They say if you would like to he next then you don't have to wait."

"No. Thank you," said Quinn.

He didn't say anything else but felt pressure inside from the sight he saw there—the girl on the table who acted as if she were not there, the men in the room, and things like ropes and wires, perhaps the most delicate parts of which they were made.

And Remal trades in this. I drop out of a box, thin-skinned like a maggot, and a cold bastard like Remal, moving the ropes and wires inside his anatomy, steps on me.

"Let's go," said Quinn, and looked for the door.

There was a door to the outside and Turk pushed it open. The girl looked up at Quinn when he walked past and then closed her eyes. There was sweat on her forehead and one of the men, with the end of his burnoose, gave a dab to her face.

And that doesn't change anything either, thought Quinn. It looks almost human, that gesture, but it changes nothing.

He stood outside in the alley, wishing he could smell the desert which was not far away. There probably is no smell to the desert, he thought. He shivered with a sensitivity which was painful. Like a goat, that's what she looked like. Even after she closed her eyes. That's how he treats everybody, like Quinn the goat, like a piece of meat hanging down from a nail—

"Perhaps you would like..." Turk started, but he didn't get any further.

"When are they done in there, with the girl?"

"Done? I don't know. The boat, I think, doesn't leave until after midnight. If you would like..."

"I want her."

"Alone? All right. But I could get you..."

"Shut up. Get that one. Borrow her. Pay the captain for the loan of the cargo he's got on the table there."

"That won't be necessary, I don't think. Just a little token, perhaps, but there is no real price."

"But there will be," Quinn said to no one in particular. "There most certainly will be," and he wiped his face because he was sweating again, feeling a sharp, sudden anger.

Chapter 10

Turk, of course, thought all along that Quinn meant to sleep with the girl.
"I understand," he said, "how you, a civilized Westerner, might feel shy
with a woman whom you love. But this one?" and he pointed at the girl
who was walking between them. "This one, as you saw on the table..."
"Stop talking a minute," said Quinn. "Now listen close." They were leaving the quarter and turned down the main street, walking towards the
lights which started a few blocks away. "You and me," he said, "maybe we'll
do a thing or two together, and then maybe we won't. I haven't got a plan,
I haven't even got anything that amounts to a notion. All I've got right now
is a bug itch and an annoyance."
"If you're worried about not having any money," Turk said, when Quinn
interrupted again.
"And don't try doing my thinking for me, all right?"
"All right," said Turk, "All right," and he shrugged.
"I was going to say, if you and I should maybe do something together,
seeing I'll be here a month or so, then I'll need your help."
This was nothing new to Turk, but he was happy to see how Quinn,
though still fresh out of the box in more than one way of speaking, how
he was starting to move and think in a way Turk understood. Turk had
known how Quinn would need help. What he hadn't known came next.
"I'm not interested in money, Turk. I'm interested only in being left
alone. I feel bugged and I itch. When I scratch myself it isn't to make an
income. You got that?"
Turk got none of it.
"All I want from you are two things. One, information."
"What do you wish to know?"
"Nothing right now. Just listen, huh?"
Turk didn't understand that either.
"And two, I might need another set of eyes, like in the back of my head,
so I don't get jumped in some dark alley."
"Ah, you are already afraid of Remal."
"I got jumped once already," said Quinn. "In return, seeing as you're a
greedy bastard, maybe I can help you in getting a slice or two out of
Remal's racket." Quinn sighed, feeling tired. "I have a little background for
it," he said.

And so he had made another small move, still without seeing which way he was tending.

Quinn showed the way to Whitfield's house, and when they got there he told Turk to wait downstairs, in the dark yard. He is shy with that child, thought Turk, as if she were a woman and he not too sure about being a man. It is a Western disease.

The light was on in the room with the couch and the door to the bedroom was closed. This meant, Quinn figured, that Whitfield was drunk and asleep in his bed and that he, Quinn, was to use the couch for the night. The couch was still full of books. The girl, who looked amorphous in her big, loose robe, stood in the middle of the room waiting for Quinn to show her what to do next.

"Sit down," he said and waved at the couch.

She went to the couch and started to take the books off, to make room.

"No, no, just sit there, goddamit, *sit,*" and he showed her by pushing her down.

Her face stayed as always, mouth closed, eyes big and dumb. Her face was thin, which made her look old, and the skin was smooth, which made her look young. Quinn didn't concern himself much with any of this.

"Now stay put. Sit. And no sound." All this he showed her.

From the next room he heard a wild splashing. And then, "I say there, is that you, Quinn?"

He even sleeps in that tub, so help me—

"Yes, it's me," he said, "I just got in."

"Are you dumping the books? I'm terribly sorry I forgot about those books."

"That's all right. Sorry I woke you."

"Not at all, not at all. But you'll need a pillow and a blanket. I say, Quinn, would you mind terribly getting the stuff yourself. Open the door."

"I don't need anything. Go back to sleep."

"Don't be ridiculous. Open the door."

Quinn went and opened the door. The light was on in the bedroom, too, and of course Whitfield was not in his bed. Everybody seems to know about this boat tonight, Quinn thought, and looked at Whitfield in his tub, face wet, knees drawn up to make room for the black-haired girl who was in the water with him. This one did not have a child's body. She was full-fleshed and she glistened. Quinn thought of wet rubber.

"I'm terribly sorry," Whitfield was saying, "but you'll forgive me if I don't get up."

"I understand fully," said Quinn, and them he meant to tell Whitfield to go on with his bath and that he himself hadn't meant to go to sleep right now, anyway. But Whitfield at that point spotted the girl on the couch and he was shocked.

"My *dear* Quinn! But forgive me, and while I don't wish to impose on your own good judgment—eh, where did you pick that up?"

"In the quarter."

"Now, Quinn, please, let me try and be friendly. We have, you don't seem to know, a terrible disease problem here, and unless you are very sure..."

"Forget it, it doesn't matter."

"Doesn't matter? *Please.* Quinn, send her away and in no more than half an hour I will send you this one. I'm quite certain of this one and I'm really trying to be friendly."

"I can hardly think of anything friendlier," said Quinn. "But I'm not sleeping with the one on the couch."

"Oh? Tell me about it. What do you do?" Whitfield showed polite interest.

"Look. Friendliest thing you can do for me right now is yell across to her to stay put here till I get back. I won't be long."

"Well," and Whitfield shrugged, "not that I understand it." Then he yelled across at the girl to stay put. He spoke in Arabic, but the girl didn't answer or even open her mouth. She only nodded. Quinn started to close the door.

"No, leave it open," said Whitfield from the tub. "I don't want her to steal anything."

Quinn stopped, then smiled at the picture. He went downstairs. In the dark yard Turk stepped up to him.

"Done?"

"No," said Quinn. "Just starting." And then he told Turk to stay in the yard and see that the girl did not leave.

"She won't," said Turk, "not if you told her to stay. Besides, I feel you may need the eyes in the back of your head tonight."

"I doubt it. Yet."

"Mister Quinn," said Turk, "I won't tell you how to think, but please do not tell me what I feel in the air. What I feel is getting darker and thicker. So I will watch out."

"I'm only going to..."

"I know where you are going. Since you did not sleep with the girl, it stands to reason."

"Maybe you also know why I brought her up there."

"No," said Turk. "In some ways you do not think as clearly as I do. This makes it hard to understand your reasons. But you go," said Turk, "and I will watch out." He disappeared in the shadows again.

Quinn wasn't sure what Turk intended. Walking in the darkness, he felt a strange sense of safety which he knew was connected with nothing real.

Bea's house sat in a dark garden and no light showed anywhere. Like a midnight visit which once happened to me, it struck him, but then he rattled the gate to make a noise because he could not find a bell. Nothing happened for perhaps a minute, but when Quinn got ready to call out a servant came running up to the gate. He spoke no English but understood that Quinn wanted in. He opened the gate because there had been no orders to keep it closed.

He took Quinn to a downstairs room where he lit a lamp. After that, nobody showed for about fifteen minutes.

The room looked dull, drapes too dark and heavy, furniture dark and heavy. There was also a vase of large flowers, but they did not make the room gay. He saw a box of cigarettes on a round table and without thinking about it took one, lit up and smoked. He watched his hand, how it held the cigarette, flipped ash. The damnedest thing, he thought. It's really the damnedest thing to forget that I used to smoke. And what else did I forget—When he was done with the cigarette he felt tense and hostile. He could recall nothing else which he might have forgotten, but it had suddenly struck him that he had no clear idea of what he wanted with Remal. Then he heard the footsteps coming down a hall. I'll let it go till I see him, he thought. That should help—

But when the door opened it wasn't Remal who came in. Beatrice smiled at Quinn as if she was really pleased to see him. She brushed her hair back with one hand. She wore no make-up and looked as if she had been asleep.

"What exciting hours you keep," she said.

And you too, he thought. And she's not wearing a thing under that dress, which is why she looks this soft and slow. Or the no-lipstick face does it. A real face in bed on a big, deep pillow—

"I didn't come to see you," he said without any transition.

She sat down on a couch and didn't know what to say. But then she laughed. She took a cigarette from the boy and kept eyeing him.

"It was about the last thing I expected you to say, Mister Quinn," and she gave a low laugh again. "Not the way you were looking at me."

"I'm sorry."

"So am I. Do you have a light?"

He lit her cigarette for her, watching the end of the match and nothing else.

"If Remal is here, I'd like to see him for a minute."

She leaned back and blew smoke.

"You must have been talking to one or the other of everybody, seeing that you know exactly what goes on in my house." She made a small pause and then, "He won't like it."

"I know he won't," and Quinn smiled.

She had not seen him smile before and had wondered, after the one time she had seen him in the hotel, how he might smile. She had speculated what a smile might do to his face which she remembered as looking still or indifferent, the eyes in particular. That's the difference, she thought. The eyes changed. They had not been looking for anything, but now they were. And the smile? It smiles at something I know nothing about, and that's why it bothers me—

She got up and said, "I'll get him for you." When she was by the door, she added, "I thought you were on a curfew?"

"You must have been talking to one or the other of almost everybody, too," said Quinn.

"No. Just Remal." She came back into the room and stubbed her cigarette out in a tray. "Quinn?"

I wish she'd go, he thought. I don't know what to think of her. She's less simple than anyone here—

"You know, it would be easier if you had come to see me. I'm much easier to see."

"I wouldn't come because you're easy."

He had said it without thinking. She started to smile but then didn't because he was not smiling. They looked at each other with an unexpected quiet between them. Then she took a quick breath and turned away. Of course, he wants to see Remal. And I want anything I don't know. So, of course—

She walked out and Quinn did not watch her. He did not have to watch her to know what she looked like, how she walked, how she felt. She feels like me, he thought. Or the way I did those first few days here— And Quinn almost felt as if he had lost something.

When she got to the bedroom she saw Remal standing on the other side
of the open French doors. He stood on the dark balcony and was stretch-
ing, and at the end of the stretch he made a sound which was a lot like a
purr. He is a big cat and needs a jungle. No, he is too sly and too educated but he is a big cat in bed. I like him there but nowhere else. A big cat
in bed. What a way to think of a man: a cat.

"*Cheri,*" she said, "it's for you."

He turned and when he saw her he smiled and came into the room. "For
me? What is it?"

"Quinn is downstairs."

She thought she could hear something snap when his face changed. The
smile was gone, as if his thin mouth had bit into the smile and made it
break into pieces, and his black female eyes became black the way Chinese
lacquer is black and cold. He said nothing and walked past her, out the
door.

Remal's face had not changed at all when he walked up to Quinn, and
Quinn saw the same thing there which Beatrice had seen. But he reacted
differently than she had—not with a fright which was kept still with
silence, but clear dislike. Remal kept standing.

"Since you left your quarters after dark, I will place you under house
arrest, Mister Quinn."

I don't exist for him. Except as a violation of law—

"Sit down, won't you," Quinn said. He was surprised at his own calm.

"This can't possibly take long. I'll stand."

Quinn shrugged. He said, "I'll be here about one month, no more. If for
that length of time you want to stand like that, look like that, then suit
yourself. Except I don't like it."

"I'm too polite to laugh," said Remal. "However, I will have you jailed."

"I don't think you can afford that," said Quinn.

"Are you blackmailing me?"

"Of course." Quinn got up, walked around the small table.

"And you want?" said Remal. He said it only because it was the next logical question, but not because he was really concerned. He must go, of
course. Perhaps I will have him killed.

Quinn stopped walking and turned. It was suddenly all very simple. And
if the mayor can feel as straight as I do now, all this can be over. It felt
almost as simple as coming out of the box.

"I want you off my back," said Quinn. "You understand the expression?
I want you to leave me alone."

"Are you leaving me alone?"

"It comes to the same thing," said Quinn. "I want no part of your troubles. I want no part of your schemes. I'm not interested in you."

"You make me sound like I don't exist," said Remal, and he thought again, I may have to have him killed.

"I wish to hell you didn't exist, that's a fact," and Quinn meant it. "But while you do, I don't want to get jumped in the dark, I don't want your curfews. That's what I mean by getting off my back."

It was that simple. Quinn took a deep breath and knew this: if he gives the right answer now then he *is* off my back. I don't even feel angry any more. He can be of no importance. If only he gives the right answer now—

Upstairs, Quinn could hear someone walking, then the sound of a chair. That's the woman, he thought. What if Remal were not here at all—

"I don't think you finished," said Remal. "You didn't say 'or else'. Your kind always says 'or else'."

The bastard, thought Quinn. The ugly bastard—

" 'Or else' what, Mister Quinn?"

Quinn sat down on a chair, put his arms on the table and looked at his hands. He didn't give the right answer. He's still on my back, no matter if I put him there or if he jumped on by himself, and now— He didn't finish the thought. He didn't have to. He felt the dislike creep in again, like cold fog. The straight talk is over. I didn't know I could talk that straight, but it's over now and back to the conniving.

He looked up at Remal, and this was the first time that the mayor really saw the other man. He had missed everything that had gone before. He might have been looking at Quinn some time back, somewhere in New York, and there would have been no difference. I'll kill him, of course—

"Mayor," said Quinn. "For my information: let's say a man, some man who lives in the quarter, comes up to you and says, 'Sir, give me ten dollars or I go to the authorities and tell them everything I know about your shipping business.' "

"Who knows about it?"

"Don't be naive. Everybody does."

Remal let that go by. He conceded the point by closing his eyes. When they came open they were on Quinn again, taking him in with great care and interest.

"What would you do if some man came up to you like that?"

"Kill him," said Remal.

Quinn smiled. He was starting to like the game.

"Now let's say I come up, just like that rat from the quarter." Quinn stopped smiling and leaned over the table a little. "You think you can do the same thing to me *and* get away with it?"

Remal thought for a moment because he had never considered that there might be a difference.

"I'm under official protection," said Quinn, "of official interest. I'm a citizen of another country. I'm an active case with my consulate, and then suddenly I *disappear.*"

There was a silence while Remal folded his arms, looked up at the ceiling. When he looked back at Quinn, nothing had changed. Neither Quinn nor Remal.

"Yes," said Remal. "You will just suddenly disappear." He shrugged and said, "It has happened before. Even in your country it happens, am I right? And you have so many more laws."

Now the bastard is laughing at me and he's right and I'm wrong.

"Was that the blackmail, Mister Quinn?"

"No. And all I wanted from you..."

"Come to the point."

There was a magazine on the table and Quinn flipped the pages once so that they made a quick, nervous rat- tat-tat. Then he looked up. "I've got some of your merchandise."

"Also a thief, I see."

"And this merchandise talks. She was going out on a boat tonight, white slave shipment to some place, which would interest anyone from your local constable to the High Commissioner of the Interpol system."

This time Remal sat down, but he was smiling. "All this, Mister Quinn, so I don't put you on a curfew?"

"That's how it started," said Quinn, which he knew didn't answer the question. That's how it started, he thought, but I don't know any more. I might like to go further.

Remal threw his head back and laughed loud and hard. When he was done he did not care how Quinn was looking at him.

"You found her where, Mr. Quinn, on my boat?"

"In the quarter."

"Ah. And she was being used, no doubt, somewhere in an alley."

"The point is I have her."

"Was she thin and young, Mister Quinn?" And when Quinn didn't answer, Remal said as if to himself, "They usually are, the ones Hradin brings in."

"Maybe you didn't get my point, Mayor."

"Oh that," and Remal sighed. Then he said, "More important, you're not getting mine. I know the trader who brought her, I know from which tribe she comes, and I know something else which seems to have escaped you. She, her type, has been owned since childhood. One owner, two, more, I don't know. Uh, Mister Quinn, have you talked to her?"

"I don't speak Arabic."

"Neither does she. But have you talked to her?"

"Get to it, Mayor."

"I will. The ones Hradin brings in, the women of her type—" Remal, in a maddening way, interrupted to laugh. He got up and kept laughing. "Mister Quinn," said Remal from the door, "when or if you see that little whore again, ask her to open her mouth. She has no tongue, perhaps not since she was five."

Remal slammed the door behind him, but even after that he kept laughing.

Chapter 11

First Quinn sat, and it was as if he were blind with confusion. But this did not last. He sat and was blind to everything except his hate for the laugh, and for his own stupidity. Because, for a fact, Quinn was not new to this. Neither to the contest with the man, Remal in this case, nor to the simple, sharp rules of the game: that you don't go off half-cocked, that you don't threaten unless you can hit.

Quinn got up, left the house fast. His teeth touched on edge, as if there were sand there and he needed to bite through the grains. The garden gate was locked. He went back to the house, stumbled once on a stone in the garden.

"Quinn?" he heard in the hall.

One light was on over the stairs and Beatrice stood on the first landing, no longer looking half asleep. She came down, saying his name again.

"Open the gate for me," he said. "It's locked."

She stepped up to him and put her hand on his arm. "Perhaps—" She didn't seem to know how to go on.

"You got the key or not?"

"He's gone," she said. "He went out the back gate. If you like, you can stay here."

He looked at her and felt surprised that she could seem so hesitant.

"What did you do?" she said. "He came back cold as ice."

"I asked him to get off my back and he laughed."

"Quinn, stay—"

"I'm getting out. I've got to."

She misunderstood. "Can you leave town? If you let me help you..."

He stepped back, not to feel her hand on his arm. He felt sorry he had met her like this and had a small, rapid wish—it only leaped by, nothing more—that she might be elsewhere, and himself, too. But then he sucked in his breath to interrupt, because unless he knew why he had this wish about her, he would not permit it.

He thought he knew, of course, why he felt anger with Remal, so he stuck to that.

"I'm going out there and don't worry. Open the gate."

"What are you going to do?" she asked and ran after him into the garden.

"Have you got the key?"

She went back into the house and brought the key. She said nothing else, brought nothing else, just unlocked the gate and let him go out. She wished she knew what to say, what she wanted. Then she locked the gate.

It was no darker now than it had been before, but as Quinn walked hack to Whitfield's he thought it was darker, and colder. I have to see Turk and set something up, he kept thinking. Whitfield? No help there. But I'll need help. Either because of what the mayor does next or what I want to do next. What? I'll see. First, check out that girl, check out Turk, even Whit-field—he knows the mayor, he can help make this clear if I'm imagining that something's going to break—

He walked fast, which preoccupied him, and got to the yard out of breath. He stood for a moment there in the dark and called Turk. There was no answer. There was only the pump sound of his blood and the hard sound of his breathing. You listen to that long enough, he thought, and you get scared.

"Turk?"

Nothing. He's with the whore, of course.

Quinn ran up the stairs and the first door was open. The light was on inside and the room was empty. No girl, no Turk. In the next room, Whit-field was asleep.

Quinn did not know what to think and did not care to think. He ran to the bed and started to shake Whitfield awake.

"Listen, listen to me," he kept saying, until Whitfield opened his eyes.

There was an empty gin bottle on the floor and Quinn kicked it out of the way.

"How was she, huh?" said Whitfield. "Okay?" He sounded thick.

"Shut up and listen to me."

"Once a week. Back next week. Okay? Nice girl—" Quinn tried a while longer but was too anxious to give Whitfield a chance to come out of his drunk. Quinn was so anxious he could feel himself shake inside.

Everybody gone, he thought. I'm imagining something, but not this. Everybody gone and me alone here. End up dead in an alley this way. That's no imagination. Like the first time wasn't imagination. End up dead in a coffin, next end up dead in an alley. That's twice. That doesn't happen to me, twice— And he let go of Whitfield as if he were a bundle of laundry. But Quinn didn't race out. He felt alone but now this did not give him fright but strength. He picked up the gin bottle and left Whitfield's apartment. In the yard he cracked the bottle against a stone wall and held onto the neck. He looked at the vicious jags on the broken end and heard his own breathing again.

"Turk?" he called once more.

Only his breathing. It didn't frighten him this time, only made him feel haste. He left fast, to go to the only other place which he knew, which was Beatrice's house. He didn't get there.

On the way he saw shadows, imagined shapes, and fright played him like a cracked instrument. He bit down on his teeth, held his bottle, and with a fast chatter of crazy thoughts going in and out of his head, he had to stop finally or come apart.

It was very quiet, and except for a cat running by some little way off he seemed to be alone. His jitters embarrassed him now, but not much. Stands to reason, he thought. Stands to reason getting worked up like this, but no more now. Ninety-five per cent imagination. Try sticking with the other five for a while. He wished he had a cigarette, and the wish was ordinary enough to take the wild shimmer off his imaginings. In a while, standing by the wall of a house, he felt better. He moved on.

As he turned the next corner, he stumbled over a man lying on the ground.

Quinn saw everything very fast. The man was dead and bloody, throat all gone, and something went padding away, fast, in the dark. The sound wasn't a dog or a cat. It was a person running.

But no panic this time. The act was so clearly wrong it pulled Quinn together. He ran after the sound of the feet.

At the next corner Quinn slowed. He did not think he was making a sound and then he saw the man waiting by a wall.

Knife, thought Quinn. He could see it. That would be twice, wouldn't it? But not for me, Jack the Ripper, not for me— In great haste Quinn thought, why run after him anyway, why think he means me with that knife, why think that the dead man in the street has anything to do with me—

Suddenly the man with the knife stepped away from the wall and slowly moved towards Quinn. He said something in Arabic and stopped. He spoke again and came closer.

"And the hell with you, too," said Quinn and didn't wait any longer.

He thought the man was startled, that he moved back, but then the man with the knife never had a chance to start running. Even before he got his weapon up Quinn was on him like an animal and with a sharp hack tore the bottle across the dark face.

The man jerked like something pulled tight with wires, spun and screamed. He screamed so that Quinn swung out to cut him again. He felt so wild he heard nothing until the last moment.

He heard fast footsteps, then the voice. "No, Quinn. No!"

It was not the man with the ruined face. Quinn spun around and saw Turk. Confusion and Turk. Bloody face falling down on the stones, knife clatters, and Turk now.

"Come on. Run," Turk hissed. "*Run.* Now the others will come—"

"Who?...."

"Not now!"

Quinn hadn't meant who are the others, he had meant who was the man whose face he had cut and who was the man who was dead just yards away and who in this night town knew anything to explain anything—

And there wasn't any more question about anything when two more Arabs came running. At first Quinn could only tell they were there by the white rag wrapped around the bead of one of them and the long white shirt fluttering around the other. And he felt how Turk tensed. They ran.

The other two got distracted by the man in the street whose face had been slashed, and when Turk stopped sharply and turned to run up the stone steps between two houses, Quinn looked back quickly and could tell what the two others were doing. They stooped over the man on the ground, a motion of white cloth and then they leaped up.

Quinn followed Turk up the steps and saw they were in a dead end. There was a blank wall and a door which was recessed deeply.

"In here," said Turk. "It's all right. You'll see."

They squeezed into the doorway and watched the other two come up the stairs.

"You got a gun?" asked Quinn.

"Too noisy. Besides, they can only come up one behind the other."

They did. They seemed to know where Quinn and Turk must be hiding. They were going more slowly now.

"You know how to throw a knife?" said Quinn.

"I would lose it."

"When I throw the bottle we jump them," said Quinn.

Turk only nodded. When Quinn stepped out, to block the steps, the two men below looked up and stopped. It was slow and weird now, because Turk talked to them and they talked back.

"What goes on?"

"I am bargaining."

"And?"

"The one in front says he'll let us run again and the other one says he doesn't care. They are both lying."

Quinn suddenly threw the bottle. He threw the bottle because a new figure had showed at the bottom of the stairs and startled him. The bottle hit the first Arab's arm and the man gave a gasp. He staggered enough to get entangled with his friend. Turk rushed past Quinn now, knife field low.

When Quinn got halfway down the steps the two Arabs were scrambling, or falling—it was hard to tell which—back down to the bottom. One lost his knife, the other was holding his arm. Turk was over them and the third man stood there, too. They were talking again when Quinn got there. Then the man with the rag around his head made a hissing sound and Turk pulled his knife out of him.

Quinn sat down on the bottom step, head between his knees, and threw up. When he looked up again only Turk was there and he was smoking.

"Better?" he said.

"Gimme a cigarette."

"I thought you didn't smoke."

"Just gimme."

Turk gave him one and explained, "Remal sent somebody for the girl right away. It was stupid of you to take her to Whitfield's house. Remal figured as much. But no matter."

"Huh?"

"She had no tongue. Did you know that?"

Quinn put his head down again but nothing else came up.

"I didn't know it either or I would have told you. Anyway, here we are."

"What else happened?"

"I sent a man with you. All the time. A friend of mine. Didn't you know this?"

"No."

"You cut his face. It's too bad, but then you didn't know."

"Who was the dead man in the street, the first one?"

"One of the three that Remal sent after you. He waited for you, he had seen you, but then the one whom you later cut, my friend, killed him there. It was very unfortunate that you hurt him."

"You should have told me."

"Yes. Would you like a drink?"

"And the two who came up these steps, they were Remal's men?"

"Yes. One is dead, the other, you saw, is with us now."

"And the one at the bottom of the steps, that last minute?"

"Another friend of mine. He and Remal's man are now cleaning up."

"Huh?"

"The dead must be disposed of. Everything will be much more quiet that way."

Quinn threw the cigarette away and thought, yes, how nice and quiet.

"Except when Remal finds out," he said.

"On the contrary. What does Remal gain by making a noise over something he already knows? He will soon know that you are not dead, that two of his men are dead and he has lost another."

"Yes. Good old reasonable Remal. Now he's scared and won't lift a finger anymore. I'm sick laughing," Quinn said.

"You need a drink," said Turk.

"Where is Remal now?"

"He is busy. He has to attend to the boat."

"What else? Naturally. Must attend to inventory."

"You need a drink," Turk said again.

"And Whitfield slept through it all?"

"I told you Whitfield knows how to live within limitations."

Quinn nodded and got up from the steps. He felt shaky and hollowed-out. He steadied himself by the wall for a moment and took a few deep breaths. He thought how he had started out on this walk and where he had been going. I was going to her house, but just as well. She probably would have been asleep. And of course going to her house would have meant ignoring everything else. And that can't be. That can't be any more.

"Turk," he said. "I've got to plan something now. Find a place where we won't be disturbed."

They walked off.

At this point Quinn had just about everything back that he had ever had.

Chapter 12

Where the main street ended and the quarter began there was also a dirt road which went down to the water. They went down to the water, past the rocks, and sat in a black shadow. Only the night sky seemed to have light. Turk said nothing because he was waiting and Quinn said nothing because he was trying not to think. I'll start with the first thing that comes to my mind—

"I've changed my mind," he said.

Turk didn't know yet what that meant, but the voice he heard next to him in the dark was hard and impersonal. It was impersonal with an effort and Turk felt uneasy.

"I told you once I'd help you to a slice of Remal if you helped me."

"I know. I remember."

"You came through and now I'll come through. Except for this."

Turk bit his nail and wished he could see Quinn's face.

"I want a slice, too," said Quinn. "I really want to carve me one out now."

Turk grinned in the dark, grinned till his jaw hurt. He was afraid to make a sound lest he interrupt Quinn or disturb him in any way.

"Did you hear me?"

"Yes, yes! I see it. I can see how..."

"You don't see a thing. Now just talk. Tell me everything that goes on with this smuggling operation. And don't be clever, just talk."

Turk went on for nearly an hour. Where the girls came from and where they went. It was, Quinn found out, a fairly sparse business and needed connections which he could not make in a hundred years. He learned about the trade in raw alcohol, black market from American bases, and how it left here and then was handled through Sicily. And watches which one man could carry and make it worth while. And inferior grain, sold out of Egypt.

None of the operations were very big and there wasn't one which was ironclad. Remal, with no competition and with his thumb on a lethargic town, ran matters in a way which looked sloppy to Quinn—unless Turk told it badly—and ran them, for the most part, pretty wide open.

Quinn smoked a cigarette and thought of chances. He thought business thoughts about business and once he thought of Remal who was an enemy. But he stuck mostly to business.

Taking a slice here or there was ridiculous. Remal would hit back. But to roll the whole thing over, and then leave Remal on the bottom—

"Stuff leaving here goes mostly to Sicily?"

"Yes. Not tonight. Tonight there are just the women, and they go just up the coast. And the silk..."

"Never mind." Quinn picked up a pebble. "Does Remal run the Sicily end, too?"

"Oh no. He never goes there. Sometimes the Sicilian comes here."

"What's his name?"

"I don't know. He sees Whitfield. Sometimes Remal."

This could mean anything. It could mean Remal runs the show at both ends, or the Sicilian comes down with instructions for Remal, or he comes just to coordinate. Turk didn't know. Quinn couldn't tell.

"Is it important?" said Turk.

It is most likely, thought Quinn, that the two ends are run independently.

"Remal ever send anybody over there?"

"No, he never does."

And put that together with the Sicilians and their reputation in a business like this— It is likely, thought Quinn, that they're bigger at the other end.

"Now tell me again about the alcohol. All the details," said Quinn. "You mentioned something about tonight."

"Yes. Tonight he went down..."

"But there's no alcohol going out tonight, you said."

"I know. I said twice a month, like tonight. Remal goes down to the warehouse to see about the alcohol in cans. It comes in by truck and goes out by boat."

"Does it come in tonight?"

"No, it comes in and goes out, all in the same day. Tomorrow."

"Then what's Remal doing down there tonight?"

"To send the driver out to the pick-up point. Remal always counts the empty cans, and when the truck comes back the next day he counts the full cans or has Whitfield count them. And he gives instructions to the driver, about little changes in plan."

"What kind of changes?"

"Little changes, like time and place and so on."

Quinn sat a moment and started to play with a pebble. "On the truck," he said, "there's just this one driver?"

"Yes."

"Kind of careless, isn't it?"

"Who would dare interfere?"

Quinn nodded. Who indeed. "As far as I know," he said, "there are only two ways out of this town. One east, one west, and both along the coast."

"For trucks, yes."

"Which way does this one come and go?"

"Both ways the same way, west. Because the alcohol is black market from Algerian ports. It comes overland, and then this driver picks it up out of town."

After that, the talk became more and more detailed, about how many cans and how large, time schedules and distances, and while none of it came out as precise as Quinn might have wanted, it was enough. Enough for a fine, hard jolt.

"Now something else," Quinn said, "and this time I don't have questions but you do the listening."

Turk noticed the difference in Quinn and paid attention.

"With no more effort than you put out now, doing nothing, you can pick yourself off the street and no more handouts, like the kind you've been taking all your life."

"Oh?" said Turk, because he had not understood all the slang.

"Here's what. You told me Remal picks his help as he needs it."

"Yes?"

"This is good enough when there's no competition, but not good enough when the opposition is organized."

"Are you discussing a war?"

"Just shut up a minute. Remal doesn't have a gang. I'm going to make one."

"Gang?"

"A few men, always the same men, working their job not for pennies, but a cut."

"Ah," said Turk. "No war. You are talking now like a *brigande.*"

"Call it what you like. The point is we run it a new way. This leaves out the knife play in the street, it means picking our men with care, and it means no talk whatsoever. Everybody knows of Remal's operation. Nobody knows of yours and mine."

"Ah," said Turk. "Anything."

"For a start we'll need three men. Whom can you suggest?"

"There is my friend," said Turk, "the one who you saw by the steps."

"Can he be trusted?"

"Absolutely. He is my friend. Then," Turk said, "there is the man whose face you cut. He has..."

"Him?"

"Not him, he will not be able to help us for a while. I was going to say, he has two brothers..."

"They'll work for me?"

"They will not hold it against you that you injured their brother. Especially after I explain that it was an accident and they hear there's money to be made."

They then talked details about what they would do in the morning. What most impressed Turk was that Quinn would start all this new life immediately in the morning.

"Can you have the men ready on time?"

"Of course. I have already thought about..."

"Don't of-course me. Remember, we're not setting this schedule ourselves. We've got to follow one."

"Understood."

"Make sure your help understands it."

"I will."

Quinn threw the pebble away and got up. "I'll stay at the hotel tonight. You got somebody to watch me?"

"Of course. The man who got hurt in the arm. He is a very good watcher."

"You're of-coursing me again. He just came over from Remal and he's going to watch *me* sleep tonight?"

"Well. I feel..."

"And he's going to sit there in the hotel with blood all over his arm?"

"I have a great deal to learn, about watching in hotels."

"Then say so in the beginning and don't make stupid suggestions instead."

"I'm sorry."

"Don't be. What you know you know well, I think. Walk me over."

Turk walked with Quinn to the hotel and they said nothing else. I could love him, thought Turk. If he'd let me. I really could— And after Quinn had gone into the hotel, Turk got a boy from the quarter who had only one eye. He told the boy to sit in the street all night and to kill anyone who went into Quinn's room or he, Turk, would dig out the boy's other eye. He forgot to explain how the boy was to know, while sitting in the street, who would be likely to go into Quinn's room.

At ten in the morning Quinn had an Occidental-type breakfast downstairs, and while he was drinking his coffee Remal walked in. He came up
to the table and asked if he might sit down. Quinn nodded.

"And how are you, Mister Quinn?"

"Alive."

"Yes, I heard. And now I see."

"Coffee?"

"No, thank you."

"You see what, Remal?"

"I see you in a new light, Mister Quinn."

"In the cold light of dawn?"

"You make small talk almost as well as our Whitfield. Only less amus-
ingly."

"Then let's drop it."

"Very well." Remal folded his arms on the table and looked out the window. "You have indeed demonstrated," he said, "that you can draw attention."

"We cleaned up all the mess lying around."

"Yes. Thank you. That was thoughtful of you and, I suppose, in the
manner of a *beau geste.*"

"A what?"

"You could have left the bodies there and made it difficult for me to
cover things up. It was generous of you."

"Welcome, I'm sure."

"And of course the meaning is that it will not happen again, but the next
time you will draw as much attention as possible."

Quinn hadn't thought of the last night's corpse-dumping that way but
he let the impression remain. He said nothing.

"And of course, in the same night's work you have demonstrated something else I had not known, that you have help. Rather good help, as it
turned out."

"I'm alive."

"Yes. We discussed that," and Remal wiped his mouth. "I have learned
to be flexible in my position, Mister Quinn, and will make a new propos-
al."

"I know."

"We are not friends, but we are not yet enemies. Let us choose something in between."

"What's that?"

"A gentlemen's agreement."

"The thought is new to me, but go on."

"You sit still, Mister Quinn, and I will sit still. You stay in sight and you will come to no harm. Maybe I can harm you with more success than I had last night, but for the moment why risk it? In the meantime, I will do what I can to expedite what needs to be done to get your papers and passage."

"A truce?"

"For the moment."

"Why should I trust you?"

"Why? Because I no longer underestimate you."

They parted as politely as they had talked, each wishing that the other would do nothing else.

At eleven Quinn met Turk. This was different. No hotel hush, no polite conversation, no touch of imported European culture. The narrow streets of the quarter were so full of screaming that Quinn thought something terrible was about to happen. But the noise was normal—only he felt excited. Neither he nor Turk talked at all. They walked. They left the street after a while and went through a courtyard, through an arch, then more courtyards, through a house once, and then came out into the open.

This was the back end of the town where the desert started. It was not all sand or large sand dunes, the way Quinn had thought of the desert, but there was gray and black rock strewn around and the sand was not really sand but rather bare packed dirt with nothing growing in it. The last sirocco had blown sand against the backs of the houses, fine and loose like dust, but the expanse of the desert was hard, hard as the light and as hot as the air.

"The jeep is here," said Turk, and they walked to an oval passage which had no gate.

The jeep still showed army markings. It showed no signs of care and at first glance looked like four over-sized tires with two seats and machinery hung up in between. There was no windshield and the fenders were gone.

But the motor worked. Turk drove and Quinn sat with his eyes squinted tight. Turk was whistling.

The trip, Quinn knew, would not take very long. A short trip across the desert to catch the West highway away from town. Turk whistled and drove like a lunatic. Quinn appreciated the breeze but not much else.

"Look. You got all this land here. All this open space, like air to fly in. Stop going back and forth in zigzags like this was fun or like we had all the time in the world."

"I am going the shortest way," said Turk.

He spun the wheel and made Quinn fly sideways and almost out of the jeep. "I will explain to you," said Turk, and drove straight for the moment. "Open your eyes more and look at the colors."

Quinn opened his eyes and in a while he saw the colors. The sand was not yellow. It was brown, grey, whitish, and—a trick of light—sometimes blue.

"The colors show the way." said Turk. "Some are too hard and some too soft and that big patch there, you can drive in it without sinking in but you can drive only in a very slow creep. All right?" and Turk laughed. Then he said, "I drove oil trucks for the French, from the Sahara fields to the coast, in Algiers. Then came the fighting, so I left," and he laughed again.

Quinn grunted something. He held onto his seat and tried to squint the sun out of his eyes. A lieutenant I got, a real right-hand man. Then the fighting came and I left, haha.

But he did not worry the thought and just kept squinting, which drew his face into a constant grin. In a while he grinned for real. He was starting to look forward to the thing he had set up.

Turk swung the jeep around a large boulder and after that they could see the road. The heat on the road turned the air to silver which shimmered, waterlike.

Turk bounced the jeep on the road and drove North a short while until they came to a ruined house. It was four broken walls by the side of the road and the roof was gone. Turk left the road again and drove into the walled space by ramming the jeep through the door frame which had no top and one incomplete side. Turk let the motor die.

Now the air was very still, like water in a pond. They could not look out and from the road they could not be seen. It was important that the jeep should not be seen.

A dirty burnoose lay in one corner and a large pile of skin bags which were full of water. On the rubble floor of the house was old camel dung.

"You brought the tool?" Quinn asked.

"The tool? Ah, the tool, yes," and Turk reached under his seat and came up with a wrench.

"And the rag," said Turk.

Turk did not have a rag. He had seen no reason for a rag and so had forgotten it. But then he went to the corner where the dirty burnoose was lying and tore a piece out of that for a rag.

They had time and Quinn smoked a cigarette. Then Turk got on top of the jeep and from there to the top of the wall. He sat there and looked. Quinn wrapped the rag around the wrench.

"Anything?"

"I can see the camels."

He could see three camels walking, one behind the other. They were crossing where the jeep had been driving and then they disappeared behind the boulder. Only one camel came out on the other side, head up in an angle of disdain, knock-kneed lurch of a walk. It went slowly, as if thinking about other things, but the Arab who was leading the animal had to trot to keep up.

Turk stayed on the wall and Quinn went out to see. The camel and the man had stopped on the other side of the road. Those two figures stood there and Quinn stood opposite. Nothing else happened—only grit itch prickled Quinn's back.

"Tell him to put that beast down, the way we said," Quinn called to Turk.

Turk yelled Arabic and the man with the camel walked into the road. He left his animal and walked alone to the middle of the road where he put his hand on the pavement a few times and then walked back to the camel.

"He says it's too hot. Ah! I saw the truck for a moment!"

"Tell that goddamn animal..."

"He won't listen. He says it's too hot."

Quinn started to sweat a new sweat, which was thin and rapid. He did not argue or curse now but ran back into the broken house, then came out again with a water skin. He ran with it, so that there was a gurgle sound from the skin. The skin was black and moist and made inside water movements under his arm so that it felt alive. On the pavement Quinn pulled the wooden plug out of the bag and let the water run out. He trained the stream all over the road and pressed pressure into the stream with his arm.

"You see him?" he called to the wall.

"No. It means now that he will come out of the dip when I see him the next time."

Quinn licked sweat from the side of his mouth. The moist pavement was starting to steam.

"Get off the wall," he said.

The skin was limp on his arm now and the water sputtered. Turk got off the wall.

"All right," said Quinn and stepped back. "Tell him to put that animal down now. It isn't hot any more."

The Arab brought his camel over and made it stop in the middle of the road while Quinn ran into the broken house. He came back with the dirty burnoose on his arm, and with the wrench.

"He says you are very clever," said Turk. "Very clever about the water."

"Tell him to put that goddamn animal down. And you come over here and help me with this sheet."

Turk showed Quinn how to wrap the burnoose and the Arab with the camel was hitting the animal's front legs with a stick. This made a wood on wood sound and in a while, like a building collapsing, the camel folded down and sat in the road. It showed its teeth and made a groan like an agonized human.

There was nothing else to do now except wait. The Arab talked to the camel, or cursed the camel, Quinn stood inside his sheet, and Turk was gone, inside the house.

The truck, Quinn saw, was a Ford pick-up. Because there was a camel in the road, the truck stopped. The driver came very close, made the brakes and the tires scream, but he stopped. The talk, which came next, was all in Arabic and Quinn did not understand a word. But he knew what was supposed to go on and he could see how the screaming got more and more violent. The point was, get that camel off the road and, I can't get the beast to get back on its feet. And then the driver, in an excess of violence, was supposed to jump out of his cab to give the camel a kick or to give the man with the camel a kick.

But the two men just kept screaming. Quinn stood by and sweated under the big burnoose. What else could go wrong now? The driver backs up, leaves the road, and bumps across the desert. Or he just keeps sitting there and screams for another hour. If that idiot with the camel would stop tugging that halter rope, would stop putting on such a convincing show—At that moment he did. Quinn was sure the man had worked himself into a genuine rage and only at that point did he think of the next thing. He dropped the halter rope, threw up his arms, screamed something which was probably very obscene, and then he too sat in the road, legs folded. It took another second before the driver decided to get out of the cab.

Quinn stood still by the truck and watched the door fly open. He stood still while the driver jumped out, turned toward the camel, and then Quinn hit him.

He let go of the burnoose flap with which he had covered his face, got his right arm free, and tapped the wrapped wrench on the back of the driver's head.

It is hard to judge the right force of a blow like that, unless the purpose is murder. Quinn wanted the man out cold for perhaps half an hour. This was important, because the man should later drive his truck for the rest of the trip.

When Quinn caught the man he turned the head up and saw that the eyelids were fluttering.

From here on in, a number of things were supposed to happen like clockwork.

Quinn put the man down on the ground, slowly, leaned the man back and felt the tension. This was the natural tensing of trying to balance one-self while leaning back. Quinn hit the man again because he had not been entirely unconscious. He used his fist this time, a sharp uppercut, feeling much more certain about what he was doing now. When the man sagged in the right way Quinn was done.

Turk, by the house, was whistling.

The man with the camel got up, yelled at his beast, and tapped his stick under the animal's chin.

Quinn dumped the driver on top of the canisters in back of the pickup, got into the cab, and maneuvered the car off the road and behind the ruined house. When he got there Turk was ready with the tools.

So far, nice and smooth. Quinn felt nervous and happy.

While Turk pushed the jack under the front axle Quinn started to undo the nuts on one wheel. By then the first camel came around the corner of the house, and then the other two, each led by a man. Quinn did not know any of them but they're working out, he thought, maybe they'll work out. He hardly looked at them, no time now for this, and told Turk what he wanted each of the others to do. Then he took the first wheel off. He let the air out of the tire while he took off the second wheel. He let the air out of that one too. Turk was coming back out of the house.

"Check the driver," said Quinn.

Turk went to the back of the truck and said, "Do you want me to hit him again?"

"I said check him! I want to know if he's still out."

"He sleeps."

"Make sure."

"I did."

Quinn did not ask how Turk had made sure. He only told him to put the driver into his cab and they should get busy with the cans on the truck. The three Arabs came out of the house, carrying the skins. One camel was lying down by itself, one stood, and one was grinding its teeth.

Then Quinn pounded the tires off the front wheels, and then he bolted the bare wheels back on the wheel-drums. After that he got the jack out and put it under the rear of the truck. There he did the same thing he had done to the front. He took the tubes and tires off the wheels and then put the bare wheels back in place. Make them think there's a gentleman thief around. Puts the wheels back on, after the deed.

Turk and the three others were pouring alcohol into empty skins and water into empty canisters. Quinn smoked a cigarette, standing back a little. It smells like a hospital, he thought, or a brewery. I can't decide which.

The men put the canisters full of water back on the pickup and they tied the skins full of alcohol to the packsaddles of the three camels. They were all scratching themselves and they were grinning while they stood around because none of them knew what this was all about. Quinn checked the driver again and then walked to the Arabs.

"Tell them what I say, Turk."

He gave all of them a cigarette and they all smoked. Turk smoked and so did two of the others. The third split the paper open and ate the tobacco.

"Tell them they can sell the tires as soon as they wish. And I don't care to whom they sell them or where."

"The best place..."

"Shut up and listen. Make it clear that it will go badly with them, if Remal finds out who stole his tires. Tell them."

Turk told them and they all talked at once. Then they listened again.

"Tell them that I will do nothing to them, if the tires get traced, because Remal will take care of them good and proper if they aren't careful."

"That will be difficult," said Turk, "to sell the tires and Remal knows nothing about it."

"It can be done."

"But how?"

Quinn picked up sand from the ground and rubbed it in his hands. It took some of the grime off and then he wiped his hands on the dirty burnoose.

"I want them to figure that out by themselves. Because I can't use them if they can't sell stuff without getting traced. Tell them."

Turk told them and there was much discussion while Quinn got into the truck. He leaned out and told them to move the camels out of the way, he wanted to back up. Then he said, "Do they know about the alcohol?"

"Oh yes. They are to hide it, not sell. They know."

Quinn nodded, kicked the starter, geared into reverse. It was a clanking, hard maneuver without tires on the wheels, and gave a weird motion to the truck. Once the truck hit the highway, it sounded like a tank clattering over the pavement. Quinn stopped with the truck pointed towards town. It had been twenty minutes since the driver had gone under and Quinn was a little bit worried. He propped the man up and then got out of the cab. Behind the house the Arabs and Turk were still arguing.

"Since it might take them a while to figure a way of selling the tires," said Quinn, "give them this as an extra."

He handed bills over to Turk which amounted to about one dollar apiece. Then he said that the three men and the camels should go.

Quinn did not watch them leave but sat in the jeep, inside the ruined house, smoking. He said nothing when Turk came and thought, I hope I did that with a sufficient, imperial touch, stalking off that way.

"Quinn," said Turk and started the motor, "did you like the men I picked?"

"I don't know yet. We'll see how they'll work out with the tires."

"That was very clever of you, Quinn, and they too thought you are very clever. And generous." Turk drove out of the building and crossed the highway.

"They'll make more, if they stick."

"Yes, but they thought you very generous. They know how much you got for the cans which you sold to Whitfield and that you have no other money."

Quinn did not care to show that this irritated him and said nothing. When the jeep was on the other side of the road Quinn looked back, worrying about the driver in the pick-up truck. The man sat in the cab as if he were asleep.

"And they want to stick with you," Turk was saying, "because they believe you will do great things."

"That's very devoted of them, I'm sure."

"They know how little money you have and they are sure your greed will make all of us rich."

The jeep bumped and leaped and made so much noise on the rough terrain that Turk could not hear how Quinn was cursing.

Chapter 13

Quinn got some of his humor back when he stood on the pier and heard the noise come from the distance. It was a clattering metal noise which nobody could place.

"How come you're still here?" said Quinn. "Isn't it siesta time for you?"

Whitfield looked up from his clipboard and said, "I never saw you smoke before. When did you pick up that habit? I'll be damned, Quinn, if that doesn't sound like a tank."

"It does sound like a tank. A sort of tinny tank."

"Odd," and Whitfield did checks and crosses on the forms he held.

"How come you're still here, Whitfield, and not home in bed?"

"I take a bath, for siesta."

"How could I forget! Yes."

"Some damn transport is late. Wait till I talk to that man."

Quinn thought about this and grinned. Then he said "I think the tank is coming this way, by the sound of it."

"He's on the cobbles. All along the piers we have cobbles, you know."

"I'm going around the building," said Quinn, "to see what the cobbles are doing to the tank."

"To the driver. Can you imagine that driver?" said Whitfield.

Quinn said no, he could hardly imagine such a thing, and the two men walked from the pier through the warehouse and out on the cobbles.

"Oh, sainted heart!" said Whitfield.

The wheels of the pick-up were still round, but this had no visible effect upon the truck as a whole. Each spring—there were four—worked like a pogo stick, and no pogo stick would have anything to do with any of the other pogo sticks. Inside the cab a man was fighting to keep from flying into the roof. What kept the canisters in back from rocketing away was the thick tarp that had been tied across the bed of the pick-up, and this tarp was ripping through at one end. When the pick-up stopped by the warehouse there was a silence of exhaustion.

"Quinn," Whitfield said quietly. "We are both seeing the same thing, aren't we? Say yes."

"Oh, yes."

"Quinn, have you ever seen anything like it before? Don't lie to me, Quinn."

"I won't lie. I've only seen this once before."

"Thank you, Quinn. I now need my siesta, but first," Whitfield cleared his throat, "first I must speak to the sainted driver."

The sainted driver had not yet come out of the cab. He was sitting behind the wheel, gripping the wheel, as if uncertain that the ride was over.

"You can come out now," said Whitfield. "You've made it."

The driver did not move.

"You can let go of the wheel," said Whitfield, "and nothing will happen, really."

The driver moaned, and then got out of the cab. He moved with care and disbelief. Then he closed the cab door carefully and sat down on the running board. Seen from the top, there was a visible lump on his head.

"Will you look at that," said Whitfield. "Must have struck his head against the roof for some reason or other. Now then, Ali. I say, Ali?"

The man looked up carefully. This showed a bruise under his chin.

"Must have struck his chin on the wheel, repeatedly," said Whitfield. "Ali, can you hear me?"

"Yes, sir."

"You have no tires on these wheels, Ali."

"Yes, sir."

"Will you tell me where they are?"

"They took them."

"Who?"

"The two who took them."

Whitfield breathed deeply. Quinn said, "Must have struck his head against the roof repeatedly."

"Don't confuse matters, Quinn. Ali?"

"Yes, sir."

"Did anything happen that you can explain to me?"

"The camel wouldn't get out of the way and then he hit me."

Whitfield nodded. Then he took a handkerchief out of his pocket and blew his nose. "Naturally," he said. "It would be a he. A female camel would never beat a man over the head. Now then. Ali."

"That's all I know, sir. Everything."

"Well," said Whitfield, and slapped the clipboard against his thigh, "it is now clear to me that somebody stole the sainted tires."

And then he thought of something else and went quickly to the back of the pick-up. He unlashed the tarp, pulled it back, and sighed when he saw the canisters. He reached over and lifted two of them at random and sighed again.

"Thank you, sainted heart," he said.

"Didn't touch the cargo, is that it?" said Quinn.

"Thank God."

"What is it, liquid gold?"

"No, but it's convertible. Ali, drive that stuff into the warehouse. Do you realize you're two hours late?"

"Please sir, please—" said the man on the running board.

"I think he doesn't want to drive any more," said Quinn.

Quinn drove the truck into the warehouse. It is, he thought to himself, only poetic justice that I should do this. What with the jumping and the rattling, all of which was transmitted directly into his skull, it took him all of the fifteen yards which he had to cover before he had formulated the whole thought.

When he got out of the cab he could see the driver walking slowly away from the warehouse, slow like a farewell walk, but straight and steady, as if he would never come back. Then Whitfield came around a stack of bales and brought two Arabs. They immediately began to unload the canisters and wheeled them out to the pier on little wagons.

"Tell me," said Quinn. "Where's Bea this time of day?"

"Hotel most likely. It's just before her siesta."

Quinn smiled and left the warehouse. Two days, he thought, with hardly anything to do.

Chapter 14

She was drinking something orange and oily and when she saw him coming to her table she was not sure whether she liked seeing him or not. Of course he was new. But it seemed to her there had been something else before, something she missed.

"You looked," she said to him, "as if you were heading straight for my table."

"I was. May I sit down?"

She nodded and watched him sit.

"You look positively like you'd had a good day at the office."

"I did," he said.

They did not talk while the waiter took his order, and when the waiter was gone they still had nothing to say. Bea sipped and then licked her lips, which were sticky and sweet. She concentrated on that, trying to forget the platitude she had used on him, and that he had answered it in kind. Quinn lit a cigarette.

"I didn't know you smoked," she said.

"Now that I'm in civilization I'm taking up all kinds of civilized habits."

She put her glass down and looked at him. "You say that without a smile and it sounds nasty. You say that with a smile and it sounds cagey."

"Which did I do?"

"Don't you know? You did both."

Quinn waited till the waiter had put down the drink and left the table. He made out to himself that this was the only reason he didn't say anything right away. Then he folded his arms on the table.

"You know what you sound like, Bea?"

"As if I disliked you." She gave a small laugh and said, "Strange, isn't it? I don't know why."

Quinn did not know what to do with that answer and looked into his glass. He drank and thought, how did I used to do it? I don't remember ever sitting like this, not knowing what next.

"And then again," she was saying, "if you were to ask me right now, now I don't dislike you at all."

This did not help him at all. He lost all touch with her and felt only suspicion.

"Look," he said. "Naturally you don't like me. First of all, you don't know me from Adam. Second of all, what you do know you got from somebody else."

"What was that?"

"You're thick with the mayor, aren't you? So naturally, listening to him—"

He knew he had missed as soon as he heard himself say the sentence. Bea sat up and looked at him as from a distance.

"You know something, Quinn?" She flicked one nail against her glass and made it go *ping.* "I just caught why I don't like you. When I don't like you."

"I'm interested as all hell," he said. The anger he felt seemed to swell his face. She went *ping* on the glass again and that was the worst thing about her, he thought idiotically.

"Here you sit talking to me, but not with me. Oh, no. It's not even about me. It's about the mayor. You have some thing with the mayor and nothing else matters, and when you get around to going to bed with me, that will probably be from spite too."

Quinn sat hunched with his arms on the table. Then he pushed away and picked up his glass. He kept looking at her when he tipped up the glass and let the ice cubes slide down so that they hit his teeth.

"You don't have to look at me like that," she said.

He put the glass down and lit a cigarette. I'll give her this silence, he thought, so she'll be as confused as I am.

"And now I'll tell you why I like you when I do like you," she said, but he could not let her finish. He did not want to hear what she had to say about liking.

He exhaled and said, "Are you drunk?"

"No." She frowned, and he thought it could have been anger. "I'm not drunk," she said, "but I think I'm going to be."

"You're sweet," he said. "Oh, are you ever a sweet female."

"Reserve judgment, Quinn. Wait till I'm drunk."

He now found that everything went very much easier. It was now easy to show her his anger, though he had no idea what he was angry about. He made out it was she who caused the anger and that game was fine with her. It was fine with her because now she felt animated. She was not bored. She ordered another drink for him and for herself and tried to insult him by paying for them. He let her pay for them and so insulted her back.

"For a pushover," he said, "you sure do all the most repulsive things." The liquor was starting to scramble his thinking and he sat wondering what he had meant by the remark.

"But I'm no pushover," she said. "For that you'd have to ask me to go to bed and then I'd have to say yes, just because you asked. None of that has happened, you know."

"And it won't either."

"You are very drunk, Quinn, very drunk," and she looked slightly past his left ear. Then she got up. "I'm going home," she said.

"And you're not going to ask me if I want to come?"

"No. You're no pushover, Quinn. You're a hard man of principles." Then she laughed and walked away from the table.

He watched her walk away and how her hips moved under the dress. The dress made a fold over one hip and then over the other. Quinn suddenly felt he had never seen anything more exciting in all his life.

He sat and wondered if it was the liquor making him dull and stupid, letting her walk out this way, letting her hit him in the head with her lousy insults, swapping insults back and forth like two idiots. He sat a short while longer and enjoyed disliking her. Then he left.

When the servant showed him into the room she did not even look up. She sat on a very red couch in the sunlight, because she had opened the shutters. The sunlight made a glow in her hair, it caused round shadows under her chin and her breasts, and the brown liquor in her glass looked almost like gold. When the door closed behind Quinn he felt the heat in the room. She did nothing about it. This heat was just there.

"God," he said, "you look sullen."

"I'm getting drunk."

He swore again, feeling stupid. A bottle of bourbon sat on the window sill and when he picked that up she nodded her head in the direction where he could find a glass. He poured straight liquor which felt warm. Then he walked around in the room.

"More small talk?" she said. "You working up to more small talk?"

"No," he said. "It's simple. I don't want to be with you and not have you talk." He took a gulp from his glass and felt the liquor make a hot pathway inside him.

"Go ahead," she said. "Get nasty. I invite it. Always do."

He turned around and saw her drink from her glass He watched her throat move.

"You don't invite a thing," he said. "That's why you irritate so." He listened to her exhale after the drink, a heavy breath making him think of moisture, and he felt excited.

"All the time," she said. "All the time like that," and her sullenness fit the warm room, went with the body curve which she showed sitting there. "You bastard," she said. "Why don't you go away!" She never raised her eyes but kept looking down, past her lap where she held the glass.

Quinn went to the couch and sat down next to her.

They did not touch and she did not look up. "Listen," he said. "Let's start all over."

"Bah!"

"What's 'bah' here?"

"Let's start all over. That's all I ever do, Quinn."

"Listen. I didn't mean any big discussion by that."

"I know. Just little remarks for you. Just nothing."

He suddenly felt like reaching over to touch her, to touch her with an unexpected emotion. He wanted her to feel comfort from his hand. But then she looked up and he didn't move.

"Bea," he said.

She looked half asleep. She looked at him while he put out his hand and then he touched her arm. He put his hand around her bare arm and after one slow moment of this touch she closed her eyes and tears ran out. They rolled down her cheeks and glittered in the sun. Quinn pulled his hand back as if he had been bitten.

She opened her eyes and just stared at him.

He drank from his glass, finishing it. "I don't know why I pulled away like that. I'm even sorry. You know that?" He shook his head, to get rid of the fog. "I'm even sorry. And I'm sorry that you have to cry."

She nodded her head but said nothing. She leaned way over the arm of the couch and reached for the bottle on the window sill. Quinn watched how her body stretched.

"You pour," she said and gave him the bottle. "I need to get drunk."

"No," he said. "You don't need to."

"Yes, I do. Because I know why I'm crying."

She was not actually crying but there were still tears in her eyes, though she seemed to pay no attention to that. She held her glass out and said, "I'm crying because I have absolutely no idea why I am here. You understand that, Quinn?"

He poured for her and then for himself and then he took a swallow. For a moment there was a muscle fight in his throat but then he swallowed.

"I was going to ask you," he said. "Why you're here."

"I told you. I don't know. Do you know why you're in this town?"

"I came in a box."

"What makes you think I didn't come in a box? What makes you think everybody gets out the way you did?" She gave a drunken smile. "Anyway, for a while it *looked* like you got out."

"What's that you said?"

"You think anybody comes here of their own free will? Everybody comes here to get rid of what's best left behind. That's why Okar is so dirty."

"I wish you'd said that while I was sober," he said. "I really do. Or not at all." And he took a long swallow.

When he looked at her again, he thought she was going to start crying again, not because of her voice or some look in her eyes, but because he thought she was on that kind of a drunk. But she had not been drunk when she had cried before, and now instead of crying she started to laugh. Now she was drunk. This made Quinn angry again and he watched her throat while she laughed. Her throat came in and out of focus and it moved with her laughter, as if a large pulse was pumping in there. Quinn watched this and felt there had never been anything so exciting. He put his hand on her throat and she stopped laughing immediately.

It was very quiet now and again very warm and the throat moved under his hand like a pulse.

"Quinn," she said. "Not so hard."

"No," he said. "Gently," and moved his hand gently. She leaned back so that he could move his hand on her.

"You have a heavy hand," she said. "I like your hand. Hold still."

He held still and felt the fabric between his hand and her body and for a moment he had the serious thought that he might now go crazy. Then he clamped his hand into her and the feeling went and became excitement.

"Quinn," she said. "You're too quick. This is the Orient. Slow, Quinn. Slow."

He laid his hand on the round of her thigh and imagined that his hand was sleeping there. It was not sleeping, but it was something to imagine this and to be so awake. He took liquor in his mouth and let it run down his throat. He thought of hot oil. She suddenly reached for him and ripped the front of his shirt. She only moved her arm and her hand, doing this, and then she put her hand on his chest so that it lay there very quietly, like a bird sleeping.

"You," he said. "Listen." He put his glass on the floor very carefully, hoping not to get dizzy. "This slow is too slow."

"Yes," she said, "open me up."

"Yes. Not here. Where's the other room, the other, goddamm it—"

"I like you on this couch, Quinn. Your black hair on the red couch."

The heat poured into the window and made the couch seem more red than it was. He leaned over to open her dress and felt her move under him. He fumbled and saw that his hands were shaking.

"Take my glass," she said. "I'll do it," and gave him her glass.

He took the glass and threw it across the room while he watched her. She tore something but could not get the dress open and then he grabbed her and said, "To hell with the dress," but that turned into a fight. She scratched the back of his neck and then he found that he was biting her arm. From somewhere the anger was back now, or a weird mixture of muscle strength and sex strength and they held each other apart, trying hard to focus. This might have been because of the liquor or because of a true confusion, and they had to let go of each other. I'm breathing like an animal, he thought, but an animal wearing clothes. He hunched on the red couch and watched her get up. She went to the door, rattling it before she got it open. Then she yelled something which he thought was like a scream. All this Arabic is like a scream in the ear, he thought, and therefore I don't understand the language— He shook his head and wanted to get up, go after her, when he saw that she was back in the room and the servant was with her.

He was an old man, with beard stubble looking very white on his prune-dark face, and his fingers were nothing but bones.

"Hold still, Quinn," she said. "Any minute now."

And then Quinn saw what the old man was doing. He was opening her dress while she stood there and then he peeled it up and over her head. He now walked around her, to her back, looking like a crab. He unhooked her bra and slid it down off her arms.

What else are servants for, Quinn thought, yes, yes, what else when the lover is too drunk to move. Those bone hands are rattling on her, goddamm it. He looked at her body, and his eyes were stinging.

"Listen," he said. "You."

She was kicking her shoes off and the old man went after them, again like a crab.

"Listen," said Quinn. "You going to send him out or what?"

"You look weird, Quinn."

"I look weird!"

"I'll send him out, if you want," and then she laughed. If she comes close now, if she were close now, and he felt his arm jump and his fist get hard.

Then she stood by the couch and her belly looked soft. The old man was gone or the old man was not gone. Quinn remembered shaking his jacket off, and then the touch of her up against him, standing or lying, except that the red of the couch hurt his eyes, and then a blood roar inside him when they came together. The drunkenness was like veils between them but they came together.

Chapter 15

Quinn did not leave that day. The first time he woke up he saw Bea asleep on the couch and his hangover was as bad as a disease. He closed the shutters of the window, took one violent drink straight from the bottle, then managed to go back to sleep.

The second time he woke up the shutters were open again and he could see the sun, low and red. He sat up carefully and localized the pains. One was in his head and one was in his back, but there was no more malaise like the first time when he had come to. He was alone in the room and sat looking at his clothes on the floor. They lay there in various ways, flat and wrinkled. I feel like they look, he thought. He put on his shorts and sat down again. The sun, he thought, was turning blue.

Bea came into the room holding a wrap around herself. She had a cigarette in one hand and when she closed the door she had to let go of the wrap. She did this without special haste, and without special slowness. The movements were simple and Quinn's reaction was simple. She is beautiful, he thought. Then she came to sit on the couch.

"Bad?" she said.

"Not too bad. And you?"

She shrugged and smiled. Her face looked quiet and the eyes were a little bit swollen, but bright. She looks like a cat again, thought Quinn. She sits like a cat.

"I feel suddenly helpless not knowing the time," said Quinn.

"Fifteen minutes and it will be dark. The light falls quickly now."

"I came at noon?"

"Later." She pulled on her cigarette and then did not exhale. When she did, she made a bluish feather of smoke and a sigh. "We drank, and argued, and made love, and then slept, and woke up, and Whitfield was here, and now we'll have coffee, if you like."

"Whitfield was here? You mean in here?"

"He comes sometimes."

"He comes sometimes," be said. "Did you sleep with him too?"

"No."

"Why not?"

"He was too drunk. You feeling nasty again, Quinn?"

"*He* was too drunk. Ha."

She said nothing to that and just smoked. The smoke had an odor which reminded Quinn of queer teas, sweet liqueurs, and strange candies.

"Is that a reefer?" he asked.

"A local kind. Want one?"

"No." He looked at her and how her skin showed through the stuff of the wrap where the wrap was tight over her. "No," he said again. "I don't think I want any more interference."

He touched her arm with two fingers and stroked down the length of her arm, over her wrist and the hand. She watched, moving only her eyes, and then she did a sudden thing, like the one she had done once before with his shirt. She moved her hand and was suddenly holding his fingers. And then, like that other time, she was done moving as suddenly as she had started. She sat holding his fingers with no more pressure than to make him feel the warmth in her hand.

The old man with the bone hands came into the room and brought a tray with cups and a coffee urn. Nobody talked while the old man was there. He made sounds with his robe and once he made a sound when his hand touched the low table. It did sound like bones, thought Quinn. Then the old man closed the door and that sounded like wood.

"You going to pour?" said Quinn.

"Not yet." She sat holding his fingers and watching smoke.

"You keep working that smoke like that," he said, "and pretty soon you're going to go up like that smoke."

"Oh no. Try?"

"I told you why not."

"It's no interference, Quinn, it just slows everything down. Sometimes it slows things so much, nothing runs away any more." She closed her eyes and held his fingers.

The sun was now halfway into the water, far away, very big and rich-looking, but far. The room was in shadow already.

She put out the cigarette when it was very short and had turned brown and then they drank coffee. She said a long ah, and that she enjoyed coffee more than anything now. Quinn looked at her over his cup, wanting her.

"You look greedy," she said.

"I am. I like nothing better right now than feeling greedy."

"Good. Because you owe me one."

"What?"

"When we made love, you left me way behind."

"I don't remember, you know that?"

"You were full of tricks but it wasn't any good."

"Tricks," he said and drank from his cup.

She put one hand on his leg just as the old man came back into the room. She left her hand there and pressed while the old man said something in Arabic and then he left the room.

"Whitfield is back, maybe?"

"No. He said he fixed the bath."

"You got one of those tin things, too?"

"No. Mine is tile and all black. I look very white on the black," she said and got up.

The sun was no sun any more but was all red water. She wanted to look out for a while or wanted to close the shutters, but he took her arm and said, "Come on. To hell with the shutters, come on," and they went upstairs.

That room had a big white bed and was very dim. In a while Quinn did take the drug she had smoked and he smoked that while she took her bath. Quinn stayed that night, and the next day, and the night after that, but he knew this only in the end. What he knew was that the room was dark, that the room was light, that the woman smelled warm, that she was there or wasn't. Once there was wild laughter, and then there were screams. He was sure he saw Whitfield one time and there were other people. He was holding a woman once and she turned out to be somebody he did not know. Then Bea came back again, crying, then laughing. *God, you didn't leave me behind that time,* she said, then wept again. *I feel like slush. God, how I hate slush.* Some of this came and went in a way which reminded him of the time in the box, except this time it was really the opposite.

Chapter 16

The first thing Whitfield saw from his bed was Quinn, shaving. Whitfield did not have a hangover but he did have a delicate routine in the morning and the razor sounds went through him. He broke routine and started to talk while still lying in bed. This way he would not hear the razor sounds.

"Ah! Good morning!"

"Hum," said Quinn, doing his chin.

The good morning had sickened Whitfield and he wished he had said hum instead.

"Why are you shaving?" said Whitfield. "Got a date?"

"Lend me some money."

"How will I get it back?"

"When I get my job."

"You're getting a job?"

"Today, if the thing is on schedule."

The exchange left Whitfield a little limp and he had no idea what it was all about.

"Why do you need money?"

"Because I got a date."

Which is, of course, Whitfield thought, how we started. And better avoid confusion and not ask how come a date at this hour in the morning.

Quinn was toweling his face and Whitfield closed his eyes. There was too much activity. When he opened his eyes again he saw Quinn stand by the bed.

"You look terribly awake," said Whitfield, feeling threatened.

"You going to lend me that money? Five bucks or so."

Whitfield sighed and closed his eyes again. "I'd rather not," he said, "though it seems I might, any moment."

"You'll get it back, Whitfield. Really."

"I point out to you that you are not permitted to hold a job in this country, not with your status, and I point out to you that it is barely daylight and no time for a date at all, and if it's Bea, then of course you actually don't need any money at all. This exhausts my arguments. I am exhausted."

"I haven't got a date this early in the morning but maybe I haven't got

time to ask for the money later. And don't tell me about legalities. You
know they don't mean a thing around here."

"All right," said Whitfield, "all right," and then he got out of bed. He
gave Quinn some bills which actually came to about three dollars and then
said he was not too interested in discussing legalities, not with an active-
type crook such as Quinn, he himself being a passive-type crook only, and
that there was a great deal of difference. He, Whitfield, did not enjoy the
activity as such but only the rewards, and that was quite different from
Quinn's situation. And would Quinn please leave now, so that he, Whitfield, might wake up in peace.

"Be seeing you," said Quinn, and left.

Whitfield thought about the way Quinn had grinned, and about this
disturbing electric quality which the man could muster at this hour of the
morning. And I'll not be seeing you, not today, if I can help it.

But Whitfield felt apprehensive from that point on without bothering to
try and explain this to himself. He knew that he could always find explanations for anything, several explanations for anything, and that it did not
help him one bit. He went apprehensively through the entire forenoon,
consoling himself with the thought of his siesta.

He was reasonably busy with bills of lading, and at eleven the cutter
came in. The cutter had tear streaks of rust down its sides and looked to
be built about fifty years ago. Which was true, except for the engine. This
was the cutter from Sicily and eleven o'clock was a very nice time of
arrival—the cutter did not always come in on schedule—but eleven was
fine with Whitfield because by eleven-thirty he could start his siesta. With
this thought Whitfield forgot his apprehension for a while and watched
how the cutter sidled up to the pier.

Then Whitfield saw the Sicilian. The man stood, arms akimbo, where
the gangway would come down from the ship's side and Whitfield went
back into apprehension. Oh no, he thought. First I lose five dollars, while
still in bed, and now this has to happen. That man there never comes
along on a trip unless there is trouble, or at any rate, hardly ever unless
there is trouble, and of course there is trouble today. I feel it. I know my
siesta is shot all to hell. Why did I have to be in such an exciting business
like shipping in Okar.

The Sicilian was the first off the gangway and came across the bright pier
to the warehouse door where Whitfield was standing. Let him walk all the
way over, thought Whitfield, I am used to apprehension and besides, that
one loves to walk.

This seemed to be true. The Sicilian walked as if preceding an army. He also reminded one of a bantam, except that his face was a monkey face. He wore an Italian suit, the jacket leaving some of the rear exposed in fairly tight pants, and the shoulders flared out as if there were epaulettes. He walked, flashing his shoes. Where an American buys a showy car, Whitfield thought to himself, a Sicilian buys that kind of shoes.

"Whitfield?" said the Sicilian, as if he did not know whom he was talking to.

"How are you, Cipolla," and Whitfield smiled, hoping that this might influence fate.

"You got troubles, Whitfield. Come on."

Cipolla talked English whenever he could. He did not talk English, according to Whitfield, but a type of American. Cipolla had learned the language during his few years in New York, before he had been shipped back for illegal entry.

Since the Sicilian went to the warehouse without saying another word, Whitfield had to follow. When he got to his office, Cipolla was sitting in the only chair.

"What kinda monkeyshines goes on here?" said Cipolla.

It would be useless to try to answer that, so Whitfield said, "I beg your pardon?"

"And don't hand me that Boston accent. You know what you done?"

"No, and you are here to tell me. What I done," said Whitfield.

"That shipment of alcohol—you know what shipment of alcohol?"

"Yes," said Whitfield and rubbed his forehead. "The one without tires on the wheels, I'm sure."

"Che dice?"

"Never mind, and you needn't give me any of your Sicilian accent, please. It affects me similarly as my..."

"I'm gonna tell you your troubles, Whitfield. That alcohol, friend, was just like water!"

Thank God, thought Whitfield, no alcohol is just like water, and let us soon be done with this dismal day. "In fact," Cipolla yelled suddenly, "it *was* water!"

"It was?"

"And besides, it still *is* water!"

"Oh no," said Whitfield. "I knew it—"

"You *knew* it?"

"Will you stop crowing at me!" and Whitfield got up from the window sill.

For a moment he felt pleased for having known that of course something bad would soon happen. How could one ignore the signs, being of average intelligence: the five dollars lost while still asleep in bed, the truck without tires, the creature from the box, the bad run of siestas. And now it had all come true. Whitfield knew well that there was trouble, but before he could get depressed he thought of a bathtub and became indifferent.

"Come on," he said. "Might as well see Remal."

Quinn had just one highball, even though he had to sit with it for almost an hour. He did not want to feel dull, or feel happy, or indifferent. He wanted to sit there for whatever time it would take and feel sharp like this, nervous like this.

When Bea walked into the hotel he seemed glad enough to see her come up to his table, and he gave her a quick smile.

It was too quick, she thought, but then I'm too apprehensive. She sat down, looking at him, wishing he would look at her too so that she could tell how he felt.

"Buy you a drink?" he said.

"Thank you. Is yours Scotch?"

Quinn did not answer but waved at the waiter and called Scotch across the room.

"Quinn?"

"Huh?"

"I wanted to say something to you about this morning."

"There's Whitfield," said Quinn and pointed out to the lobby. "Who's that with him?"

"I don't know. He's a Sicilian. Quinn?"

"I guess they're not coming in for a drink," said Quinn. He folded his arms on the table and looked at the woman. "You were saying something?"

He even smiled, but she did not feel that the smile was for her, not for anyone even, it was that kind of a smile. She took a deep breath and said, "I wish it were morning again."

"What?"

She made a small sound which was almost a laugh.

"I wish I knew myself what I'm saying."

"Listen, Bea. Here's your drink. You excuse me for a moment?"

She watched him get up and said, "Are you coming back?"

"Sure." He was buttoning his jacket.

"Quinn, I don't know exactly how but I'm trying..."

"Later. I'll be back, huh?"

He waved at her, or he waved at the chair, and when he walked out he was not thinking of the woman at all.

He went to the desk in the lobby and put his hands on the marble top. This felt cool, and he felt cool. He said to the clerk, "Would you tell me where the mayor is?"

"Who?"

"Remal."

"He is talking business at the moment."

"I know, and I'm late. Where do I find him?"

The clerk told Quinn to go up the curved staircase to the only room on the next floor which had a double door. That was where the mayor was talking business. Quinn went up and the brass railing on the staircase felt cool, too. He did not go very fast and he did not delay either. Just about now, he felt, they should be in the middle of it.

He came to the double door and both wings had open slats, for ventilation. He could hear them talk in the room. Quinn knocked once, heard the silence, and walked in.

Quinn had no trouble at all in sizing up what went on in the room. Even without foreknowledge. The Sicilian looked most actively interrupted. Little Napoleon laying down the law, thought Quinn, little punk with big shoulders which he bought from the tailor. Whitfield had a crestfallen look, but Whitfield had never very far to go in order to look that way. And Remal, Quinn saw, was not wearing his cap. First time Quinn had seen the Arab without the cap on his head. It was on Remal's knee and his left hand was making nervous plucks along the stitching.

"Who in hell is that?" said Cipolla.

Quinn looked at the Sicilian the same way he would look at the furniture. He ignored Remal. Let him stew, good for him, and then he used Whitfield for his wedge.

"I've come to help you," he said to Whitfield. "I thought you could use a hand."

"You have? You can?" said Whitfield and his face lit up with total belief.

"Now just a minute..." Cipolla started to say, but Quinn said for Cipolla to be quiet and never looked at him while he said it. He sat down at the table and then he looked at the Sicilian.

"My name's Quinn. I'm new here and you and I don't know each other, but maybe if you get off your horse for a minute, maybe there's something in it for you." Quinn did not wait for an answer but turned back to Whitfield, "This is about that alcohol shipment, isn't it?"

"God, yes. Never in my entire..."

"What in hell do you know about this?" said Cipolla, and then, to get the meeting back under his own thumb, he was going to say something else.

Quinn interrupted him again. "I stole it."

Cipolla got up from his chair and sat down again. Whitfield giggled and Remal let go of his cap. He started to frown very heavily which was about the most intelligent thing anyone did at the table.

"Mister Quinn," he said, "I have underestimated you. My original impulse about you was correct, but then I did nothing about it. I underestimated you."

"You can have the stuff back," said Quinn.

"I know that. I know the shipment as such is of no interest to you."

"You're right."

"Of course. I no longer underestimate you."

Now, thought Quinn, for the first time, the man is getting dangerous. Now we start. Quinn sat back in his chair and felt right.

"Before anything else," said Cipolla, and his voice was too high, "I want to know what in hell goes on around here and what's the doubletalk around here."

Whitfield translated doubletalk for Remal and then Remal explained to the Sicilian.

"Mister Quinn is here temporarily. He is nevertheless interested in business, that is to say, in my business, and this is his way of involving himself."

Remal seemed to be on the point of saying more, but then he looked at Quinn and Quinn felt certain that the other man was puzzled. Then Remal looked away and said, "That is all."

There had been no rancor and there had been no sound of danger, and Quinn could not gauge Remal any more. Remal was down and Quinn could not gauge him. He hunched his shoulders and put his arms on the table. He hooked his fingers together and for a moment imagined that one hand was he and the other was somebody else and these two were having a fight. Then Quinn relaxed, and now Remal did not puzzle him any more. Just watch him. This isn't his dance, but mine, and he knows it. He's just learning that now and isn't sure what to do yet and that's the reason why he doesn't show something clear-cut, like anger.

Cipolla, in the meantime, got everything just as wrong. He got it wrong in a different way and for different reasons, and the most important thing was that nobody should think they could gang up on him.

"Hold it," he said. "Just a minute." He squinted his eyes because he wanted to show that he too could be conspiratorial. "I'm getting an ugly picture," he said. "I'm getting an ugly feel here like you two are cooking up something around here, something between you two, and maybe you think I'm gonna get left out."

Remal was too surprised by this diagnosis to say anything, and Quinn sat still.

"All I get from the doubletalk with you two is that one steals from the other, and the other one knows it, and the other one says you can have it back, and all that polite crap with nothing else showing, to me, you know what that looks like? Like maybe you two are trying to pull something over on me. And when that happens..."

"Really, Cipolla," said Whitfield, "you must be quite wrong."

"I must? How?"

Whitfield did not know how and shrugged. "Quinn," he said, "before he speculates us all into a disaster, would you kindly explain what goes on here?"

"*He* should explain?" and now Cipolla felt he had his feet back under him. "I took the run over here to get it straight from you and Remal how in hell you ship water across and don't even know it. And I'm here with the message..."

"Before you give the message," said Quinn, enjoying his trick of interrupting the other one, "I'll explain it. They couldn't explain it because, like you said yourself, they didn't even know what they were shipping."

"So?" said Cipolla. He was not sure whether he had been corrected, or reprimanded, or what.

"I hijacked the alcohol and sent along the water. How I did it isn't important. What is important—and this is why you are here—is the fact that it was possible to cut into the line of supply."

Cipolla said, "So," and waited for more.

"You got a sloppy set-up over here, on this side of the run. I'm here no time at all and pulled this thing off without any trouble. I can do it again. I can do it in different ways. But the main thing right now, Cipolla, the set-up here stinks."

"Who sent you?" said Cipolla.

"Nobody."

"Who sent him?" said Cipolla to Whitfield this time.

"Well, in a manner of speaking he *was* sent, though the explanation wouldn't help you a great deal. In Quinn's sense of the word, of course he was not sent, though..."

"I'm sorry I asked," said Cipolla. "Where you from, Quinn?"

"The States."

"Who you with?"

"I'll tell you what I'm going to do, Cipolla. I'll talk to whoever you are with. Okay?"

"Listen here. When it comes to trouble-shooting..."

"All you got is troubles. You got nothing to shoot with. You got a wide-open line of supply at this end, and I can run it better."

The tone of the talk decided Cipolla to pick another victim for the moment. He looked at Remal and said, "What have you got to say about this?"

Remal sighed and put his skullcap back on.

"Mister Quinn," he said, "is of course right. At the moment I cannot say much more. I have two problems here. One is you, and the other is Mister Quinn. I am frankly confused at the moment and don't know what else to say."

Cipolla took a cigar out of his pocket and looked at it for a moment, so that he would he doing something. When he started to talk again he talked at the cigar.

"All this time," he said, "we been thinking you were running things over here. Remal is a pretty good end at this point of the line. We been thinking that. Now, what turns out, he sits here and is too confused to know what to say or to know what goes on." Cipolla looked up and talked straight at Remal. "I'm gonna go back," he said, "and explain to cut you right out of this set-up. We got other ways, you know that, and right now you look washed up to me."

There was some more talk back and forth, but Quinn wasn't listening. He had the fast image of Remal becoming a nonentity in this thing, a collapse much too fast, the whole thing self-defeating. He saw it this way, that with Remal out there would be no deal for Quinn. He did not think beyond that, but thought only that his whole effort in Okar might now go down the drain. No Okar set-up, no nothing. No Remal, and nothing.

"You got it wrong," he said to Cipolla. "You don't know what you're junking here, what part's good and what part's bad."

"But you know, huh?"

"Yes," said Quinn, and then the rest came out as smoothly as if he had practiced this kind of thing for a very long time. "I can give you the details some other time, but the no good part in the set-up isn't that big."

"How big?"

"Whitfield here. That's all."

Whitfield gaped. He sat up in his chair as if he hadn't heard right and then he started to stutter something, but Quinn was not looking at him. Quinn was looking at Cipolla to see if the right impression was made.

"Quinn," Whitfield got out, "what did I ever do to you?"

Quinn did not answer. He kept looking at Cipolla and then he said, "Well? You going to go hog wild on this thing or am I going back with you and set this thing straight?"

Cipolla put the cigar back into his pocket and got up. "Okay," he said. "We're leaving after dark."

Chapter 17

They all seemed to be leaving the room alone because nobody looked at anyone else or talked. Quinn stopped on the landing and lit a cigarette and then walked down the stairs slowly. No rush now, and feeling a little bit tired. But it had worked. He was getting in, right on top of Remal, and the little panic of losing this thing was now almost forgotten. When Quinn got downstairs the Sicilian had gone and Remal was walking out the front door with Beatrice. She looked back at Quinn and then away again. Her face had not changed while she had looked at him but Quinn had not seen too clearly, or had not cared too much. He watched the two walk down the street but he actually saw only Remal. Then he walked through the arch to the bar.

Whitfield was there and when he saw Quinn he quickly tossed down his drink and started to leave.

"Hey." said Quinn. "Listen a minute."

Whitfield stayed where he was because very quickly he felt too indifferent to argue.

"You know there was nothing personal in that, you know that, Whitfield. Buy you a drink?"

Whitfield pulled his empty glass towards himself and said very slowly, "Damn your bleeding eyes, Quinn, I have never seen anything more contemptible in my life. And I hope you get yours."

"What?"

"You won't get it from me, because I'm not the man or the type and don't understand any of this anyway, but let me make clear to you, Quinn, I despise you."

"Now listen..."

"I cannot say that I dislike you. That would involve some sort of activity on my part, and any sort of activity on my part is of course rare. But I despise you. I would go so far as to spit. Thank you, I'll buy my own drink," and Whitfield waved at the waiter.

The two men did not talk while the waiter first made a gin drink for Whitfield and then poured Scotch over ice for Quinn. After that Quinn had to haul himself out of a deep, heavy dullness in order to say something or other to Whitfield. He wished the other man would understand him.

"Whitfield, look here. Maybe you've heard about business. I know you'll have nothing to do with it but you must have heard of it."

"Spare me," said Whitfield and looked away.

"Don't you know I have nothing against you?"

Whitfield looked back at Quinn and said, "That's what makes it so surprising."

"Look. When I get over there and talk to whoever runs that end of the line, I'm going to make it my business..."

"Stop saying business to me."

"I'll see to it they don't get the wrong impression about you. Only reason I used you for the goat up there in the room was to keep that idiot, what's his name..."

"Cipolla. It might interest you to know that's Italian for onion, and perhaps you shouldn't bite into that one too hard."

"I know his type from way back, Whitfield. Don't worry."

"But I *am* worried!" Whitfield took a hasty drink and then he talked with more animation than Quinn had ever seen in the man. "You know his type from way back," said Whitfield, "and you'll be sure to use that type very properly too. And any other types which you may meet around here and which may prove handy. See here, Quinn. In this half-blown-over town we all lead a fine useless life. All the people I know lead a most useless life. And we are bastards, and we cheat, and there's all manner of laxness and laziness for all of which you have one highly developed nose. And now I will even tell you what's going to happen and since I never do anything about these things which I know ahead of time, they therefore usually happen. Here's all this no-good worthlessness which I've been describing to you. Very well. Not much harm done. But you, Quinn, you're going to organize all of that! You're just apt to take advantage of all the worst in us and *organize* it, you rotten—rotten something or other from a box!"

Quinn felt surprised and angered and agitated by Whitfield's long talk. He felt like saying a great number of things himself, about how right Whitfield was and how wrong Whitfield was, but he felt unsure and said nothing. He thought, the only thing he's left out is some preachment about Remal not being such a bad sort, as Whitfield would put it, and why don't I lay off Remal? Because I got sucked in and I've had it. Simple answer.

Whitfield finished his glass and then he finished his speech. "And that's why I much prefer to remain drunk because then I'll *never* be organized. Good night, Sir," and he left.

When Quinn got outside he saw Whitfield standing with Bea. Then

Whitfield started to walk again and waved his arms once or twice, which seemed to have something to do with finishing the conversation.

First he, now she, thought Quinn. Naturally, she'll wave this way in a moment and then it's either of one or the other: let's go to bed, or, what kind of a bastard are you anyway, Quinn.

Quinn fumbled for a cigarette and found that he had none. He then discovered that he had only stood fumbling there to give Bea a chance to look up and see him before he, Quinn, would turn away. Why not, he thought, I've got nothing else to do until evening.

She waved at him from the distance and he waved back. Then he stood by the steps and waited for her, watching her walk.

"What's gotten into you, Quinn?"

Yeah, yeah, sure, he thought, and to hell with it, this is all about what a bastard I am.

"You know I *like* Whitfield?" she said, and stopped in front of him.

"You got a cigarette?" he said. It did not sound tough or off-handed and was not meant that way, but he did not know what else to say at that moment so he said the prepared thing.

It surprised him when she said, yes, and nothing else and he waited while she felt around inside the big pocket on her skirt and then pulled out—this habit she had—just the one cigarette.

"This will surprise you, Quinn," she said, "but I like you too. Only you make it hard for me to show it."

"Oh hell," he said, and threw his cigarette away.

She gave a yank on his arm which made him stop and she had stopped too. "Look at me Quinn. Not down the street. You're like that thin dog running there except you want to run and be fat."

He nodded, not knowing why. He knew he felt a direction when talking to Whitfield, or to that bum from Sicily or to Remal or anyone else, but not with her. Not with Bea, no direction with her, but he did not want to leave.

"I don't know why you're running or what got you into that box because you never mention either one or the other," she said, "but then again maybe you never had to mention a thing but made it clear just the same. Just by doing all the things you've been doing. Whatever got you here, you never made that too clear, Quinn. But somehow, when you came out of that box, you looked like you were well out of it." She took a breath in between, without talking, as if she might shout next, or as if she might just sigh the rest away. Either would fit. But then she just talked again, though it sounded as if she did not like this ending. "And now," she said, "you're going right back into that box."

When she let go of his arm the change startled him. She had told him something and had now left him alone with something which felt harsh enough to remind him of the truth. He took a deep breath, the way she had done a short while before, but he did it to brace himself.

"Don't ever say that to me again." He was surprised to hear that his voice was hoarse.

"Quinn," she said, and started to put her hand out to him. Then she dropped it when she saw how he moved back. "Quinn," she said again, "please don't run from me and please don't jump on me."

"All I said..."

"But you were listening to me this time, weren't you?"

He looked away, down the street, and this meant yes both to him and to her.

"You remember how you came out of that box, and never used to look away?"

He looked back at her and then down, as if thinking about what to say, or how to say it.

"Bea, listen. When all this is over—" Then he thought some more.

"When?" she said.

"I was just thinking when."

"Any time, Quinn."

"Just a minute, just a minute," he said. "Don't screw me up now. Any time what?"

"Anything."

"You thinking about yourself or me?"

"It doesn't make any difference, the way I was thinking, Quinn." Then she said, "I would like to leave with you, Quinn."

He looked down at her and then put his hand to the side of her face because now she was turning away. There was a great deal of warmth in his hand and he felt she must feel this.

"You know," he said, "you say this to me and you still call me Quinn."

"That doesn't matter to me. It can be strange and it can be right all at the same time."

He put his hand down and said, "I can't leave because I don't have any papers."

The remark was as asinine as it was correct and he wished that he hadn't made it, because of everything it left out.

"You know I saw Remal before," she said. He was glad she was talking, but now he did not want to listen.

"Where is he?" Quinn said.

"I was just going to tell you. He's phoning. He's making all kinds of calls..."

"Like, maybe Sicily?"

"Sicily?" she said. "Your consulate. I don't know about Sicily."

Now Quinn tapped himself for a cigarette again and she held one out to him. He took it without looking.

"Sure," he said. "Sure that's one way of trying to get ahead of me," and he did not see her hold out the lighter to him. "Where is he?" he said again.

"I was to tell you he'd like to see you in the hotel a little later."

He looked at her now and saw her hold the lighter but ignored it.

"You came running down here just to tell me that?"

"No, Quinn!"

"Am I supposed to be stupid?"

"Yes you are! I did not come down here because he sent me. He didn't send me, Quinn. Please!"

"But if you just should happen to run into me, is that it, you should give me this kindly message to show up at the hotel and get the good word from Remal himself about all the preparations he's made about keeping me here in the country, with the help of consul and what not, and then, that failing, what preparations he's made for my Sicilian reception, once I get over there."

"Oh my God," she said and turned away.

She walked back up the street, toward the hotel, and he followed her, walking next to her. They did not say another word. They went into the hotel; he went to the bar and stopped. She did not stop but kept walking to the back of the big room; she sat down at the round table where he had seen her that first time. He looked at her once from the bar. She did not look like the first time to him, or like any other time. In fact, he hardly saw her at all, only something sitting there. He looked away and hated her guts. He was not done with his first Scotch when Remal walked in and that was just fine with Quinn, that was just fine and as expected.

"I'm glad you waited for me, Mister Quinn," Remal said as he stepped up to the bar.

"Your messenger got to me just in time. Just as I was walking out of here to do something dangerous and heroic, she came running and begged me to wait for you instead. To lie down under a table here and wait for you. You'd come over to the table and give me a soft little nudge with your soft little slipper and then I'd know it was you, come to talk to me."

"Are you very drunk, Mister Quinn?"

Quinn, in fact, did feel drunk, but knew no reason why he should be, on two widely-spaced Scotches.

"I would like us to sit down," said Remal. "I have some good news for you."

I can't tell whether or not he's hopeful or worried, thought Quinn. Maybe he's neither. And I'll take another Scotch, on him, and might as well catch up drinking to the way I feel drunk.

He ordered the drink and sat down at a table nearby and Remal did the same. Remal looked back and forth from this table to the one in back where Bea sat alone, but said nothing. I bet he's puzzled as all hell, thought Quinn, and can't understand how anyone can take offense at a woman for any reason at all. Such a gentleman, this one, and with good news yet.

Quinn picked up his fresh glass and Remal said, "I would like to tell you and discuss the news before..."

"Before I get any drunker?" said Quinn, and then he took a good swallow from his glass.

Remal said nothing while Quinn finished. When Quinn had put down his glass Remal said, "If this was meant to offend me, Mister Quinn, you cannot offend me."

"Like you wouldn't be offended at a dog that pissed on your rug because that would be just too foolish, to think of the brute as if it were a human being."

Remal sucked air through his nose. It's just like he's sniffing this whole thing out, thought Quinn.

"It's precisely this kind of remark, Mister Quinn, which keeps me from understanding you. I've been wondering whether or not you do it on purpose."

"What's the good news?" said Quinn.

"Yes. It is better to talk about that." He smoothed his skirt affair and then he looked up. "I have been on the phone, Mister Quinn, to inform myself and to expedite."

"Yes, yes?" said Quinn, and thought of the Arab who stank so much and had a donkey face.

"I spoke to your consulate, and a passport has been issued to you!"

Goddammit, thought Quinn. He's smiling!

"Mister Quinn?" and Remal cocked his head. "I thought you would be pleased."

Quinn picked up his glass, looked at Bea in the far corner and, for a moment, held his breath. Then he put the glass to his mouth and drank all the liquor down.

I stick the pig and make it, he thought. I stick him good and he's down! Then why do I feel like the pig that got stuck. Why now, after making it!

"Mister Quinn. I do not pretend to understand you, but I do understand this. You and I cannot be friends, though there seems some hesitation about our being enemies. I do not pretend to know why. Or you may reverse the sentence and it comes perhaps to the same thing. Under the circumstances, for you and for me, the best has really happened. You now have your papers. You can now leave."

Quinn still did not answer. Something just went down the drain, he thought. I'm drunk. Or something just opened up and like only once before I can be rid of him. He looked up when he heard the heels on the tile.

"I just told Mister Quinn that he has his papers," Remal said to Bea.

"Yuh," said Quinn. "He just gave me my traveling papers." He watched Bea sit down.

"Yes, as I just said," Remal added.

"He didn't mean it that way," Bea told Remal. "The way he used the phrase, it means you just threw him out." Then she turned to Quinn and saw how he sat there, as if hiding behind drunkenness. "On the street," she said, "you told me you couldn't leave. You had no papers." She put her hands on the table but didn't know what to do with them. She put them into her lap. "But now, Quinn, what is there to decide?"

"You don't even know my first name," he said and felt really drunk.

"Please—" she said.

Remal coughed. He understood little of this but suspected it was some private language, the kind lovers might have. He got up, smoothed his shirt.

"I will leave you alone," he said. "I will leave the papers at the desk of the hotel. In addition, I will leave you some money." And then he added the part which made everything wrong for Quinn, though it made him suddenly sober. "Because I want you out." He made his bow and left.

Quinn watched him go out and then turned back to the table. He felt small and pushed and he felt he looked ugly sitting there, but that Remal looked large and the woman, Bea, was terribly beautiful.

"I'm thinking," he mumbled, "that it was easier in the box."
She got up and took his arm. "Walk with me," she said.
He got up and they walked out.

Chapter 18

With unusual suddenness the white light of day had changed into the
yellow light when siesta is over. Okar was no longer quiet, empty-looking,
but full of voice sounds, feet sounds and motion. But Quinn heard mostly the sounds inside: indecision like a squeak, anger a noisy scratching getting louder, and the hum, the constant hum, of his tenacity. To stay put
and not jump.

But this is the time to decide, he thought, and please, Bea, do not interrupt me. To leave or to stay. And to go with Cipolla means no new change
at all.

They walked down to the quay, saying very little.

Once he said, "Maybe I look like a bastard—"

"I think you act like one, yes."

They walked the length of the quay, away from the warehouse and the
town. Quinn remembered having been that way once, with Turk.

"You want to know something, Bea?"

"Yes."

"Sometimes I don't enjoy any of this, you know that?" She nodded,
which was enough.

They walked through the rocks and then on the pebbles. He held her
arm and said there was a scorpion, she should step around it. They walked
around it and when they were by the water the reflections jumped and
darted at them and they turned away. There was a rock big enough for a
black hood of shade and they went there and sat down. The water had
been full of sun flash but on the rocks which tilted away the sunlight
seemed gray. Sun-gray, he thought. All day long like a heat death under
the light and now everything is ashes. I'm tired.

"Quinn?"

"Yes."

"You asked me if I thought you were a bastard, you remember? I don't
like the word and feel awkward with it and only used it because you did.
And to tell you that I don't think you are now."

"I don't feel like one now." And he looked at the rocks and they did not
remind him of ashes any more. They were just rocks. "And I want to tell
you something else," he said. "Not for apology or anything like that,
because what's done is really done, but that thing I did to Whitfield, using

him like that, it happened so smoothly and I did it so well I'm frightened about it."

"Why frightened?"

"Because I didn't like it. Not even when I was doing it."

She looked at him but said nothing.

"I hurt him and didn't care. All the circuits were set, and then after pressing the button it's out of my hands, because that's how I'm set up. You know what I'm talking about?"

"No. Not yet."

"I'm talking about Remal. I'm set for him, all set up, to get him down and out of my way, and then I press the button and after that nothing can be done about it."

"And tonight," she said, "you'll take the boat to Sicily."

"Yes," he said. "For the same reason."

She saw now that he had never acted from nastiness or because he was stubborn, or from total blindness, but that this was something else.

"You sound like a condemned man," she said.

He waited a moment, not looking at her, and then he said, "Yes, that fits."

She said nothing else to that, though she wished she could tell him, there are other ways, even better ones maybe, and why don't you try— She dropped that, because it made her feel like a hypocrite. How much did she herself try, and still ended up with the same things she had done before, a hundred or more times.

She took his hand and put it over her breast, holding it there. They sat like that and looked at the gray terrain tilt away.

"You know what will happen to you, if you go through with all this?" she said. It was a real question, the way she asked it, not an admonition or a trick introduction for working up to a lesson.

"I probably do," he said, "because it's happened before."

"Back into the box," she said and gave a small, disconnected laugh.

"I don't think I've ever been out of it."

He got up and brushed at his pants. Then he held out his hand for her and helped her up. When she stood next to him she put her hands on his arms and her face into the side of his neck. If there were nothing else now but to feel the skin warmth there, she thought, his and mine, and other simple things like that—

"You're wrong," she said. "Once, at one point there, you were out of it."

She stepped away from him a little, to see his face when he would answer, but he did not say anything. He isn't saying anything, she thought, because he's afraid to say yes, I've been out of it, I can be out of it.

Her hands were still on his arms and she curled her fingers into him very hard for a moment and said, "Please stay."

It was as artless as anything which comes at the wrong moment, which comes too late.

His face was in the sun now, the sun yellow now and his face looking not very alive. His eyes were closed. "And what do you want from me?" he said, but even when be opened his eyes he was not looking at her.

For a moment she did not know what to answer, feeling helpless trying to make sense.

"What?" he said and looked at her.

"I don't want anything, Quinn," she said. "I love you." He held her for a moment. It was as artless as the phrase she had used.

Chapter 19

After the sun had gone down there was still light for a while, a very fugitive light to which no one paid much attention because it would soon be gone. On the pier the lights went on and made an immediate night even though everything still showed where the orbs of the lights did not reach.

And then, when he stood with her on the pier, he had one other chance.

"Have you heard about Turk?" she said.

"What?"

"Some children found him behind the town, in the desert. They recognized him by the army jacket. The dogs had already been there."

All the softness went out of Quinn with the shock. And then he stayed that way, stiff and hard.

"Never mentioned a word, did he, the mayor? Too polite. He could have said, take the passport or else. For example, like Turk or else. But no. Much too polite to pressure a man right to his face."

"Quinn, you don't understand him. He is not playing word games and he doesn't think that way. He kills Turk because Turk is staying. He tells you nothing because he does not even assume that you might stay."

"I'll show him," said Quinn. He looked over her head, at nothing.

"There is nothing to show him, Quinn. Don't you understand? Look at me."

He looked at her, not really wanting to.

"Don't go with the boat," she said. "Go with me."

He was stiff and cold and made no decision. Making no decision, he muffed his chance. And he saw this.

"And you," she said, "you can't be shown anything either, can you, Quinn?" And she walked away without waiting for an answer.

The water was black and slick like hot tar and the sky was losing the red of sundown and moving into the no-color dark, a very solid dark of night sky without moon. There would be no moon this night. In this shift of color there is the point where the sky is a heavy gray, gray being no color at all but still light, so that on the other side of the bulbs on the pier Quinn could see the fences where the warehouse ended. There was a child at the fence at one end. Quinn was sure it must be a child because of the size. It hung on the fence like a spider and seemed to be looking at him. The child made no sound and there was just the wet slap and suck of the water now and then, under the pier.

At the other end of the warehouse, on the pier, lay the box. It was on its side, as before, with one edge broken, as before.

Quinn smoked and watched the sky turn from gray to blue, and then it was dark.

No one saw him off because after all, he would be back.

When Cipolla came, he did not say anything but just went to the edge of the pier where he whistled for someone on the water to come rowing across to the pier. They had moved the boat when the loading had been done and it lay somewhere in the dark. There were no lights. Quinn walked over to Cipolla and listened for sounds.

"How long does she take, to Sicily?"

"Why?" said Cipolla.

In the afternoon, when Quinn had walked in and interrupted the conference, there he might have felt uneasy about this. Here was Cipolla being suspicious in order to add character to his store-bought status. But now on the pier Quinn felt bored with the man.

"I just asked," Quinn said, and listened for sounds from the water again.

"I mean," said Cipolla, "so far you're not taking over anything, Quinn, so why in hell should you know how fast she can make the trip."

Quinn did not discuss it, feeling as before. The lights on the warehouse wall were behind him. They showed the bare pier very clearly, but beyond that they reached a limit which was much like a wall, so that Quinn could see nothing at all on the water. He thought he heard oar sounds now.

"She doesn't look it," said Cipolla, "but it takes just a night and part of a day."

Quinn could see the rowboat now. It came out of the dark and a man stood in the bow, skulling. He came out of the dark the same way he might come gliding out of a curtain.

"For the whole run, from here to the South coast of Sicily," said Cipolla.

"Fine," said Quinn.

Cipolla had his cigar out and was fingering it with small, rapid movements. Quinn was not watching.

"You got any kind of interest in this thing?" said Cipolla. "Don't it strike you funny we get there in the middle of the day?"

When he was five, Quinn thought, I bet he was a brat and used to whine.

"That's all fixed up," said Cipolla. "We got that all fixed up. Yessir."

"You're shredding your cigar all to pieces," said Quinn, and then looked elsewhere.

Cipolla started to curse to himself for any number of good reasons and then the rowboat bumped the pier where the ladder went down to the water. Cipolla climbed down first and then Quinn.

Now the pier was really empty. There was no child hanging like a spider on the wire fence any more. The two men no longer stood at the edge, and not even a dog trotted out, to watch or to look for something.

This was the first time Quinn had been on a boat since the time in the box and the motion underfoot reminded him of it. Then the motion no longer reminded him because the boat, once out of the bay, revved up to a great speed and seemed to lunge through the water rather than roll or sway. A black wind cut into Quinn on the deck and he went below, to a small space with a leather couch and a table and a desk in one corner, captain's quarters perhaps. The captain must be on the dark bridge, thought Quinn. He had not seen anyone else either. Cipolla was in the cabin, but when Quinn walked in Cipolla left. Quinn sat down on the couch. It smelled of office—a small country office for an old lawyer, perhaps—or like a photographer's waiting room. In the same country town. Quinn did not think of the country town and stretched out on the couch.

There was a vibration in the stuffed leather. Two big diesels, he thought. Two big diesels in the root cellar of the same country lawyer's house in the small town. I once had a relative. I called him uncle. I know he wasn't my father. He lived elsewhere. He was a lawyer and the uncle was a lawyer and every Christmas he gave me five dollars. God, I'm tired. And once, later, when I really needed money, he said, wait till Christmas.

Quinn took his jacket off and put it under his head so he would not smell the leather so much. When he closed his eyes there was the motion again, and more of the vibration, and it reminded him of the box. It was not the same motion and not the same vibration, he knew that, but he was reminded. Without transition Quinn went to sleep.

Cipolla looked in once and muttered something and left again. Once the captain came into the cabin, wanting to lie down on the couch, and he left. At one point there was a sudden drop in speed and the boat wallowed and rolled with the water motion entirely. Then came a surprising jump in speed with no let-up for a very long time. The pitch of the diesels was new now, which Quinn could have felt through the stuffed leather, except he slept. He woke up once and ate with three other people—one was Cipolla, he saw—but that waking did not make much of a difference. In fact Quinn was unaware of the light from the portholes, unaware whether it was day or night. Then, as long as the boat was in motion, he slept again. Once he knew he was sweating inside his clothes and once he knew that he was dreaming. That stopped the dream. He knew he felt cold from the sweat on his skin and right after that his sleep became deeper and he no longer knew how he felt but just lay there, on the couch.

The trip lasted longer than Cipolla had said and they did not dock until sundown. When the engines stopped Quinn woke up and when he went topside he saw the pier next to the boat. The sun was down just behind a black line of mountain, and with the half light in the cool air Quinn had a moment's impression that nothing had happened since the time he had stood by the warehouse in Okar, waiting for the day to be over and for the trip to start. This lasted a moment and then Quinn saw what there was.

The pier and the railroad track were close together; the dominant building was the railroad station. It was timeless with ugliness and could have fit Scranton, Pennsylvania, or Bangor, Maine. Though here it was uglier, trying to put the rest of the town to shame.

There was not much of the town. Narrow-chested gray buildings clapped up against the drop to the sea, all this on the North side of the bay, so that gloom seemed built into the town. Quinn saw how everyone stared on the pier, but then he decided it was the national habit. They stared at each other too. Police in blue and police in gray; they most likely had different jobs but they also just stood and stared.

"You going to unload whatever you got on this boat right here in the open?" Quinn asked Cipolla.

"While you were asleep," said Cipolla, wishing to make a point of that, "we transferred at sea. I told you we got it all set up. Come on."

They walked down a gangplank and then along the pier.

"For all I know," said Quinn, "we could be in Scotland. I haven't heard a word of Italian yet."

"They know their place," said Cipolla.

"Huh?"

"This is Mafia country."

If this was an explanation, thought Quinn, it was a pretty gruesome one. Cipolla, the way he walked down the pier, seemed to take pride in his sentence, but the short, black-eyed men and the thick, leather-skinned women who stood around with their stares depressed Quinn and made him wish that he were some place else. Any place else, he thought, any place that's not on the North side and where somebody screams now and then.

They walked down a narrow street, dank like a back alley, but full of the shops and stores which showed that this was a main street. Now there was noise, of course, men talking in cafes, women talking in shops, but to Quinn there was no ring to the sounds. There was no space for sound, really, on this North side of the mountain, and the eyes staring and the mouths hanging open, they said more, actually, thought Quinn, than any sound.

"Happy little community," he said. "You like it here?"

"Lots of money around, if you know the ropes."

If this is an explanation, thought Quinn, but then he dropped the thought. They stopped at a cafe with an awning over the sidewalk. If the headman holds forth here, Quinn thought, I'm going to be reminded of Remal in his hotel. Though the hotel looks better.

Cipolla talked to one of the waiters—it was rapid Italian or perhaps rapid Sicilian—and then they walked again.

"He told you what today's password is, right?"

Cipolla only shrugged.

They walked. Lights went on in some windows and in some of the stores, the naked bulb usually, and sometimes a kerosene lamp which threw more shadow than light.

"We're almost out of town," said Quinn. "Where does he live, in a cave?"

Cipolla stopped in the middle of the street, and if there were enough light, thought Quinn, his face would now show red like a turkey's wattles.

"You listen to me, bum," said Cipolla. "You come down here knocking this place right from the start and you don't get nowhere. I like this place. People here like this place, and if you know what pride means..."

"Yeah, yeah, yeah," said Quinn. "When you're poor and dirty you can always say, I got pride. Lead the way."

Cipolla said something filthy in Sicilian—the language, Quinn had noticed, did not have the ring and the sing of Italian. Quinn thought, you can probably say something filthy better in Sicilian than in any other language. They walked, and Quinn wondered whether the man they would see knew as little about Quinn's coming as Quinn knew about the thing he was going into.

There was a big wooden door which opened right from the street into somebody's windowless apartment. They walked through that past a woman in black who stood at a stove and past an old man in a bed who was looking at a lit candle which stood on a chair next to the bed. They walked out through a back door scaring five cats away from a garbage pail,

and, on the other side of this yard which was made by the backs of old
houses, a yard like the bottom of a shaft, they walked into a whitewashed
kitchen. This kitchen seemed as naked as the bulb which hung from the
ceiling and the place smelled only from the damp. No food around, no
smell of food, no sign of use.

"You wait here," said Cipolla, and walked on through a door.

This could definitely not be some place in Scranton or in Brooklyn or any
other depressing place I know, Quinn thought while he lit a cigarette, but
this could definitely be the place which all the others—with bad light and
bad air and bad altogether—have used for a model. Patience now, he said
to himself, patience. Wait till you meet the educated animal that lives here.

Cipolla opened the door and jerked his head and then disappeared again
down a dark corridor.

When Quinn walked into the room at the other end he thought, yes,
now this on the other hand could be in Scranton or in Brooklyn. There
was mail-order furniture and there was a big console TV. Then the man
got up from the maroon couch and Quinn was really surprised.

He was short, just like everyone else seemed to be in this town, but he
had a pink face, white hair, and he was smiling. He said, "Hi, there," with
no accent at all and held his hand out in the friendliest way. Only wrong
note, thought Quinn, is that ring there. Big diamond with collar of
baguettes, all on one little finger. Santa Claus wearing jewelry.

Quinn shook hands and said he was Quinn, and the other one said, "Yes,
I know. My name's Motta. Just like the ice cream."

Quinn did not know that Motta was an ice cream but he thought that
was a nice, innocent comparison to make and who might Motta be.

Cipolla came and went while Motta and Quinn sat down on the maroon
couch. The couch creaked and it smelled of moth balls. Quinn smelled the
moth balls and looked at the antimacassars on the arm-rests of the couch,
wondering who the woman in the house might be. There was a brown
photo of a couple on the wall and behind the framed photo somebody had
stuck a palm frond at a slant. This palm frond was as brown and yellow as
the young couple in the picture. The man was stiff with starch and waxed
mustache, and the woman stiff with whalebone and laces.

"Mother and Dad," said Motta. "They died in the States. Poor as church
mice, but proud. Never took a dime from me, rest their souls."

The woman who came into the room now looked like the grandmoth-
er of the couple in the picture, though she was really the daughter and
Motta called her Sis.

Sis put three espresso cups on the round table, a small pressure pot full of hot coffee, and a white jug which held hot milk. Cipolla came in with a bowl of sugar and then the old woman left without having said a word.

"Half and half?" said Motta. "I take mine black."

Quinn took half milk and half coffee and Motta took half coffee and half sugar. Cipolla had nothing. He sat and watched.

"Well," said Motta, and smiled into his cup. "Here we are." He slurped coffee and said, "Ah!"

The dead TV screen looked gray and shiny and Cipolla's skin looked like a dry leaf. A wind had started to whistle outside. If there's fog, thought Quinn, I wouldn't be surprised.

"Yessir," said Motta. He looked like the most alive thing in the room. "I do miss the States some, now and then, but they sure never learned over there how to make coffee. Like it?

"Born and raised right here, Quinn," said Motta, "but got took to the States when I was maybe three years old. Those were the big immigrant days. Everybody poor tried to get there." Motta laughed. "Then, them who got rich got throwed out again. Hahaha!"

It wasn't a stage laugh but sounded like real amusement.

"Yessir," said Motta and put down his cup. "Made my own way over there. Just like you, huh, Quinn?"

"I didn't really make it," said Quinn.

"But you got deported just the same, huh, Quinn?" and Motta laughed again.

Can't get sore at that kind of a laugh, thought Quinn. How can you get sore at Santa Claus?

"You heard about that," said Quinn.

"Oh sure." Motta folded his little hands on his stomach. "While you were asleep on the boat, Cipolla told me some, with the radio. Some of that TV over there," said Motta, "is a short-wave. TV, of course, we ain't got yet, down here. Not that I miss it."

"I miss it," said Cipolla.

"He's not taking his deportation with deportment, like me," said Motta, and the way he said the sentence, Quinn was sure he had used it before. "Not that I wasn't low and all that when I first got here. I mean, it's my home town and all but what's that to me, after all these years and having made a life for myself in the States. I mean, Rome let's say, okay. Naples. Okay. Palermo even. But no. They got to stick you with a home town that nobody even twenty miles from here ever heard of." Motta sighed at the

TV and then he nodded. "Well, then it turned out all right, after all." He smiled and looked at Quinn from the rim of his coffee cup. "Gotta get your hand in, you know, Quinn? Like, I come down here and pretty soon it shows there's a real set-up, a real opportunity. *That's* what the States taught me, boy. How to spot opportunity. Get your hand in."

He put the coffee cup down again—it had been empty for some time—and looked at Quinn with real interest. No smile, this time.

"That's why you're here, right, Quinn? To get your hand in."

"Yes," said Quinn. "That's just about it."

"You walked in over there and spotted a real opportunity. Right?"

"Stared me right in the face," said Quinn.

"Good," and Motta got up. "You and me, Quinn, maybe you and me can get along, huh?"

When he walked by Quinn he gave him a little pat on the shoulder, nothing overdone, just a friendly pat. Then he went to the bureau with all the vases and shepherd figures inside and took a cigar out of a box on top. Cipolla came up with a match, and while Motta got his cigar started he discussed things like, what time is it, time for an aperitif at the cafe, dinner still two hours off, and more small talk like that.

Here, thought Quinn, is a strange break, but a break perhaps, nonetheless. Old gangster deported from the States, running a little thing for the action of it, and to keep in his hand. Out of boredom. Boredom in a town like a handful of mud thrown against the side of a mountain, and twenty miles away nobody knows about the place, and Motta, by the terms of his deportation, must stay in his home town. Apt to drive a man crazy. Like being nailed into a box. Except that Motta has managed it differently, has kept his pink complexion, his easy ways, his good temper. This one, unlike Cipolla, thought Quinn, might well be the man with whom he, Quinn, could work. Finally. Quinn felt a small kick of excitement.

"So they gave you the trip around the world, huh, Quinn?" and Motta came back to the couch, sat down, puffed a blue cloud which smelled like clubs and good leisure.

"Yes," said Quinn. "Except I got out ahead of schedule."

"Must have been bad, huh?"

"I don't remember too well, Motta. I think I'm glad I don't remember too well."

Motta shook his head slowly and watched a blue cloud make a belly and then turn into lace.

"I never thought much of that treatment," he said. "Heard about it, of course, but, well—" and he shook his head again. "Who did it?" he asked next. "I been out of the picture in the States for a long time—how long is it, Cipolla?"

"Twenty-nine years," said Cipolla. "On the fifteenth, next month."

"Long time," said Motta to the picture with the young couple who were his parents. "Who was you with, Quinn? It's been a long time for me, lots of changes over there, but maybe I know."

"His name is Ryder."

"Ryder?"

"The numbers and unions. New York State, Pennsylvania, Ohio, and some Illinois."

Motta shook his head. "There's a new crowd, I guess."

"Maybe Ryder's isn't much of an outfit," said Cipolla. "I just been outa the States five years and I never heard of him. And I was in New York."

"The big ones, Onion, don't get seen by the little ones," Quinn said to Cipolla. He was starting to feel hopped up.

"You must be an educated man," said Motta, to change the conversation. "I mean, listening to the way you talk, things like that."

Quinn shrugged and thought about his education.

"You been to college?" Cipolla asked.

"I'll bet he was. What was you in?" asked Motta.

"Law."

"Hey, that's funny!"

"Yes. It was."

"And from that maybe labor relations or politics and from there, well, you either get to be a politician or a crook, right, Quinn?" and Motta laughed again.

It was the same laugh as before, showing good humor, and Quinn did not mind it. He did not like to think about the subject they had been talking about, especially when Motta had guessed fairly well how he, Quinn, had drifted from one intention to another. Though it had not really been so much a matter of intention, but almost all drift. There had been no zest, not much zest at any rate, in his switch in direction or in his taking a new one. Except, of course, the matter of clawing his way ahead, in spite of Ryder. That had been the spice. If he and Ryder had been in the leather business, in the paper business, it would still have been the same.

"Well," said Motta, "what say we go down to the cafe and talk business, huh, Quinn?"

Quinn had wondered when they would get to it and if Motta was stalling. But Motta simply did not care for speed; he had his evening routine, and business is discussed over a glass in a cafe.

"You notice," said Motta and got up, "that I just lit this cigar, and if you know anything about cigar smokers who care about the product they smoke, you'll have noticed they don't like to walk around with the cigar in their mouth. Cipolla, find me the cane with the bone handle, huh?"

Cipolla left the room to look for Motta's cane.

"I was saying," and Motta smoothed his vest down in front, holding the cigar in his mouth, dead center. "Now, I'm the kind of cigar man I've been describing to you, Quinn, but here you see me walking out with more than half of the Havana still good."

"Yes," said Quinn, a little bored with the gentle small-talk.

"I do this," said Motta, "in fact I do this every day this time of evening, because of the humidity."

Cipolla came back with Motta's hat, which was big-brimmed and light colored and had a black band—this hat, thought Quinn, no doubt goes on the head dead center—and also brought the cane with the bone handle. It was a beautiful, shiny handle, and there was a little silver band where the bone joined the wood. Maybe he'll have forgotten about the cigar talk by now—

The hat went on the head dead center and the cane went in the left hand, because the right hand was for the cigar. Motta looked like somebody happily retired, modestly happy and entirely done with the rat race. They walked out to the street through somebody else's apartment, the same way Quinn had come. Outside it was dark now and miserably damp.

"This dampness," Motta said, "slows the smoke, cools the coal, and brings out tobacco flavors like you don't get in any other way. *That's* why I do this."

Then they walked. Every time they passed a corner there was a street lamp sticking out from a wall and around the light there was always a milky halo of dampness.

"Very important for our operations," said Cipolla, who had been suffering from not saying anything. "This fog every night is like part of the business set-up."

"Now, some would say," Motta went on, "that a cigar, damp like this, gets to be like rotten leaves or the comer of a basement or something like that."

"Of course," said Quinn. "And nonetheless, they keep cigars in a humidor."

Motta ignored that. "But I say, and I think there's something to this, Quinn, I say, don't you eat cheese and like it, and that's rotten? Don't you grow mushrooms in a basement, and that's delicious?"

Quinn got the impression again that Motta had rehearsed this. It did not sound like his usual kind of talk, and of course it did not fit the Santa Claus thing any more. Santa Claus, Quinn thought, would not talk about cigars like this. Somebody who collects butterflies might talk this way, or someone who collects recipes from Greenland and Ceylon, or maybe instructions on how to grow mandrake roots without benefit of gallows and moonlight.

The cafe had an outdoor part and an indoor part. In spite of the weather there were few people inside. Most of them were at the little round tables which stood by the sidewalk. The men were wrapped in their overcoats and the table tops were damp from the evening fog, but to sit inside would mean not to be able to see anything. They sat with their hands in their pockets and stared at the street, at the leaves dripping on the potted tree, at each other.

"Tell me something," said Quinn, "you use any local people in your organization?"

"Christ, no," said Motta, and then he crossed himself.

They walked to the inside of the cafe where two waiters started to scurry as soon as Motta showed in the door. They pushed tables, they jabbered, and they bowed like two pigeons doing a mating dance.

Motta was affable about all of this; he nodded his head, he nodded his stick, and when he took off his hat and one waiter lunged for it Motta smiled at the man and said something in Sicilian.

They took a table which had been pushed to the fireplace, where Motta could warm his back and look at the rest of the room which was almost empty. The usual bare bulb hung from the ceiling, a velour curtain with grease on it covered the kitchen entrance, and the tables were the same as those outdoors—warped wood tops and rusty legs. On Motta's table was a white tablecloth.

The waiter brought wine without being asked. He poured from the same bottle for Quinn and Cipolla, and all this, Quinn felt, was the usual routine, a nice evening, a nice fire, and a cold fog outside. Maybe, thought Quinn, I shouldn't have anything to drink.

Chapter 20

Motta held the wine in his mouth and then he swallowed it. While doing this he dipped the end of his cigar into the wineglass, just the tip of it ever so gently, and when he swallowed the wine he immediately put the cigar into his mouth. And now, Quinn thought to himself, something else about new taste sensation.

"So tell me, Quinn," and Motta took the cigar out again. "Our set-up on the other side, what's it look like to you?"

"Lousy."

"It's making a lot of money for us, Quinn."

"If I can shake it up..."

"Did you?" said Motta.

"Well," said Quinn, "just a little tilt. Enough for you to sit here with me and talk about it."

"That's true," said Motta. "That's true."

"I'm not here to shake anything up for you," Quinn said very slowly. My own Santa Claus voice, he thought. Listen to the kindly rumble. "But I am here, Motta, to tell you that the other end of your operation can slide right out from under you, make less money, you know, instead of more."

"You think it can?"

"Make more?"

"Slide out from under me."

"Motta, look. I was over there for a few days and saw enough and did enough to start up a take-over, if that's what you're asking."

Motta sighed, stretched, and stroked his vest as if he were stroking a baby. Then he patted it some.

"What I'm asking, Quinn, do you think we can do a job together?"

"I don't know," said Quinn. "I can't answer that because I don't know enough about your operation."

"*Right* answer!" said Motta. "Very good, boy. Very good."

Cipolla spat on the floor next to his chair and stepped on it. Quinn lit a cigarette.

"Now I," said Motta, "got naturally an idea of the set-up, me having made the set-up, but before we go into that, and before you make suggestions—you got suggestions about the other side, don't you?"

"Of course."

"Before any of that, Quinn, let me ask you a question."

"Go right ahead," said Quinn, feeling hopped up from all the delay.

"This is about how well you covered your tracks. You got dumped by an independent tramper, didn't you?"

"That's what I'm told."

"That's what I was told. You know the name of that captain?"

"No. I was..."

"Name of the tub?"

"Why do you ask? I don't know the name, but why do you ask?"

"Simple reason. By rights, that captain has to report what happened, back home."

Quinn sighed and then he said yes, he had thought about that too. He didn't think the matter important. He wanted to start talking business. He wanted that more than anything in the world so as to be done with waiting, and doubting.

"And what did you do about it?"

"Not much. Just some questions. Upshot was, I didn't think it very likely that the captain would report back the whole irregularity, just for his own sake."

"Makes sense," said Motta. "That makes sense." He nodded his head and sipped a little wine. This time he did not keep it in his mouth but started to talk again right away. "Reason I bring this up, Quinn—what if you start operating out of Okar and then your friends from way back move in on you, not the operation, I mean, but on you?"

"Should that happen," said Quinn, "I expect to be set up by then in such a way—there are ways—that no outsider can do very much to rock my boat. Speaking of the set-up on the African side, what I'd like to discuss..."

"Later," said Motta.

Then he waved at the waiter and ordered a meal. Quinn had no idea what was being ordered and did not care. He sat smoking and looking around while Motta went through a long ritual, as if this dump, Quinn thought, was Maxim's or Antoine's, unless Antoine's is a hairdresser's and I got the names mixed up.

When Motta was done ordering he threw his cigar into the fireplace behind him and folded his hands on his belly. He smiled at Quinn and stroked the belly twice.

"I know you got ways," he said, as if nothing had interrupted the conversation, "but on the other hand, Quinn, couldn't any of this interfere with our operation on this side?"

Quinn thought for a moment and then he explained that he did not think so. He thought, first of all, that no one from the States would come looking for him, second, that he could take care of any eventualities, and third, that none of this would interfere with the business, Motta's business, Quinn's business, any business. Quinn sighed when he was through, feeling like a schoolboy who had gone through a recitation. And when a schoolboy recites, the teacher always knows everything ahead of time, so this whole talk was sham and useless. Quinn lit another cigarette and felt he smoked too much.

Motta, he was sure, had something entirely different on his mind. I'll just have to wait, even if I bust.

"I was thinking this," said Motta, and poured more wine. "I was thinking this because I know the whole operation, of course, and maybe once you do, you'd see it the same way I do, but I'll explain the details some other time. Antipasto," he said, and watched the waiter come with the big plate.

Quinn did not wait for the waiter to get done.

"I didn't understand a word you said," he told Motta. "Maybe because I don't know the whole operation?"

Motta laughed and put a pickled cauliflower in his mouth. He kept it there and sucked.

"Ever taste it the way it tastes when you suck?" he mumbled.

No, said Quinn, he had never tasted it the way it tastes when you suck, and what exactly was Motta talking about before. Quinn rubbed his nose because it had started to itch nervously.

Motta swallowed—Quinn had not seen him chew—and talked again. "I was thinking this," he said to the ceiling. Then he looked at Quinn. "I think I can use you on this side better than on the other. Maybe Cipolla told you, but I can drop that Remal character any time, and ship out of other ports."

"Work with you here?" said Quinn. "It's a proposition. Tell me more."

Quinn reached over to the antipasto plate and picked something up which looked green and wrinkled. He chewed it and did not like the sourness. He himself felt prickly.

"And I tell you," said Motta. "If I were you, Quinn, you know I'd just keep worrying and worrying about that captain floating around some place, and who knows what he'll do about this queer business with the undeclared box."

Motta talked more, always between mouthfuls, and by the time the pasta and meat sauce came, Quinn was worried. Santa Claus has a strange effect, he thought. Like a snake charmer.

During the veal the talk shifted to Remal, and who knows what a foreigner like that is up to, and what would the reception be, if Quinn were to go back. Ever think of that yet?

And maybe, thought Quinn, no longer tasting his food, maybe there's an entirely different reason behind all of Motta's pink-cheeked advice. Maybe all of this has to do with his wish to keep Quinn nearby, to keep Quinn under close check. He doesn't act like Ryder, and he doesn't act like Remal, but who knows Motta, except that he likes moist cigars?

The greens were served separately from everything else and Quinn now had to eat a plate full of greens. They were not very hot, they were warmish, and very slippery with oil.

"I'll tell you what I'll do," said Motta. He burped behind his napkin and explained that this green stuff always made him burp, but how healthy the green stuff really was.

"I'll give Whitfield a call," said Motta, "with the shortwave, and find out from him where that tramper has his ports of call."

"I know that already. Tel Aviv, Alexandria, and then down to Madagascar. From there, home. I don't know if he goes around the Cape or how, but I remember those ports."

"Well," said Motta, "I think Whitfield will remember better. It's business." He sucked his teeth and spat something out, all done discreetly behind the napkin. "That is, if you want me to, Quinn."

"I don't know what good it would do."

"If that captain is still in the Mediterranean basin, I can maybe get in touch with him. I got friends here and there, and with a bottle of something or other, maybe we can get it out of him if he's reported about you in that box, if he intends to do so, and we could even explain to him he should better not report anything, just like you were figuring."

Quinn nudged his plate away and wondered why Motta was so interested in all this.

"The reason I'm worrying, besides from being a worrier," Motta said, "is because I'd like to be sure the guy I work with is gonna be as safe as me, seeing he and I, what I mean is, you and I, will be sort of hitched up with each other. Which is true if you work on the African end or here. Right?"

Yes, answered Quinn, he could see that point of view, and he agreed with Motta so he would drop the matter. It was not business.

"Cipolla," said Motta, "you've eaten enough."

"Huh?"

"You get on this right away, Cipolla, and see if you can raise Whitfield this time of evening and we get this thing rolling. Okay, Quinn?"

It was now okay with Quinn. Cipolla seemed to be used to this kind of treatment, as who wouldn't be, with Motta pink-cheeked and smiling—a retired hood who likes to be friends.

Cipolla left. Motta ate the next thing, which seemed to be something from the sea, and Quinn sat in the dim room, angry at having to wait through a revolting meal.

"How long will all this take?" Quinn asked.

"If he's still in the Mediterranean, Quinn, maybe just a few days, you know?" Motta looked up and smiled, to give reassurance. "My guess is we can still catch him. Those tramps are slow. And besides," he said, with the next piece of gray-looking stuff on his fork, "the next run out of here isn't for five days anyway, so you'll be stuck here till then whether you decide to take Okar on or whether you decide to team up on this side." Motta nodded and said, "I still wanna talk business with you, you know. A few days, you and me, and we might do each other some good."

Then he ate.

The next morning Quinn was surprised to find that the sun was shining, as if sunshine did not belong here and it was a mistake. There was finally business talk with Motta, and that went very well. When Motta talked business he talked only business, he did not insist, the way Cipolla did, that he, the speaker, was the big thing in the talk. The smuggling set-up, Quinn found out, was extremely well organized, and the reason Motta had allowed Remal his own slipshod methods was because there was no point, at the Africa end, to be any more careful. However, should Quinn take over there, they could make much more money. Quinn worked on plans as if studying for an examination.

The captain had not been located.

On the second day Quinn slept until late in the morning. There was no point in getting up early, but there was a point in staying asleep. The subject of the captain and what his reporting might do to Quinn had become a bothersome worry.

On that day the sun turned watery by noon and Quinn sat in the cafe and missed Bea. This surprised him, and by late afternoon Quinn was drunk.

At ten that evening, at the end of Motta's meal, Cipolla came into the restaurant and reported that the captain was tied up in Alexandria.

On the third day Quinn woke up very early because the captain was now an insistent preoccupation.

Motta was reassuring. They discussed where Quinn should work. Quinn wanted Okar. Motta thought Sicily better. He said he liked Quinn and his hustling ways.

That evening, in bed, Quinn thought of the box for the first time with any feeling. He lay sleepless for a very long time, with the window open and the light turned on.

I had not thought about the box, it came to him, because for a while that matter was really finished. I am thinking of the box now because for the first time it's clear now, clear and true, the way Bea explained it, that I'm not out of it.

But that no longer matters. In this business, I know my way. I'm not bucking anyone and I know my way. He said this like counting sheep and fell asleep. He fell asleep the way a body falls off a cliff.

On the fourth day Quinn saw in the mirror how his collar was loose around his neck. The sleeplessness, he said to his face. The goddamn sleeplessness of lying in bed with thoughts and without any feelings. This eats me up.

At noon that day Cipolla had a talk with Motta in the cafe, and when Quinn walked in Motta waved to indicate Quinn should wait just a moment. Then Cipolla left and Motta waved again, Quinn should come over.

"Good news," he said. "I got a friend talking to the captain in Alexandria, you know, friend talk with a bottle, and the captain says he hasn't reported the stowaway thing and he's got no intention of reporting it, that it's too much trouble." Motta grinned and folded his little hands on his belly. "What do you think of that?"

Quinn felt weak. "Am I relieved!"

Motta laughed and slapped Quinn on the back, causing a pain like a cramp on one side.

"You're free!" said Motta. "Just think of it!" Motta's laugh went stab, stab, stab inside Quinn's ear.

Then Motta bought Quinn a cognac and left.

Quinn did not get drunk that afternoon but had only one more cognac which he charged to Motta. He charged it to Motta because he had no more money. And because he, Quinn, felt that Motta would not mind.

He is a Santa Claus after all and if I drink more I shall cry—

At four in the afternoon the sun came out, surprising Quinn. He sat where he had been sitting because Motta had sent word he was busy.

The threat of the captain reporting the box, that was gone. But Quinn felt on edge, as ever.

I must decide about here or Okar. Makes no difference to Motta. Fine. Does it make any difference to me? Now that Remal is out anyway, the way Motta described it—

On the fifth day Quinn woke up, having decided. He would run the Okar end of the business. It was underdeveloped, and there was more sun.

By four in the afternoon, Quinn had still not been able to discuss things with Motta. Santa Claus was out of town.

Nerves, thought Quinn. I'm beginning to imagine a plot. He had decided on Okar, but—it struck him—he felt as jumpy as before.

Half an hour before the boat was to leave, Quinn stood on the pier. The fog was there as expected. Nobody else was.

Then a car rushed down. Motta, with hat and cane, leaped out and hurried onto the pier.

"Quinn boy, I'm sorry. This other thing couldn't wait. Now look, we went through all the details, all about this end and the other end, and if you wanna stay here..."

"I want the Okar end. You don't need me here."

"Now boy, I wouldn't say that."

"We talked about how I can build it up."

"Right. And about your friend the mayor?"

"I'll not only take my chances, but I'll take your advice."

"What was that, boy?"

"I like people, you said. I'm going to tell Remal I like him, or else. He's going to like me or I move the operation to the town of Tagen."

"The one we talked about, yes."

"Okay?"

"Quinn, I like how you work. Best to you over there." Cipolla came running up but Motta waved him off.

"I'm talking," he said. And then, "Quinn, lemme ask you something personal. You mind?"

"No, I don't mind." Quinn felt nervous about getting away.

"Lemme ask you, may I, Quinn?"

"Yes, sure, sure, go ahead."

"Have you got a woman over there? I haven't seen you looking at any women over here and the way you been acting like a young 'un and rubbing your nose and not talking much, I mean not very much after all the business detail talk we been through..."

"No," said Quinn. "No, it's not that."

And I'm a liar, he thought, for leaving out Bea, this one woman over there who knew what I went for. The one who knows how it feels to build a box and that the worst things that happen are the things you do to yourself. And if you have to—she knows this—and if you have to go and take it like a sentence, then I have respect for you, that's what she might have said. Respect for you because you know how you're under a sentence, your own, which is the worst. And I respect you for knowing what you do, and I won't interfere because, she might have said, I don't know right or wrong any better than you do. Bea never said all of this but she did all of this. And I'll be here, she might have said, if you come out of it.

"Time to go," said Cipolla.

Motta held out his hand and smiled. "I like to see a man with a serious interest, and that's you, Quinn. Hate to lose you. Goodbye," and Motta walked off to his car.

Now that was a queer thing to say, thought Quinn, but then there had also been the smile and the shrug and the nice pat on the arm, touch of tolerance, good old Santa papa, and to hell with you, too.

Why so irritable, having decided everything?

"Let's go," he said to Cipolla, and the two men went to the end of the pier and the boat.

Chapter 21

On this trip he did not sleep.

There was part of the fake cargo on deck: several rows of large drums with cheap wine inside, destination a legitimate port which was one day's run from Okar. The Okar stop, on the books, would be for engine repairs.

At first the drums were wet because of the fog off the Sicilian coast, then they were dry because of the fast blow during the night, then they were moist again, making the black metal look a great deal like velvet. Just south of Malta they met the sirocco. Dry again, all day under the sun, and then toward evening Quinn did not watch any more. He knew how many drums there were, having paced back and forth where the rows were strapped down, back and forth, back and forth, like counting his canisters in the dark, and for the same reason, to know all there was to know, just as long as it was simple.

But by the next night he had quit the pacing. He felt cold and clear and he thought, anyway, it's good that it's clear. Shame though that it also has to be cold.

There was a perceptible change in the temperature as they got close to Okar, but Quinn paid little attention to that. Thinking about cold had nothing to do with the temperature.

The boat slowed before Quinn knew why but then he saw the lights of Okar, far away, just a few lights, which slid out from behind the land tongue which made the bay. There was also a beautiful moon. Quinn did not notice. Another half hour of deceptive distance and then Quinn could make out the pier.

The first one Quinn recognized was Bea. There were other people on the pier but Quinn saw Bea first.

Some people, he thought, look stupid waiting, or they look somehow silly, or like cattle standing around.

I've always thought she looks beautiful. She looks exciting now, and she must be excited the way she stands there in the light, she doesn't see me on the dark boat, but she looks for me.

The boat docked and the first one down the plank was Cipolla. He headed across the pier towards Whitfield who stood by the warehouse with the clipboard under his arm.

At first Quinn went fast, going down the plank, then slowly. He wanted to see everything, he wanted to see everything there was to see in the way she stood, walked toward him, waited.

At first they stood close by each other, not touching, then she put her hands on his arm the way she always did, and then he bent to put his face into her hair. He put his hands on her waist, feeling her, and then straightened up again.

"You're back," she said.

Maybe she had said it as a question? He said, "Yes."

But as soon as they had started to talk, the words had taken over for him and he found everything difficult. She is too beautiful and perhaps that's why, he thought. Why do I have to think this and not say it to her.

"Warm here," he said and felt the sweat creep out on him, from the sheer awkwardness and stupidity of his remark.

"Quinn," she said, "are you done?"

"Hell, yes, I'm done over there."

"What?"

"Done working for Santa Claus. You should see him." She did not understand him and waited. "I'm staying here, Bea."

"Here?"

"It's the best I can figure. It'll be all right with Remal. I think I can handle him now and I got a good relationship at the other end."

He thought she was going to cough, the way her breath went, or perhaps she could not get any breath for one reason or another. How can anyone catch a cold in this place, it went through his mind. But she was not coughing or gagging at all. It had been a deep painful breath, all dry, no tears, a dry shaking inside her, so that she sounded hoarse when she talked, and he almost had to guess what she was saying.

"My God, Quinn," she said, "I thought—maybe you'd be done and, and it's over, but you're only starting all over."

"Bea."

She stepped away and then she walked away.

"Just a minute now," he said and caught up with her. "Where are you going?"

"I'm going away, Quinn."

"Why?"

She did not answer. There were several people on the pier and the boat made low sounds against the pilings but Quinn knew only the pier in the spotty light, big stretch of pier, and black, quiet night. Then he saw the box. Bea was gone and there was the box.

The first thing he had seen had been Bea and now the first thing he saw was the box. It was as if having a choice of one first thing after another.

The box was upright and the crack had been repaired. There was a new lid, all white wood, set to one side and the box was still open.

Everything that happened next happened, in a manner of speaking, without any succession. Everything that happened next was all life and death. Something that is always immediate, that does away with all past and future. There is only now, and so there is no succession.

All the things that came next happened with Quinn and there was a death in it every time.

To lay all of it out, there was a dead man who floated by the pier in the water. There was a dead man lying face up on the rocks where the desert started. And then there was a dead man who lay curled up in a box which was shipped to New York.

The way fever makes the vision shimmer and draws all the color and sharpness out of seeing, that was how Quinn saw the pier in a moment. Everything was holding still and there was no meaning anywhere, until Whitfield happened to drop his clipboard. This made Quinn jump. He did not jump visibly but on the inside in some way.

"You dropped your clipboard," said Quinn.

"Oh."

Quinn smelled the gin. He watched Whitfield pick up the clipboard. It was now all very quiet again and Quinn felt no haste. And now, he thought, now for the finish. And I care very much how it turns out.

"Whitfield," he said. "You know where anyone is?"

"If you mean just anyone, then the question..."

"Whit, don't just talk. Not this time."

Whitfield looked at Quinn and immediately took him very seriously. It felt a lot like respect.

"Only the box is here," said Whitfield.

They both looked at the box which stood by the edge of the light. White, new wood on top, the rest stained as before. The contrast was obscene.

"What do you know about it, Whitfield?"

Whitfield took a breath, feeling the air was too thick.

"Quinn," he said. "I know they fixed it, I saw them. That's all. Quinn, I even want to know less than I do know."

"Yes. You're always like that."

Whitfield wiped his face. "I never sweat. I think I'm afraid. What do you do when you're afraid, Quinn?"

Out of nowhere Quinn felt a very clear affection for the other man, so clear that he was sure it must show and therefore he need say nothing. Perhaps Whitfield caught this. He wanted to say something, but the habit of keeping things dullish and pleasant made him think of some platitude. He did not want to say it and kept still.

Then Quinn turned, walked to the box. He moves like a cat, thought Whitfield. When Quinn reached for the crowbar which leaned by the box Whitfield held his breath with sudden excitement.

Quinn hauled out the iron bar very steadily for a long, wrecking smash into the side of the box, but then he never hit. He suddenly spun around and stared at Whitfield.

"Quinn, what..."

"Out of the way," said Quinn. "To the wall."

Quinn wasn't looking at Whitfield at all and when Whitfield had moved, as if hypnotized, he saw where Quinn had been looking.

Cipolla was coming out of the warehouse. He walked slowly, as if wading in water, and the water was very cold.

"Spread out," he said, and then Quinn saw the two sailors whom Cipolla had brought along.

Quinn was not winded but he now started to breathe in an inhuman way. He crouched forward a little and breathed with a sound which was deep and loud. He reached back with one hand and touched the box behind him. He barely touched and then pulled his hand away.

"It's no good," he said, "unless I'm alive. You know that, don't you, Cipolla?"

"That's why," said Cipolla. "That's why you're still standing there."

"You going to take me alive, Cipolla?"

The small man didn't answer. He showed his teeth for courage and he swung his arms like an ape, a big ape twice his own size. For the moment he did nothing else. What crazy eyes, thought Cipolla. And he moves like a cat and maybe got nine lives—

"Ah," said Quinn and smiled very slowly. It was hard to tell by the high bulb light over the pier what the smile meant, but Whitfield, by the wall, thought the smile was sad. "Ah," Quinn said again. "And Santa Claus knew Ryder all the time, didn't he?"

"I told you that was Mafia country," said Cipolla. The remark made him feel strong and no longer alone. "All right!" he said to his helpers.

Whitfield, by the wall, closed his eyes. He was therefore almost startled out of his skin when the box gave a sudden drum bellow of a sound because Quinn had swung the crowbar into the wood.

"Now!" Quinn yelled. "And remember, Cipolla, whatever is going to happen now isn't going to happen to my corpse! Try me!" and he hit the box again, sharp and heavy, breaking wood. He spun back around to Cipolla and held the bar in both hands. He stood like that and looked like a killer.

The two sailors, with the true hireling's caution, hung back and looked everywhere except at Quinn.

"Rush him!" yelled Cipolla.

Quinn laughed. He stood with his back to the box and laughed.

"Rush him!" Cipolla again.

"Shut up," said Quinn, and then, talking quietly, "Shut up and turn around." His smile was back. "You've got friends there."

To Cipolla, of course, this was the oldest trick in the world. Except that Whitfield looked past Cipolla and gasped.

"Or maybe I'm wrong," Quinn said. "Maybe you've got enemies."

Cipolla couldn't wait any longer and had to turn then. He saw Remal standing there very quietly. Remal had one Arab along and held a gun. He was holding it down by his side, as if it were not important.

"Cipolla," he said, "you will please step aside."

"What?"

"He's mine," said Remal and made a small flick with the gun in Quinn's direction. Aside from that he hardly looked at him.

Oh God, thought Whitfield, what do you do when you're afraid? Then he began to tremble. And then, because everything happened so fast and so violently, Whitfield started to scream. He stood by the wall like a child and screamed.

It seemed to Quinn that nothing mattered for the moment but Whitfield's screaming and his fright and that he, Quinn, must now give that man a hand. The thought struck Quinn as weird and out of place even while it happened, but it was also true that with Whitfield full of fright, Quinn felt none. After that, it went fast.

One sailor got knifed by Remal's Arab, Cipolla whipped out a gun, Quinn threw the crowbar and saw Remal stagger. And there was a shot and Quinn ran.

He had Whitfield by the arm and yelled, "Run, Whit, run!" and when they were in the warehouse there was another shot back on the pier. They ran across the cobblestone square when Whitfield started to cry.

"Run, Whit, I'll help you—I'll help you—" Quinn kept panting while Whitfield cried like a child, not like a drunkard, because no drink was strong enough for what Whitfield went through.

"I can't—I can't any more—"

"Run, Whit, the quarter, shots no good there, Whit, let me help—"

They ran through the quarter, one way or the other, and came out into the desert where the moon was like a white stone in the sky.

"Oh God," said Whitfield, and Quinn let him stop. "God, I'm too tired to be afraid any more." He could hardly breathe, but he made a small laugh. "And so sober," he said.

There were two shots. In the open like that it was simple murder, though with the light as it was it was hard to tell who was shot—

But as if to a magnet which never lets go he had to come back to the box a while later. He went slowly this time, creeping through shadows, though by the time he crossed the square he no longer cared if he were seen or not. Because it was almost over and he was almost there. I've got nine lives, he thought, and I'm going to use all of them—

In the warehouse he could hear the voices and walked no further than the nearest stack of bales.

"He's out there," said the voice which was panting hard.

"You shot him and left him? Did I tell you to shoot, you son of a bitch?"

"Listen, all you said..."

"Shut up and get the tools and get the thing fixed up!"

Voice high and tense like a mouse and then Cipolla's hard step on his extra-high heels, that too a high, tense sound coming closer.

No haste now, thought Quinn by his bale. He'll freeze all by himself.

Cipolla did. One chopped heel sound and he stood very still by the dark bale. Quinn did not hit him. He reached out and dug his hand into Cipolla, high on the neck. This was pure satisfaction. There was no talk.

Cipolla, though small, turned out to be very strong. He started to see life and death come and go, nine lives come and go, and he now had all the strength of all his hate for everything he had ever hated.

It seemed to Quinn that he cared less than the other man. The silence of their grip on each other was much like a drug to him. I see nine lives go, he thought, and don't care. I only care that I have none left over—

Then came a death, slow like a sigh.

When they found the body in the desert, very dry and the eyes staring up, there had been no doubt about this one because of the hair. Nobody in Okar had had hair like that; only Whitfield had blond hair, which was the only thing which had not changed on the corpse.

The one with the hole in the skull, the one who had been in the water for such a long time, there was some delay and some doubt about the identification, because so little was left. But of all the ones missing, only Remal used to wear the long shirt which was still floating around the thing.

And much later, in New York, where Ryder made a special trip for the occasion, there had been no doubt or delay when the box was opened. Ryder gave one look, stepped back quickly, and said, "I thought he was going to get back here alive."

"Accidents happen," said somebody.

"Stupid punk," said Ryder and got into his car. "They don't shrink that much, you idiot. That one's maybe half of Quinn's size."

Okar, except for the missing people, did not change very much. There was talk for a while, but no change. About where the woman might be, the one who had left suddenly after having known everyone, and where the man might be, the one who had come in a box.

THE END

Journey into Terror
BY PETER RABE

Anybody coming down one of the three streets had to end up at Truesdell Square. One street had crosstown traffic, the other one was lined with cheap, neat residences, and one looked old, with trees and clapboard houses. They joined on Truesdell Square. There was a bus stop, grocery stores, a five-and-dime, and in one building on the second floor there was a sign which read *Office Space For Rent.* The sign was up there all the time and meanwhile the space was used for storage. There were empty crates, long rows of pinball machines, and a safe—

The heater in the car didn't work. Two men sat in front and two were in the back. They sat very still, bent a little forward, so that they would not disturb the warm air inside their clothes. The car drove slowly because the street was full of slush.

"How much further?" said one of the men.

"We'll make it. They're moving the books at three," said the driver. "We got five minutes."

They didn't talk for a while. A clump of wet snow slid off a tree and smacked on the hood of the car. It made the men start and some of them cursed under their breath.

"It could make a mess, Tarpin," said one of them. "What you're trying."

The driver grunted. He made a gesture to look at his watch, but he knew the time, anyway.

"What do you say, Tarpin, maybe you just try talking to the head once more? This could make a mess—"

"I got to mess," said the driver. "I get squeezed out, all I got left is a mess, anyhow. So let him regret it." Tarpin said this without any emotion. He had black hair, very thick, and it started low on his forehead. When he was tense he would move his scalp and then it looked as if he had no forehead at all.

"Maybe you don't need the books. We could..."

"I want them."

"But the trouble..."

"No trouble," said Tarpin. He moved his scalp and then rubbed the back of his head. "No trouble at all," he said and squeezed his left arm against his side so he could feel the shoulder holster.

They would be at Truesdell Square at about four o'clock....

The girl could see the square at the end of the street and walked faster. The sidewalk looked black and neat with the snow scraped to one side. If I hurry, she thought to herself, I can shop and then meet him at the bus. She smiled. The street was empty, but when she smiled she rubbed her face into her collar as if it were best to hide how she felt.

The girl had very white skin and large eyes, a frail look about her, and her wrists, showing out of the heavy coat, were small and frail. The girl tucked her hands into the bend of her folded arms, walking that way to keep out the damp. The gesture made her feel enveloped, keeping her happiness close to herself.

"Well, well, well—" said the voice.

The girl gave a small start. She looked at the woman in the driveway and did not know what to say.

"You *are* way off somewhere, aren't you, Miss Jackson?" The woman laughed with a maternal note.

The girl smiled back. She didn't want to talk, she didn't even want to smile at anyone, but did not know what else to do. "You are shoveling the drive, Mrs. Pollin," she said.

"Why, yes," said Mrs. Pollin. She looked down at the shovel and held it suddenly to show that she rarely did this sort of thing. "The Mister will be late," she said. "Inventory time, you know."

"Ah yes," said the girl. She wished she could walk on, but felt too shy to end the conversation.

"And tomorrow it's going to be Mrs., eh, Miss Jackson?"

The girl felt suddenly abandoned, as if the question was so personal that it amounted to an attack. She did not want to talk about her husband— tomorrow's husband—and wished that he were here.

"Are you going to settle here?" the woman asked.

"Perhaps," said the girl. "I haven't—we haven't—"

"That would be lovely," said the woman. "Such a lovely neighborhood."

"Yes."

"And you such a nice, lovely girl, Miss Jackson. If your Mister is at all like you, why, you should have nothing but friends in our neighborhood."

The girl just smiled again, to cover up the same feeling as before—that the woman was attacking. Her husband—tomorrow's husband—needed no explaining. John wasn't something to discuss when in a hurry, with strangers—

"Whom does he work for?" said the woman.

"Kessler Equipment."

"Oh, that's a wonderful company," said Mrs. Pollin, but since Kessler Equipment was at least five times as large as the company for which her husband worked, she was quickly losing interest. "What's he do? Machinist? Electrician? My Mister is in the office, you know."

"He's an engineer. Electrical engineer."

"Really? That's almost a professional man, isn't it?"

The girl just nodded, offending Mrs. Rollin. They had nothing else to say to each other and the girl, Ann Jackson, got away saying a quick good-by.

If she hurried she could still shop and then meet John when he came in on the bus. It wasn't busy on the square this time of day.

She would reach Truesdell Square at about four o'clock....

The yard between Building Four and Building Five was "restricted to all unauthorized personnel," a phrase that had been introduced at Kessler Equipment with army contracts, but John Bunting didn't care. He wasn't sure what time it was but he was in a hurry, so crossed the yard because it was the shortest way out to the gate. "Oh, wedding day in the month of May..." he sang, and looked up at the wet January sky. It made him step into a puddle and since he had been going fast his pants got wet tip to the knees. "...wedding day don't go away," he started again. "Come here and stay so I can say..."

"Hey, Bud!"

John Bunting stopped long enough to look around and see the plant guard in front of Building Five.

"I'm authorized personnel," Bunting yelled back. "I'm getting married!" and started toward the gate again.

The guard didn't much care one way or the other and, not wanting to chase after the man, he went inside the building and put a chew of tobacco into his cheek. Besides, he knew John Bunting. He had recognized him by the unkempt hair and by the arms.

John Bunting's hair was brown with red in it and his arms, as the guard had seen from far away, seemed much too long. It was either that, or

Bunting always bought his clothes with sleeves too short.

He stepped into another puddle and this time started cursing. He kept going and wished he knew what time it was. He would have to start carrying a watch. Maybe Ann would give him one on their first wedding anniversary, one day and one year from now, in fact he would speak to her about it later and one day and one year from now she could surprise him with it. But for now, if the sun were out he might have a notion if it was late or early. "Oh glorious sun, where have you gunn..." he started to sing, but stopped when he got to the gatehouse.

"Checking out, Clint. Lemme have the book," and he smacked his hand on top of the counter.

"This hour?" said the guard, but he knew why Bunting was getting off early. It was just after three.

"Lemme sign out, man. I'm getting married."

"You are?" said the guard, because it was a joke by now. Bunting had told everyone for months.

The guard brought up the book but didn't hand it over yet. "Maybe you ought to wait and think this over, John. Maybe I'm doing you a favor not letting you rush into this."

"Jeesischrist, Clint, hurry up! Don't you know what it's like? You're married."

"Thirty-five years."

"Oh. Well, you're the wrong man for this type argument."

"Think of it," said the guard. "All them women you're going to miss. Ever think of that, boy?"

Bunting looked at his hands on the counter. Then he said, "I'm no lady's man."

The guard laughed, because that was the joke behind his comment. Bunting was fairly shy with women. "Hell," he kept laughing. "You're embarrassed!"

"Sure," said Bunting.

"What are you ashamed of, huh, John?" and the guard kept laughing.

"I'm not ashamed," said Bunting. "I'm just embarrassed." He reached across the counter, holding his hand out for the book. "Lemme sign out."

The guard stopped laughing and gave Bunting the sign-out register. When Bunting was done the guard smiled at him and said, "No harm meant, John. And good luck."

"Thank you," said Bunting. "Nice of you," and went out.

It started to rain, a fine spray sharp with cold. John Bunting ducked his head down and waited for the bus. It would take him close to an hour to get across town. He huddled close into himself to shut out the feel of the coldness and the gray scene, and once he was on the bus he stayed that way, disturbed now because he couldn't find the warmth inside him. Nothing but a tension growing. The bus went stop and go and stop and go, the same as Bunting's feelings: a strong happiness, a sense of warmth about Ann, and then impatient anger about not being with her. Before this tension went, one or the other of the opposites would have to disappear.

When Bunting saw Truesdell Square ahead his jumpiness got worse. He bit his lip, he smiled, he even tried to count the people in the distance. There was a traffic jam or something, a backfire. The picture wasn't clear, because the light was fading fast this time of day.

When I see Ann, he thought, the tension will all go, like always.

The bus stopped to let him off and then went on. The taillights went away. It was quiet. Bunting then discovered that the square was empty, no people on the street, no moving cars, except way in the distance. A feeling like a lull.

Bunting coughed, wondered if it was four. What confused him was the square being so empty. He frowned, hated to think that he was late, and was about to walk across the sidewalk.

He had almost missed her. He stumbled across an orange which had rolled out of a paper bag and stumbling he saw the bag, split open, and then Ann.

She lay still and very small in a tight angle of two buildings where the snow had not yet melted.

He suddenly saw all the people coming out of doors and entrances but that meant nothing to him. He mostly saw Ann's face and the round hole in her white forehead.

Chapter 2

The lieutenant switched the light on and said Bunting should sit down at the table. He had to say it twice before Bunting crossed the bare room and sat.

"I know you want to get away, Mr. Bunting, and I can understand. I'll take maybe five minutes and that's all... Mr. Bunting?"

"Yes," said Bunting. The lamp over the table gave a yellowish light and it seemed to Bunting that the whole room was colored in mustard. Except for himself. He himself felt so much apart that he didn't think there was any color in him at all. "What's that?" he said. "What you say?"

"... about the girl. Just a few questions, formality, and that's all."

Bunting was afraid that he might faint The mustard-yellow was fuzzy and he didn't hear very well.

"The girl," he said.

"You know what I'm talking about," said the lieutenant. "Pull yourself together, will you?"

The lieutenant did not mean to be curt but he was in a hurry. He excused himself without Bunting hearing it and went to the door. He called down the hall for somebody to come and take notes. Then he stayed in the open door smoking a cigarette.

Bunting closed his eyes and sat very still. A tear slid down his face, shocking him, but he did not wipe it away. "All right, Mister Bunting. You ready?"

"Sure," he said. He watched the two men sit down, the lieutenant and the uniformed one with the notebook. "Miss Ann Jackson was your fiancée?"

"Yes," said Bunting.

"When she got shot, you were..."

"Why—" said Bunting. "Why?" He did not recognize his voice.

"Mister Bunting, we went through all that. An accident. She got in the way of a gunfight. It was an accident and she had nothing to do with it."

That wasn't what Bunting had meant. He couldn't say exactly what he meant. This felt suddenly like a too easy discussion, like discussing a blueprint with circuit systems, all very clear and uninvolved. He looked at his hand on the table and could see the skin and muscles with surprising clarity. The sight offended him, felt cold, like hand wax—

"The young woman's address was Four-Two-One Maglin Avenue, this city?"

"Yes."

"Where do her parents live?"

"Parents? Out of town, I think."

"You don't know?"

"Small town. I've never been there."

"Her place of work, you know that? You understand, we're trying to get a line on her nearest relative."

"She works—" Bunting coughed, then changed it into a laugh, on rather what sounded almost like laughter. "At Kessler. Next floor down, she used to work."

"What's that?"

The lieutenant's voice reached way through, too sharp, too much. Bunting had given a start.

"Look, I'm sorry," said the lieutenant. "Just answer me this one thing. Her place of work. So we can check—"

Bunting answered intelligibly, but was not thinking about it. He was thinking of one floor down from his office, through the drafting room into the blueprint library where Ann had been, how they had never talked the first few times he had come there and how they had suddenly loved each other without any transition, or without any preambles that he could remember, as if nothing else could be imagined. They wanted to marry, and tomorrow they would finally marry—

"Bunting. You all right?"

All night? What the hell. The weirdest thing was the feel in his throat, a small tensing inside his throat which would go away if he were to laugh. He might laugh any minute.

"Would you come along now, Mister Bunting? The morgue is next door— You've been very patient—"

"I'm no relative of hers," said Bunting. It was the most patient thing he had said, ever. It was the dullest and the most far removed thing ever in all his life.

"Just an official expedient. Till the dead girl's relative can be located. After that you can go."

"I can go? That's all?" Bunting started to roar with laughter.

It took care of that small tightness inside his throat, Bunting roared and roared though he soon knew that this was not laughter, with tears full in his eyes and wetting his face and the big spasms shaking his body. "That's all—" he kept shouting. "That's all—"

"Bunting! Cut it out!"

Like before, it drew him up short. He sat up, seeing everything clearly, and rubbed one hand over his face. He kept doing that because suddenly—though he saw everything clearly—he did not know what to do. He felt interrupted.

"Come on," said the lieutenant, "let's go." He was gruff and short. He was not only in a hurry but also embarrassed.

It was much colder outside now and old snow crackled under their feet. They went into the morgue building, past the office and down a long hall, and when they went through the double doors in the back, it was cool again. The large room was oil-painted white and the cool air felt smooth after the outside.

"All right," said the lieutenant. "All right, this way." The covered corpse was on a table with thin, high legs. "Just take a look, identify her, and that's all." He stood at the table, waiting and tapping one foot. "All right. Here."

But Bunting wasn't ready. The covered shape meant nothing to him and he did not want it to mean anything.

"All right, Bunting. Take a look." The lieutenant flipped back the sheet.

A short silence and then Bunting said, too quietly, "You lousy sonofabitch—"

"What?" And then the lieutenant looked up and saw Bunting's face.

Bunting thought he could smell the oil paint on the bare walls and the faint sting of Lysol. But also a sweetness in the air, an odor which stopped once you walked out into the hall.

"Bunting, what in hell is the matter with you?" The lieutenant saw that Bunting was starting to tremble. It wasn't a trembling from fear or weakness, but the small shiver of self-control before breaking loose.

"You lousy sonofabitch," Bunting said again, "say something else. Say something—" and Bunting was waiting.

The lieutenant dropped the sheet back over the face and walked out of the room without saying a word. He didn't look back and he didn't rush, just walked out leaving Bunting alone.

In a short while Bunting left, too. He looked normal enough, walking down the street, but he again had the small, airless feeling of having been interrupted.

Chapter 3

John Bunting slept in his room one more night and then he moved out. He moved to a place he had never been before, a street with narrow hotels, long pool halls, and grocery stores next to small bars. He moved into a room which looked dead and cheap during the day and which, at night, gained a weird life from the flashing neon sign under his window.

He started to drink the first day, in the forenoon, and when he found he could not sleep when night came, he kept drinking then, too. In a short while it became a routine of staying in bed all day and staring up at the ceiling. There was nothing to see. He felt the deep empty feeling of loss. It lay under his ribs like a black hole. He stayed on his bed and suffered it, knowing nothing else that could fill his loss.

When he could not see the ceiling any more he was in danger of falling asleep, in danger of dreaming. He could not see the ceiling any more and saw the girl Ann instead. He saw the park where they had gone in the beginning, the leaves gray with city dust and the Sunday sun not very cheerful. In the beginning they had been very cautious with their feelings, very careful not to let each other know too much.

"You go to all these picnics?" she said.

"What?"

"These company picnics," she said, and when he looked up at her she laughed quickly so that he should not misunderstand. "I mean, they're a lot of fun. Everybody is having such fun—" .

Bunting looked around at everybody having fun with softball, with radios, and with burnt hot dogs. Then he remembered he had not answered.

"Uh—no, I haven't been. I've often thought about it, though."

"Oh, yes ?"

It was a difficult conversation for her. She wondered how everybody was managing to have so much fun.

"I— To tell the truth," said Bunting, "I feel a little awkward here."

This made Ann feel so terrible, suddenly, she first laughed again. But it wasn't enough and she had to get up and take a few steps.

"Oh," she said, "perhaps you would like to go over there—" she waved at the others—"over there to the games? You know, the only reason I'm not playing ball over there, I hurt my ankle a week ago. It's been a whole

week now and I can still feel something hurting in the joint, in the ankle—
" And then she stopped talking because Bunting had gotten up too and taken her arm. He took it and made her sit down again.

"I didn't mean it that way, Ann. I see these people in the plant all week long."

She laughed and he wished she wouldn't, but she had to laugh brightly, and then said, "You know everybody? I wish I knew everybody. I hardly know..."

"I don't know everybody. I just want to know you." This time he was the one who covered with a laugh, but Ann had heard him.

She said, "Would you like to walk over there? My ankle isn't so bad." And then they walked even further away from the picnic and didn't say much more to each other. They walked along the concrete, which was bordered with pathetic bushes, and every so often a strategically placed tree.

Bunting said, "You know, Ann, I hate city parks."

She stopped when he said that and Bunting was worried sick he had offended her. She looked at him and said, "I do too. I really hate them, John." She was very serious....

When he could not see the ceiling any more he sat up and stayed like that for a while. It was getting too dark now. The reflected light blinked on and off at the edge of one wall and this was his picture of wakefulness. The wakeful blink of the light beat at him, one strike after another.

Bunting left the house and went to the first bar he reached.

They knew him, but Bunting, at this point, didn't see anybody. He went to a booth in the back and sat down.

"Your sucker's here, Mooch," said the bartender.

Mooch was small and frail and had no teeth at all. His face flapped when he talked. "You're so big and clean you can talk to me like that?" he said to the bartender.

They looked at each other with dislike and the bartender poured two drinks. He dumped a double into each glass and put ice over that. "Go hustle," he said.

"You're so damn rich and beautiful you can do without me hustling for you?" said Mooch, but before the bartender could turn and answer, Mooch had turned toward the booth.

He put one glass in front of Bunting and held the other one up. "Health and cheers, Johnny!"

Bunting put his hand around his glass and didn't look up. He knew who it was by the voice. The man said health and cheers the same way he would have said, "Mud in your eye."

Mooch sat down in the booth and kept grinning. "You all right today, Johnny?"

"Sure."

"Fine," said Mooch. "That's fine."

He watched Bunting take a long pull on his glass and quickly did the same so he would be ready for the next round when Bunting was finished. But Mooch didn't calculate right and he was drinkless while Bunting still had some left in his glass.

"Whaddaya say, Johnny, feeling okay this eve?" Mooch badly wanted a conversation. It was a fact which meant a great deal to him, which proved that he was not one of those simple drunks who could sit for hours and do nothing but drink. It proved to Mooch that he was no drunk at all but a person with a mind, with ideas, a man who had things to say.

Bunting was swirling the rest of his liquor around the inside of his glass and wouldn't drink it. He was looking at Mooch and wouldn't talk.

"I can tell, Johnny, I can tell," said Mooch and forced a laugh. "I can tell something's eating you, huh?"

"Like what?" said Bunting.

Mooch kept grinning and laughing. It was now automatic. "A guy what's hoarding his drink is broody, Johnboy, which means bad disposition, huh, John?" By this time of evening Mooch needed regular sips, no interruptions, or else his scalp started to prickle and anything might irritate him. He could not afford this, not at this time, with only one round hustled so far. "Maybe you see something wrong? You thinking something is wrong, boy?" and Mooch giggled.

"No," said Bunting. He did not move his eyes though, which made Mooch even more edgy. And he couldn't afford this. There never had been anything like this John. There never had been such a touch like Bunting, one night after another, buying the drinks and never insulting Mooch or making comments on the way he looked or how he lived, just sitting there—

"Johnny," he said, "know something? You're good people."

Bunting had never heard the expression before and he thought that it was revolting. He said, "Get another drink, will you?"

Then there were two drinks, Mooch at ease now, feeling free to make conversation, because Bunting never interrupted, didn't care when Mooch lost his thread because of trips back to the bar, and Mooch had a lot to say.

"...so me, trusting the bastard, I say to him, okay, I'll take the mount, I'll ride him in to win or, anyway, *show.* You unnerstand, John, this—coming from me!—meant something. Not for nothing was I been—" He lost his sentence structure and took another drink. He looked sober as ever. The only thing showing his state was the emphasis he gave some words. When Mooch drank he felt that there was never enough emphasis on anything.

"So after twenty five years of me jockeying mounts all around the country he does *this,* to me! He *dopes* the nag, to *lose!*"

"What do you know?" said Bunting into his glass.

He wasn't watching Mooch or he would have been surprised. The man's toothless face turned lax, with eyes lidded, the whole face seemingly helpless in an attack of evil. "Twenty years now and *me,* I don't forget. I'm seeing to it, before he dies, I'm seeing to it he dies to regret crossing me up."

"Vindictive bastard, aren't you?" said Bunting. He finished his glass which meant Mooch had no time to answer. Mooch finished his and then got two more.

"Like when I switched from sports to entertainment," he started to say as soon as he sat. "You didn't know I used to be an entertainer? *Yes sir!* This kid and me we had this act, *bigtop* act I tell you. She'd be dancing with this snake and me making with patter all about the *danger* of this act and also playing drums. *Bongo* drums, with her dancing. Stop hooring around after working hours I tell her. You got your *snake* for work and *me* for play and no extrakirrikeler shag *needed.* Or I feel like a *pimp,* I say to her face. You won't, she says, 'cause I ain't giving *you* no *money.* I'm mad, John, I'm *mad. That* night, before the act, I heist every *stitch* of clothes she's got except that snake. She wants to hoor? Let her go hoor in *that,* I says.... So the act is over. So I see her running to the wagon where we *bunk,* she running over there with nothing *but* that snake; so *fine, I* say, I'll let her stew there for a while, she with no clothes and all and meanwhile go and have a *beer.* Just *beer,* in those days, seeing I was in entertainment.... *Yes sir.* At maybe one or two o'clock I go back *to* her. *Teach* her something. Inside the wagon *she's* got the lights off and the bed all bunched up with the blankets so I start to smile and then *take* off my clothes. Devil bedamn that girl, you know what she *done?* I get in bed naked and *all* that's there is this *bechristed* snake! I never seen that girl again. And what she run off with I don't know, she being naked—"

The barroom was crowded now and much too warm. The din of voices rose and fell.

"You hear me, Johnboy?"

Bunting looked up. He had heard everything Mooch had said, but he had not been interested. He looked up now, because the small man's voice had become low.

"That was funny, maybe? You got an idea I'm telling it funny?" And Mooch's face changed again. "It wouldn't be funny, boy, if she walked in here. Right now, for instance. You wouldn't see anything funny, I tell you." And Mooch emptied his glass, not caring that it put him ahead of Bunting.

"Vindictive bastard," said Bunting.

Mooch leaned way forward and had he had the nerve he would have grabbed Bunting by the front of the shirt. "You give it the name you want, any high-sounding name you want to name it, but you listen to this: anybody rubs me wrong is on my list permanent. Nobody gets away with nothing as long as they live. They maybe think they do because I'm here and they's somewheres else, but I'm thinking about it and don't forget. I hate the sonofabitch who thinks he's getting away with something. That don't happen to me. Nobody gets away with nothing in my book, and I lose a nickel means somebody owes me a nickel. Get that? Somebody owes me!"

Bunting was drunk, but the sharp voice and the sharp venom in the man's voice reached him. The words nudged at him. "You got a tiny little itch somewhere, runt," he said. He had never before called a man runt. "Or maybe you're sore because you lost all your teeth and can't afford any new ones... Wanna drink?" he added.

Mooch sat hack. His small butt was tense under him and if Bunting had made a move, reached for Mooch, the small man would have been out of the booth in no time. Mooch sat that way and didn't seem to have heard the offer. He watched Bunting without making a move. Bunting, he thought, wasn't the same. The simple drunk had stayed with it too long, night after night, and was turning into a mean drunk. The prize sucker who paid for all the drinks and never said anything was getting himself off the floor and was starting to look for trouble. Put him down, before he turned so mean he got sober

"Keep talking," said Mooch. He carefully stayed where he was. "Because that's all *you're* good for." He waited to see if he were reaching Bunting. "I know your trouble, beau, you think taking it out on me is going to make it better. But it don't—"

"Huh ?"

"You don't care, do you, Johnboy? You don't remember crying into your beer and telling me how sick you was with your troubles—"

Bunting was listening carefully now, trying to keep the drunk waves out of his brain.

"You don't care, huh? You don't care somebody gets away with murder!"

"Runt—"

"You don't care somebody shoots your girl right out from under you, huh, Johnboy?"

Mooch was halfway out of the booth before he saw Bunting give any sign of having heard, and then Mooch couldn't breathe.

Very briefly Bunting was aware of the loose skin under his fingers and how small Mooch's neck felt in his hand, but this awareness went quickly. With an aimless rage he kept pounding the small man's head against the back of the booth, enjoying the feel of the strength in himself.

He let go of Mooch when he got hit himself. He didn't care enough about the small man. He hit faces and bellies and cut his knuckles on wood and for the first time he found something to fill the hole which had been left by his loss. With this great heat inside him, it didn't matter that he got the worst of the beating and was thrown out on the street. He got to his room, spitting blood, and never thought of the runt at all. He did not think that, in a way, he had taken the runt with him.

Chapter 4

When Bunting woke up he ached very badly and remembered little. He stayed on his bed. He lay there and waited for the day to go by, the way he had done ever since he had moved. He stared at the ceiling and waited. He even hunted for the cold, empty feeling inside, and it didn't come. He tried to force it, but it didn't come. He sat up gritting his teeth, and suddenly he kicked at the chest near the bed. The sound incensed him and he kicked again, breaking the wood. That reminded him. He remember the night before and how the toothless runt at his table had turned him from a sick drunk into a boiling maniac.

Bunting got up and washed his face at the sink, cursing when he saw his cut face and cursing all through the painful job of washing it clean. A sick drunk. He was getting sick from it. No. The other way. He was sick and then started drinking, sick from lying there on the bed, sick from doing nothing but wait—wait for what?—and sick of feeling empty. He went back to the wrinkled bed and the sight of it revolted him. He went to the window and the sun in the street beat at him like a fist and that too made him angry and when he turned back to the room with the peelings walls and the gray bed he couldn't see how he had stood it so long....

It had snowed during the night and turned colder, but the sun had a lot of heat. Bunting walked down the street and at first he walked by the bar, because he hadn't thought that it was this close to his house. He went back and saw that the place was empty. A bartender was tapping a keg and an old woman was mopping the floor. In the back booth where Bunting always sat some plaster was knocked off the wall.

"I'm looking for a guy, about so—" he held his hand out for height— "and he's got no teeth. You know..."

"He means Mooch," said the old woman behind him.

The bartender said, "What happened to you? Your face."

"I got sore," said Bunting. "I get sore and I break out like that."

"Oh."

"I thought he might be here, this Mooch." Bunting looked along the empty booths. "You know where he lives?"

"He don't get here till just before noon or along there," said the old woman.

"I'll wait," said Bunting.

"What are you drinking?" the bartender asked.

Bunting went out to the street and crossed to the diner. He bought ham and eggs and a cup of coffee, but before he was halfway through he had to go out to the back where he threw up what he had eaten. He went back in and had one glass of milk. When he lit his cigarette he saw Mooch coming down the street and into the bar. Bunting finished his cigarette, then went across.

The bartender was there, dusting the bottles, and the old woman was having a beer. "In the can," she said, pointing.

Bunting went to the toilet in back. It smelled moist because the woman had mopped it, and a powerful hyacinth odor was in the air. The little man's stiff-shouldered jacket hung on a hook, and with the hat over it, it looked like a separate person. Mooch himself was by the sink. He was bare to the waist and when he saw Bunting he jerked around and crossed his thin arms over the chest. The gesture made no sense, but Mooch kept standing that way.

"I want to ask you something," Bunting started, but Mooch was so nervous he seemed to be fluttering.

"Christ—" he said. "Hi, you all right, Johnny—Christ— Wait a sec, will ya? Lemme just—" and he snatched his shirt off the radiator.

"Last night, you—" Bunting started again but gave it up; Mooch wasn't listening. The small man skittered around putting on his clothes and kept turning away from Bunting. He kept mumbling, "Wait a sec, wait a sec."

"Just listen," said Bunting. "I'll look someplace else."

"That's all right, John, that's all right. I'm all dressed. We can go and..."

"You got soap on your face," said Bunting, and Mooch rushed back to the sink.

Bunting did not want to wait. He did not want to sit down in the bar with Mooch and start buying drinks to make the small man talk to him. He didn't have to ask much, anyway. Just one question.

"You made a big speech yesterday," Bunting started. "You got all riled up."

"Listen, Johnny, I'm sorry I got you sore. Honest, I didn't mean..."

"I'm not sore, I'm asking a question. You listening?"

Mooch was wiping his face with a paper towel, kept wiping and dabbing long after he was dry. This Bunting was no longer the same, not just an empty skin you pour full of liquor—

"The way you talked," Bunting said, "it sounded like you know something."

"Know something? Cheez, Johnny, all I ever do..."

"Just listen," said Bunting. Mooch stopped dabbing his face. He picked small worms of paper off his cheek and listened. Bunting said, "The—that woman, Ann Jackson. Who shot her?"

More than the words, it was Bunting's new manner that frightened Mooch. The way Bunting asked was like reaching for a man and yanking him up close.

"You know who?" Bunting asked.

Mooch dropped the paper towel and didn't know where to look. What they should do is go out that door, leave this damn toilet, and sit down with a drink. That way they might discuss this thing. There were a thousand angles involved. Mooch had to prove his great knowledge of things, to disguise the fact that he knew nothing specific, to keep Bunting from getting violent again, to keep him close and not let him get away, because Bunting no longer acted like Mooch's personal sucker.

"I haven't got much time," said Bunting.

"Johnny, listen, I can tell you a lot of things. I can maybe give you a line— Let's get outa here, Johnny. My clothes is starting to smell like hyacinth. Honest, John, I..."

"You don't know?"

"Listen, maybe I can find out..."

"Forget it," said Bunting, and opened the door.

Halfway through the bar Mooch had caught up and taken Bunting by the arm. If he could get Bunting to sit down, have at least that first drink; this time of morning, all this excitement—

"Johnny, you're rushing outa here halfcocked. You don't know what you're running into when you start messing with Saltenberg's crowd—"

Bunting stopped and turned around. "Who did you say?"

When Mooch saw Bunting's face he knew he hadn't lost his man. Mooch looked back and forth along the empty room, then walked up to the bar. Bunting would follow him. "Hair of the dog," he said to the bartender, and then to Bunting, "Yours?"

"Nothing."

The next step would be to get Bunting to pay for the drink, but Bunting had already put the money on the bar. Mooch took his drink and carried it away. He sat down in the booth and watched Bunting follow him. Mooch was okay now. He sat back, a little exhausted, and smiled. He looked at Bunting with slow care, almost loving the man for being there, at this time, first thing in the morning, his once-in-a-lifetime sucker who listened to conversation and bought all the drinks. And Bunting meant even more now. Bunting the Novice, and Mooch the Master. Bunting, who sat there boiling, ready to get going, and Mooch, the brains.

He started his delivery. "Nobody gets away with nothing in my book." He stopped to take a careful sip of liquor, but then he noticed Bunting wasn't with him...

"Who's Saltenberg?" said Bunting.

"Trouble," said Mooch. It didn't work, though. Bunting stayed specific.

"What's he do, who is he? You know or don't you?"

"He is the most important..."

"Cut it out. You know him?"

Mooch didn't know him. Mooch maneuvered all he could, he tried to make it conversation, he sat there with his drink all gone and Bunting not buying any new ones, and in a short while he knew that he had lost his man. He started answering, short, depressed, without much interest.

"Who's Saltenberg?"

"He heads this combine. They make gambling machines and run them."

"Why did you bring him up?"

"Because you asked me. You asked me about this girl."

"Saltenberg shot her?"

"Jeesis ! He's the brains!"

"You know who shot her?"

"No! I told you."

"What?"

"Don't you read the papers?"

"I haven't lately. What happened?"

"Well," said Mooch, and leaned over the table. "Not all of this was in the papers, but since you ask..."

"Just tell it!"

"All right. They split. Saltenberg, the old one, and his sidekick Tarpin. Some squabble, the way those big shots do, but Tarpin gets the short end of the stick. See?"

"No. Go on."

"Tarpin gets pushed out. He's got the dough, he's got the men, but he don't have the connections. He gets pushed."

"That's behind the shooting?"

"Right. Tarpin goes to heist some books—who knows what books?— and there's a squabble. With Tarpin that means, Johnboy, shooting it out. Nothing to lose, you know. Anything to make a stink for Saltenberg."

"Get to the point."

"What point? I'm giving you points all along. I'm discussing personalities, you understand? Hey, wait—"

Bunting was leaving. Mooch didn't know a thing.

"Wait up! You didn't ask me about any of the rest. This outfit, Johnboy, this outfit is big— Wait up! Where you going?" Mooch, the empty glass before him, was dying at the thought of losing Bunting.

"I'm going to the police," said Bunting and walked out.

Mooch sat down again. Now he was positive that he had lost his man.

Chapter 5

The fine snow was cold enough so that it didn't melt and the wind that blew around the building threw powder into Bunting's face. Bunting lowered his head and went inside. There was a marble hall and a small, wooden booth in the middle. After the outside, the hall seemed quiet. It was cool, the way the morgue had been.

The man in the wooden booth had an electric heater by his feet. He had his feet turned up to catch the glow, and sat there looking at them. He didn't bother to look up when Bunting spoke to him, just said, "Homicide, Two-Three-One."

Two-Three-One was a large office with flowers on some desks and mostly female help. Bunting went to the desk that said *Information.* "My name is John Bunting," he told the girl. "I want to see somebody about the Ann Jackson case."

He said this fairly fast. It got him over the excitement he was feeling, the conflicting emotions which he didn't want to understand. It had been easy. Perhaps because he had called it a case.

"May I ask your business?"

"Business? I'm an engineer. What's that got to do with it?"

"What I meant was, for what reason do you want..."

"Ann Jackson got shot in the street. She was my fiancée."

This time it had been more specific. First, the quick pain and then, to cover it, the rage.

"Oh— I'm sorry—"

He was too busy to think of some fast platitude, because he had to get this straight. How did he feel? Which was it going to be: staring at the ceiling from the wrinkled bed in the gray room, or, like last night, not feeling a thing except the heat that had suddenly been back inside him?

"I'm terribly sorry, Mister Bunting. I'll get someone right away." She hid her face with the phone.

She needn't have, because Bunting wasn't looking at her. He wished he had a cigarette. It would distract him.

"Room Two-Three-One-A. Lieutenant Dolphin will see you." She tried to smile at Bunting, but gave it up.

The room was small and much too hot. A row of files made it look crowded and the moving shadows in the frosted glass partition on one side made Bunting feel he would get interrupted any moment.

"I'm Dolphin," said the man behind the desk. "Please, sit down, Mr. Bunting."

Bunting sat down. He saw that the lieutenant looked very young. The man wore civilian clothes and one of his arms seemed to be crippled.

"Won't you take off your coat?"

Bunting didn't take it off. "Are you in on this Jackson case?"

"No," said the lieutenant. "I only do desk work now." He smiled. "The man you ought to see should be back at any moment. You know, as a matter of fact they were looking for you a few days ago. Some point of information."

"Oh?"

"They dropped it. I don't know what it was, but it was cleared up, anyway."

There was a brief pause. Dolphin smiled at Bunting and offered him a cigarette. Bunting took it, then took the light. He dragged a few times and looked only at his cigarette. He felt tense, full of pressure, but suddenly aimless. They had talked as would any two people who did not know each other, just chitchat, very far away from anything personal.

A door banged behind the partition and Dolphin turned around. "Let me see if that's him." He picked up the phone.

Whoever answered the phone wasn't the right man, because Dolphin just said, "... No. I have a man here, a Mr. Bunting... Flinn? All right," and hung up.

He pushed something around on his desk and then said, "Would you like some coffee? I'm going to order some for myself—"

Bunting didn't want any coffee. Most of all he didn't want to wait. Maybe they were stalling him— Why should they? He hadn't even said why he was here, he himself didn't know why he was here. This was the most important thing: to know why he was here and how he felt. He suddenly felt drained. Thinking of how it had started with Ann, the sick, familiar feeling tried to come back—

"Mr. Bunting, are you all right?"

Bunting straightened up and took a breath. His face was moist with sweat and he felt sweat prickle his skin under his clothes. The heat, he thought, or rather, Dolphin would think it was the heat, since Bunting hadn't taken off his overcoat. And Bunting didn't give a damn what Dolphin thought.

"How about calling Flinn again?" he said. "Or somebody else."

Dolphin smiled quickly when Bunting looked at him. He might have been mistaken, but this man Bunting had looked as if he were holding his breath. And he was sweating. But that was the overcoat. Bunting didn't look sick. He looked like he was getting mad.

"I'll try again," and he took the phone.

Bunting listened closely this time. He was sure that Dolphin must be talking to the same man that had answered him before. "Flinn isn't there yet?... Oh. I'd like to send him in to you, Krakow...." Dolphin looked out the window. "No. I think it's important... Fine." He hung up. He turned to Bunting and told him to go through this door and then the first one on the left.

It sounded as if he wanted to get Bunting off his neck, and the other one, who had been answering the phone, he didn't want any part of Bunting either. Bunting was sure of this.

This office was a cubicle with two glass walls and a desk, and wirebaskets on a table. The heat was stifling, and just across the top of Bunting's head there was an icy draft. The man behind the desk had pushed the window partway open. He said, "Hi, Bunting. Remember me?"

Bunting remembered. Krakow was the lieutenant with whom he had gone to the morgue.

"Yes," said Bunting. "I remember." He took off his coat.

"I'm a little rushed right now," said Krakow, "but anything you want to know, let's have it." He looked worn out. He hadn't shaved yet. "Sit down if you want," he added.

Bunting sat down. He put his coat over his lap and folded his arms on top of that. He looked like a football player starting to run.

"I haven't been around much. I want to know what happened with that case, Ann Jackson."

"We're on it, Bunting. We're not done with it."

"I want to know who killed the girl."

Krakow got up and pulled his tie down. He didn't like the tone of voice Bunting was using. He thought Bunting had changed a hell of a lot. "We haven't found him yet, Bunting."

"Why not?"

"Why? Because it ain't easy, that's why. We got..."

"Listen," said Bunting. "You're in this and you know all there is to know about this case. I'm in this too. I don't know a thing. I want to know..."

"Okay, okay." Krakow rubbed the back of his neck. It looked as if he were hitting himself. "The girl was walking west on Truesdell Square when the brawl started, some men coming out of a building there. Miss Jackson probably stopped dead—I mean stopped there not knowing what to do. Right then, we figure, was the time when those punks cut loose. She was far enough off not to be sure what was going on, but too scared, maybe, to run. She hadn't even turned away when she got hit. That's how the shot got to her—hit her the way it did."

"In the forehead."

"Yeah, like you say." Krakow looked disgusted. He pushed some folders around on his desk and found a cigarette. "I'm telling you so you know we figure all the angles. Why she got hit, where the shot came from, things like that."

"I know she's dead." Bunting paused, waiting for Krakow to finish lighting up, and then, "I want to know who killed her."

Krakow exhaled. It sounded exhausted. "I know that's what you want to know." He changed his voice, maybe because he'd changed his mind about what to say, and talked as casually as he could. "I'll tell you what we'll do, Bunting. Give me your address, your number, and just as a favor to you I'll give you a ring as things develop, and let you know. I think I know how you feel and even though we don't often do this sort of thing..."

"You don't? How come you don't?"

Krakow got up again, went to the window. He wanted to feel the cold draft. "Take it easy," he said. "Just take it easy."

"Easy? All I know is she's dead and whoever did it isn't!"

"Bunting, listen to me. I told you how it happened. I went into details, just for that. It was an accident. There were six shots. Two one way, four the other. We found all the shells and she got one of them. A stray, Bunting. An accident." Then he went to the table and took his hat out of one of the wirebaskets. "I don't want to rush you, Bunting, but the way things have been going here..."

"You're tired, I know. You haven't slept in days. I appreciate that," Bunting managed to say, but then his voice got rushed again. "I'm tired too! I haven't slept in days either! All I'm doing now is asking one simple question and what I'm getting is the heave."

"You got it wrong, fellow—"

"And you don't like it. But let me hear you say something about the killing. Let me hear you say the sonofabitch is running because you're after him. How about saying that? How big is this town you can't get a line on some punk murderer who..."

"He's out of town. Whoever he is."

"Whoever he is!"

"Yes! I told you what we know. One bunch was on the street, the other bunch was coming out of a building and the way that fight was going we even know which bunch fired the shot that hit this girl. And they're all out of town!"

"Who left, Tarpin or Saltenberg?"

Krakow dropped his hat back on the desk and said, "Well, you do know something."

"Who left?"

"You're so smart, Bunting, and you have to ask that one? Not Saltenberg. You couldn't pry him out of here…"

"Where did they go, this Tarpin and his bunch?"

"Are you pumping me?"

"And Saltenberg, where's he?"

"What is this, damn it! I'm going to feed you information so you can go and act like an avenging angel? Let me tell you something, Bunting…"

"I don't care to hear it! I came to hear what you had done! Nothing! That's what I hear. The killer skips and you're too busy with something else to go after him. Did you say you have a line on him? No, nothing like it. Did you say you're going out of town to chase him down? Nothing like it! You got a desk full of ragged-looking paperwork and haven't slept in days over it! And you expect me…"

"I expect you to keep your lousy head and not yell at an officer of the law! I expect you to have enough sense to keep your lousy temper and not try meddling with the works of an organization that's big enough…"

"Big enough?" said Bunting. "Hell, you haven't even got a place to hang your hat!" and Bunting left, slamming the door.

Chapter 6

From now on, Bunting knew, it would have to go different. From now on it wouldn't be enough to have intentions, even with all his Jheat behind it. From now, everything he did would have to make sense.

The sun had gone. It made the snow look less white and the sky heavy and close and gray. Bunting walked back to where he lived. He walked an hour. The wind had stopped but the still air had bite in it. Back at the bar they even had the lights on because it was so gray, but Mooch wasn't there. It was early afternoon and Bunting went home. From now on, everything he did would make sense. He felt ill-tempered and cold, but everything he did from now on would make pure sense.

Nine o'clock at night they turned the steam off in his room. Bunting woke up and shivered. Nine was early to look for Mooch but there wasn't any point staying in this room. Bunting stretched and kicked his blanket off, looked up at the familiar ceiling. There wasn't anything to see and he felt nothing. The neon wink flashing on the wall disappeared when Bunting put the light on. His face felt better. It was a little puffed, but better. Bunting washed with cold water and then he shaved. He changed his clothes. The cold material felt stiff around his skin. Then he went to the bar.

Mooch, because of what had happened, had found two new ones. He sat at the table close by the stove, and the two men with him were drunk. Mooch, who never fell behind a customer, showed nothing. The bar was so crowded and foggy with heat and smoke that nobody saw Bunting till he got to Mooch. He stopped behind his chair and said, "I want to see you."

Mooch turned and yelped. There were a lot of customers who remembered Bunting from the night before and everybody looked. Nobody moved.

"Mooch," said Bunting, "I want..." and then he felt the man behind him.

"Out," said the bartender. "Just out."

Bunting turned a little.

"This place is full of friends of mine," said the bartender, "and you haven't got a one."

"Don't worry," said Bunting.

"And looking at you, I see you aren't a drinking man no more. So, out."

"I'm waiting," Bunting said to Mooch. "I'll wait five minutes," and went outside.

Mooch shot out of the door as soon as Bunting had reached the curb. Mooch seemed beside himself. "Johnny, for heaven's sake, you trying to..."

"Who are they?" said Bunting. The two drunks from Mooch's table came weaving out of the door.

"Customers! That's what. I got an obligation to..."

"This won't take long."

"I can't, John, I can't. What do you want?"

"Open up when ready," said one of the drunks. "Damn the torpedoes. I haven't begun to sink," said the other one.

"Conversation," said Bunting. "Like we had this morning. Come to my place."

"For heaven's sake, Johnny, you see I can't. I got these customers along. They don't know where it is and I got an obligation. I gotta take them."

"They look like they've been. Come on."

"I have not begun to sunk—"

"Johnny, you ruining my setup. I don't recognize you. You was such a nice..."

"I changed my attitude. Let's go."

"Damn them slippery torpedoes—"

"Johnny, please, listen. If I don't bring 'em I'm out one buck each. Two bucks!"

"I'll give you the two bucks."

"Open up when ready, Griswold, because I'm ready—"

"Please, John. My reputation. Lemme just bring'em in."

"I have not begun to stink—"

"Where?" said Bunting.

"The house. The cathouse. And if you wanna talk we can talk. They got a room I can use, nice warm room, nobody bothering us, just lemme..."

"When you're ready, I'm ready, Grinelda—"

"All right," said Bunting. "You take one, I take the other. Let's go."

"But I collect for both of them."

"You collect."

"When ready, call—"

"I haven't begun to sink—"

The house was nice and warm. It smelled of bacon in the hall because the kitchen was nearby. Once through the drapes which hid a parlor with old-fashioned furniture the smell was incense. Mooch held the drapes and Bunting pushed the drunks ahead, but once into the parlor he didn't have to hold them any more. A girl came from the right and took one, and a girl came from the left and took the other one. The third girl took a hold of Bunting, but Mooch explained why he was there and the girl went back to the couch. The madam, wearing glasses and a business suit, came into the room, and Mooch went with her to collect his two dollars. There was another couch in the parlor and Bunting sat there.

The couches were wine-red plush and there were small, black tables inlaid with chips of white mother-of-pearl. Somehow this even gave the Grand Rapids furniture an Oriental touch. There were two hookahs on the mantelpiece, together with a cupie doll.

The girl in the other couch sat very quietly, smoking a cigarette.

"If you're going to wait," she said, "we got time."

"No," said Bunting and looked away.

The girl picked up a woman's magazine and turned pages. It was the only sound. Once she spat a little, to get tobacco off her tongue. She wore high heels to give bounce when she walked, and she wore black shorts to make her look that much more naked. She wore nothing else. Her skin was powder white and her plump nipples, Bunting thought, were rouged. She notice that Bunting was watching her but aside from one brief look at him she did nothing. Bunting didn't really see a woman, only a body.

The drape flapped open and Mooch came back. He felt much better. "Miss Karen says we can have a room for a while." He held the drape for Bunting. "You want the kid?" he asked when Bunting was close.

Miss Karen came in. She looked from Bunting to the girl and back and said, "Guess not." The madam nodded at the girl and said, "There's time. Go to the kitchen and have your breakfast."

Mooch took Bunting upstairs. The room was plainly for business. An immaculate bed, no covers, a simple dresser. There were no chairs. Mooch sat on the floor and looked up at Bunting. "She says about fifteen minutes. We can have the room about..."

"All right. Now listen."

Mooch listened. He felt fine.

"I went to the police and didn't find out a thing."

"Ha!" said Mooch. "Surprise!"

"They haven't got the killer."

"Ah—you don't sound like you mind, huh, Johnny?" Mooch snickered.

Bunting controlled himself and didn't say a thing. He thought Mooch and his sounds disgusting.

"What I mean is," said Mooch quickly, "I know they done nothing."

"You know this?"

"Sure. Look. When I was..."

"Before you start," said Bunting. He took his coat off and sat on the floor. "I don't want to know how you feel, I don't want your life history, or what you want me to do, just say what you know and that's all."

Mooch didn't miss the tone. It was cold, decided, and it filled Mooch with admiration. "I'll help you all I can," he said.

"Tell me what you know."

"I know this," said Mooch. He looked up at the ceiling, then back at Bunting. "This Saltenberg outfit has been bugging the cops for years. Big operation, makes slot machines, pinball machines, you know. They also place their stuff and run it. Mostly pinball machines in this area, which is no crime, except maybe when Saltenberg makes it so with fancy wiring and under-the-counter bets on the machine. Not to speak of what else. Like Saltenberg might be in—on this house, maybe— I'm not saying, you understand, but..."

"Get back to the point."

"Yeah. So he bugs the cops and they, of course, are slow. What can they do! Slow and careful. And now they're close. They're so close it even makes the combine nervous and Saltenberg and Tarpin split. So close, Johnboy, why should the cops scramble their deal with a loud murder investigation? Why should they push finding some hood who shot somebody accidentally and scare old Saltenberg? I ask you!"

It fit. To a machine like the police it would make sense. But not to Bunting.

"Who's Saltenberg? Where does he live?"

"Who's Saltenberg? Johnny! He is only..."

"Never mind that. Just answer."

"Mr. Saltenberg," said Mooch, "is a businessman."

"Yeah. Sure. Where is he?"

The door opened and the girl from downstairs came in. The young fellow with her couldn't keep his hands still, coming in close behind her and wanting to touch her back.

"Miss Karen said for me to use this room," she said to Mooch. She was still chewing something. She had been interrupted in the kitchen. "And if you aren't done to go to Number Three."

Mooch and Bunting got off the floor while the girl walked to the dresser and kicked off her high heels. The boy stayed close. He ignored the two men and tried to help the girl with her shoes by holding her arm and her bare waist.

Bunting closed the door. He heard the girl say, "Ease up, honey, ease up—" and followed Mooch down the corridor.

Number Three was downstairs and looked exactly like the room they had just left. An old maid was in this one, changing sheets. The two men waited till she was done. She gave them a disgusted look and walked out of the door.

"Traffic problem," said Mooch and sat down on the floor.

"Where do I find Saltenberg?" Bunting asked.

"Listen. When we're through talking, Johnny, how about..."

"Forget it."

"What I mean is— Hell, didn't you think that little girl upstairs..."

"I'm going to pay you for your time," said Bunting. "You don't have to try and make a buck on me, pimping."

"Oh, I didn't mean to make a buck." Mooch grinned. "You got an idea how old she is?"

"Twenty-one," said Bunting and sat down on the floor.

"Twenty-one! When she's twenty-one she'll be through here." He started laughing but stopped and changed his tone. "All right. Saltenberg. I don't know where he lives."

"You know where I can find him?"

"Sure. Lots of places. What you gonna do, walk in on him and say, look here, mister, which one of your punks done in my girl so I can go over there and find justice? Ha!"

It sounded raw. It suddenly gave Bunting a feeling of tiredness, making him want to lean against the wall and close his eyes. He waited a second and then killed the feeling. It wasn't hard. It went because this was true: he himself would go dead if he couldn't hold on to the hate.

"Where's the other one," said Bunting. "This Tarpin. Maybe you know that."

"That's a secret," said Mooch.

"You don't know?"

"He's out of town, I know that much."

It checked with what the police had said and Mooch didn't seem to know much more. "Okay," said Bunting and got off the floor. "You've been a great help. I'll give you..."

"Wait a minute, Johnny, wait up. I don't even want your dough. Look, Johnboy, I got connections, I know people..."

"Who?"

"Well, for instance, I know a guy what used to run with Tarpin. This guy and me— No, honest, Johnny. Hear me out."

Bunting put his coat on and waited. It gave Mooch a chance to think. "Johnboy, don't it mean something to you I'm not even taking your money?" He stepped close and sounded confidential. "I'll think of something. Now you just go downstairs, sit in the parlor—"

"Listen to me," said Bunting. He took a bill out of his pocket and slapped it into Mooch's hand. "This is ten bucks. Now listen while I tell you what it's for. You know me from the bar, and you and me are drinking buddies. That's all you know. You don't know who I am, why I've been talking to you, or what I'm after. You get that clear? That's what the money's for." Bunting buttoned his coat, said one more thing. "I don't have very much money. I can't afford this very much." He nodded at the bill. "And you," he said, "can't afford not to take it."

Bunting turned away, went to the door, but then he stopped when the small man talked again. The voice was almost a whisper and very urgent. "I want to see you win, John. You understand that? I want to see you make out."

"Yes?"

"So I'll help you all I can. I get you guns, a knife—maybe you like a knife—and I can..."

"You make me sick," said Bunting and went out the door.

The disgust did not leave him for a long time and he lay on his bed in the cold room wishing he could see the ceiling. The disgust and the sudden dislike for the small man gave Bunting an anger which was quite different from the anger which made him hunt for a killer; it was aimless and testy, and full of revulsion. And this, because Ann was dead. Ann had said, "Why do you love me?" and he had not been able to give her an answer in words. He had later been able to think of a great number of reasons why he loved her—she was frank; she was shy; and this to Bunting, had not been a contradiction; above all she was "yes" to everything he could think of wanting, and none of his wanting had to be checked first or thought about when he was with her.

"I used to be very cautious," he said to Ann, "in everything, almost. I'd forget to be cautious sometimes, but now it's different. Now, with you, there just is no such thing"

She nodded and understood everything.

They sat very close together and watched the rain hit the window. They could see a street lamp from where they sat on the couch and the rain going past the lit globe of the lamp.

"That is one sorry-looking bulb over there," said Bunting.

"A bulb?" and she turned against him a little to see where he was looking.

"That street lamp out there. Imagine you were that solitary street bulb hanging there and rain all around, and way down below wet pavement. Isn't that the most solitary sight you ever saw?"

"Oh yes," she said.

It surprised Bunting that he was thinking in this way about a bulb in the rain, and that he was able to spin out a feeling just by looking at anything ordinary, because he had never done that kind of thing before. He held Ann close and remembered that sometime in the past he had wanted to think and to feel that way but there had never been anyone who would have understood him.

"I don't even have a thought in my head altogether," said Ann. "All I am with you is warm and close."

Except, it did not stay that way. It was not warm enough and not close enough for them and Ann began to tremble.

Bunting held her and said, "Ann, please, don't worry—" She held herself close to him so that he could not see her face. He could hear her breathing.

"Darling," he said, "don't worry, it's all right, darling."

She kept her head close to his chest. "I'm not worried," he heard, "I feel—I feel awkward, so awkward—"

There was much of this feeling of awkwardness between them, always at a certain point. It gave a very special sense of passion to them, an excitement which Bunting had never known, except with Ann. This was the sum of his love for the girl, this expectation and this knowing how much they would soon be together.

Chapter 7

John Bunting woke up very suddenly. He lay still in his bed and stared into the dark. His blanket was like a cocoon around him but the cold touched his face, feeling like glass. He did not know what had awakened him. He lay very still, hating being awake.

There was a knock on the door; the one before must have wakened him. He heard, "Johnboy? You in there?"

Bunting lay still for another moment and then got out of bed. The floor was cold under his feet and the light from outside made nervous flashes.

"Johnboy, you hear me? I got news!"

Bunting hated the sound, but at least he was no longer dreaming. He opened the door.

"You been sleeping?" said Mooch. "Christ, it's cold in here."

Bunting closed the door and sat down on the bed, lifting his feet off the cold floor. "What have you got?"

"Johnny, I just had an idea. I think..."

"Come on, what?"

"Listen. You want a line on Saltenberg? Where you can find him?"

"Come on," Bunting said again and tried to see the small man's face.

"There's this girl back at the house," Mooch said, but by then Bunting started to hate himself for his own eagerness; he hated the cold touch of his own feet, and every time the light made a flash he could see Mooch's face, full of eagerness and expectation.

"What time is it?" said Bunting.

"Six in the morning. Now listen. Back at the house..."

"You mean to tell me Saltenberg is back at that cathouse at six in the morning?"

"What I mean is, Johnboy..."

"Get the hell out of here. Get out!" Bunting got off the bed and started pushing the small man back to the door.

"Johnboy, I can get you a line..."

"I can find his address in the book tomorrow or I can go to City Hall and find out there. Now move. Come on!"

"No you can't. Listen to me. He isn't listed, and even if you go to where he lives they wouldn't let you in. You got to find him where he works. You even..."

"Tomorrow!"

"Johnny, please. Maybe tomorrow..."

Bunting stopped at the door and said, "Maybe you think I'm still your sucker, because I offered money before, and for nothing."

Bunting bent over to see Mooch because he thought he had heard the man giggle. It was true, and when the giggle stopped Bunting saw that the small man was embarrassed.

"That's right," said Mooch. "I just thought— I think you paid for nothing, too. That's why I want you to come."

"The cathouse?"

"Serious, Johnny. I asked around and maybe one of the girls knows something. Where Saltenberg is. I just thought, seeing you was so anxious—"

"All right," said Bunting. He turned on the light and squinted his eyes painfully. He didn't look at Mooch.

Had this happened a while ago, about a week earlier, Bunting, quite naturally, would have felt grateful, or he might have felt touched by the small man's rare show of an uncomplicated feeling. Bunting got dressed. Now he only felt greedy to get done with his job.

The morning was raw and the two men had to lean into the wind. There was no daylight yet but the frozen snow made a false dawn.

Bunting would have walked by the place. All the windows were dark and the front of the building was different only because it looked in better shape than the other houses.

They went into the hall, where only a dim wall light was burning, and past the dark parlor. It wasn't as warm as before but the kitchen odor was there again. It smelled of roast and Bunting could hear the sound of forks and plates.

Everybody was in the kitchen. It was warm and bright, and eight girls sat at the table and the madam was wearing an apron over her suit, stirring things on the stove.

"Hi," said Mooch. "We're back."

The madam nodded and the girls looked up. They all wore wrappers or colored kimonos and when they saw the two men they tucked themselves in the front. Then they ate again and talked in low voices.

"Here's the one I want you to meet," said Mooch and walked over to one of them. "This is Joyce. This is John," said Mooch and showed Bunting the same girl with whom he had been in the parlor. The girl Joyce, like the others, looked tired, and nodding at Bunting, she seemed almost shy. She held the top of her wrapper closed and started to get up.

"You sit and eat," said the madam. "You and your friend," she said to Mooch, "go sit in the parlor." She turned hack to the stove. "Little privacy—" she said. "This is suppertime."

Mooch and Bunting went to the door. "Take some coffee, if you want," said the madam, and they each took a cup of hot coffee along.

They found one of the pink lights and sat on the wine-red sofa. It had started to snow, Bunting saw. The flakes came by the window and seemed to disappear on the glass. The glass looked blue-black in the dusky room.

"What about this Joyce," said Bunting. "She know Saltenberg?"

"No, but maybe her sister. Joyce goes home after supper and you can go along an meet her sister. Now, this sister, she ought to give you an idea."

Bunting put down his cup and took out a cigarette. "How come this is so complicated? The way you act nobody sees Saltenberg unless you know a secret word."

"I told you," said Mooch. "This Saltenberg goes from one place of business to another. One day here, one day there. And this sister, maybe she knows where he is today. I explained to you..."

"All right. All right."

The drape opened and the girl Joyce looked in. She was still wearing her wrapper and said, "I'll be right down." Bunting paced the room while he waited and Mooch got up after a while. He went out into the hall and talked to the girl coming out of the kitchen and later, when Joyce came for Bunting, Mooch was gone.

They went out into the snow. The girl walked unsteadily on the ice and Bunting took her arm. She didn't acknowledge it.

"Will your sister be up?"

"She'll have to be. We got one bed."

"Tired?"

"My back's breaking," she said.

There was no make-up on her face and Bunting could see how young she was.

They lived in one room and a kitchen alcove. The one room was crowded with furniture.

"This is my sister Linda," said Joyce, "and this is— What's your name?"

"John."

"Okay. John. He wants to ask you about Saltenberg or something. Mooch brought him over." She turned away, taking off her coat.

Linda stood in the kitchen nook and the bare bulb over her showed up the black hair rumpled from sleep and face etched with sharp shadows. The light made her look sullen. Actually she did not care enough to act sullen.

"How are you," she said, and put her coffee on the table. "You want to sit down?"

Bunting did not take off his coat. He said, "I'm trying to find Saltenberg and I hear you may be able to help me."

"I hardly know him," said the girl.

She was wearing a loose blanket robe, which made her look slovenly. She did not care.

"Christ," said Joyce, "you know enough to show this guy where he is, don't you?"

"I guess," said Linda. She sipped coffee.

"You his girl?" Bunting asked.

It made Joyce laugh. Bunting couldn't see her because the girl was somewhere behind him, but her laugh showed how irritated she was. "Hell," she said, still forcing her laugh, "she's a widow. She mopes around being a widow.°"

"Why don't you dry up," said Linda.

"Soon as you get out of here I will," and Joyce came to the table hoping that Linda would say something else. But Linda didn't. She sipped her coffee and didn't even look up.

"All right, just a minute," said Bunting. "All I want to know..."

"I'll tell you," said Joyce. "Her departed was one of Saltenberg's men, went around with him everywhere. That's how she knows where Saltenberg is because he's got a schedule. Ask her!" Joyce gave her sister a fast, dirty look.

Linda seemed to be used to the tone, or just didn't care, but Bunting got irritated. "You got it in for each other, wait till I'm gone. I want..."

"Why in hell should I? I don't live here? I don't pay the rent?"

Linda didn't bother to answer, just got up and went to the closet.

"Lazy bitch," said Joyce, and then, "you know something— what's your name?"

"John."

"Okay. John. Take a look at her. You'd think she could earn a living. I even told Miss Karen back at the house—not that Linda would try—I told her to take a look at my sister and you know what she said? She said, 'You ever see a piece of meat so dead?' and wouldn't have any part of her!"

Bunting looked at Linda and it made sense. The girl was well built, her breasts high and round, and judging by the place where her hips curved under the robe she had long legs. The girl looked back at Bunting but there was no expression. Perhaps her eyes were swollen from sleep. There seemed to be no movement in them. She stood there, the robe looking careless, and in some way—perhaps the bare neck or one sleeve pushed back showing her arm—she gave an impression of nakedness. There was no movement in her.

"Just tell me where Saltenberg is, will you?"

"What's today?" Linda asked.

"Wednesday, for heaven's sake. Wednesday!" Joyce kicked her shoes off and started to unbutton her dress. Linda had soap and a towel in her hand.

She said, "He's at a place in Steuben today. I don't know the name of the street." She turned to the door, wanting to leave.

"Damn it, describe it, will you?" Bunting's voice was sharp.

"You know where Steuben is?"

"Will you turn around please so I can get into bed?" said Joyce.

Bunting turned around.

"What's Steuben? You mean the suburb?"

"Yes. That little town."

The bed made a sound and then Joyce sighed.

Bunting said, "Where in that town? Can't you..."

"Am I going to get some sleep? It's almost daylight!"

Bunting bit his teeth together and yanked the door open. He took Linda's arm and pushed her out. When they were in the hall he said, "Now just wake up enough to give me one clear answer. How do I find that damn place where Saltenberg is?"

"I don't know. It's just a house there and he's got a shop in the basement. Let go my arm, will you?"

Bunting looked down at her arm and watched her push the sleeve over it. He took a deep breath. "Go wash. Get dressed. I'll wait downstairs and when you're ready come down and show me where he lives."

"He doesn't live there. It's one of the places where he..."

"All right! Are you coming?"

"Okay," she said, "if you want," and went down the hall.

Chapter 8

Linda had a new car. It was a two-tone sedan with a lot of automatic gadgets. The girl drove and Bunting sat next to her, smoking. She had changed somewhat. Perhaps the expensive car and the fact that she was driving—doing it well—changed the impression. She was not really slovenly. Her face looked indifferent, but vague enough so that her indifference could mean composure or could mean carelessness. The slightly sullen look was still there, the look that didn't come from sleepiness. Her eyes showed no upper lids and, as before, there was no movement in them.

"Your kid sister pay for the car, too?" said Bunting. His own manner startled him. He didn't know why he had talked this way.

She said, "No. My husband left it."

"I forgot about him," said Bunting. He realized he did not like the girl.

After a while it got very warm in the car and the girl tried to take off her coat.

"You want some help?" said Bunting. He sensed she would never ask for help.

"Would you?" she said.

He helped her, then moved away. Her arm was bare halfway up, a smooth female arm, and that, too, made Bunting feel mean.

"What happened to your husband. Shot in service?"

"He died in the hospital. He had a gall bladder ailment."

Bunting thought of his cruelty, but it did not upset him. Because she took it, he said to himself, that's why it doesn't matter.

"I never heard of a hood dying from gall bladder trouble. They get shot, or something."

"He was Mr. Saltenberg's accountant," she said.

The morning had daylight now, a shadowless light coming from nowhere, and the car made no noise on the new snow. They drove through the city and didn't talk until Linda said, "I haven't had breakfast yet. You mind?" She slowed down, pulling the car into the lot next to a restaurant.

"You're doing the driving. How long will you be?"

She parked, turned off the motor. "Aren't you coming in ?"

Bunting got out of the car and followed her. He saw that she did have long legs, shaped well, but the sight gave him no pleasure.

She ordered a spread. Bunting had never seen a woman do that before.

She ordered juice, pancakes, sausage and eggs, and coffee after that. He himself had eggs, toast and coffee, just the amount he knew would take care of his hunger. They ate and said nothing. She ate some of each dish she had ordered, never finishing any one portion, and then she had her coffee. She drank it black and smoked two cigarettes.

Bunting knew he disliked her, but now he thought she was also disgusting. They had been driving for half an hour when Bunting had to say something. "You full?" he asked her.

"Yes," she said. "Thank you."

"How come you didn't finish any of it?"

"I couldn't very well eat all of that," she answered and then they didn't talk any more.

She stopped the car in front of a house which had little bushes in front of the porch and a small lawn. Everything was covered with snow and looked neat. Bunting saw there were ruffled curtains behind the windows.

"We'll go to the basement," she said. "I think the shop is there."

They walked down the drive which was swept clean and to the side door where two empty milk bottles stood. "He's here," said the girl. "That's his car."

Bunting saw the black car in back, square and expensive.

The homey street and the ruffled curtains had given the wrong impression. For a while, seeing all that, Bunting had fooled himself and had almost relaxed. As if Saltenberg wasn't a racketeer, as if he might be an elderly, kindly man, and as if Bunting himself didn't need the ferocious tension inside himself, and the questions he wanted to ask were just casual things, chatty.

"Watch the bottles," said the girl, and went through the door and down the stairs to the basement.

It was an electrical shop with workbenches where two men did assembly, and two others were soldering. Another one was tracing a blueprint on onionskin. They assembled small parts which they handled with tweezers and they soldered thin wires which were red, yellow and blue. The sight, the smell of the solder, was so familiar to Bunting that he felt confused. This did not feel like the moment when he would meet Saltenberg—

"What is it?" The man got up from a chair and walked over. He hadn't been working. He was wearing a suit.

"Aren't you Henry?" said Linda. "Maybe you remember..."

"Oh, yes. Linda. How you been, Linda?" He looked back at Bunting. "You want something?"

"He's looking for Saltenberg," Linda said. "He came and asked me if I knew where he could find Saltenberg, so I thought maybe he could find him here. I remembered Wednesdays he showed up here—"

"That's right," said Henry, "he still does," and looked back at Bunting. "Mr. Saltenberg isn't seeing anyone here. He's busy."

Now it felt more like Bunting had imagined: a cold face saying no, Saltenberg never in sight, and Bunting with no tricks to bluff his way in, only his pressure.

"It takes me five minutes, if I see him. I stay here all day, if I don't," said Bunting. He talked very quietly, all the time thinking what he might have to do next. Because he wasn't going to leave without seeing Saltenberg.

"You don't say," he heard. He thought he would hear more, and worse, the next time, and soon he, Bunting, would lose his temper.

"What's your name?" said the man.

"John Bunting."

"John Bunting?"

"You got it right. And now get..."

"I'll ask," said Henry and left Bunting and the girl Linda standing in the basement.

Saltenberg sat in the front room, upstairs. He had gray hair and a ruddy skin color that had been massaged into his face. He sat at a desk, in shirt sleeves, and when Henry came in he took off the gold-rimmed glasses he wore. "Did I see Linda come in?" and before Henry could answer, "I thought she had left town a while back."

"Yes, that was Linda. She..."

"Who was with her?"

"Bunting, Mr. Saltenberg, John Bunting."

Saltenberg put down his glasses and looked out of the window. He even lifted the ruffles aside and then dropped them again. "John Bunting?" He turned back to the room.

"That's right."

"I wonder why—" Saltenberg got up and opened a pasteboard file he had brought along and looked through it. "Is that folder here, or back at the office?"

"I think..."

"Never mind. I got it," said Saltenberg and sat down to open it. He didn't look at the folder very long, then dropped it back on the desk. "Ask Linda in for a minute, will you, Henry?"

When she came in Saltenberg got up and smiled at her and took her hand. Linda barely smiled back. Saltenberg said, "How have you been, Linda. Everything all right with you?" His smile, a little bit vague, was there all the time.

"Yes, thank you," she said.

"The fact is," said Saltenberg, "I had heard you'd left town after Tom died."

"I did, for a while. I came back."

"Fine, Linda. Fine. I'm glad to see you're getting around a little hit more. Making friends?"

"No," she said.

Saltenberg shook his head at her, offered a cigarette. She didn't take it.

"Linda," he said, "it's not good for a young woman to shut herself up the way you do. You can't grieve forever."

"I'm not grieving."

"You used to be such an open person, my dear. You used to enjoy yourself, do things and so on—"

The girl didn't bother to answer. Saltenberg kept his smile. "But I'm glad to see you're making friends, anyway."

"Yes."

"Have you known John long?"

"Who?"

"John Bunting, your friend."

"I don't know him at all."

"Oh?"

"I just drove him over. He was looking for you."

"Linda," said Saltenberg, "I'm not saying you did wrong, and of course your husband and I were quite close, but why did you bring this man over? You know I don't see just anyone."

"He asked me."

Saltenberg smiled at her, shaking his head. "Yes. I'm sure that's all it was. But you know nothing about him? You just brought him?" Then he patted her arm and said, "You used to be much more alert, Linda, and..."

"I'll take him back. You don't want to see him, why talk to me?"

"Now, now. No harm done. I just don't like to see you getting this way." Then he laughed. "Maybe you're pulling my leg, eh? And you finally made a friend." Before she could answer he said, "It's time you tried, Linda." He put one hand in his pocket. "How's your money holding out? You know, if you need anything—"

"I'm all right."

"Fine," sand Saltenberg, "fine." He took his hand out of his pocket again and led Linda to the door. He did not want to give her any money and had just wanted to talk. "If you'll leave me now," he said and opened the door for her. She said good-by and left.

Henry came to the door. "You want him now?"

"Linda lives with her sister?" asked Saltenberg.

"That's right."

"Find out who pays the rent, will you, Henry?"

"Sure. Today?"

"Yes. Her car out there, I suppose, is paid up."

"I'll find out. You know," said Henry, "if she needs any money, all she has to do is sell that thing and make a good..."

"I don't think her mind works that way," said Saltenberg.

"I don't think it's working," said Henry. "You know, if there's anything I don't like in a woman is when she acts dead like that.... You gonna lend her money?"

"I wasn't thinking of that," said Saltenberg. "Send in Bunting, will you, please?" and he sat down at his desk and looked out the window.

Bunting walked in fast, straight to the gray-haired man in shirt sleeves sitting at the desk. Bunting didn't bother to try and figure Saltenberg, what he was like and how to talk to him. He said, "My name is John Bunting. I came..."

"Yes, Mr. Bunting. Won't you sit down. I'm terribly sorry about what happened to you. It must have been a bad blow."

Bunting hesitated, tried to see Saltenberg's face against the light from the window, and then it occurred to him that Saltenberg must have read about the killing and seen Bunting's name in the paper. He said, "I won't take your time, Mr. Saltenberg. I have two questions."

"Won't you sit down, Mr. Bunting."

"I have two questions. Do you know who shot her?"

"No," said Saltenberg.

"Do you know where Tarpin is?"

"Yes," said Saltenberg, and then he smiled. "You are a little abrupt, Mr. Bunting, and a little bit ahead of me. Perhaps..."

"No. I'm behind. The girl I'm talking about got shot and then nothing else happened. I've been to the police and nothing happened. I want..."

"Justice, Mr. Bunting?"

Saltenberg seemed to be smiling all the time. Bunting clamped his teeth and when he let go he said, "I don't give a damn what you call it."

"Of course. And whatever you call it, I think I understand, John. I may call you John?"

"I want to get back to what I asked you. All I want..."

"I know," said Saltenberg and got up. He started to walk the room, made a careless gesture with his arm. "But don't you see, John, you are hardly equipped. You know nothing about these men, you don't talk their language, and I doubt whether you can think and feel the way they do. You see, there is a difference..."

"Forget that. All I'm asking..."

"Let me make my point, John," Saltenberg started pacing again. "All you have ever done is work and I don't think you should underestimate that. You worked part time while you were at home, because your father wanted you to and perhaps, I'm guessing, because it kept you out of the house."

"What's this?"

"I'm saying that a nice, normal, though perhaps strict upbringing, is all you have behind you. No variation. After school, college. Electrical engineer from the start. Then, during five years of work you changed jobs five times. I mention it only because it happens to be the only show of inconsistency in your whole background. Maybe it shows you're restless. It would be the only sign..."

"What in hell is this?"

"I'm showing you," said Saltenberg, "that you're not equipped. Engineering, yes. And I was coming to that. You could..."

"That's all? That's all you know? How about the time I ran away from home, to the corner drugstore and stayed five hours. That's nothing? Or the time I almost drowned the little sonofabitch who was buying candies for my girl with the pigtails. Or when I played basketball when I was..."

"I know. I understand you could have been a very good basketball player."

"That's just because I got long arms," and then Bunting started to laugh. He had to do something. It had to be something close to violence and his laughing was like that. He felt confused and angry. "You know something else I've forgotten, something not in my background?"

"No. I don't think there is anything."

"So why bother? And how come you know? Why..."

"It's simple. I have a large organization."

"I'm going nuts! For all I can tell you're offering me a job!"

"I am," said Saltenberg. He sat down, to give Bunting time, and flipped the folder he had lying there a few times. "Perhaps you don't know," he said, "that my operation, as far as the need for electrical engineers is concerned, is not much smaller than the Kessler Company's, though I pay, on the average, twice as much. I can offer you..."

"Are you out of your mind?" Bunting was up. "Didn't you get it why I'm here?"

"You can't go as you are."

"You trying to stop me?"

"No," said Saltenberg. "I'm going to help you."

The man at the desk had not changed in any special way, but suddenly Bunting saw him as a new being. Like a spider. Like a spider with a net that curved all around, wherever you looked.

For a moment Bunting said nothing, but then, before the confusion would get too large, he started to shout. All he could do was shout. "Tricks? Tricks! Coming at me no matter which way I turn! What do you want? What are you trying to do? Hire me, fire me, use me, throw me out— What, Saltenberg?"

"Simple. You do what you have to do. You go after Tarpin or whoever it is you hate..."

"Who? You know who? I asked you!"

"I told you I didn't know. As I was saying, you go ahead and go down there..."

"Where? Where are they?"

"A small town in Florida. Manitoba. Now please don't interrupt me again. You go, do whatever you want, and I'll help you to get in. I can provide you with background, the kind that would recommend you to Tarpin. I could arrange it for you to go with someone who knows them. For instance, this young woman, Linda. Did it occur you she would be of help? You can go as exactly what you are, an electrical engineer. Tarpin will be able to use you. He wants to set up as an independent. And you join. And now and then, we'll discuss how, you let me know what goes on, you see? You help me keep tab on developments there." Saltenberg smiled, pleased by Bunting attention, and said, "When it's over down there, believe me, John, I can always use you up here. My need for your talents is as great and as legitimate..."

"Are you out of your mind? Do you think by planning my future you can take..."

"You're shouting, Bunting. I can understand why, but you're still shouting. All you have now is this—your insulted rage. That's all. And it's starting to set, like cement. You think that's enough—"

"Think, talk, plan! Why don't you shut up, Saltenberg!" Bunting jumped up from his chair and grabbed the coat he had taken off. "You don't get it, do you, Saltenberg? You're talking and planning as if I were human. I'm not!"

The door slammed and for a moment Saltenberg sat there alone. He turned away from the window when Henry came in.

"Did he hire?"

"No," said Saltenberg.

"Oh. A shame."

"That's all right," said Saltenberg. "He's going down there," and for the moment discussed it no further.

Chapter 9

The girl Linda drove home alone because she hadn't given Bunting any thought one way or the other. She drove, smoked a cigarette, and looked out at the snow. She looked at it and thought she felt like the snow, vague and cottony and without any color. It had been that way for a while and she thought it was best. She smoked another cigarette and looked forward to getting back home. If Joyce was up she would go to bed and take a nap, maybe.

The sun had come through and the air was glassy and bright when Linda got out of her car. It hurt the girl's eyes.

Joyce was still in bed. The dark curtains were drawn and there was an odor of sleep in the room. When Linda closed the door the bed creaked and Joyce turned slowly.

"You want some coffee?" asked Linda. She wanted to lie down.

"Don't do me no favors," said Joyce and scratched her head. "What time is it?"

"One."

Joyce sat up in bed and looked at one of her arms. She rubbed it slowly and looked at the skin.

"When are you getting up?" Linda asked.

"Why? You had a rough day?"

Linda didn't answer. She went into the kitchen nook and put on some water.

"I can understand how rough it was," said Joyce. "Driving all the way out to Steuben and back. Gimme a cigarette, will you?"

Linda took a pack out of a carton and tossed it on the bed.

"Especially rough, I'd say, seeing how you spend your days doing nothing."

"Leave me alone, will you?"

"Why in hell should I ?" said Joyce.

Linda took off her dress and then her slip. She was thinking of taking the bra off too but didn't like Joyce looking at her. She kept on her underwear and put the robe over that. Joyce laughed, but made no comment,

"I got the coffee made. You want some?"

"I don't get it," said Joyce, "unless you're doing this to get me out of bed. I don't get all this sudden taking care-of-your-kid-sister act."

"Why don't you shut up."

Joyce stopped smoking a moment and watched her sister. The sharp irritation in Linda's tone was something that Joyce knew how to handle. She just sat it out. She knew that Linda would do nothing more once she was left alone. Linda didn't want anything else, and got irritated only when pushed out of her groove.

And then, in a short while, Joyce could start again.

"Tell me, dear, speaking of work, are you finally going to..." She got no further. She had misjudged her sister and talked too soon.

"Shut up! Turn off that daily, constant, always-the-same dribble and leave me alone! Can't you? Just leave me be!"

"Well, dearie—"

"Work! Yammering about getting out and doing something. Are you any different? You sleep all day and lie on your back all night and haven't done a thing besides ever since we left the Sisters, so don't talk to me about get up and go. With all the laying you do you're so far from being grown up it's a wonder..."

"You knocking my trade, you bitch?"

"You make me sick!"

"I do? I really do? Then how come you're sticking around? One more crack outa you, Linda, and you're out on your ear."

"You couldn't do without me," said Linda. "Who would you call names? Your customers?"

"How come you take it?" asked Joyce. "How come you walk around the way you do, honey?" Joyce started to smile. "You used to be a lively one, I remember, when you were around eight years old."

Linda tried not to hear. If she did, if she answered, it would get worse and would start to hurt.

"Ah, yes," Joyce went on, making it sound as if she were thinking. "Until around eight or so, isn't that right? That's when love came into your life. Isn't that how it was?" And Joyce laughed, with satisfaction.

Joyce had come close. Maybe it had been around eight, though the date didn't matter. What Joyce meant, though—that mattered: Joyce, the kid sister, had managed to muddle or louse up every friendship Linda could remember.

"Can I help it men like me better than you?" said Joyce, and grinned as if this were a tremendous joke.

"You don't know any men. You just know customers," Linda said.

"Oh, no. That didn't happen till I got business-minded. That didn't hap-

pen until I got through with your boy friends. Until then it was love—
pure, big-hearted love. Like you had, huh, Linda?"

Linda sat down at the table and turned away from her sister. If Joyce
would only get up and let her go to sleep. If she would stop talking nonsense. But only the words Joyce was using were nonsense. The rest, what she
meant, came close. A competitive little bitch with a bouncy body who liked
nothing so much as making out with her sister's friends. What worked best
after a while was to care less. What Joyce had said, was true. Except for one
bright interval, Linda had been dull and distant for a very long time.

Joyce sat up in bed, folded her arms, and watched her sister's back. Before
Linda slipped off again, to wherever she went when nothing mattered to
her, before that, Joyce wanted a little more conversation. She wanted a little bit more of that fine friction between them, to put life into her day, so
that the rest of the day and the night would hardly matter to her.

"So tell me," she started. "Is all this going to change now?"

"What?"

"You and your Zombie routine, I mean. Now that you've taken up with
that what's-his-name."

No answer.

Joyce said, "How far did he get?... He did? And now, of course, knowing
my sister, comes marriage? Like the last time?"

"You can stop talking."

"Why? I gotta find out, don't I ? I might want what's-his-name myself."

"Take him."

"Ah! Not like the last time. Not like with Tom."

Linda went to the hot plate and poured herself coffee. She took it back
to the table and dipped her finger into the warm liquid and then sucked
her finger.

"I don't grudge you Tom," said Joyce. "After all, he's dead."

Even that didn't seem to work. Linda sat very still and said nothing.

"But just as a historical fact," Joyce went on, affecting a fake tone of
indifference, "the reason you got him, Tom I mean, was because I never
tried."

"Sure," said Linda into her cup.

It piqued Joyce. She talked very fast and sharp now. "What puts you up
on a high horse? You built any different from me? You look any different
than me except fatter and older? You got any thoughts in your head I don't
have? And vice versa? Just because you got married, picked up that sick
pencil-pusher of yours..."

"He's dead!" Linda suddenly screamed. "He's dead, dead! Can't you get that through your head?"

The outburst startled Joyce for a moment, but it was, after all, what she had been digging for. She didn't often succeed as completely as this.

Joyce was now satisfied. She stubbed out her cigarette and swung her legs out of bed. All she said was, "You know, that's very funny, coming from you," and put on her housecoat.

The two sisters didn't talk after that and then the phone rang. Joyce picked it up and said, "Yes?... What?" Then she listened and when she talked again her tone was different. "Yes, Mr. Saltenberg." She gave a quick look at Linda but saw no reaction. Linda was rubbing her face.

The rest of the conversation was a few yesses and Joyce listening. When she hung up Joyce was smiling, but not for Linda to see.

"You going to sleep now?" she asked her sister, but didn't wait for an answer. "Do that." She laughed. "I'll see that you wake up."

It was late, five o'clock, before Bunting got back to town. It took him three bus changes and a taxi to get out of Steuben and back to his place— a long, irritating trip. Bunting tried to think but that made his mood even nastier. He tried to think of nothing and that was worse. He itched and prickled with all the unfinished business that wouldn't turn clear and solve itself. And no help from Saltenberg.

At the first bus change Bunting had twenty minutes. He went into a bar and drank two shots.

And what if Saltenberg would do something against him? Stop him? Bunting gave an unnatural laugh and people in the bus looked at him. Bunting didn't notice, as if the balled-up rage put a film over his eyes.

He drank more at the next change. He realized that he drank like a greedy pig, but he had to calm down, think this thing through.

What was changed? Nothing. Except he knew where that Tarpin crowd was. He know more than before he had gone to Saltenberg. Much more.

Saltenberg was a reasonable bastard and if there was anything that got under Bunting's skin it was low-pitch, reasonable talk coming off like the tape on a recorder. "You're going to set like cement," was Saltenberg's phrase.

Not he, not Bunting. He was going to move like lightning. Saltenberg was a crooked businessman with a holy voice. Vicious thoughts churned through Bunting's head and made his gut feel as if it were full of knives—

Then he didn't want to go home, upstairs to his room. He had a weird urge to see Mooch. He looked for him in the bar, but the little man wasn't there, so Bunting sat there a while and drank. Nobody bothered him. The bartender acted as if he didn't know Bunting. He came to pour and then would leave to the far end of the bar. There were very few customers. Maybe the cathouse—

The cold snap had settled solidly over the city and the wind had picked up again. Bunting didn't feel anything, walked with his overcoat flapping behind him.

"I'm looking for Mooch," said Bunting when the cleaning lady opened the door.

"Who you say?"

"That's right, you got it," and Bunting pushed her aside and walked in.

It wasn't like the night before. There was no warmth in the air, no store-bought incense or kitchen odors. A vacuum cleaner was going and the hall was moist from mopping. There was an open window some place, airing the place and making the house unfriendly.

The madam stopped him. Same suit, same glasses, same manner. She said, "Yes?"

"Where's Mooch ?"

"I don't know. We're not open right now."

"Don't slam your business. This is a very cozy and wholesome place twenty-four hours a day. I can tell."

"You're drunk. What do you want?"

"I want the runt."

"I just told..."

"Can I wait?"

It wasn't six yet and the house wouldn't open till eight, but three of the girls came in from the street, wrapped up to the neck, their faces pink from the cold. They said, "Hello, Miss Karen," and "How are you, Miss Karen," and one of them said, "Brisk, isn't it—business, I mean." She laughed and looked at Bunting as she walked by.

"I could sit in the parlor," said Bunting. "You got any liquor?"

Miss Karen left him in the parlor. She had the cleaning woman close the window and then he sat there alone. He almost left.

The girl who had made the crack about brisk business came into the room, bringing a bottle and two glasses. She put them down in front of Bunting and then left to bring a bottle of Seltzer.

"Mind if I join you?"

"Sit." He picked up the bottle and poured for himself. The girl had to make her own.

"How come you aren't naked?" he said to her. He looked at her dress, then her legs, then her face.

"You know," she said, "it isn't evening yet. I thought you just wanted to drink first."

"First?"

She tried to laugh, but his voice was so mean she felt frightened.

"How much you cost?"

This was more familiar. She said, "Sawbuck. That is, if it doesn't take longer than..."

"Not at all. We'll just hook ourselves up to the gas meter and watch the dials, okay?"

She didn't understand any of this, except the okay. She smiled, got up, and said, "Okay."

"Sit down."

"What?"

"Sit. I don't want you!" He took a long drink, "Besides, you're too skinny."

She wasn't skinny at all. She was plump and pink and Bunting rattled her.

"You mean, you want me to send somebody else?"

"Oh no. I'm craving to have you sit right there on that couch pillow there, denting that couch pillow in that forceful, cruel way, and give me more of your conversation. I don't often get a chance to talk to such a bright, pink mind like yours. Here, drink something." He poured for both of them and waited till she had taken a swallow. "You know how it is." He leaned close, very confidential. "You know most girls. You know what they want to do all the time."

She thought it best to laugh.

The sound irritated Bunting. "Stop laughing."

She stopped, looked at him expectantly.

"Now let's see you cry."

"What?"

"Cry. Press the other button, the one that says *Cry,* and we'll have that for a while."

"Gee—"

"Aha. Pressed the wrong button. You pressed the one which says *Conversation.* Very well. Let's speak of something vital. How are you?"

"Me?"

"No. I mean the old man sitting on your shoulder there, the one with the peaked hat."

"You're— You know something? You're getting me..."

"I am? Where?"

"Please... can't we just—just sit peaceful—"

"Right. Peace is now descending upon you, your eyelids, my dear, your blue eyelids are getting very heavy— Feel it? Heavy like lead, like a bag of sand so heavy and tired, and the sand is getting in your eyes. You can feel it gritting there—"

The girl started rubbing her eyes involuntarily and Bunting laughed. Perhaps the laugh disturbed the girl more than anything else. She drew back on the couch and held one hand to her bosom.

"That worked very well," said Bunting. "Now we'll try something else. Put your hands up over your head. That's it. Hold it there and repeat after me. I—'

"I."

"I am."

"I am."

"I am a—"

"I am a—" She stopped, feeling rushed and confused. "I am— Why— Please, can't we do something else? I—"

"You what? You're what?"

She suddenly put down her arms and covered her face with her hands. Her shoulders shook and she was crying. "There now. The right button at last. What's your name?"

"... Effie."

"Get up, Effie."

She did. She blinked and stood there.

"You don't have to tell me," said Bunting. "Instead go upstairs. What's your room?"

"Five. Miss Karen..."

"Go to Room Five, take off your clothes, lie down on the bed and wait there. Go!"

The girl ran out of the room.

Bunting took a drink and walked around in the parlor. He stopped at the window, he stopped at the mantel, looked at the cupie doll for a while.

All he was doing, waiting for Mooch, was a waste of time. Hang around long enough and you start to set like cement. Mooch would be all right now, because there was a runt who liked conversation and was used to getting it in the neck. A nice brilliant conversation about the difference between Bunting himself and Mooch the runt would be just the thing now— Wasting time. What he really wanted was dead. And the next best thing was miles off, somewhere in Florida with the bugs in the swamp.

Bunting kept staring at the cupie doll. Then he reached up, took it, and broke it.

Linda. If he wanted to find Tarpin and whoever else was there with him, she was the one—

A moll. Bookkeeper's widow, my foot! She knew that bunch. She was a coyer, a front, his intro. Necessary as baggage and just as dead.

Bunting kicked at a piece of the cupie doll, then stamped it with his heel. He went to the couch where he took a straight pull from the bottle and then went out to the hall.

"Are you leaving?"

"Yes, Miss Karen," said Bunting. "How much for the bottle?"

"Did you finish it?"

"Just half."

"Four-fifty, please."

Bunting gave her four dollars and fifty cents. "And twenty-five for the girl."

"You nuts? Five buck a trick, she told me!"

"That's a straight trick. Perverts are more."

"Listen here, you bitch! All she and I did was sit there, having conversation!"

"I know. And she's up there on the bed right now, crying."

"I didn't touch that hooker!"

"I said in the beginning. Perverts cost more."

Bunting thought about hitting the woman but his hands were already feeling around in his pockets, getting stuck there trying to reach the money. He yanked out three tens and grabbed the woman by the neck. He jammed one bill into her teeth and stuffed the rest down the front of her neck. Then he left. His hands were flying, so he stuffed them into his pockets, and he shivered all over. He thought it was the cold wind.

The light was on behind the door and Bunting went in without knocking. Linda was at the table. She was dressed to go out and was packing a suitcase.

She just stood there and waited.

"You don't remember me?"

"Sure. John Bunting, wasn't it?"

"What a sharp, retentive mind. Where you going?"

"Are you drunk?" she asked.

"No. I just have a happy gift for living life to the hilt. Up to here!" he said and held his hand under his nose.

"You want to see Joyce, or did you want something else from me?"

"You," he said, and when she mistook his emphasis he sat down and said, "I mean it, you."

"What now?"

"Man," he said, "what armor-plating," and looked at the suit she was wearing. It was a suit like the madam wore, buttoned all the way up, the buttons making a curve along her body. "Where you going?"

She didn't think she needed to answer, rather she didn't think about it at all.

"Joyce throw you out? Or maybe," he added, "you got somewhere to go?"

"Yes," she said.

"You got anything to drink?"

She went to the kitchen corner and brought back a pint bottle. It was almost full.

"And two glasses."

She brought them and when Bunting poured for her she didn't object.

"You look in severe shock, Joyce girl."

"I'm Linda."

"I know. I know," he said and then he reached up and ran his thumb over the top of one of her eyes. "You haven't got any lid there, you know that? Like a fish."

She pushed his hand away and took a drink.

"What's the shock you had," he said, "so I'll know how to behave."

She hadn't thought anything would show in her face.

But there had been a shock, the first one since she had gone to live in her cocoon, since the death—

"I got to move out. Joyce threw me out."

"That all?"

"Yes." And then she said, "I have no money."

Bunting didn't say anything. He was smiling and twisting the glass in his hand. He was suddenly paying attention.

Linda got up and tried closing the lid to her suitcase. It was too full.

"You got a big, expensive car," said Bunting. "You can sell that."

"Sure," she said.

It was what she would have to do, only the task seemed so complicated to her, the whole thing repugnant. But she needed some money. It would buy a room with four walls and a shaded window. It would buy the kind of existence she wanted. Linda made a grimace, as if she were under a sharp light, and stopped thinking about it. She felt irritable again.

"Your sister time this? Throwing you out with no money?"

"You got a cigarette?"

"Yes, she timed it."

Bunting poured liquor into Linda's glass. "Thank you, Joyce," he said.

"My name's Linda, damn you."

He looked up and exaggerated his surprise at her tone of voice. Then he said, "I meant Joyce, though. I was thanking Joyce for the timing."

Because of her peculiar eyes he couldn't tell whether there was special meaning in her expression. Then they both looked at the radiator under the window. The valve had kicked open and steam hissed inside.

"Cozy sound, isn't it?" said Bunting. He took off his coat.

Linda nodded. "Give me another cigarette," she said. She lit the new one on the stump.

"You're a slug, half dead," said Bunting.

She looked up. She spat a piece of tobacco out while she kept looking at him.

"You misunderstand," he said. The liquor in his head kept him smiling all the time. "I respect that state so much I'll even help you keep it."

Then he poured her more whisky. Every time he poured for her, she took a drink.

She had one arm on the table, her head in her hand, and her eyes, he was sure, were much narrower now. The steam hissed and they both felt too warm. "What do you want?" she said. "A trick?"

Bunting stopped smiling. He lit a cigarette, to recover himself. Then he said, "No. A business proposition."

Linda tried closing the suitcase again and when it didn't work she unpacked some of her things. She got the suitcase closed, hefted it off the table, and knocked her glass down, spilling the liquor.

"Try mine." Bunting handed his glass to her.

She sat down and took a drink. There was a big stain on her skirt now from the spilled glass.

"Look at your skirt," said Bunting. The stain annoyed him.

"I saw it."

"Well? Aren't you gonna clean it up or something?"

"Leave me alone," she said. Her head had started to hurt and there was too much heat in the room. Too much light—

Bunting moved his chair up to hers and leaned close. "A slob and a slug. I couldn't ask for better." Then, without moving away, he took a drink. "I tell you though, from close up there's a hell of a lot more to see." Their eyes were quite close. "I just thought I saw something move in there. Did I?" She hauled out at him, but was too close to hurt him. Bunting stayed where he was. "Not that dead, are you?" and he poked a stiff finger into her soft flesh.

She tried to get up, to get clear, to get air, but he was in the way. She grabbed him by the arms. Then she knocked into him with her head and bit his neck.

The room too hot and the light too bright and everything much too close to her— She went cold again, and hung on to him in order not to fall on the floor. Then he tripped her—a drunken mistake and the bed seemed to shriek under her.

They stayed there, both with their clothes on. Neither of them had ever done that before. Like rape.

Chapter 10

Bunting drove Linda's car and Linda sat next to him, smoking. She wore wool slacks and had one foot on the seat. There was no conversation. At first Bunting thought that the girl was making an effort to avoid talking to him, that she looked straight ahead, out of the window, so that she wouldn't have to see him and remember the night before, but none of this was true. Last night hadn't really happened to her, just as nothing else had happened to her for a long time. She smoked one cigarette after another and sometimes she hitched herself around to be more comfortable. Once when her foot touched his leg she left her foot there and then Bunting was the one to move out of the way.

They drove south out of the city, and Bunting felt restless, wishing the trip was done. He read road signs and he read mileage and if Linda had been someone else he would have said irritable things about any subject at all. But not to Linda. She would stay blank and unimpressed even if he insulted her. Her blankness was a constant rankling with which he could not come to grips.

It would be a long trip before he could start his hunt. He read signs along the way and the names of towns: St. Mary, Bolton, Marksburg, and one that was called Alton. Bunting drove slowly, as the traffic required, holding the wheel hard and feeling his heartbeat jumping around on the inside. Alton was the town where Ann had come from. He was almost sure it was Alton. Ann had said, "My parents live in a small town not very far from here. Next Sunday, John, let's drive down and tell them our news."

She was so happy thinking about this and saying this to Bunting, it surprised him when he heard himself answer her. "No," he said.

It was the first time they had ever looked at each other with misunderstanding.

"No? But, John, we're going to get married!"

"That's right. You and me. You see what I mean, don't you, Ann?"

He was sure she would, but she didn't.

"But my parents—"

Bunting did not know what to say. He sat down next to Ann and reached for her hand and then dropped it again. He was startled to see that she didn't know what he felt.

"You and me, Ann. Can you see what I mean? It's got nothing to do with

parents or home towns or somebody else's wedding preparations or anything like that." He had explained more and had somewhere in his explanation said something that had made Ann change her mind, or at least
had made her give in to him.

Alton was a small town which seemed to be built entirely of red brick
and the cement urns and ornaments which were built into the false fronts
of the downtown buildings. One of the stores said, *Jackson's Plumbing Supply.* Ann's father? Bunting shot around the car ahead of him and made the
light further ahead. Ann's father? He didn't remember. All he saw were
buildings and strangers walking around and snow melting.

"Did you ever see so much brick before?" said the girl next to him.

It was better, thought Bunting to say something to Linda than to
remember Ann, to say something that would take care of the whole
rankling mess inside him. It would probably come out as curses.

He swore, long and heavy.

Linda frowned at him and Bunting saw it.

"You'll love Florida," he said in the same tone of voice he had used for
his cursing. "You'll love every little dump in it. There won't be a brick in
sight. And while I'm out hunting—while I'm out hunting a job—you can
sit and imagine how many bricks..."

"What's the matter with you?"

He didn't answer her. They were leaving Alton and the straight road
ahead knifed all the way to the horizon, a clean, sharp sight which could-
n't have looked any better to Bunting. It could only have looked better if
Manitoba, Fla., would have been visible where the road touched the horizon.

You are now leaving Alton, said the sign.

Bunting could not remember what he had said to Ann so that she had
changed her mind about seeing her parents. And he couldn't remember
how they had got over that first disagreement. Their last disagreement.

Manitoba wasn't very big, but like most of the towns in the state it made
a mighty effort to look like something a two-week tourist might like. To
keep the bugs away there were hardly any lawns, the trees were all imported palms, and for the rest, the town was mostly plaster, tin, and cin-
derblocks.

Manitoba was inland. However, the favored sections of town could see
Lake Okeechobee, or anyway, could see the prison gangs cut down the
swamp grass that grew along the lake. The lake itself was beyond the tall

grass, a large, oily reflection of sunlight, spreading to the horizon.
The season hadn't started yet. When Bunting drove into town it looked
empty and blank under the big sun. *Pleased to Meetcha,* said a sign across
the street. It was a permanent sign which had just been repainted.
Bunting said, "Pleased to meet ya." He stopped the car and spat out of
the window.

"It's hot," said Linda. She lifted up her hair in back and twisted it. "I wish
I had a rubber band."

They sat a while, looking around, but there was nothing to see. They sat,
glad that the motion and the wind noise had stopped.

"You want a cigarette?"

"No," she said. "I would like a bath, though."

Bunting nodded. It was early afternoon but he felt stiff and tired from
the three-day drive and the empty sight in front of him; the shut look of
a strange town depressed him. He nodded again and felt relieved because
Linda had suggested a delaying action.

"Next motel," he said, and started the car.

Linda shook her hair down again and sighed. She wanted a bath and was
glad there had been no argument about it. Two days earlier, even yesterday, he would have argued. He was almost human, she thought, letting her
have her way

They took a room together after three days of driving and sleeping in the
car, of sitting side by side and not wanting to touch each other in any way,
of being two bodies each wrapped in his own skin. But in this hot, empty
town they knew only each other—somewhat.

They stood in the small, impersonal room for a moment and heard the
air conditioner hum. The floor was terrazzo and cold. A hooked bedspread
with a leaping fish in violent colors gave an intentional touch of old-fashioned cheeriness.

"You want to go first?" said Linda.

"Huh ?"

"The bath."

"No. You go ahead." He dropped his grip on the stone floor and then
went to the bed. He lay down and sighed.

"You mind if I turn this off? I'm suddenly cold," said Linda.

"What you say?"

"The air conditioner. I..."

"Oh, sure. Go ahead."

He watched her turn it off and walk across the room to her suitcase. She showed a softness that came from being tired.

Bunting sat up and pushed off his shoes. He took off his jacket and dropped it on the floor and then he yanked off the bedspread because the knobs of the design bothered his back. He lay down again and stretched hard. He looked at the window and noticed for the first time that the glass jalousies were frosted to give privacy. He got up, turned the crank that pivoted the glass sections into a slant, then went back to the bed. He saw a blue strip of sky now, several leaves of a palm, and a geometric section of roof. He closed his eyes and felt the ache in his muscles.

"You have a rubber band?"

"Rubber band?" He opened his eyes, sat half way up.

"For my hair."

"No."

He lay down again, closed his eyes. He then remembered that she had been standing there in her panties and halter. He heard the girl pad into the bathroom, but did not open his eyes again. In a while he heard the shower and thought he could smell the warm steam—

"... go in now," he heard. "You can go in now."

He jerked up and opened his eyes. For a second he felt very sharp and awake, but the feeling left him. He looked up at the girl standing by the bed, then let himself sink back again. "Okay. I'll go later."

She kept standing there. She was fluffing her hair with a towel. "Do you good," she said. "It's a good shower."

"That's all right. Later."

He sensed she was still there and opened his eyes. Linda looked away and then back at the bed.

"You want to lie down?" he said.

"Could I?"

"Go ahead. Go ahead." He moved over, lay there with his eyes on the ceiling.

He had to brace himself and then shift when her weight changed the contour of the mattress. He smelled her fresh-washed odor.

"Got enough room?" he said.

"Thank you."

She had put on a slip. She lay with her back turned to him and he saw that she was just wearing the slip. He looked up at the ceiling again, but he now had the image of softness, female softness under the nylon.

He felt heavy and dull, and strained because of the slant in the mattress. He did not want to move.

The woman breathed regularly and seemed relaxed. He could hear her breathing. When he had to move he touched the nylon, then moved again to avoid it. It was like glass.

"You want to turn around, so the light won't be in our eyes?" She sat up, leaning on her arms, looking at him. "We could..."

"Get up."

"Get up?" she said.

"Yes. Up. Out of the way." Her skin, it seemed to him, glistened. She wasn't wet or moist, but a shine from the window highlighted her skin.

He looked away while she got off the bed and then he himself got up and bent to the floor for his jacket. She had stepped back to let him pass, but one foot was still on his jacket.

"Get the hell off that and out of my way!"

His voice startled her, making her move quickly, but she said nothing. And he didn't look at her. He put on the jacket and when he went out of the door he could tell by the sound of the bed that she was lying down again.

There was a dog sleeping in the shadow of Linda's car and across the street, leaning against one of the palms, stood a man. He wore the hat and the khakis which most of the farmers wore in this section and his face looked wrinkled from the sun. He looked across at the motor court and the closer Bunting came, crossing the street, the more the man smiled.

"Say, fellow!"

Bunting looked up, but kept walking.

"Howdy. Glad to meetcha," said the farmer. All his wrinkles were smiling.

Bunting didn't stop until he saw the man come after him. He waited by the curb, and while he stood there he slowly took his hands out of his pockets. He even felt himself bend forward slightly, as if ready for something—anything almost. He acted as if he had already committed a crime—

"Howdy," said the man and held out his hand. "You from Steuben? You ever been in Steuben?" He smiled all the time.

Bunting put out his hand and let it be shaken. He stood like that and said, "Steuben?"

"Yup, Steuben." The man shrugged, looked down at his feet quickly, and said, "Well, it ain't much, just a small town, suburb by now, most likely— Used to live there. And I saw your license plate. That's from up around there, ain't it?" The man looked expectant.

Bunting muttered an "Oh, yes," let go of the man's hand and took a deep breath. He felt shaky.

"Ain't been up there in fifteen years," said the man, "but let me tell you, I still get the home-town paper. Yessir!"

"Yessir," said Bunting and then laughed quickly because it had sounded as if he were aping the man.

"My name's Collins," said the man. "I ain't been up there in fifteen years, love it down here, but I still get the home-town paper. Yessiree. What's yours?"

"What?"

"What's your name?"

"John... And your name is Collins?"

"Yessiree, love it down here. Feel like a native, at times. Tell me—"the man leaned closer—"any snow up there at all?"

"Oh yes, quite a bit."

"Izzatso."

"Yes." Bunting felt awkward. He took his foot off the curb and stepped onto the sidewalk. He had no idea what to say next and was angry at himself for feeling forced to say something.

"This a vacation for you, Johnny?"

"Oh yes. That's right." He thought about walking away.

"I'll walk with you a ways. Okay? I been living here—" Bunting started to walk and Collins fell in. After a few steps Bunting stopped.

"I'm going the other way. I'm going to... going to have something there." He nodded at the restaurant down the street.

"It's on me!" said Collins.

The restaurant was an open-air counter. Fish were mounted on the walls; there were novelty games, lamps made out of shells, magazines, and the weird picture postcards you send home to show what a time you're having.

"How about a milk shake?" said Collins. "They make a milk shake in this town, made with orange juice. You never tried anything like it, Johnny."

"No, thank you. I'm going to have coffee."

"But let me tell you—"

"No, really, I'll just have..."

"It's on me, Johnny!"

The counterman came up and Bunting said, "Coffee." Collins ordered his milk shake.

They sat in the shadow and Bunting looked down the street at the squat, white houses, the sun on the palm trees and flower bushes. This would be, he knew, a warm night and a unique one.

"Now you take this town," Collins was saying. "Don't look very active, does it?"

"No. Looks pretty flat."

"Yessir. And you know why? I'll tell you why." Then he waited, trying to see if Bunting was interested. Bunting sat there, feeling nervous and annoyed. "Because you don't know this town," said Collins.

"Uh-huh." Bunting slurped coffee.

"You listening, Johnny? Now me, take me, I know this town good."

Bunting disliked being called Johnny by a casual stranger. He felt it should come only with familiarity, affection. He looked at the man next to him, trying not to show anything in his face.

"You looking at my hat, Johnny?"

"Yeah. Very nice." It was sand-colored and had a flat brim like a platform, the kind of hat Bunting hadn't seen in the North. Farmers and sheriffs wear them, he thought. Maybe this sonofabitch is a law man, casing a stranger.

"I'm in the tourist business myself," said Collins. "Trailer park. But I know everybody here."

It struck Bunting that this wasn't true. Collins didn't know the man behind the counter, for instance, or else they would have called each other by name and said a few things to each other.

"Like there's a part of town here you got to see, Johnny. Tourists hardly ever do. We got industry there. You listening?"

"Yeah. Industry. You said industry."

"That's right. Look around there. Go down Denver Avenue till you get to the produce sheds. Around there."

It had taken a repulsive codger who talked and talked and didn't care whom he talked to, to awaken Bunting. Bunting put his cup down and turned to look at the man. "That's interesting," he said. "What all goes on here, besides tourist trade?"

Collins laughed and folded his arms. "I been trying to tell you. We got year-round activity here. Like for instance, you look at this street. Don't look much alive, does it? But you go down Denver and take a look. This here is a produce center. We got a railroad going and coming!"

Bunting thought that a railroad was certainly unexpected in a town this size and in this location.

"So anybody wants to open a business here, man, you got the spot!"

Bunting nodded. He thought that Tarpin might well have been thinking of this.

"And cheap labor! You know," said Collins, "every month somebody
comes down here and looks the place over for industry."

"Is that right—"

"That's right. You in business, Johnny?"

"No, I'm—I'm employed. This is a vacation."

"Well, if you like it here, maybe you'd like to stay here—vacation weather all year round—and get yourself employed here, huh?"

"Maybe. Except I don't know anything about produce. What else is
down here?"

"Nurseries, tin shop making gadgets of some kind, and the way I hear
tell, new industry moving in any time."

To Bunting's surprise Collins got up. He put his money on the counter
and fiddled with his hat. "You go down Denver and look around. There's
out-of-towners down there all the time, not tourists, I mean, and if you
want business, why, Johnny, this town's got a future. See ya," he said, and
walked away.

Bunting lit a cigarette and smoked nervously, hardly inhaling. He tried
to focus on the man walking down the street and on what he had said.
This man was too much coincidence; it confused Bunting and made him
feel wary. But he didn't know what to be wary of. And the longer he'd sit
and think the worse it would get, and the longer he would be delaying
what he had come down for. Meanwhile, that girl Linda was sleeping with
no thought in her head, sleeping there after a bath, like a slug, and she the
one that had slowed him down in the first place, saying that they should
stop, take a rest, interrupt what he wanted to do—

He paid and went to the motor court. Linda was still sleeping.

"Hey you." He touched her bare arm, took his hand away. "Wake up!"

She didn't wake up easily. After having recognized Bunting, she stayed in
a half doze, not wanting to wake all the way.

"Don't you hear me? Get up now! Listen!"

"Yes," she said and sat up. She slid a strap back onto her shoulder and
said, "All right, I'm up."

"I'm going to take a shower. You get dressed in the meantime and be
ready to go. Understand?"

"You can stop yelling," she said.

"So get off the bed!"

"Just stop yellin." She wrinkled her forehead and kept her eyes closed.

Bunting was going to tell her more. He saw the way she had tightened up her face and he thought it looked ugly that way. He just looked at how ugly it was and no longer felt the need to say any more. He went to the bathroom.

She was waiting for him outside, smoking. She sat on the stoop in front of their door and looked up when he came. "I'm hungry," she said. "Do you want to..."

"Now listen to me." He crouched down next to her and talked close to her ear. "I told you once, before we left, and I'm telling you once more. I'm here for a job. A simple job, doing wiring. I told you. I didn't get the job with Saltenberg, so I'm trying to get it with Tarpin. And you," he said, "you're living with me, as far as they are concerned. As far as I am concerned you're here to help me find that crowd, to look like you're with me, and that's all. Simple business. Understand?"

"Yes," she said. "I do. But I don't understand why you have to act..."

"Because I got a lousy kidney stone bothering me!"

She sucked in her breath, but then she looked away. She got up and brushed her skirt off in back. "I don't see why you have to try and insult me. Or hurt me."

"Leave me alone. Just stay away!" He looked around quickly, because he had shouted, then lowered his voice. "That's what we said. Remember? I get you out of that town, I feed you and find you a bed, and that's all you want out of it, right? Just that and to be left alone."

"Yes," she said. "But you're not leaving me alone."

Bunting didn't answer. She was right and he hardly recognized himself. He took her arm and they went to the car. Then they drove off.

"You didn't say how long I can stay with you?" she said.

"Till I get my job. After that, if I got any dough left, I'll give you some. And you're on your own."

"Yes," she said. "I know."

"What's the matter? Not good enough for you?"

"You're doing it again," she said. "Why don't you lay off me. At least with Joyce..."

"All right. I'm sorry."

Since she didn't answer he wasn't sure how she took it, but he hoped it was all she needed then. If he didn't keep himself in hand, she might even leave. There was really nothing to keep her here, except her own inertia.

He came to Denver Avenue which looked like the main street of town, with shops, a bank, some taxis and benches. Bunting stopped and nodded out of the window. "We'll eat first. You eat."

She said, "Thank you," and got out of the car.

Bunting drank coffee again and Linda ate, unaware of the food, knowing only that it filled her stomach. Once, looking at Bunting, she felt like talking to him, asking him something, but she let it go. She saw he was trying to leave her alone and she also saw that it was hard for him. Or something was hard for him. She wished there would be no more quarrels. With Joyce, at least, it had been really no more than needling. But Bunting didn't needle. He fought.

With a real sense of surprise, it struck her that she was paying attention to him. It was no wonder, in a way. He forced contact.

She had finished eating and now she sat back. He hadn't noticed. She could look at him for a moment, seeing him with his face turned to the window. He was the first, she realized, with whom she had been in contact since her husband had died.

"You done?"

"Yes. I'm done," she said.

"All right," he said. He leaned toward her, over the table. "We start now. We start looking for out-of-town license plates and you start looking for faces you know. As far as I know, there are four men. Tarpin is one of them. You'd recognize him?"

"Yes. Him I would. I don't know about the others. If they're new, during the last half year or so— I haven't seen anyone for the last half year, about."

"And you and me," Bunting went on, "we're close. We're together. Clear?"

"Yes."

Then they left. They got into the car and drove down Denver Avenue, going slow like any tourist might who had just come to town. The sun was low by now and reddish, making shadows deeper and giving the air a dusky look. For a moment Linda felt the thick air wrap her like a physical presence. But then it went. She saw Bunting clearly and she saw the street clearly. She saw his long arm angled down from the shoulder and up to the wheel, and his elbow was touching his leg, looking as if he were poking himself.

"Here's a motel, on your side," he said.

But there were no cars near it. They drove on and came to the produce sheds which ran along both sides of the street. One of them had a railroad siding running the length of the front. Then came a concrete building with a sign saying *Trixi Inc.*, which could mean anything. A semitrailer was backed into the building and on the second floor was a sign: *Space For*

Rent. Next, a diner and a laundromat, then a trailer court.

"Somebody's waving," said Linda. "Is he looking at you ?"

Bunting saw Collins sitting back on a tilted chair near one of the posts where the drive went into the trailer park. He had a small girl on his lap. He was holding one of her arms, waving it at the car, and grinning all the time.

The street split. The railroad yard was in one direction and down the other fork were more houses. They drove all the way down that way until they got into the country and close to the lake. Bunting turned back.

"I didn't even see any cars," said Linda. "Except the pickup."

"I'm trying the other fork."

Bunting drove back fast and sat behind the wheel as if he were going even faster. Linda braced herself at the dashboard when he made the turn into the fork and then, halfway towards the railroad yard, they saw two more motels.

They were side by side and had been hidden. There was a row of Australian pines and their feathery heads made a screen.

"There are cars in there. I'm turning in."

"Wait. What about that one?"

A car came out of one of the courts, but the sun was against them and they couldn't see it clearly.

"He's coming this way—"

"I can't tell what it is," said Bunting. "but there's a plate in front. In this state they don't have a plate..."

"I know him," said Linda. "That's Morgan."

Chapter 11

They caught up with Morgan in a drugstore. Bunting had pulled the car up next to Morgan's and they followed him into the drugstore. Morgan sat at the counter drinking a root beer.

"You sit on his right, I sit on his left," Bunting said to Linda. "And then you introduce me."

"All right," she said and they walked along the counter till they got to Morgan. Linda sat down on his right and Bunting sat down on his left. Bunting accidentally bumped into Morgan while sitting down.

"Excuse me," said Morgan. He turned his head toward Bunting and smiled.

"That's all right." Bunting sat down. He looked past Morgan and tried to catch Linda's eye. She put her hand out and touched Morgan's arm.

"Excuse me," Morgan said again. He barely looked at Linda, nodding at her, and then turned back to Bunting. "Bumped her too. Little clumsy today." He smiled again.

The counter girl had come up and asked Linda what she would have. She wiped the counter in front of Linda and recited the kinds of sandwiches they had.

"You new here?" said Morgan. "You got no tan," he explained. "Like me." Then he laughed. "And you look like you could use a vacation."

Bunting was suddenly unable to talk. He was conscious of every muscle in his face, and his throat was glued shut so that he couldn't talk.

This was one of them. Maybe the one he wanted. Morgan was blue-eyed and soft-looking, the fat under his skin giving him a large, soft look, the smile friendly. The blue eyes made the pupils look sharp and black, which was—to Bunting—the only hard thing about the man. Bunting could not talk because he didn't know what kind of man he was talking to. Here sat a man drinking root beer and smiling to show he was sorry for bumping his neighbor, a fellow with friendly fat making his cheeks round and smooth— Or a bland man with only his eyes, with only the sharp little holes in his eyes, showing the mean, thoughtless brute inside.

"You know, the nicest thing about the heat down here," Morgan said to Bunting, "you can come in here, for instance, and sit in the cool. There's nothing nice like sitting in the shadow and looking out at the light there and knowing it's really hot. Ever think of that?'

Bunting didn't have to answer. For a moment Morgan was looking at him, waiting, and then Morgan turned away.

"I thought it was you," Linda was saying. "Morgan! Don't you remember me?"

"Well," said Morgan. "Well! It's Lindy! What do you know, it's Lindy!" He laughed and put his hands on her arms.

Bunting looked past Morgan's shoulder, saw Linda's face talking and laughing. He had never seen her laugh before and felt a small jolt when he saw the ease with which she pretended. He kept looking at her face laughing, and if her laughter were real, he thought. How far away it was from him—

"And how long you been here? Where is—" Morgan stopped very suddenly and Bunting could tell by the man's back and his head moving that he was deeply embarrassed. "Christ, Lindy, I'm so sorry— honest. How I could forget—"

"That's all right, Morgan. I'm trying to myself. Look," she said, and put her hand on Morgan's back to turn him around, "I want you to meet somebody."

Morgan turned and saw Bunting again.

"You mean—you mean I been talking to him—"

"This is John," she said, "and this is Morgan."

Bunting found he was shaking hands with the man and that Morgan was looking at him.

"Nice to know you, John, very nice. Like it here?"

The pause was too long and Morgan was looking at him.

"Yes. Nice. Very nice." Bunting heard himself aping Morgan, felt himself push the words out like a cough.

"You here for vacation?... John, hey, fellow—"

"What! Yes. What did you say?"

"What you here for?" said Morgan, and he laughed at Bunting's behavior.

"He's been driving for days," said Linda. "You know how you get, sort of bogged, when you're overtired?"

"Oh, sure," said Morgan. "I know what you mean." And then, "Hey, John, have a root beer. There's something in that stuff gives me a real..."

"Fine," said Bunting. "I'm fine. No, no root beer," Then he took a deep breath and the stalemate was over. He was very conscious of Linda's help, explaining for him and giving him a moment to breathe, and now he saw just the man Morgan about whom he knew nothing and who would take him to the rest of the men.

"Reason I'm here," said Bunting, "is a job."

"Yeah? What you..."

"And meeting you here wasn't all chance." Bunting saw how Morgan got very still, just his eyes with the black dots stayed active. "And lucky that Linda knew you, because I didn't."

"You're not making sense," said Morgan.

"I'm looking for Tarpin."

"Tarpin?" Morgan said it immediately. It kept him from showing any reaction.

"Tarpin. I'm looking for a job and I have to see Tarpin about it."

Morgan nodded and smiled, and turned around toward Linda. "Who is he, Lindy?"

"He's with me, Morgan. He's all right."

"Sure," he said and winked at Linda, but only because he liked her.

Bunting tapped the man on the back and when he had turned again he said, "What's there to decide for you? Why do you act like the gate between me and Tarpin? All I'm asking..."

"He's my boss," said Morgan, which to him explained everything.

"That's why you shouldn't decide," said Bunting. "And besides, I can find him without you."

Morgan laughed when he saw the point. He had acted by training and habit, but he wasn't suspicious by nature. He laughed and said, "Hell, yes, you could at that, and why not," paid for his root beer, which he finished noisily with a straw, and then led the way to the street.

"You driving?" he said. "Follow me. It's five minutes from here. Christ, look at that sun go down. The way it gets dark here fast!"

They followed him west, toward the motel, where the sun was thick and red on the horizon. It seemed to give no real light any more.

The motel consisted of one large building in the front and long rows of one-story houses further in back. There were streets between the rows of houses and each row was a different color: one pink, the next azure, the next white. It added no life to the sight, just pink, azure and white on rows of flatroofed plaster houses.

Bunting stopped where Morgan had stopped and looked down the street. There were cars here and there and two kids were playing near a washing machine. Transients didn't live in these rows.

"We got both sides," said Morgan and waved at the two doors of the flat building. "If Tarpin's here, he'll be in this one."

The same builder had done all the motels: terrazzo floors, oil-painted walls, jalousie windows with frosted glass. This house had two bedrooms, a front room, a bath and a kitchen. Clothes and magazines were all over the place but the cold look of the rooms stayed the same.

"Who's home?" Morgan yelled.

"Us mice!" said a voice from the other room. Morgan laughed, looked at Bunting and then at Linda.

"He always says that—and I always have to laugh."

"I'm receiving in the bedroom," it said.

"Are you decent? I got a woman—"

"Jesus Christ, bring her in!" it said and the bed made a noise.

They went into the bedroom and a curly-haired man sat on the bed, making a great rattle with the magazines he had there. His black curls were shiny, his black shoes were shiny, and his face didn't keep still a minute. "I thought you said—" he started and then shrugged so they all could see that he was resigned.

"Remember Linda?" said Morgan.

"Linda, Linda— Yeah, yeah. You and Tom," he said and held out his hand.

"I forgot your name," said Linda.

"Jesse. No reason you should remember." The man got off the bed. "You were married." Then he looked at Bunting. "Married again?"

It was up to Bunting to talk, but he didn't. He was watching Jesse, and as once before, didn't know how to act.

"No," said Linda. "But I came with him. This is John."

It was necessary to cut down all feelings, to act without any at all, because he didn't know where to direct them, what to allow.

"Yoohoo, John—" said Jesse.

Linda laughed to take the weight off the moment and then she said something to explain about Bunting, which made the others laugh too. Morgan sat down on the bed and patted himself for a cigarette, Jesse went over to Linda and made a joke about something. Linda looked at everybody, back and forth, trying to laugh through it.

"When's Tarpin coming back?" said Bunting.

They all looked at him and Jesse said, "Shouldn't be long. Half an hour maybe."

"All right," said Bunting. "We'll be back. Come on, Linda."

There was an empty moment while everything shifted.

"You can wait here," said Jesse, and Morgan nodded his head. He wasn't smiling though. He just nodded his head, and his face looked fat and innocent.

Bunting turned to the door, and Jesse was there now. He was shorter
than Bunting and lighter, but none of at stood out. What showed clearly
was that Jesse wouldn't let anyone out of that door.

"All right" said Linda. "Might as well. All right?"

Bunting didn't want to relax because he was afraid he would slump, but
he turned, stiffly and slowly, and went to the bed. He sat down and took
out a cigarette. He did this as if the movement were difficult. "We'll wait—
a few minutes."

Morgan turned his head toward Bunting and asked, "Do you carry a
gun, John?"

Bunting shook his head, lit the cigarette. Then he said, "No, I don't." A
whole lot more went through his head, about not having a gun, never having thought about needing one, about his plans which were no plans and
how hard it all was, how hard it was to be hard and unchanging.

"Pat him over," said Jesse from the door.

Morgan said. "Lindy, does he..."

"Of course not," said Linda.

"I don't think he does," said Morgan. He saw Linda come closer and he
got off the bed to let her sit down next to Bunting. She sat down and put
her hand on Bunting's leg. She sat like that and looked from Morgan to
Jesse. Morgan smiled at her and opened the door. "Just a few minutes," he
said. "Won't be long," and went out with Jesse.

In a while Bunting became aware of the hand on his leg and as soon as
he did, Linda took it away.

"I'm all right," he said to her. She had done all this better than he had
expected. She was the most double-faced acting female he had ever seen.
Even now, sitting there watching his face. He thought this, but didn't look
at her.

"John," she said. "You're not doing well. You made them all look at you."

"And you," he said, "just don't overdo it."

She moved away. She said, "I don't know why you're here. You said you're
here for a job, and I'd just as soon believe it, but you're making them all
look at you as if there was something else."

When he turned his face to her, she felt like drawing back as far as she
could. She had never seen a look that hostile. "Just carry your end and shut
up," he said. "Just shut up—"

She hadn't imagined it would be this hard. She had imagined she would
go with him, be the figurehead for him when he introduced himself, and
then she would be through. She would then have no more to do except

sun herself in Florida or sleep. She hadn't thought she could get this involved.

"Understand that?" he said.

"You do any damn thing you please," she said. She turned away and felt more as she wanted to feel.

Bunting took a deep breath and got up. He opened the door and went out.

"Want something, John?" said Morgan. He was right there in front of Bunting.

"A glass of water."

"Sure. Right there in the kitchen. Is Lindy all right?" He craned his neck and looked at the girl on the bed. She sat there, rubbing her face.

"She's all right."

Bunting went to the kitchen. He drank his water, and then Jesse nodded him back to the bedroom. Morgan was there, giving Linda a pat and saying, "A good night's sleep, Lindy, and you'll be all right." Then he smiled at Bunting and left the room.

Suddenly it was dark; there had been no twilight. Bunting hadn't realized the light had changed until the headlights swept through the room. A fast, big flash swept through and then was gone. Like the light flashing into his room where he used to lie on the bed till dark. That wink on the ceiling had been his sign of wakefulness—

A car door slammed and Bunting got up. He turned on the light and waited.

"See me?" he heard.

"Linda brought him. You remember Linda—Tom's wife—"

"Why'd she bring him?"

"He brought her. I just meant she's here too—"

Bunting heard steps and more murmuring and then he didn't want to wait any more. He heard water run in a sink and a man snorting, and then Bunting opened the door. They all looked at him, watching him come out of the bedroom, Jesse and Morgan and a new one. A fourth came out of the bathroom. He had a towel up to his face, rubbing himself, and only his eyes were visible.

"You're looking for me," he said through the towel.

"Tarpin?" Bunting came into the front room.

"Yeah," said the man with the towel. "And you're looking for me."

He paid more attention to his towel than to anything else, only giving Bunting a look now and then. Then he ran his hand through his hair and threw the towel at one of the men.

"Sit down."

Somebody else pushed a chair at Bunting.

Tarpin looked very dark. He had close-cut black hair. Sometimes he moved his scalp, and then his forehead was no more than a thick, creased ridge. He kept standing there, rubbing his scalp, barely looking at Bunting. Then he paced a little, got a cigarette.

"So?" he said.

It took Bunting a while to realize that Tarpin wasn't going to hold still or sit down but that this was the way he meant to conduct the interview. If he had meant to irritate Bunting, he couldn't have found a better way.

"If you got the time," Bunting started, but Tarpin interrupted.

"You're wasting mine right now."

They all stood around, waiting, and even Tarpin had stopped moving around. Bunting sat on his chair. He looked at the four men—one of them was his. He looked at each one of them and for a second he thought he would die from not knowing—

"You want me to leave, John?" said Linda from behind him.

It brought him back He shook his head and got up from the chair. It made a nasty sound on the terrazzo floor.

"I went to look for a job up north. I'm in electrical work. I saw Saltenberg just when you and him were having your troubles and Saltenberg couldn't use me. I found out where you were and decided I'd come here and ask you."

"Why?"

"You can use me better than he, seeing you're just starting in."

"Who told you that?"

"Nobody had to tell me. Stands to reason."

"How'd you know I was here?"

"It's no secret."

"I thought it was."

"Then how would I be here."

"That," said Tarpin, "is what I'm asking."

"I remember you people by sight," said Linda. "That how I found Morgan."

Tarpin started moving around again, pacing, patting his foot, rubbing his hands on his pants. He made his scalp move in a sharp jerk and when his men saw it they all got a little more tense.

"Wait outside," said Tarpin, nodding at Linda. Nobody said anything else until she had closed the door.

"Roll that window shut, Kuntz."

Kuntz was slight and nervous and everybody waited while he struggled to roll the jalousies shut. Bunting had a hard time breathing. He just kept watching Kuntz whom he hadn't seen before. Maybe Kuntz was his man—

"Sit down," said Tarpin.

Somebody pushed a chair into Bunting's legs from behind and when Bunting sat two hands touched his shoulders lightly, waiting for him to move. Bunting sat still.

"How'd you find me?"

"I asked around—"

"Who?"

"I just heard. I..."

Bunting's head jerked hard and his cheek stung where Tarpin had back-handed him.

"Maybe he did," somebody said. "You know how things get around."

"Sure," said Tarpin, and then hit Bunting again.

Blind with the sting in his eyes, Bunting kicked out, but hit nothing, and then nothing else happened to him. He sat tense in the chair, held there by the two hands from behind, his head down and tense. But nothing else happened. Nothing moved and there was no sound. The tap in the kitchen dripped, but there was no other sound.

"You hear me?" said Tarpin.

Bunting could see his shoes now, standing a little ways off, not moving. Bunting sat up and saw that Tarpin was lighting a cigarette. Tarpin wasn't waiting to fight or to hit him again.

"Where'd you used to work?" Tarpin asked. And then he was ready to hit again. This was the way he had decided to run it.

Bunting tore loose from the hands behind him. He flew out of the chair, stumbled, and when he was up he saw Tarpin waiting for him. "You'll answer," said Tarpin, "in a while—" Then he pulled his punch. "Why mess it."

They grabbed Bunting and he couldn't move. They gave up forcing him back into the chair, but they held him there, standing, and then Tarpin said, "I'm gonna ask again," and hit Bunting in the stomach. "Where'd you come from?"

Bunting retched.

"Hold him up again."

They did and Tarpin waited. Again nothing moved and the tap in the kitchen made the drip sound. Bunting thought he might faint. He might faint to make his impotent feeling complete, to shut out his aimless hate and his task which seemed suddenly impossible. The only thing possible was to kill all of them after a while. It struck him as being absurd even then, but gave him back the focus: one of them. He'd get one of them—

Tarpin missed that time. It didn't upset him. He just started a new swing, slow and wide, all a part of the way he meant to make Bunting talk. Then he hit him and then he asked again. There never was any anger—only monotony, so that, in a while, Bunting felt very strange, felt that this was the dullest moment he had ever been in—

They all turned at the shrill sound and when it stopped they kept standing, waiting for it to come again.

"Answer that damn phone, somebody!"

Morgan went. Everyone else was waiting.

"Yeah?" said Morgan into the phone. Then he listened.

"Is it Miami?" said Tarpin. "Tell 'em I'll call back."

"No," said Morgan, "it isn't Miami. Wait a minute—"

"Who wants me?" Tarpin sounded impatient.

Morgan put the phone on the table and said, "Nobody. They want Bunting."

Chapter 12

When Bunting went to the phone he thought there was a buzzing sound in the room, as though the men were talking rapidly and whispering to each other.

Nobody was saying a word. The silence didn't hit Bunting until he had the phone in his hand, halfway up, not wanting to bring it any further. There was a faint crackle in the earpiece, like a taunt, and then Bunting lifted the phone all the way and said, "Hello."

"You Bunting?" said the voice.

"Yeah."

"Fine. Listen, Bunting, you remember that snowstorm the day you came to Steuben?"

"What?"

"The snowstorm. Remember? You came to..."

"There wasn't any," said Bunting. "The sun was out."

The other voice laughed and said, "That's the boy. Little primitive, but all I could think of to check on you. To check if it was you, Bunting."

"That's why I said so." He took a deep breath. He could have played dumb, he knew, but then he would never have found out a thing. "Who is this?" he asked.

"Anybody else listening in?"

"Nobody."

"Don't let on, Bunting, don't react or anything. This is Saltenberg."

"I see."

"Better say something now, something like, 'Oh, how are you, Jack!' But whatever you say, put the name Jack in it."

"Oh, you! You, Jack... What is—"

"Just listen, Bunting. This call, whoever is with you there, it's got to sound to him like this call is from Jack Eckstein. Anybody listening in the room?"

"Yeah. The works—Jack."

"I'm Jack Eckstein to them," said Saltenberg. "Jack Eckstein is an operator like me, in the New York area. You've been in New York, I gather from your record—"

"You got it," said Bunting, and in spite of the pressure and the confusion he had to marvel at Saltenberg.

"You worked for Eckstein for a whole year, ending a month ago. Supervising assembly and repair of machines, and doing some purchasing. I gather by your record that you can do that kind..."

"Yeah, yeah, yeah—"

"I'm Eckstein and I'm right now calling you to come back and work for me. You don't want to. We had a quarrel about some minor thing, something about costs, but you don't want to come back. You're through with me. Come on, Bunting, say something like that for the benefit of your audience!"

"All right! No! The hell with you. I won't!"

"Very nice. You are doing very..."

"I want to know what— I want to know why this, all of a sudden!" It was right for both ends of the phone, right for Saltenberg who hadn't explained anything yet, and right for Tarpin who would think it was just anger over the call.

"The why is this," said Saltenberg. "Eckstein and I are not friendly. If you have worked for Eckstein you'll be that much more right in Tarpin's book. Understand? And— "

"How in hell..."

"Don't interrupt. This is 'how in hell': I have made an arrangement with Eckstein. He will corroborate the background I've just given to you, and to prove it you can suggest to Tarpin to give Eckstein a call." Saltenberg coughed slightly, then said, "It should make an easier introduction for you, Bunting."

For a moment Bunting said nothing. He saw how Saltenberg was saving his, Bunting's, hide and he saw how Saltenberg hadn't given up, how he was hanging on for his own reasons.

It didn't stay a conflict for long. Bunting looked at the four men in the room, standing there listening—and one of them was going to be his.

"All right, you—Jack. And what's the tag? I'm sure there's a tag."

"You remember Collins, of course," said Saltenberg.

"Collins? I never heard..."

"Hold it! And no more names!" Saltenberg lowered his voice again. "The cracker you met today. He'll be your contact man. He'll be in communication with you..."

"You sonofabitch," Bunting said without thinking.

Saltenberg laughed. Then he said, "That all right. That'll sound quite proper at your end. Well, Bunting, I think we better hang up now. By the way, I see you got off quite nicely with Linda. Everything all right there?"

"Scram out of my sight!" Bunting shouted, and with a strong burst of profanity he slammed the phone down.

He hadn't thought of it as an effect, but it made an impression. The four men in the room waited till Bunting, breathing hard, sat down in a chair. Only then did Tarpin ask "Who was that?"

Bunting muttered something and took out a cigarette. He wanted one badly and he felt he now had the time for it.

"And how did he know you were here?"

Bunting exhaled and then he got up. He stepped closer to Tarpin and said, "I told you maybe five times before, lamebrain, that you being here is no secret! And my coming here to see you is no secret mission either. I'm here for a job, and if you've ever looked for a job yourself you know that a man asks around when he tries making a contact. I asked around where you might be and the reason I asked around is because I need a job! And that's no secret either!"

Bunting sat down and watched how it went over. Tarpin took it. He gave a brief look at his men, but they showed nothing, so Tarpin didn't feel he needed to play it up. He just said, "Who was that, on the phone?"

"That was Eckstein," said Bunting. "Jack Eckstein." He took a drag, for effect, and added, "I used to work for him."

Tarpin put his hands in his pockets, said, "You did," and waited.

"And if I don't get to work here, I'll go back to him. That's what he wanted." Bunting jerked his head at the phone.

It went easy after that. Tarpin called New York, to get Eckstein on the phone. It took a while, and during the time, Bunting went to the door and looked out to find Linda. She was standing by one of the cars and came in when Bunting called her. Then Tarpin got Eckstein on the phone and Eckstein played it the way Saltenberg had paid him to, so that Tarpin got the new picture on Bunting. Bunting was now a valuable man—no need to ask details—and when Tarpin hung up, the whole thing was settled.

"You give the word," said Kuntz when Tarpin turned back to the room. Kuntz looked small and worried and wanted to know where he stood.

"It's the way he said." Tarpin nodded and then he went to the plastic couch and sat down.

"Am I in?" asked Bunting.

"What's he do?" asked Jesse. He asked Tarpin, as if Bunting weren't there.

"Shop man," said Tarpin. "Everything with equipment."

"So he's in. We can use..."

"Wait, Tarpin hasn't said—"

"Tarpin, listen," said Morgan.   "We haven't moved at all and mostly because we didn't have..."

"But maybe there might be..." Kuntz started when Tarpin said, "Shut up. All of you." They did. Then Tarpin gave just a brief look at Bunting and nodded. "I can use you," he said and got up to go to the kitchen. He stood at the sink, and ran one hand through his hair. His scalp moved, so that his forehead, for a quick moment, was small and compressed. But nobody had seen it. They all saw Tarpin come back with a liquor bottle and a few glasses. They all relaxed and they all had a drink.

Bunting said, "How about telling me..." but Tarpin shook his head and said he didn't want to talk business now. He didn't talk about anything else either, never mentioning a thing about the way he had started to beat it out of Bunting, and Bunting said nothing about it either. It had been a personal matter and Bunting didn't want any personal feelings involved. Not at this point.

"What I want to know is," said Jesse to Linda, "how come you changed the way you did, huh, Linda?" He watched her over the rim of his glass and smelled the raw liquor inside.

"I don't know what you mean, Jesse," she said. She kept a stiff smile on her face, trying to act as if she were at a party.

"It comes back to me, honey," said Jesse, "that you and Tom was like *that*. You know? Nobody even tried making a pitch any more."

"Christ," said Kuntz. "He's dead. What you gotta talk about him for—"

"I'm not, I'm not even trying." Jesse sat down next to Linda, on the plastic couch, sliding close and grinning at her. "What I meant was, I'm happy to see how you changed, honey."

"I don't think you ever knew me well enough," said Linda, but then Jesse put his finger over her mouth.

"But I can see," he said. "I see no sooner you lost one, you take up with another, huh, Linda?" He smiled close into her face.

She pulled back because of the liquor odor. She tried to think of nothing else.

"Leave her alone," said Morgan. "Come on, Jesse."

"Why? Johnny don't care." Jesse looked across the room where Bunting was standing. Bunting was talking to Kuntz and wasn't looking anywhere else.

"You get up now," said Morgan. "You be nice and get up now," he said and took Jesse by the arm.

Jesse got up without objecting and winked at Linda's face and then at the

V of her dress. Perhaps he thought Morgan was much too big for him, or that he'd talk to Linda again later, or—anyway, she was going to be around a while longer. Because of Bunting.

The light in the room was unfriendly, the cold floor and the practical furniture made out of plastic and painted wood, all this, and the men themselves, made it no party at all. Morgan sat on the couch and looked slow and heavy. Jesse drank because he felt fidgety, Tarpin had started to read a paper. And Kuntz by the wall, with Bunting looking down at him, felt nervous and small. "Was I in on what?" he said. "The split with Saltenberg? Yeah, sure. I'm Tarpin's man. All the way—"

"He looks like he might be fine to work with," said Bunting. "Steady guy. Gets what he wants—" It was bored, mechanical talk to Bunting. It bored him because it was not the real question. He took a nip at his glass, not tasting, and said, "Musta been good to have him around when things went haywire that day."

"What? Haywire?"

"Truesdell square. When you had to shoot it out."

"Oh Christ, yes," said Kuntz, very uncomfortable.

"Were you there?"

"Where? You mean that time? Christ, we were all there—"

"Ah," said Bunting. He looked around the room and this time, for the first time, he really saw the four men. And one of them was for him.

"Look," he said. "Listen, Kuntz. The way—the way that girl got shot in the head..."

"Christ, don't even talk about it," said Kuntz and tried to get away.

"You want another drink?"

"No. Never mind. I got to go to the can."

Kuntz went to the toilet and Bunting kept standing there for a while, nothing to do. It wasn't a party at all.

"You just met him, you mean?" said Tarpin to Linda. He lit her cigarette for her and kept holding the newspaper in his left hand.

"Depends how you mean that, Tarpin." She tried very hard to let none of this mean anything to her.

"I mean," said Tarpin, "are you his, or why are you here?"

"Or maybe you don't want to be with him at all," Jesse cut in.

Tarpin gave him a look and Jesse went back to the bottle. Then he said it again to Linda. "Are you..."

"Yes," she said, "yes, I'm with him. Why the questions? Why do you keep..."

"You're jumpy," said Morgan. "I bet you haven't had enough sleep."

"Or maybe just jumpy." Tarpin kept looking at her, never changing his tone. "You used to be different."

"Well—you know. Things change." She even laughed.

"You mean Tom dead?"

"I mean—just time—"

"You used to be one steady, happy kid," Tarpin insisted. "You looked twice as gorgeous then. You still got the same build, but you were twice as gorgeous."

"Leave me alone, will you, Tarpin?" she said in a dull voice. It was a formula.

"I'm just asking."

"Just leave me alone."

"That guy give you trouble? Bunting, I mean? What's he like, anyway?"

"If he's any trouble to you," Morgan cut in, "you just...."

"No, no! What do you want from me? I haven't slept in two days, I come in here and get sent out, you start pumping me with all kinds of..."

"Don't get excited, honey." Morgan touched her arm. "I'm not, I'm nervous. I just want to..."

"What?" said Bunting. Linda had raised her voice and Bunting had given up waiting for Kuntz. "You all right, Linda?"

"She's nervous," said Tarpin. "It bothers her getting asked all kinds of questions."

"What questions? You got questions, ask me," said Bunting.

"Oh. I don't know if you'd be able to answer," said Tarpin. "We were talking about— When was it, Linda? maybe half a year ago? You weren't even around then, Bunting. Where were you half a year ago?"

"I don't think," said Morgan, "you should keep at Linda like that. Maybe half a year is half a year ago to you, Tarpin, but maybe for Linda it isn't over yet. So maybe..."

"Whyn't you let her talk?" said Tarpin.

"That's enough." Bunting stepped forward. "I'm taking you home, Linda."

At first nobody said anything and Linda just got up, let Bunting take her arm and lead her to the door.

"Where you living?" said Tarpin.

"The other end of town. Nighty Night Nook, or some crap like that—"

"You can take the place next to ours," said Tarpin.

"Fine. Tomorrow—"

"Much better that way," Tarpin interrupted as if Bunting hadn't said a thing. "More convenient. Morgan."

"Yes," said Morgan and got up.

"Run down to that Night Nook or whatever the place is called and pick up their things. Save you a trip," he said to Linda. "You look beat. And so do you."

Morgan was at the door, holding his hand out to Bunting. Bunting gave him the key. He didn't want the evening to last any longer. It was a cold group in the room, there was some kind of disgruntled attitude in the behavior, and Linda, Bunting could see, would not be good for much longer. He sat down on the couch and sat next to her. There was another drink for all of them, a few flat phrases back and forth, then Kuntz left to go to bed, Tarpin read his paper, and Jesse cursed in the other room about something that had to do with a sport shirt or a necktie or both.

Bunting and Linda sat it out, sitting next to each other without ever touching. But Bunting, perhaps for the first time, was very much aware of the girl. She seemed restless, though she hardly moved, and instead of her dull indifference she seemed on the alert for any next thing that might irritate her. Her face was tight and she was biting her lip a lot.

Finally Morgan came back and waved at them from the door. When Bunting and Linda went out nobody said good night.

"I hope I packed things okay for you, Linda," he said. "I just..."

"Fine, Morgan. I'm sure it's all right. Thank you. I'm glad..."

"Right here," said Morgan and showed them the small efficiency they were going to have.

Bunting noticed that Linda had not liked being interrupted.

"You go in and I'll set the bags right here by the door," said Morgan.

He was already on his way to the car but Linda had started talking again and it seemed she didn't want to stop. She said, "Thank you, Morgan, that'll be fine. Don't really have to bother, if you don't want to, because John and I, I mean John or I, we can easily..."

"He can't hear you, Linda. He's in the car. His head is in the car."

"Oh, yes. All right. Oh. The bedroom. Twin beds, this time. Actually, you know, twin beds are supposed to be much better for persons when..."

"I'll get the bags," said Bunting.

When he came back she was getting undressed. She watched him put the bags down and kept undressing with quick little movements. "If you'll open that bag and just throw me the little plaid pouch in there with all my things for the bathroom, and that calico there, that's a nightshirt—actual-

ly very hot, you notice, very hot tonight. I keep forgetting we're in Florida after all that snow up there. Would you just give me— Thank you. Oh,
here, help me unhook this, please. Do you mind? I just as soon sleep this
way, with nothing, because the heat—" Then she laughed, remembering
something. "Remember in my room, in Joyce's room? Drunken rape, was-
n't it? I hardly remember. But I had clothes on at the time and you've never
really seen me naked, have you? Here I'm supposed to be... "

"Linda," said Bunting, "you're not supposed to be anything now," and
walked to the bathroom.

"But you said before, you said this morning again, about the reason—"

He pushed the door shut slowly and then turned on the tap. Linda was
still talking, she had to keep talking, but he could not hear what she said.
He washed his face violently and his body, feeling somehow that his own
effort and the shock of the water on himself would interrupt and stop
whatever went on.

After he had toweled his head and turned off the water it was very quiet.
He went into the room with the two beds and Linda sat there, on her bed.
She had stopped talking. He walked by, hardly seeing her. He did not see
that her body was beautiful, that her skin had healthy highlights because
it was young, or that her face was tired. He saw a naked woman sitting on
the bed, one of her feet making small, mechanical pushes at a fold in the
sheet.

"I'm going to turn off the light," he said.

"Good night," she said.

The room was very dark and after the bed noises stopped Bunting lay
still and wondered for a moment whether Linda was still sitting there or
whether she had lain down too. He heard nothing and closed his eyes. He
felt aware of his bones and wanted to sleep very much. But an active jum-
ble of images kept his closed eyes awake and after a while he saw the main
thing. There was Tarpin, and Kuntz, and Morgan, and Jesse. He saw their
faces and felt their moods, the way he had seen them till a short while ago,
and one of them, Bunting knew, was his. He watched all of them, kept the
images going, hunting for the right feel and the right focus.

Suddenly his attention shifted. Linda, he saw in the dark, was still sitting,
crouched now, and the sound he had heard was from her. It was harsh
breathing cut off at the end so that Bunting did not know she was crying
until he himself had sat up and leaned closer.

"Linda?" he said.

She didn't answer and the rhythm he heard didn't change. He got up, his only impression that of a woman there in the dark, trying to cry.

"Linda," he said again and put out his hand. Her back was smooth under his hand and for a moment he had an image of cold silk. He sat down next to her on the bed and gave a small pat to her back. "Linda," he said, "what is it—" and when she did not seem to respond, "—why, why this?"

The spasm in her throat was painful and all Bunting could understand was, "—I have to— I have to—" until finally she found a deep breath. "I have to do *something,*" she broke out and then started crying hard.

Bunting held his arm on her back and let her lean into him. He started to say, "Now, now—" and when he heard how soft the word sounded he kept saying it to her over and over."

When she stopped crying, she felt warm and limp.

"I'm tired," she said. "Will you lay me down, John?"

He did this gently. He moved her hair out of her face and spread it on the pillow. He covered her with the blanket so that there would be no folds or holes to let in cold air. He said good night, moving his hand away.

Before he fell asleep he thought that he had understood her quite well, because he once had walked away from the morgue, crying and shaking, and walking like that all night.

He was wrong, though. He did not really know how Linda felt, didn't know that she wasn't crying because Tom was dead half a year. Her dullness was no longer protecting her, and that's when she had noticed that even her mourning was no longer real. That shock made her cry because she was now left with nothing.

Chapter 13

When Linda woke up she stretched and rubbed her back on the sheet under her. She felt the heat of friction on her skin. The frosted windows kept the light bland, giving her no idea of the time, but she felt awake. She wanted to get up right away and turned toward Bunting's bed. But that was no test, because Bunting had left an hour ago.

They sat on the plastic furniture and, though it was daylight now, the room looked exactly the same as the night before, with the same air of nobody living there, and the same blind windows. And the men were the same as Bunting remembered them. Tarpin sullen but always alert enough to show unexpected suspicion; Jesse with an edgy temperament, which he mostly handled by making sharp and irrelevant comments; Morgan, who always smiled first, either because he was slow and needed time, or because he wished somebody would smile back; and Kuntz, to whom everything seemed to be trouble and who mostly looked scared.

They sat around in a circle and it seemed to be hard for them to talk to the point. They ate sandwiches from the corner store and sharp coffee in paper cups.

"If Miami doesn't call back," Tarpin said, "that means a few days extra before we get the supplies. That's all it means."

"Means no supplies from that outfit," said Jesse. "Just means we scrounge some place else."

"You can't take it?" said Tarpin. "You can't stand it somebody says no?"

"To me," said Kuntz, "he's got a point. To me it looks like nothing but troubles and they don't want any part of us, Tarpin."

"Maybe we ought to..."

"Don't think," said Tarpin. "I got the money to hold out and I got the money to buy supplies anywhere."

"When you say supplies," said Bunting, "you mean you're going to build pinballs from the ground up?"

"He means he'd like to know what else he can do," said Jesse.

"You mean you don't save by buying pre-assemblies, like the whole cabinet, the board, the pegs, separately, maybe, and then you just..."

"Where you gonna get that?" said Kuntz. "Musical Co. won't sell to us—"

"Crap." Tarpin put his paper cup down and said it again. "The first touch of winter and you crawl in a hole. I want you guys to get used to the fact this here is now an independent operation. No more Daddy Saltenberg and right away nothing but cold feet. This takes waiting and it takes finagling. You have an idea..."

"I'm getting one," said Jesse. "It smells like..."

"Exactly what I been saying," Kuntz started, but then there was an argument, a petty thing, like chickens bickering over a bug that had scuttled off anyway, while Bunting sat there and slowly got a new picture. He didn't want to believe it at first but it got worse and his anxiety grew.

"...settle this whole thing with a clean sweep," Jesse was saying.

"I'm getting this new, this repulsive angle on you guys," said Tarpin.

"Face it!" Kuntz suddenly yelled. "We can't make it. Why don't you face it." His own voice disturbed him and he quickly looked from one to the other.

"You mean drop the whole thing?" said Morgan. "Look, Tarpin, they saying we should drop..."

"What do you mean we?" Tarpin cut him off. "All these turds think of is which way to run."

"Tarpin," said Morgan. "Just in case you want to know, you and me—" He didn't know how to put it and smiled. He nodded, hoping it would give his loyalty emphasis.

"Don't gimme that act," said Jesse. "Don't act the sidekick."

Tarpin himself didn't give Morgan any more satisfaction either. "Just shut up and sit down," he said.

Kuntz, having been the one who had brought the point out, felt conspicuous and ill at ease. He said, "Look at it this way. All I meant was, why butt into a wall. We got Saltenberg to buck and we got Eckstein to buck, maybe, and if not now, then sooner or later. Look at it this way," he started to plead, "there's a million other things. There's casinos we can get into, there's horses and dogs, there's always the numbers. We can even..."

"I don't like any of those. I like a racket that's got a future but not much of a past." Jesse stopped there because he liked the sound of that sentence.

Tarpin got up and they all watched while he stood for a moment before he opened his mouth. "For that I need you guys?" he said very evenly. "For that I need a bunch of drifty bums like you?"

"Maybe you got something there, Tarpin. Now, I'm Just thinking *maybe,* Tarpin." Kuntz didn't look at anybody. "But maybe, each of us looking around for a while, you know, feeling our own way—"

He let it hang, hoping nobody would make anything bad of it, hoping he hadn't gone too far this time. But there was no comment. Everybody had thought the same thing.

Bunting felt his voice shake before he even said anything, but he didn't care. He talked very loud. "You mean split up?"

They still said nothing, each for his own reasons, so that Bunting was sure. He was now more upset, more afraid, than any of them, because he had the strongest reason of all to keep them together.

"You can't do it!" he said.

"We're just talking this thing around," Tarpin said. "And whatever we can and can't do..."

"You haven't even got enough details to decide this thing one way or the other!"

"But you have," said Jesse, "is that it?"

"Why don't you shut up a minute and look at this thing like a business, not like a jump in the dark. All that throws you is what? The market? Distribution? Supplies? I don't know a thing about any of that except I know about some of the supplies that go into one of those machines. Are you thinking of building your own?"

They all looked at Tarpin. "Maybe," he said.

"Maybe what? Maybe yes? And if so, why? You..."

"Where do you come off, Bunting? How come..."

"You got me to be your man who knows about the machines and I'm working at it. You gonna build your own?"

"No. I don't have the shop for it. And to get a shop together..."

"And to buy outright is no good either because you would have to ship too far or something like that?"

"The real thing here," Kuntz started but Tarpin waved him off. "You got nothing new, Bunting, nothing new. The best way is buy parts and put them together and that's what got us stalled. They're too high or we can't get them."

"Look here," said Jesse, "who is this guy telling us to stick around on a sour deal. Who?"

Bunting had the answer. He carried it with him inside and it started to happen the way Saltenberg said. Bunting started to set, like cement. He stuck with his main intent, badgered them, questioned them, gave answers that sounded convincing, kept at it with the kind of conviction that an upcoming businessmen might have about a young venture. It almost sounded like that and it convinced Tarpin, at any rate. The rest went along. Kuntz because he was afraid to say any more, Jesse because he didn't want to lose out just in case, and Morgan stuck by because he actually had no ideas of his own.

"You give me the authority, the way I explained," Bunting finished up, "and I'll get you the electrical stuff that goes into the machine for half of what you figured on. That way you can afford to pay for the rest easy, buying from anyone. And I'll set you up an assembly system where all the wiring can be done by you, in your own shop, and for less than buying the board all wired, or buying the machine knocked down, or any old way there is." He took a breath and looked around. "That's what I'm here for. And that's how this thing can be licked."

It would take, Tarpin knew, just one trip to Miami to see if it would work; Bunting could make one trip to Miami to show what he could buy and how good his contacts in purchasing were.

"Go ahead," Tarpin said. "I'll expect you back by late tomorrow."

"Maybe sooner," said Bunting.

"And Morgan is going along," said Tarpin.

Morgan got up, and when Bunting looked at him Morgan just shrugged and tried to smile. Then the two men left.

The highway followed the side of the lake curving east and the sun glared into the car. Bunting drove and Morgan sat next to him. Morgan sat with his back to the door, arms folded and the hat pulled down against the low rising sun. The air in the car was not very hot yet but the sun had a contact heat that made the men's skin feel hot and dry. They drove and nobody talked.

The lake shimmered like oil and the swamp growth looked black in the sun.

"You should have sunglasses," Morgan said.

Bunting just nodded, didn't take his eyes off the road. His face was creased from the effort to keep his eyes as slitted as possible and he felt an ache in his jaw. His face, he thought, must look almost as if he were grinning, or as if he were gnashing his teeth. But he just sat there with his face stiff and the excitement going out of him slowly. It was all right. It felt fine to make everything hard, keep everything clear.

Tarpin's bunch, Bunting knew, didn't want to hold together. They might hold for a while but not for long. Bunting would have to hold them together, the way he had managed that morning, until he had found his man. He would have to go faster than he had thought. He would do exactly what was required even if it meant he would have to do things which he had never done before.

"You sore at me, John?"

Bunting looked at Morgan and just barely shook his head. Either Morgan hadn't seen it or it hadn't been enough.

"You know, me coming along the way Tarpin wanted—"

"Not your fault he's a suspicious bastard."

"That's right," said Morgan. "I was hoping you'd feel that way."

Bunting didn't see the lake any more. They were going through the flattest, the most naked-looking expanse of land he had ever seen. Thin pines stood alone here and there, and there were occasional low mangrove tangles. A few times Bunting caught the glint of dead swamp water in the brown landscape.

"You do feel that way, don't you, John?"

Bunting couldn't ignore the tone. Morgan, gunman with the look of baby fat in his body, was talking like any human being, not at all like one of Bunting's targets.

"Sure, sure, Morgan—"

"I had—" he laughed— "I don't know why, but I had an idea you might be that way. You know what I mean?"

"You did? How come, Morgan?"

Morgan sighed and shifted the holster under his arm. He did it the same way somebody else might adjust a tie, and then said, "I just gotta feel that way when I see—when like you—you know Linda, of course, and she—" He lost his sentence and covered up with a laugh. But then suddenly he said, "I just got to feel that sometimes. To know that somebody is nice." And then he waited, hoping that Bunting would understand and that it hadn't been something too weak.

When Bunting got it he finally nodded. He didn't talk yet. One of the maybe killers had said that he sometimes has to feel people are nice, so that he too could sometimes feel that way—

Bunting remembered that nothing like that should impress him.

"Why pick on me?" he said. "How about Tarpin? You know him better."

"Yeah— He's fine, you know? He's always hard, and not even trying," but there was no admiration in Morgan's voice. Then he changed and said, "But when I seen you with Lindy—I mean Linda. I guess you call her Linda, don't you?... Uh, anyway, anybody with her is all right in my book, you know what I mean? When she was married to Tom, same thing. He was—he was nice, that's all." Morgan finished by laughing again, a little bit hesitantly.

"I never knew him," said Bunting, almost to himself, and then they drove for a while without talking.

The mangroves moved in from both sides, and there now was a drainage canal that ran next to the road. The water was black glass and mangrove roots dipped into it like old curved fingers.

"If you see a log there," said Morgan, "you know, a log half in the water and it looks like a gator— That'll be a gator." He waited for Bunting but then he laughed about it by himself.

The road was the straightest Bunting had ever seen. It looked like a smooth groove wiped through the tangle that showed on both sides. The sight tired him, the stillness inside and out tired him, made him feel dull the way Linda felt. Next to him was the man, the gunman whose favorite word and favorite wish was *nice*—

Bunting stopped thinking about that because he had to find out.

"None of you guys," said Bunting, "look very happy." He kept his face front. "But that Kuntz, he's more nervous than any of you."

"Oh, yeah. That little guy. He's that way most of the time, you know?"

"No. I didn't. All the time, you said?"

"Well, you know—an expression." Morgan shrugged.

"Especially lately, I guess. All this pressure."

"Yeah, you know—" Morgan took out some gum, started chewing it.

"When did it start, when you left that town up North?"

"What start?"

"Kuntz being so nervous. When did it start?" Bunting kept right on talking, not daring to change his tone of voice, not daring to stop. "I thought, maybe, seeing the way he is like that anyway, a thing like that Truesdell Square business could really rock a guy."

"Truesdell Square?... Oh, Truesdell Square! Where we tried heisting the books." Morgan nodded to himself. "We sure flubbed that one."

"Hmm?"

"Flubbed that one, I said. Didn't get the books at all."

Bunting had started to sweat. He wiped the wetness on his face.

"And the killing—don't forget." It was like a low-tone afterthought.

"Christ, yes. Was a girl, wasn't it?"

"It was a girl," said Bunting.

The sun had climbed, or the direction had changed enough, so that Bunting's face was now in shadow. But he kept his eyes squeezed like before. "She got killed."

"I know," said Morgan. "I know that." He turned to Bunting. "I was there, you know."

"Oh ?"

"Yes. We all were." Then he sat up and pointed. "See that place? How about stopping. You been making good time."

"I think we better..."

"Looks like they should have something cool. Root beer, even. You ever notice they don't have root beer down in these parts like they do up North? Not as much, I mean, you know?"

"I hadn't noticed."

"I have. Hey, slow down—"

Bunting slowed and stopped at the roadside place, to Morgan, afraid to ask any more.

They sat down at the counter and both had root beer because Morgan wanted Bunting to try it, and Bunting drank the sweet stuff because he didn't know what to say next, how to go on.

They got back into the car and Bunting drove. He was so preoccupied with his effort to think of a new opening that he didn't hear all that Morgan said.

"...who got that girl," Morgan was saying.

"What you say? What was that?"

"I said, do you know who got that girl?" Morgan waited. "I mean is, did the papers ever say who it was? We left right away, you know."

Either Morgan didn't know, or Morgan wanted to know whether anyone else knew the killer.

"You need the paper to tell you?" said Bunting.

Morgan, when he heard that, had to laugh.

Bunting, without being aware of it, drove more and more slowly. He held the wheel like before, very hard, but he was barely paying attention.

"You know, I'm laughing," said Morgan, "because that's funny, you know?... You don't see it? Funny because I was right there and I'm asking to see the paper to find out what went on."

"You mean you don't know?" Bunting felt he was working for breath and that his breathing made a great deal of noise.

And when Morgan talked again his voice had changed completely. There was no laughter, just a low voice. "I feel like telling you this, John. You're with Lindy, and you're the kind I can tell this." He hesitated and kept looking out of the window. "You know, John, I'm sorry that happened."

This was so honest that it was hard for Bunting to keep on thinking the way he had to think. It was either that honest, or it was sicker than anything Bunting had seen, because to talk about being sorry the way Morgan had, and to act so bland, as Morgan acted, was the sickest: *if* Morgan had killed her.

"You're crawling," said Morgan. "You want to stop for something?"

Bunting speeded up immediately and said without waiting, "Kuntz kill her?"

"What?"

"You kill her, Morgan?"

Bunting had to turn his head, he had to then. He had to see Morgan.

He was throwing his gum out of the window and when he turned back he gave Bunting just one, brief look. He said, "You oughtn't to ask that, John. That good I don't know you."

"You said you were sorry," Bunting pressed. "You said that!"

"I know. I oughtn't to have." He folded his arms and leaned back to rest.

Chapter 14

First stop in Miami was a bar near the Greyhound station. The hot air
of the city sat wedged in the narrow street, and the bar had nothing but
one big-bladed fan to swish the air around a little. It was hot, but it was-
n't vacation weather. The sun shone, but it looked dusty coming into the
windows. There wasn't a palm tree in sight to make all of this tropical. It
was just hot.

"Two beers," said Bunting.

"Two beers?" said the bartender. "How about..."

"Two beers."

"All right," said the bartender and put two bottles and glasses on top of
the bar.

He got embarrassed and talked a lot when Morgan reminded him that
he hadn't uncapped the bottles. Bunting, in the meantime, had gone to the
telephone booth, and since the directory was secured by a short chain he
had to sit in the close cubicle while he copied names and addresses out of
the yellow pages.

"All this in one day?" said Morgan when he saw the list.

Bunting drank half of a glass of beer before he answered. "Maybe not.
Maybe I'll be lucky enough to find a good source after the first three or four."

"Three or four? Why don't you go to the first wholesaler in the list..."

"Because I want the lowest price. I've got to shop." They drank beer for
a while and then Morgan ordered another round.

"Don't," said Bunting. "There isn't time. But if you want to sit I can pick
you up later..."

"Don't tempt me," said Morgan, and got off the stool.

They got a city map at the Greyhound station and for the first stop
picked the address which looked the closest and the least complicated.
They had to take a half-hour trip down Biscayne Boulevard, cut off to the
right down the Venician Way and into Miami Beach. The address looked
improbable. Between stucco hotels and fancy delicatessens they found the
small store with the sign *Entertainment Machines.* Bunting went inside the
place because he could see the jukeboxes and pinball machines standing
around.

"You're interested in pinballs?" said the man when Bunting had managed
to get him away from his ledgers. "What outfit?"

"Outfit?" said Bunting. "What do you mean by outfit?" He tried to sound polite.

"Outfit! What hotel? What bar? Who wants the rental?"

"Wrong place," said Morgan, and tapped Bunting's arm so he shouldn't waste any more time.

But Bunting stayed. "I think," he said to the rental man, "I may have come to the wrong enterprise. I wasn't going to rent a machine. I was going to order several, buy them outright."

"Wrong enterprise," said the man. "Try Royal Distributing." He started to go back to his ledgers, but then decided against it. "Uh— You opening up in this town?"

"Opening up?" said Bunting.

"You gonna rent out machines in this town?"

Bunting smiled, making it look as benign as he could, and said, "No. I'm not competition." And then, "Royal Distributing, do you buy from them?"

"That's right." The man looked much relieved, but still cautious. "You gonna buy outright and operate them? That's hardly done, you know. That's only in special circumstances." Then he waited for Bunting to explain himself.

But Bunting explained very little. He asked where the Royal outfit got their machines and found out that they were jobbers for some northern concern. Bunting could guess who the northern concern was. He found out there were only two companies in town which might furnish parts for repair and maybe assemble knocked-down machines; there was no manufacturing outfit that the rental man had ever heard of. "Up North," he kept saying. "All from up North. For all I know, every company I just mentioned belongs to the same outfit up North."

This, Bunting knew from Tarpin, was not strictly true, though who knows what the personal tie-ins might be.

Morgan and Bunting left, and drove to the Royal Distributing Co. It took an hour, going inland, and when they got there it took five minutes to find out there was nothing for Tarpin. Royal only sold to licensed distributors, licensed to make rentals.

There were two other jobbers, and one of them sold only the amusement pinball, while the other sold also gaming machines. Bunting got a commitment for the sale of one each without any trouble because he had mentioned Tarpin. Not that Bunting knew this, but on instructions from Saltenberg, the name Tarpin made the sale a foregone conclusion.

"Next, the Craft Supply Company," said Bunting, and got into the car.
"The knocked-down outfit? The guy that assembles them?" said Morgan. "John, in this heat..."

"That's business."

"Exhaust yourself and that's business," Morgan complained. "You coulda bought more than one machine each at the other..."

"We give them a profit, we lose a profit," said Bunting and drove.

"In this heat——"

It was true that Craft Supply sold all kinds of craft supplies. They sold model sets, balsa wood, plastics, and metals, and after Bunting mentioned Tarpin as a potential buyer of all manner of pre-assembly products in the amusement line, after that Craft Supply also sold pinball machines.

"I was hoping you did," said Bunting as he followed the owner into a long shop. "I'm sure we could use several parts of a machine like that for various purposes."

The owner kept nodding and leading the way to the unassembled units.

"For example, I don't know if you ever thought of this, but we have a project in mind, using the pins—I think that's what you call them—for a shuffleboard type of game; these light, hollow pins can be propelled across a board by applying a puff of air. If I don't make myself clear..."

"I get it, I get it," said the owner.

Keeping it up that way for about an hour, and showing much lay interest, Bunting got a long look at some wiring diagrams, at exploded diagrams of the electrical units which determine odds, and when the owner left for a while Bunting took notes. He even got caught up in the task enough to feel as if he were back on a job, perhaps a little elementary for his kind of training, but still his kind of work. Then he got prices for boards, glass panels, pins, cabinets. He made no mention of wired boards, but took time to talk some more gobbledegook about unique applications for some of these units.

He needn't have bothered. The owner knew about Tarpin.

They drove off and then Morgan saw how Bunting was checking addresses again.

"Don't tell me!" he said, "Don't tell me there's more!"

"A plastics place to make the pins—maybe two plastics places and an electrical jobber."

Morgan groaned.

"I'm going to lay out a wiring plan that any idiot can assemble. That's how we cut costs."

"We," Morgan kept mumbling. "We— I don't know from nothing about this. But the heat—"

The whole trip, and the business, had been a brief distraction which dropped away as soon as Bunting drove out of the city. It angered him that he had been distracted at all and the weight of his real business came back to him with renewed pressure. And he still didn't know what to think about Morgan.

Because he was driving west on the way back, Bunting had the sun in front of him, just as in the morning. The light was dark gold and very hot, hurting the eyes more with heat than with glare. Bunting could see very little. Morgan, because of his size, seemed to be suffering.

"Take your jacket off, why don't you," said Bunting.

"I'm wearing a holster," said Morgan. "I don't think I should."

"Still think you might have to shoot me?"

"John!" said Morgan, sounding hurt. "You oughtn't to say that."

"Why in hell not? You squeamish?"

Morgan tried laughing, tried sitting it out without saying anything, but none of it stopped his embarrassment. In the end he said, "I told you... I like you—"

The more time he spent with any one person, Bunting decided, the more that happened, the harder it was to go just by principle. Even a slug like Morgan could become very complicated. Not complicated like a machine, which has maybe millions of parts, because all the parts are something fixed and each one can be handled apart from the rest; but complex like a human being, whose parts slide in and out of focus. There was Morgan the hood. And Morgan the sly sidekick of Tarpin. And Morgan, embarrassed in his liking for Linda. No stereotype worked.

"I'm outa gum," said Morgan. "Maybe the next likely place..."

"Yeah. And root beer."

"You making fun of me?" Morgan looked very blank; his very blue eyes with the black dots in the middle were holding still.

"I wouldn't do that, Morgan. You know that."

Then Morgan smiled, and nodded, because he was glad he could go on thinking Bunting was nice.

"I'll tell you something else," he said later, "now us knowing each other a little better."

"You keep saying something like that," Bunting said when Morgan paused, "you must know those other guys much better, know 'em for years."

"They're all the same," said Morgan. "Like I was going to say—just
going to point out, mind you—maybe in a while, with some loot, you
know, maybe splitting outa there wouldn't be bad. You know?"

This time, Bunting felt how his back went stiff, like a stick. This time,
he thought, an entirely new Morgan was there.

"Meaning what?" he said with as little inflection as possible.

Morgan leaned closer, as if they could be overheard. He said, "You know
good as I do, John, something ain't right with this caper. You know something is sour. Don't you?"

"I—I don't know yet."

"I do. So do you." Morgan kept leaning and Bunting could see the man's
skin was suffering from heat. "But mostly, John, this is a life for Lindy? For
you and Lindy? Then he sat up again and took a deep breath. "It's my feeling, John, that's all—"

The man, Bunting saw, thought more about the girl Linda than he himself did. And when Bunting considered her now, after the few days he had
known her and after last night, there was a disturbing shifting of what he
saw—

Bunting caught his sleeve on the gearshift and yanked his arm free with
sudden violence. Then he started to curse in a low, steady voice, ranting
the vilest and the most obscene things he could think of. When he was
through he felt more the way he wanted to feel. He lit a cigarette and did-
n't say anything else.

"Jesus," said Morgan, "I never knowed half of the things..."

"Shut up, just shut up!"

They said little for the rest of the ride and by the time it was dark and
Bunting had rolled into the motel, he thought he was all right again.
Everything looked cold as stone to him and he felt just as hard.

"Tell him I'll be right in." Then he walked over to the place where he and
Linda lived.

He smelled coffee. Linda got up from the couch and smiled almost as
soon as she saw him. "John—" she said, but stopped when she saw his
face.

"I'm going to wash up," he said. "Stinking, lousy drive—" He went into
the bathroom.

She stood in the door and said, "Would you like some coffee? Tarpin said
you might be back around this time and I made..."

"Just get me a shirt. In my grip."

"I know where," she said. "I unpacked for you."

Then she brought him the shirt and stood in the door again. "If you haven't eaten yet—

"I'm not hungry."

"Oh. You'll be hungry later, though. I can have something ready."

He threw the towel on the ground, took the shirt out of her hand, and said, "You remember, don't you, I'm here on business. Right? You remember. So I haven't got time for any other plans. Pardon me," he said and went past her and out of the house.

It was bad in Tarpin's place. It was the same as before, except worse, much more tense. Jesse stood by the wall, cleaning his nails. He didn't move when Bunting came in, just looked up and winked. Then he looked down at his nails again. "Very, very nice you are back," he said. "Good news might soothe all of us." He looked up, smiling politely. "You got good news?"

"Bunting?" Tarpin yelled from the other room. Then he came out. "You got to go and kiss the bride while I'm waiting here for you to come back?"

"What in hell is the matter with you?" said Bunting.

Kuntz came in too. He looked worn out and had a dead cigarette in his mouth. He didn't come all the way in until Tarpin yelled at him. "Sit down and shut up yammering. Bunting's gonna give us his news."

Tarpin sat down himself. The springs in the cheap plastic coach twanged. "The way a little tiny sonofabitch can get under your skin," he said to nobody.

"What's going on?" said Bunting.

"Kuntz here," said Jesse, "is a little tiny sonofabitch what keeps yammering this caper's no good. All day long. And even though me and Tarpin here is strong, silent types..."

"Shut up your mouth, Jesse, because I've had all the garbage today I can stand," said Tarpin. "All right, Bunting, talk."

"Morgan?" Jesse called. "We got a conference."

They heard the bed in the next room and then Morgan, "I'm lying down. I thought..."

"Don't think, don't move, just stay there!" yelled Tarpin. He took a deep breath. "Come on, Bunting. What you find out?"

Bunting told him. He explained about prices, deliveries, how he got this cheaper and something else not as easily, how they could set up their assembly operation in little more than a week, and that he wished the problem of distribution—about which he knew nothing and which was strictly Tarpin's department—should only go as well as the manufacturing....

"Yeah," said Tarpin. "Yeah, yeah... Ever deal with Musical Co before?"

"No—I mean, maybe through Eckstein, but not me, not personally."

"But they know you—"

"I don't know. Why?"

"I just wondered. They wouldn't sell me but they sold you."

Bunting, as suspicious as Tarpin now, blew up. "Anything worrying you about that? Anything hard to understand about me knowing my business? Maybe you walked in there with that sour face and rubbed them the wrong way just because of the manner you got, and when I walked in there..."

"You don't like me to ask you?" said Tarpin.

"Ask yourself dizzy for all I care," and then, keeping in mind why he was here and that his first business now was to keep these men together, he said, "and when you're through asking maybe you got enough time left, enough sense left in your head to see that you got setup now, that you got all you can ask for because you're ready to roll! Why don't you think of that? Why don't any of you guys ever say one single thing that can start this job of yours rolling instead of jumping when somebody clicks on the light or..."

"Because that's the kind of business it is!" Kuntz cut in. "And I been in long enough to smell..."

"No question," said Jesse. "No question about that!"

"Nobody's got the jitters," said Tarpin. "Except maybe Kuntz here. And you, Bunting, better get used to answering me and not arguing, and everything will go fine."

"Fine," said Bunting. "Fine. So are we going to order?"

"We're going to order," said Tarpin.

It meant two different things to Bunting and Kuntz. It meant breathing space for Bunting, time to look these four possibilities over, and it meant just the opposite to the other man. It meant terrible pressure for Kuntz.

"You mean you're going ahead?" he said to Tarpin. "Here I been talking myself ragged all day and all this guy Bunting here has to do is come in with some figures showing how cheap he can buy wires or something and that settles everything?"

"I heard you, I heard you!" Tarpin got up, went to the kitchen and turned on the hot water. "All day you been hacking about this and now shut up!"

For a moment Kuntz just stood there and watched Tarpin put coffee powder into a cup and then run hot tap water over it. When he started to talk again Kuntz didn't feel his voice was his own. "But you never paid any attention! You're going ahead!"

"I got the figures from Bunting. That's all I want right this minute!" Tarpin came back, stirring the brown liquid in his cup, cursing when it slopped over his hand. "We're now gonna sit down and draw up these orders."

"Now wait a minute, Tarpin—"

"You gonna sit down and help? Or what?"

"I'm telling you it's wrong!" Kuntz's voice caught and he had to cough, but then he went on fast and anxious. "We got nothing planned. We got nothing but hopes, some dough, and pressure behind us."

"You ever live any other way, for chrissakes?"

"I try. I'm trying! At least we got to have some kind of commitments from the guys we're gonna deal with. We got nothing. We don't know if Saltenberg isn't going to move in where we want to sell— You haven't even tried to find out!"

"I don't have to, damnit! I got enough standing..."

"And you haven't even set up anything here! No work place, no shipping plans, nothing; but you go right ahead..."

Tarpin banged his cup down, not caring where he slopped the tepid coffee. "I'm sick of listening! I'm sick of this cautious crap and nothing done!"

"You think you got the answers, not looking at them? You think..."

"No, I don't. There's no such thing as all the answers. You gonna get that through your head?"

"How can you run things this way? Please, Tarpin, listen to me once. You think I like being nervous? You think—"

He stopped when Morgan came into the room, standing there in the door, his face sleepy. Tarpin said, "Yes, I think maybe you do, Kuntz. And it's sickening."

"Whose grip?" said Morgan. "There's a grip all packed here in the hall." They all looked from one to the other, except Kuntz. "How come, Kuntz?" said Tarpin.

Kuntz didn't know how to explain. He thought he had said everything. "How come the grip's all packed, Kuntz?"

"He's leaving," said Jesse, as if he were adding something unknown.

Bunting was holding one hand with the other, feeling the sweat sting out of his palms. Once Kuntz looked in his face, but that could have been chance. Kuntz was looking from one to the other.

"I was thinking of it. Yes, I was thinking of it, if nothing else was gonna make sense."

"You don't," said Tarpin.

"I'm trying, I'm trying!" Then, looking helpless, he suddenly changed and talked fast and disjointed. "I don't know how else I can tell you. I been telling you all afternoon— All right, you don't want to listen." Then his voice stumbled and squealed. "Maybe the stinking sunshine's too much for me— there's supposed to be snow this time of year! That any better for sense? And this, this godawful place— Look at it! You can't look outa the window, like a damn public toilet ! With this floor yet. It's getting so bad I'm looking at those damn, tiny stones in that damn raspberry floor or ter-razberry floor or whatinhell the name of that thing is—looking at the damn stone chips in there and counting 'em! And these godawful ten-watt bulbs, maybe that's the thing drives me crazy. I'm just..."

"You're all nerves," said Jesse.

"I think so," said Tarpin.

"I know damn well I am. I'm used to working where there's some system!"

"No pioneer spirit," said Jesse.

"I think not," said Tarpin.

"You can't take it," said Jesse. "That means you can't give, either."

"I think maybe not. No good at all, helping out around here."

There was silence, with everybody looking at Kuntz in the middle, and then Kuntz shrugged his shoulders and dropped his arms so they made a small clap. He talked low and tired. "So at least we got one agreement. I go."

"I think so."

"I can go right now."

"How about the dough you put into this? You leaving that? All your dough?" Jesse grinned.

"I think maybe he wants to," said Tarpin.

"I hadn't even considered," said Kuntz and went for his grip.

"How much dough you got, Kuntz?" Tarpin wanted to know.

"I got a fifty." He walked to the door.

"Kuntz," said Tarpin. "Here."

Kuntz came back, looking at Tarpin, who had his hand out toward him.

"Here's a C note. Here, take it." Kuntz took it out of Tarpin's hand. "So you can go further without stopping," said Tarpin.

"I know," said Kuntz and went back to the door.

"So I won't run into you anywhere here in this state."

"California," said Kuntz. "Like I once told you."

He had the door open, looked back at all of them, just a short look. "So— I'm off." And then, when nobody said anything, he said, "Okay," and went out of the door.

Chapter 15

The plastic on the couch made a thin, sliding sound when Tarpin shifted, and the other sound was Morgan going back into the bedroom. Nothing else happened. They all heard the car start outside and then the tires making a grinding noise on the gravel. Bunting was the only one showing anything. He still sat holding his hands, not knowing what he could safely do or say without everyone knowing that he was screaming inside. Because one of them was getting away—

"Morgan?" said Tarpin.

"Coming," said Morgan and came back into the room. He was putting his jacket on.

Tarpin nodded toward the door and said, "I want him to go far, Morgan," and Morgan, still working his arm into his jacket, kept right on going toward the door.

"Wait!"

They all looked at Bunting. He had got up and stood in the middle of the room, working his knuckles.

"I'm going after him," said Bunting.

Jesse looked as if he meant to laugh but then he looked down at his nails again and did something with the file.

"Man," said Tarpin. "You sound anxious."

"I want to go after him," Bunting said again. He could think of nothing else.

"Why?"

"I just want to go after him, I just want to go after him—"

Tarpin sat back and, to keep his frown from showing, he rubbed his face. "You take strong dislikes," he said.

"He's getting away—"

"Yeah, you hear it?" said Morgan. "He's out the gate already." He opened the door.

Bunting saw this and went to the door.

"You can go with Morgan," said Tarpin because, looking at Bunting, he did not think he could stop the man or could stop him easily.

Bunting was half out in the open when he turned back to the room. "Morgan can go with me, because I'm going after him." Then he was gone.

He made Morgan drive and they took off fast.

Morgan, from experience, turned right at the motel gate because the other way would take them to town. At the railway depot he turned right again, even though the crossroad was equally good going right or left. Right went toward the highway and left went to town again.

"Faster," said Bunting. "Come on, faster—"

"No point getting picked up." He sighed, guided the car past a rut. "Besides, this way cuts past the Everglades and there's no towns for miles."

As soon as they got on the highway Bunting saw the headlights ahead. He pointed, involuntarily, and sat on the edge of his seat.

"No," said Morgan. "That's a Ford. Kuntz drives a Packard. See the shape of the taillights ?"

"Christ—it's highway patrol!"

"Yeah," said Morgan and kept on driving.

"Don't pass him! The night limit is fifty and he's doing that!"

"John," said Morgan, "you're too strained."

"You listen to what I say or..."

"If I go sixty he'll maybe come alongside and make us stop. Then he'll ask how long we been in the state, seeing we got out-of-state license plate and then he'll explain about the limits here being different for day and for night time. That's all." And when he noticed how Bunting gave a short look at the place where Morgan carried his gun he said. "First of all he'll never notice, and more important I got a permit."

But there was nothing reasonable about Bunting's state, so nothing Morgan said changed anything. Bunting sat tense, with a fine prickle all over his skin, sat like that all the time they were edging up to the Ford when they passed him by, and then while the headlights behind got slowly smaller.

The police car didn't speed up. It turned off on a side-road that went to the lake.

"See?" said Morgan. "Most of those guys aren't really scary. They're human."

After a while Morgan went faster. The lights of the Packard didn't show until Morgan was clocking an even ninety, ten minutes later.

Bunting opened the window and held his head into the edge of the slipstream. It tugged at his hair and slapped his face, but he stayed that way till the wind made his eyes water.

The highway had swung away from the lake and when the tangle receded from the side of the road Bunting saw nothing there in the night. But he could smell the dank air from the swamp—

He turned to Morgan and held out his hand.

"The gun?" said Morgan. But he didn't give it to Bunting. "Just scare him, Tarpin said. You need a gun for that?"

"No," said Bunting. "I won't need a gun for that."

They didn't talk any more until Morgan pulled up close to the Packard in front. Both cars were doing just less than ninety.

"He's slowing," said Morgan. "You got any special way in mind?"

It was Bunting's now. First a simple maneuver to make the man stop, nothing unusual, and then the new thing. Then Bunting's new way with all the old values dead.

"Pull up and stay level. I want him to see me."

"Okay."

"After we stop, you stay in the car. Understand?"

"Sure, John."

"If he runs, or anything, you stay in the car until I come back. Until he and I come back."

"Here we go," said Morgan and the car edged up the length of the Packard.

There was nothing to see. It looked like a slow creep, like when a car edges slowly into a place in the parking lot, except that the wind jammed hard past the window, the tires made a roar, bouncing hard off the opposite car, and everything rushed out of focus except the slow, solid shape of the near car.

Bunting flicked on the dome light and Kuntz looked up. He was going so fast he dared only jerk his head very fast and then looked front again, but he knew. The Packard made a leap of speed, but it only looked like a slow, massive heaving when seen from the other car. Then the Packard slowed down, and this time it looked as if the car suddenly stood still.

"This time," Morgan said, "I think I lean on him a little."

There suddenly seemed to be no space between the two cars at all and Bunting felt himself draw back from the window. He heard a sound, like someone turning over in bed, that he couldn't place, and then the other car rocked wildly. There was space again and Bunting saw that the Packard had a crushed fender.

"He knows now," said Morgan. He went ahead and kept the Packard's light squarely behind him, and that way both cars came to a stop.

"Back up," said Bunting. "He might try..."

"Where's he gonna go? The swamp?"

When Bunting yanked on the door handle he already had heard the other door slam. He saw a flit of black next to the car behind, and then nothing.

"You want me to stay here for sure?" said Morgan.

Bunting was out of the door. For a moment he hesitated, and Morgan, much more used to this sort of thing than Bunting was, said, "He don't have a gun on him. I know." Then Bunting was gone.

Past the lights of the Packard he stopped. All he had heard was the slap of his own shoes on the pavement and the blood thumping inside his head.

Bunting stopped because all around it was amazingly quiet. There was a mess of shadow shapes on both sides of the road and one angular tree that stalked into the sky with black, very sharp lines. But no sound. Bunting stepped on the soft shoulder, and then he heard the scuffle—Kuntz was running.

The further Bunting got away from the cars the less he could see, but he heard the sound better and better, just the feet at first and then the man's breathing. And then it didn't seem quite so dark any more and Kuntz wasn't far now, just a little ahead, a black flitting, the coat he was wearing flapping behind and his head moving as if it might break off or fly off he was flailing so hard to get away.

"Kuntz— Stop!"

The man kept running.

"Just a word!" Bunting called after him, and when Kuntz kept running Bunting decided that was his last try for a simple, normal solution. Ask the man to stop, tell him you want to talk—and it didn't work. Now it would be different.

Bunting saved his breath, ran with a sudden, free anger and reached for the coat. It tore. It made Kuntz stagger and again there was the sound he had made once before, but when the coat slipped off and Bunting got tangled, Kuntz ran free.

Bunting couldn't see the man any more. He heard a dry rattle of sticks and grass to the left, a fast swishing and scraping off to the left where the tangle was.

Bunting left the road. He ran and stopped and ran and stopped because now he could go only by sound. Sometimes Kuntz stopped too; then there was the big silence, maybe the sound of dry grass righting itself, and then a gurgling.

Bunting smelled the warm moistness—

"Listen, Bunting—" It was more breath than words. It was not very far away. "Please, Bunting." And if Kuntz had said anything else Bunting did-n't hear it above the sudden crashing he made, running again.

There were strong branches now that wouldn't bend out of the way, the ground was lumpy, and the warm rot odor more heavy.

Bunting gasped when his foot sunk into wet up to his ankle, but then he heard the scream. Kuntz was screaming and screaming. Bunting heard water, heard Kuntz beating and kicking the water and screaming.

It didn't look quite so bad when Bunting came up to the canal, a small, glistening waterway because the man churning and foaming the water had taken away the look of the water.

Bunting jumped in. The water was up to his knees. He reached Kuntz, grabbed him from behind, and both men struggled to get up on the bank. They even sensed each other's relief at the feel of the ground under them. They staggered together to the level land and then both stopped. They just stood like that for a moment, breathing hard, because they couldn't move. When they heard other things again, it became different. They heard a wild flapping in the tangle nearby, which went away. They heard creaking, which could have been anything. Only then did they realize what was underneath.

The warmth in their shoes and the soft give of the ground. They could now even see the water, like the blink in a black eye—

"God! God!" Kuntz started to scream, and then Bunting clapped his hand over the man's mouth. They both fell and for a while Bunting felt only the panicky squirm of the man under him, and his own hands, like bone claws, holding on to the panic there.

In a while Bunting said, "You hear me, Kuntz ?"

"Please, pl—"

"Shut up!"

He pulled Kuntz up and made him sit. The man's face looked ghoulish with mud.

"Just one question," said Bunting, as even and low as if he were sitting on somebody's couch. "Who shot that girl, Kuntz? You?"

"What—what are you..."

Bunting hit the man in the face. It made mud splash. "Again. Truesdell Square. You were there, in the shooting. Who shot the girl?"

"The girl... who shot the girl— What do you from me, Bunting? What..."

He hit him again.

This time Kuntz stayed doubled over a long time and Bunting could feel the water again, the softness underneath, and his foot, one foot, getting stuck.

He flipped the man's head up and said, "Again."

"Yes," said Kuntz, "yes—" He said that and sat there and did nothing else.

Bunting could now see his own cruelty, and the image of it kept him steady, made him go on without a break. "Truesdell Square. Who shot the girl?"

"I don't know." The man lowered his head, but Bunting hadn't been thinking of hitting him.

"You were there. Who shot her?"

"I don't know—"

"I'm going to hit you again," said Bunting, but the man didn't move or say anything.

Bunting hit him, but not very hard. It was almost nothing.

"Kuntz. I'm going to make it as bad as can be. Better answer me soon. You shot the girl?"

"No. Why would—I mean, how could I..."

Bunting grabbed him and doubled him down and then sat on the man's back, doing all this fast. His hands were on the man's neck, then one hand moved up, cupped the back of the skull and pushed. Bunting did this before thinking or feeling could ruin the act, because nothing must stop him, no old values, no new feelings. There was nothing but this image he had of a hard steel ball, big and hard, which was he and his cruelty—

"Who did it, who did it, who did it," he kept saying. It wasn't a voice at all but a painful rasp, a spikey rasp in his throat, which pleaded and pleaded, "Who did it? Answer, answer!"

Then Bunting stopped. The head under him shot up out of the mud and water. The threshing stopped, but Bunting paid no attention. He had rolled off the man and was on all fours in the mud. The spike in his throat was now a fat lump that choked up into his mouth, killed his breath, and Bunting thought he would die if he couldn't vomit. He retched and gasped, but nothing came up.

In a while it just went away, leaving him feelingless. Bunting thought it was relief.

"Kuntz," he said. "You shot her—"

The man had sat up. He was smoothing his hair back, smoothing and rubbing his hair back with real concern. Then Kuntz stopped and said, "No. No, I didn't."

"Who did?"

"I don't know. I didn't."

Bunting got up and left.

You done?" said Morgan from the car.

"I'm done."

"Christ, you're a mess." Morgan started the motor, maneuvered the car into the other direction, drove off. "You scare him good?"

"Yes."

They drove a while and then Morgan said, "I told you you didn't need no gun. Didn't I?"

"I didn't need one."

"'Course not. He never carries one. Never shot a gun in his life—"

Chapter 16

When Bunting got back to the motel, Linda was asleep on the couch. A shaft of light from the kitchen fell across the floor and over Linda. She had on a terry-cloth robe and her feet were bare. Her slippers were on the floor. Bunting closed the door quietly and crossed the room quietly. He had nothing left in him but a great need to sleep. Everything else was painful to him.

"John?" she said, and sat up on the couch.

He kept walking, and went into the bathroom. He did not want the filthy clothes on him.

"John—" He heard the sound of the couch as she got up. "I had thought you were coming back—" She stood in the bathroom door and her voice trailed off when he saw him. "I kept some things on the stove. I thought—
"

She looked at him and said nothing else. He turned away so she could not see his face. "But you'll have some coffee," she said.

He heard her go away. He was grateful that she did not say any more.

He stripped and left the clothes in a heap on the floor. He washed himself a little and then went to the bedroom where he looked for something to wear in bed. He got a far as finding some shorts and then he quit. He was very tired and saw no sense in looking for anything else. He did not know, for that matter, whether or not he had brought any pajamas.

He had left the light off. She flicked it on when she came in. "John?" she said. "Are you hurt? I should have asked—"

"No. I'm fine. I'm tired." He sat down on his bed and looked at his hands between his knees.

"I didn't make any coffee for you. I thought that was foolish, really." She walked around her bed, sat down opposite him. "You're going to sleep anyway. Here, this is better."

"No, thank you," he said without looking up.

"Hot milk. Didn't you ever take hot milk before going to bed ?"

He remembered having sometime taken hot milk before going to bed. Then he had been sleepy too, but not with this kind of sleepiness.

"You sit so stiffly," she said. "Sure you aren't hurt?"

He took the glass of milk out of her hand, so that he would not have to answer her.

She got up—he could see her walk by, visible only up to the knees—and again went into the kitchen where she turned off the light. He could hear the click, then a click in the bathroom, then she was back. He drank the milk when he heard that, and then he heard the girl close the door. She sat down opposite him, as before, and folded the terry-cloth robe over her legs.

"If you can't drink it," she said, "don't drink it."

How had she known? He was sure it did not show on the outside—that his throat had shut on him and that one more sip would have made a soft, globular thing in his throat, like once before—

"John," she said, "why don't you lie down."

He coughed and sat up. He said, "Yes, I will in just a minute," and stretched so that she would see he felt all the normal urges of being tired and of going to bed. But then he kept sitting. He saw cigarettes on the night stand next to the bed and took one of them. Linda took one.

"John," she said, and then he interrupted her by lighting both their cigarettes. After exhaling, she talked again. He thought her voice was very soft, but perhaps he was half asleep and couldn't hear clearly. She said, "John, the job you found here, isn't it what you wanted?"

He heard himself laugh. "Oh, it's what I wanted."

"Is it a good job?"

"You know jobs."

"Yes." He heard how she exhaled and then saw the blue smoke between their legs. "You say very little," she said. "I'm talking to you so you— I mean, I know you don't like the job, John."

"You know that, huh?"

"It shows."

"How come? You watching me?"

"I am now."

"You're watching me now, all you see is I'm tired."

"I mean, *now*— I mean it differently."

"I don't want to talk," he said.

"All right."

They sat smoking a while, quietly, and then Bunting started to itch. It made him move around and puff on his cigarette unnecessarily. He sighed a few times and started to look all around the room. "You know," he said, "I feel so tired I am a little shaky."

"Yes."

"You ever get that way?"

"I know what you mean."

"It's a feeling of unusual levity." He stopped when he heard his strange choice of words, and looked at her. She was nodding at him, brushing the hair back from her face. It was a fine gesture, he thought. He had noticed her do this once before.

"You're going to burn your fingers on that cigarette," she said.

"Oh yes, oh yes." He looked at the butt and dropped it on the floor. He almost put his bare foot on it, to kill it. "Imagine," he laughed, "this habit is so strong—"

She bent down and picked up the butt, put it out in the ashtray. Then she watched him light another one.

"I'm going to smoke this one and then I'm going to sleep. Lie down and go to sleep, if you want to."

"That's all right, John. I'll sit up with you, if you want."

"Of course, yes. I—oh yes. Did you ever sleep with the light on? What I mean is, fall asleep with the light on?"

"You mean, leave it on?"

"Some people do that, you know. I once knew a person, a roommate— no, this was in the army. Restcamp."

"Oh?"

"I think it had something to do with electricity. He was from a farm, as it turned out, somewhere in—in some state way back, you know, and they didn't have electricity there. Imagine? First electricity he ever saw was in the army. Restcamp, it was."

He sighed. He had stopped smoking, but kept watching the smoke from his cigarette.

Linda got up. She went to the chest of drawers and there she took off her terry-cloth robe. He saw she was naked and he even studied the sheen on her skin. Linda pulled something out of the drawer, then shook it out. She held up the nightshirt, the calico thing—he remembered her mentioning it—and she put it on. He had never seen a woman wear one of those things and he thought it looked fine on Linda, very nice.

Then she came back to the beds. "Here," she said, "I'll put it out," and took the cigarette out of his hand.

"Thank you," he said, "thank you very much."

"Now stand up."

He did and she pulled back the sheet.

"Lie down," she said. "Move over a little, so I can lie with you."

It went through his mind, *thank you, thank you very much,* quite rapidly, over and over. It kept clicking through his mind like the sound of a type-writer, without any emotion.

Then she turned off the light.

"John," she said. "Stretch out, John. Try and let yourself."

It was so black in the room now that a man could make anything he desired out of the darkness. A man could see anything in the darkness and there was nothing to interfere—

"Let yourself lie, John, you're tired. You're so tired." Her arm was under his head and she moved his head so it would rest on her.

"But your eyes are open, John."

It was a fact that a man staring into the dark, staring long enough, would see the actual shape of the things that had to be there—

"You feel so stiff," she said. "Are you cold?"

That was from the water, from that impossible black water. Black water, no matter how lukewarm by temperature reading, was always quite cold. And when it was black enough it looked even stiff—

"John," she said, "John, John," and stroked his head and then his shoulders. His body was shivering.

"You'll be warm," she said. 'And you'll sleep. Here, John, here—"

He felt she was pushing him away, that she was making a terrible agitation in the cold bed, and he kept his eyes open wide, trying to see what was really there, wanting to move and not daring to move because of the feeling inside his body that he might shake very hard.

"Here," she said again, "here—"and she had her nightshirt off now, moved her warm body against him, held him the way she had done before. Her hand was on his shoulder, and he pressed his cheek into her. The ter-rible spike was in his throat, a dry, thorny spike, and he pressed his cheek deeper, so he would feel the softness, and when the sharp cramp in his throat finally gave and exploded, and he felt himself shake like something that didn't belong to him, she held him like that while he cried deep and hard, until he was through and fell asleep.

Chapter 17

She had rolled the jalousies open, and when Bunting woke up he could see the several strips of blue sky. He lay there warm and relaxed and then felt like getting up.

"I hear you," she called from the other room. "Are you going to get up?"

"I'll be right with you!" he called back.

In the bathroom he noticed that his dirty clothes weren't there any more, but he didn't think it would have bothered him one way or the other if they had still been there.

He remembered the night before very well. He remembered both the pain out in the swamp and the comfort with Linda, and he knew that it would take a while longer before he had finished with one or the other of those events. But the cramp inside him was gone. He got into the shower and said to himself, I think I'll live—

He did not once think about the reason for which he was here—

While he shaved he started to wonder what he might say when he saw Linda; that he was grateful, that it was nothing, that he had lost his head, that he hardly remembered—one of those things. It became very complicated after a while and the track of his thinking displeased him.

He decided to let it all go till he saw her, not to plan anything. His anger left him and he finished shaving.

Linda, he could hear, wasn't alone any more. Bunting dressed quickly and then came out.

"... so if you make coffee like that every day this time of the morning, I'll consider making this little visit a habit. You might even— Hi, Bunting," said Jesse. "Didn't wake you, did I, now?"

"No. Morning," said Bunting. He could feel the stiffness coming back. He looked at Linda, smiled quickly and thought there had been something in the glance they exchanged, but he did not feel there was the time to stay with it.

"I am merely here," said Jesse, "to see that you get safely from this idyllic little house to the next idyllic little house. Where Tarpin's been waiting for a couple of hours."

"Oh. What time is it?"

"Nine thirty, going on nine forty-five."

"All right. Tell him I'll be right there. I'll grab a bite and..."

"Uh-uh. Now."

"Here," said Linda. "Drink this coffee, anyway."

Bunting took the cup from her. He didn't like the way Linda had accepted the command, had given him coffee only because Jesse was rushing them, and Tarpin, in the next house, was waiting for him. And he didn't like Jesse sitting there, in the first place, grinning and looking at Linda.

"Aren't you gonna sit down and drink it?" said Jesse. "I'm drinking mine sitting down." The he smiled at Linda and said, "It's so good."

I shouldn't forget, Bunting said to himself, that this bastard, this monkey-mannered bastard may be my man.

Bunting burned his mouth on the coffee and stood there hating Jesse for sitting there and for what he might be—It brought the whole trip back into focus again, all the intent and his purpose, and he even hoped that Jesse was the one. He didn't think any further—just that Jesse was the one.

"Put your cup down and let's go," he said.

"Go ahead," said Jesse. "He's right next door."

"Get out—"

Jesse got up. He looked at Linda and said, "My, he's bad in the morning, isn't he?" and went to the door. He stopped there and waited for Bunting to come a little closer. Then he said, "I'll tell you what, Johnny. Next time I come here, I won't come to see you *atall!*" He laughed hard and got out of the door fast.

There was nothing for Bunting to do. He turned to Linda and gave a small wave with his hand. She waved back, but he had already left.

"Here he is," said Jesse to Tarpin. "He was there all the time." He laughed again and went into the kitchen.

"Sit down," said Tarpin, and Bunting sat down at the table. "Let's get this thing rolling, all right?"

"All right."

There was paper all over the table, with numbers and notes, and there were the catalogues Bunting had brought back from Miami. Tarpin was chewing the filter end of a dead cigarette. "I want this out today. You're supposed to make out these orders."

"I know. I'm sorry. Let's see what you got here."

"You do it. Here's my figures on how many units I want for a starter. Here. See this figure? You spend more than that on the first order, you ain't doing so good. And this one, that's for the first month, *maximum*. After that, we'll see. So start figuring."

"Wait a minute. The way you set up a production like this, the way you start ordering..."

"Do it my way," said Tarpin. "Jesse?"

"Yessir!"

"Cut out that junk," said Tarpin. "Bring me my jacket and let's go." He got up and waited for Jesse.

"Where'll you be if I need you. You know..."

"I'm going out to look at floor space. You don't wait for me. Make this out, take it to the post office, send it registered and come back here and wait for me."

Tarpin and Jesse left.

Bunting started to work with catalogues and order blanks. Once Morgan came in, asked how he was, then went out again. Later, through the rolled-open window, Bunting could see Linda walk by and then drive toward town. Bunting worked fast, without interest, disgusted with all of this because it was nothing but sham and a very complicated means to an end. When he was done he was very hungry. He took the letters and went into town.

The sky wasn't blue any more, but milky, and now had a quality which reminded him of the motel rooms with the frosted glass windows. The motor court was empty, and when Bunting came out to the street he saw it was empty too. It was a preseason emptiness, something useless. Bunting walked down the street toward town and tried not to think of anything. He kept his head down, which kept him from seeing sooner.

"Howdy, howdy, nice day."

There was the old man with the clean suntans and the than felt hat that made Bunting think of the South. He did not remember the man's name, but remembered the rest about him.

Bunting stopped by the entrance post of the trailer park, where the man sat on his tilted chair, and said, "Don't bother waiting around." He felt like adding something else, because he felt edgy, but then let it go.

"Oh, sure, not here. I'll run into you later." And then, loud enough for the street to hear, he said, "I don't think the weather is gonna hold up. G'by now—"

Bunting was already way past him. He had forgotten the man's name and most of all he had forgotten entirely that the man was still here, and would be waiting. It added one more irritation to Bunting's day and this one too, like the others, just kept floating around and didn't get settled.

He just did what was concrete—went to the post office, sent off the orders, went to the restaurant to get something to eat. Maybe later, back at the motel, after having put something inside his stomach, he would suddenly find a clear way to finish—to finish everything.

Now Bunting sat at the counter and stared at the mirror and all the decorations along the back. Every one of the decorations was gratis: each piece of cardboard or plaster advertised something. The restaurant served liquor too, so that added to the decorations along the back side of the counter.

"We haven't got sausage, I just find out, but you can have something else," said the waitress.

"All right, something else then—"

"What?"

"You got ham?"

"Sure we got ham. You want ham?"

"Ham and eggs. Can I have my coffee now?"

"Sure you can have your cof..."

"Then I want it now, please."

She scribbled on her pad while she walked away, past the coffee urn and back into the kitchen.

Bunting took a deep breath and looked at his hands.

"Susie!" somebody yelled from the door and immediately the waitress came back out of the kitchen and grinned at the man coming in. He wore a cabbie's cap, and for the rest was dressed in this and that, all of it cast off. He sat down with a thump and talked with a bellow, platitudes about service with a smile and favorite customer, while the waitress was in stitches all over—the man was so much fun. While this went on she drew a cup of coffee out of the urn and gave it to the man with the taxi hat.

"You want ham and eggs, Paul?" she said. "I got..."

"Waitress."

She looked at Bunting, but didn't come over. "I'm waiting for that coffee."

"Well, just a minute—"

"I've asked you three times. Can you remember?"

She went to the urn and mumbled something that Bunting wasn't supposed to understand, and while at the urn kept giving her friend with the hat significant glances which Bunting was supposed to see clearly. A fine string of insults came to Bunting's mind, but before he opened his mouth he suddenly felt so disgusted with all of it he lowered his head so he wouldn't have to look at the waitress when she gave him his cup. He just saw her hand, the bitten nails and the white skin, which disgusted him too. Then, because there was nothing else he could do, he looked at the decorations in back and studied each one.

A man drinking a Coke and a girl drinking a Coke, and both with a frantic smile saying that this bottle here in their hands was the thing to top off their evening. Nothing else would do it so good and nothing else, so help them, would even occur to them. Then a man with white hair and a frantic smile had just, after all his years of drinking wisely, had just come to the conclusion, so help him, that there just wasn't a whisky he'd rather he seen with. Bunting also looked at the apoplectic red face of a tomato that seemed ready to burst, grinning of course, grinning because that's what tomato soup does.

Bunting sat there and tortured himself, letting each one of the ads offend him, letting each of them jump down his throat.

"Here's your ham and eggs," said the waitress and plunked the plate in front of him so that the egg yolks shivered.

There also were grits on the plate. In these parts, Bunting remembered too late, grits was the unasked-for favor on any dish ordered for breakfast.

"You sure do look hungry!" The man from the trailer park sat down next to Bunting. "Girl," he said to the waitress, "I do believe I'll have just about the same thing, except make mine bacon, not ham." He leaned toward Bunting and said, "I'd rather have sausage, but they make the sausage too greasy here. Ever see how they fry the sausage?"

Bunting, for the sake of appearances, had to keep very still and had to answer. "No," he said. "I have never seen that."

Then he tried to eat. He found that he could put it down without tasting a thing and without even chewing. It made him feel very impersonal.

"Well sir, how you been, Johnny?"

"I got nothing to tell you. Believe me."

The man laughed, kept this up while the waitress put coffee in front of him, and then stopped to take a loud sip. " Good," he said. "Good and hot, anyway."

"I don't even remember your name. So just go."

"Collins." He drank coffee again.

Bunting said nothing. He worked on the last of the stuff on his plate, thinking about the cigarette he would smoke. Right now, eating meant just a step toward having a cigarette.

"You wouldn't even tell me about the orders you sent out this morning?" said Collins.

It gave Bunting a slight surprise, a slight feeling of respect for the man who must be, after all, good at his work. Why else would Saltenberg put him here!

"No trick, Johnny," said Collins. "You had 'em in your hand when you came by a while back. Big address on 'em, and *Attention: Purchasing Dept.* Huh?" He laughed again.

"I'll have another one of your cups of coffee," Bunting said the to the waitress. "I'll have it now."

She left her friend with the taxi cap and brought the coffee. Bunting took it and told her to take away the dirty plate. He said dirty with emphasis and that, too, made him feel puny.

"Want some dessert while I'm eating?" Collins wanted to know. "I tried this pie they got here. You wouldn't believe it by looking at it, but..."

"No. Besides, I'm leaving right after this," said Bunting, nodding at the coffee he had and the cigarette in his hand. He lit the cigarette, the first thing he had done that day with complete concentration.

Collins got his plate and started to eat. Bunting did not watch him.

"I got a little advice," said Collins, "before I tell you the other."

"What other?"

"Later. This advice is from me, not from Saltenberg."

"Thank you. Forget it."

"I'm twice your age and been making out in different ways for a long time."

"Yeah."

"Whereas you, Johnny, ain't making out very good."

"What in hell is that..."

"Not so loud." Collins swallowed something and talked without the howdy voice and the old-codger act. "I'm just looking at you and I'm telling from that. Listen," he said. "Whatever is riding you, Johnny, can't you get out from under?"

"Leave me alone, all right?"

"If you want," said Collins and pushed a forkful into his mouth.

Bunting finished his coffee, but didn't get up. "You said something before. What was it you were going to tell me later?"

"From Saltenberg." Collins was swallowing then and couldn't say more.

"I'm not working for him. I'm not in on anything here. So I don't need his messages." But he didn't get up.

"Well, it's good for you to know, anyway."

"For my own good, of course. That it?"

"Look. Don't fight me. I'm nothing to you, right? Don't fight what's nothing to you, all right? Here's the message."

"I'm sitting here and waiting for it. I'm here..."

"Leave it alone, will you?" Collins sounded tired about it.

Bunting lit another cigarette and then he meant to walk out.

"The deal," said Collins, "is off. That's the message." For one crazy moment Bunting was convinced he could walk out now and, by ignoring the old man, undo all that he had heard. Then it was gone and a very trembling excitement came over Bunting.

"What's off? What part is off?"

Collins saw how anxious Bunting was and Collins felt sorry for the young man. He didn't ride him for finally showing an interest, or for anything like that, but answered him straight.

"He called up, Saltenberg called up and said for me to tell you that he wouldn't need your help any more, that you wouldn't have to go through with anything you had arranged about giving Saltenberg information."

The excitement grew inside and became more and more unfinished.

"Yes?" said Bunting. "And that's it?"

"Why, yes. You mean there ought to be more?"

"Why? Did he say why?"

"The why is, he changed his mind. He's decided he can't bother or isn't interested any more. Saltenberg had it planned something like this, you know, to let Tarpin get going a ways, spend money, and so forth." Collins hunted around in his breast pocket and pulled out a cigar. "And then cut Tarpin down. You understand, it wouldn't be good for Saltenberg's nationwide setup to have somebody sprouting up and messing with a territory. Besides, he might have figured it was good for the soul, slapping Tarpin down. Anyway, he's changed his mind."

"Changed his mind! Exactly what..."

"Exactly this. He's cutting Tarpin down right now, without horsing around. Those orders you sent? They won't be honored."

"Christ— "

"What?"

"I mean, when? When's this going to get to Tarpin, this new plan—"

"Well, figure it out, Johnny. You just sent the orders, you should get your answers in maybe three days. Or you might get the news from somebody else, some guy who thinks he's going to buy from Tarpin and finds out different, you know?"

Collins bit off a piece of cigar, chewed it around, spat it out. "But tomorrow would be the earliest for Tarpin to know. Tomorrow the earliest."

Bunting got off the stool, left money on the counter, and got out of the restaurant without having once looked at Collins again. Collins said something after him, but Bunting didn't hear. The excitement was in his ears, in his head, everywhere inside him. He ran down the street and saw nothing. He had never felt this way before, except one other time. With a dull shock he saw the comparison come to life, the same unfinished excitement that had been his form of passion for Ann, the longing for a girl he could at this moment hardly remember. The whole thing with Ann had been a waiting, he saw.

He ran down the street to finish his hunt. He had waited enough.

Chapter 18

He saw all of them when he got back to the motel. There was Linda at the open door and she made a move to come toward him. There were Tarpin and Jesse, back early, thought Bunting. Tarpin went into his door and Jesse came toward Bunting. Morgan was further away, near one of the cars.

"Where you been?" Jesse asked.

Bunting saw that Linda had gone back into their place. She had seen Jesse come out and therefore would have to wait.

"I mailed the letters," said Bunting. He felt he had to say more because everything was very urgent now. Twenty-four hours—maybe—and it would all break up. They would all go different ways and Bunting would be left with nothing finished, not even last night— "Where's Tarpin ?" he said. "I want to see him."

"Precisely why he is here." And with some kind of theatrics which embarrassed Bunting, Jesse led the way.

"You mailed the stuff?" Tarpin said. He was lying on the couch, and when Bunting came in put his hands up behind his head.

"I did that—" He had to say more, had to bring something about— "and we're off!" His gaiety was artificial and loud.

"Yeah. Sit down."

Bunting didn't know what he was going to say, but he knew he was going to sit and start talking and something would come to him.

"You mailed them?" Tarpin said again.

"That's right. To be out of here eleven this morning and to get there by the three o'clock delivery. And sending it registered, you know, those orders are going to be read this afternoon for sure. Hell, we can expect shipments as early as two days from now. You realize that, Tarpin? We can..."

"Yeah. Everybody's excited," said Tarpin.

It gave Bunting the idea to play up his excitement, and that way to infect the others.

"I got it," he said, "I just got the idea. You know what's gonna happen here in no more than a day or so, do you, Tarpin? Business. Work. And running around and long hours and all that stuff, Tarpin. No time for anything else."

"You really think so, Bunting?" said Jesse.

"Right. Listen. So tonight I'll throw a party. On me! We can— No, that's no good. I'll take the bunch of you out to Miami, do it up right, get me? Hell, four men on the point of starting a deal as big as this deal of yours, Tarpin, hell, four of us out there in Miami..."

"You mean no Linda?"

"Huh?"

"He must mean stag," said Jesse. "That what you mean, Bunting?"

"I wasn't even thinking about it," said Bunting. "I'm just gonna throw this party. I'll tell you..."

"Miami's kind of far," said Tarpin. "Don't you think it's kind of distant from home plate?"

"All right. Fine. I got another idea. You know that place they call Freddy's Landing? Maybe you've seen it from the road going past the lake."

"Looks like a dump," said Jesse.

"Yes, it does, doesn't it? Well, it might look even more like a dump after we've had that party!" Bunting laughed forcefully. "I'm gonna rent that place for the night—you know, private parties accommodated it says on the sign he has—and we can stay right here in the heart of this gorgeous state and have our party. Huh?"

"Tonight?" said Jesse.

"Sure. I'll take care of everything."

"Where you gonna get the women? You seen any good-looking women around here yet?"

"Hell, just bring a date, if you want. I was just thinking of this as sort of..."

"Fine," said Tarpin. "Tonight." He sat up on the couch.

"No liquor either?" said Jesse.

"There'll be liquor, there'll be music—"

"All right," said Tarpin. "Drop it for now."

"Nine o'clock, how's that?" Bunting asked. "That a good time for everybody?"

"Fine. Nine o'clock."

Bunting didn't hear the tone, paid no attention to it, just thought about the party he was going to give, because there had never been anything so important. If he had to do tricks and stand on his head, this was going to be a party. And the liquor heavy. Tomorrow might be too late, but by the time this party was over he would have made his pitch. He was going to get close to these men, crawl all through their brains in a steam of liquor—

"Had a little talk with Linda," said Tarpin.

Bunting looked up. Tarpin was coming back from the kitchen and had a glass of water in his hand. He took a sip from it and then looked at the water inside the glass. "Did you hear me?"

"Yeah—you had a talk with Linda?"

"That's right."

"Well? What is it?"

"I don't know," said Tarpin. "But I'm gonna find out." He sat down opposite Bunting. He put his arms on his legs and stared into Bunting's face. "You know what she said?"

Bunting just shook his head, very carefully.

"She said you came like a real godsend, when you came."

This wasn't all. Bunting kept himself very still, waited.

"You two hit it off right quick, she said, right then and there when she got throwed out of her place."

"Her place. You mean Joyce's place, her sister's—"

"I mean that."

"Well?" And then, with some anger, Bunting said, "She couldn't have said that, Tarpin, because I met her before she had to move out. Now I can prove that, and if..."

"Fine, fine." Tarpin held up one hand, then dropped it back on his knee. "I could have got that part wrong. Not important. Jesse, give me a cigarette."

Bunting had to wait while Tarpin got his cigarette and while he rolled it around in his mouth a few times, without lighting it.

"The part I'm talking about," said Tarpin, "I know how come she got throwed out suddenly."

"I don't get any of this."

"I don't either, altogether, Bunting. And she didn't really get throwed out in the first place."

"Come on, come on, what is this?"

"I'll tell you how Linda put it. She's either real sly or she's real stupid. I never thought of her as being either, but here's what she said. She and me were just talking, you understand."

"Are you going to get to it? Are you..."

"I've been having all this trouble with my sister Joyce, she says to me, so it was coming anyway. But that day, says Linda, Joyce tells me to leave very suddenly, and then John came along." Tarpin looked at Bunting and added, "She said it just like that."

"I don't get any of this—"

"Wait. How come suddenly, I ask Linda. So she says there had been a phone call with Joyce getting some kind of good news, probably, and then, after that call, Joyce threw her out."

"That's what she said," Jesse put in.

"Who phoned, I asked her," said Tarpin. Bunting saw how the man's scalp made a sharp jump. "Then she says: 'I think Saltenberg phoned.'"

Nobody said anything for a while. Tarpin was waiting for Bunting to talk.

"Don't you get it?" said Jesse. "Or maybe you think *we* don't get it."

"Get what?" Bunting said, and then kept saying it a few times while he tried to think this thing out.

"It looks this way." Tarpin sighed and finally lit his cigarette. The filter end seemed all bitten to pieces. "Linda, dumb like most women, didn't know the first thing about phone call, shmonecall, and what it all meant. But then, sly like most women, she figured she'd tell me anyway, tell me this phone-call story to show just how naive she is and just how little she knows about all of these goings-on. That makes sense, as far as Linda goes?"

Bunting was biting his lip.

But you, Bunting, you know what I'm talking about, don't you by now?"

Bunting was suddenly up and yelling. "If you've something to say, say it, for chrissakes. Don't double-talk yourself up to it slow, just say it. If you got something to say, just..."

"I got." Tarpin was sharp now. "I got a suspicion of anything that's got to do with Saltenberg. I want to know why Saltenberg calls up Linda's sister, why Linda gets thrown out of her place, why you show up at just the right time. I want to know about that!"

"Then ask her! I don't know any more than I told you, whether you ask me polite or use a sap. All I know is what you know. I came for a job, I got the job, and I'm trying to do it. How about you and your damn suspicions waiting a day or so, huh? Wait and see how those orders come through. If I'm screwing you up, would I get you those orders? Would I go ahead..."

"I don't know," said Tarpin. "If Saltenberg is behind this..."

"I know, and he isn't! A suspicious bastard like you, Tarpin—"

Tarpin got up and went to the kitchen. He didn't even turn back to the room when he said, "I'll see you at the party tonight."

Bunting left and stood outside the door for a while.

He looked at all the identical houses, he looked at the washing machines that stood outside the houses, and he looked at the gray dust on the ground because it was easier on his eyes than the pink and azure and white of the houses.

It never occurred to him to worry about Tarpin in any of this. It suddenly no longer mattered because, one way or the other, tonight he would find his man. And he no longer felt harrassed and full of discomforts, the way he had the whole morning, but set.

He even knew why: he was rid of Linda.

He lit a cigarette and looked around. Morgan was washing his car. Bunting felt set and secure now, so that the night before and all it had started to open up was no longer a problem. He turned toward the next house, to look for Linda.

"John?" Morgan called.

Bunting turned and waited.

"You looking for Linda?"

"Yes."

"She took a walk. That way." Morgan pointed.

When Bunting walked past the car which Morgan was washing he didn't look up, and if he had he would still not have seen Morgan standing there. Morgan stopped wiping the car, and after Bunting had passed, Morgan didn't start wiping again. He watched Bunting go away, and felt worried.

She had been to the railroad depot and a little beyond that, where the country began with tall grass and with trees which had very large leaves. What she saw had not interested her, nor had she gone walking to look at things. She had wanted to leave the rooms where she was never alone with John Bunting, except for the night they had had. She wanted a while without interruptions, without someone coming in to remind her that she was here as a farce, and John Bunting leaving each time it happened. She would go home now and he wouldn't be there. She would not even expect it.

She stopped on the street and recognized him, and then she was sure he was looking for her. She walked toward him, going faster the closer she got. She felt like running; she wanted him to be looking for her; she wanted him suddenly to laugh.

He stood there and waited for her. She came up and he took her wrist. "You bitch," he said.

She couldn't say anything and she followed him when he walked away from the motel, still holding her wrist. He was hurting her.

She finally said, "John, for heaven's sake—" but he didn't answer and she was afraid to say any more.

Then was a large empty lot before the street ended at the depot, a field with trash and old lumber. Bunting walked off the sidewalk and pulled her along. Then he stopped in the weeds and let go of her wrist. For a while he just looked at her face and she, in turn, saw the sick cruelty building in his.

"You know," he said, "I could beat you and not bat an eye. I could beat you and enjoy it."

"John, please—"

The worst thing was that he had started to smile. He put his hands in his pockets and started to kick at a board, watching himself do it, so that he wasn't looking at her when he spoke. "And now, Linda—after tonight, that is— you're out of a job."

"Please, what in heaven's name are you talking about?"

"The Saltenberg thing is off, I just heard from one of his men—Collins, you probably know him—so you're out of a job. Except for one more, like I said."

Linda put her hands to her face and pressed. Then she dropped her hands when Bunting said, "I mean it. I'm on the level with you."

"What, what? Please tell me!" She was going to touch him but then was afraid.

"So you can relax the act. I know the same things you know about this. I know Saltenberg sent you along."

"No!" she said.

"Why so shocked? You did good, you know. I didn't think there was a human being could be so good like you were. And last night yet—" He said this so easily that it was the cruelest thing he had said.

When she didn't say anything, just stood there and stared at him, he got mad. "Saltenberg called your sister? He called you! What else! Why else did you come along?" Other emotions got mixed with the anger when he screamed, "Why else? Why else would someone like you go with someone like me? Why else?"

He put his head down again and kicked at the board. This time he moved it enough so that the pressed, brown grass showed underneath. A slim little newt appeared and started to wind its body and run. Bunting stepped on it, and the tail came off. The newt got away, but Bunting was already looking at Linda.

"So relax," he said. "The job's done."

Linda felt so helpless standing there that she thought she was going to cry. But her face embarrassed her, her bare arms embarrassed her, and her body under the dress.

"John, listen to me, please try to hear—" This time she did put out her hands and touched him. "You're so wrong, John, will you believe me? Please, don't look that way— You're wrong, you're sick, John!"

"Sick like cement is sick," said Bunting. He pushed her hands away.

"You are, I can't help thinking you are. Because— No," she said, "it's just that I know so little. But I know this now, John. Something is making you sick. I know this now. You're not here for any small, simple reason, for doing some wiring or anything like that. No man would act, would go through..."

"Saltenberg didn't tell you? Couldn't trust you that..."

"Believe me, John, I know nothing of this."

"So I'll tell you," he said. He said all of it low and fast. "I'm here to kill a man. I came here because one of the men in that house back there shot a girl through the head. This girl was going to be my wife, if you can imagine it, and the killer is here and I'm going to see him dead. I myself."

"God !"

He grinned at her and said, "I'm still sick?"

"God—" she said, "yes!"

He then felt like playing a game. He said, "Would you believe it? I'd do the same thing for you. Just imagine, if you can, you and me love each other and we're going to marry. Then you get shot in the head—here, that's where she got it, where you got it—and do you know what I'd do after that? Same thing I'm doing now. Understand?"

She understood everything now, everything that had happened between them. Now she didn't care any more whether he'd slap her hand out of the way or how he might look at her. She took his shirt by the front and, holding it tight, she talked close into his face.

"Listen to what I say, John, and you can't do anything then but believe me. I came because I didn't care. I was in no intrigue with anyone, with Saltenberg or anyone, and when you asked me to come I came because I didn't care. Don't you remember? Don't you remember the way I was ? So you see, I didn't come with *you*, really, but now it's you, I'm with you, and I can see how you were then and how you are now. You were suffering so, before, sick already with this—this *idea*. But now, John, please listen! Now you're sick with it and getting used to it, John ! Will you please try and..."

"Shut up. Just shut up." He stepped back and almost made her fall. He kept away from her, thinking of her as something contaminated, and backed up when she tried to come near him again.

He had the final cruelty already in his mind. He swallowed the dry grit he felt in his throat and he scratched the back of his hand very hard with his nails, the pain distracting him. He scratched, and swallowed, and coughed, and then said, "Tonight I'm giving a party. Hangman's meal. I'm going to find out which one of those three is the killer, and I'm sicking you on that Jesse. You, girl, get it out of that Jesse."

Chapter 19

There was a young woman two houses away who couldn't get her washing machine started, and after Morgan had watched her a while he went over and looked at the machine. He said, "Hi," to the woman, looked at her and then looked down the road. "This happen often?" he asked her.

"Well, no, sometimes. Henry always does something down here, here someplace, with an oil can. You see something there?"

Morgan got down on his hands and knees and looked at the motor under the tub. "It smells hot," he said. "It stopped because the motor got overheated."

"Yes, that's what Henry always says when he comes home."

"Yes."

Morgan got off his knees and looked down the road again and toward the street. Tarpin and Jesse came out and went off in one of the cars.

"You want me to find you the oil can?" asked the woman.

"Sure. Might as well."

"You want to come in?" she asked. "I got coffee."

"Sure."

Inside it was exactly like all the other houses with terrazzo floors and blank plaster walls, except here a few personal items had been added. A framed picture of a man and a boy, some figurines, and a lamp with a rotating cylinder over the bulb, the cylinder showing a waterfall which, by some trick involving the heat of the bulb, seemed to be actively cascading.

"Gee," said Morgan.

"Interesting, isn't it ?"

"You keep that bulb on all the time, daytimes too?"

"I love to look at it. It's Niagara, you know. I never been to Niagara," she said from the kitchen.

"Well, people from down here, I guess, don't go to Niagara much for their honeymoon."

"Oh, I got married in New Jersey," said the young woman. "Here's the oil."

"Thank you."

"Twelve years."

"What?"

"Twelve years married. Would you believe it?"

Morgan looked at her for the first time and thought she was very young. "Is that your boy in the picture?"

"Yes. He's eleven. Would you believe it?"

"I would about him. Not about you."

She liked that and smiled at Morgan. "Here's your coffee."

Morgan took it and sat down by the table which was close to the window. He rolled the jalousie open so he could look out.

"You staying here long?" she asked.

"Yeah. Month, maybe."

"Oh, that's nice. We been here two months already and there's just another family here that's been longer. My husband's with the tax department. That's how come we travel so much."

"Oh," said Morgan. He looked at her sitting opposite him at the table. She had her forearms on the table, crossed under her breasts, and rocked herself back and forth that way.

"You'd think," she said, "it was nice, traveling the way we do. I hate it."

Morgan kept looking out of the window.

"And on top of that, my husband's gone for days at a time."

"That's no life for a woman," he said.

"Oh, I get by."

Then he looked at her and smiled. "I guess you could."

"More coffee?"

"No, thank you. This was fine."

"Okay," she said and got up. She came around the table and Morgan got up too. She took the oil can out of his hand and then put his hand over her breast and pushed herself into his hand. "Okay?" she said.

"Jeesis," said Morgan. He left his hand there but didn't feel a thing.

"Come on," she said. "The kid won't be home till twelve. We got an hour, anyway."

Morgan just stood there. He felt her under his hand now, but he didn't move.

"Come on. There's more, you know."

Morgan looked at her face, out the window, back down at her. He wanted to move his hand but he couldn't. Just his thumb was moving a little.

"Don't you like women?"

"Jeesis—" he said, "I admire women."

"Well, fine," she said and stepped away from him. She had on a housedress and started undoing the belt when she walked away. "Here's the bedroom."

She was shaking the dress off when she went out of view and Morgan could see all she had on was her bra. He looked out the window again and saw Linda corning home. She didn't look good.

"Come on," from the bedroom. "I can't do it alone."

Morgan went quickly to the bedroom where the woman was already stretched out. She was naked now, except she had on her shoes.

"Listen," he said, "listen, uh—what's your name?"

"Fran. How's it look?"

"Listen, Fran—fine, looks fine. Listen, I got to go now. I don't want you to be sore or anything, but I got to go, really—"

"Oh, hell!"

"Honest. It's important. It's got nothing to do with you, Fay, it's just..."

"Fran."

"I'm sorry."

She sat up and rubbed her belly. "When?"

"What?"

"When? How about three? The kid'll be gone at three."

"Okay. Fine. And if your washing machine—"

"Jeesis Christ," she said, but Morgan was already out of the room.

He stood in front of Linda's house for a moment and took two, three deep breaths. Then he knocked on her door and waited.

"Come in."

He went in and saw Linda in back, lighting a cigarette. When she blew out the smoke she said, "Want some coffee?"

"No. No, thank you." He walked in slowly.

She stood very straight, and when she brought out her cup she kept the cigarette in her mouth, which made her look tough. She sat down at the table with the glassy-looking top made of plastic, put her cup down and took the cigarette out of her mouth. She looked up at Morgan, making him feel uncomfortable, though she didn't say anything. She looked away again, drank some coffee, dragged on her cigarette. She did all of this very slowly and with precision.

Finally Morgan sat down. He pulled his chair close to hers, but even then it seemed as if a wall was between them.

"Sure you don't want coffee?"

"Lindy—" he started. "I just saw you come home. I saw you through the window and that's why I came."

"Oh. That was nice of you, Morgan." She even smiled at him, a horrible, flat grimace that came and went very quickly.

"Jeesis, Lindy. You act like you don't know me at all."

"Sure I know you, Morgan. You've always been very nice."

It was almost like an insult to Morgan, though he wouldn't have thought of it in those terms. Linda couldn't have insulted him.

"Lindy," he said, "you never had any real troubles. You always had Tom and you never needed any real friends or anything like that. You know?"

She put her hand on his arm and then took it away. "You've always been very nice. And Tom liked you—"

"He was nice. I woulda done anything for him, any time."

"You were his real friend."

"He say that? He ever say that?"

"Of course."

Morgan took a deep breath. Then he said, "And that's why I'll always be keeping an eye on you, Lindy. You understand how I mean that, don't you, Lindy."

"Yes."

"And I tell you another thing, Lindy. I like your John, too. I liked him from the first, you know that?"

She drew on her cigarette.

"He doesn't act right, Lindy, what I mean is—"

"I know what you mean."

"What I mean is, he doesn't act right, some way, but you got to like him. And maybe pretty soon he'll be all right."

Linda grabbed her dress in the front and pulled it away from her with little movements, as if it would help her to breathe.

"But what I really want to say is, if you got any kind of troubles, Lindy, if there's anything..."

"Don't be foolish, Morgan."

He ignored it. He said, "I mean it, Lindy. Really, you know."

"Of course, Morgan."

He smiled at her, but she didn't seem to see it. He got up, and when he walked by the back of her chair he gave her a small pat on the shoulder. "You'll see, Lindy. Everything'll be all right, you know—" Then she broke.

With a scream and a wide sweep of her arm she knocked the coffee cup off the table, threw the cigarette against the wall, where it made a plop and a sparking. Her head was down on the table now, in her arms, and she cried with loud, angry sounds. Her fists started beating the table and only a while later did Morgan understand what she kept saying. "Morgan, Morgan, help me, God—help me!"

He put his hand on her back, wanting to pat her. A cough racked her from top to bottom, and Morgan could feel it under his hand. In a while her head went down on the table again and she seemed to slump. She lay like that and could only mumble, "Help me, help me—"

He didn't know how, but he knew that he wouldn't leave Lindy like that. He put one arm around her back and one under her legs and lifted her up. She fell into the pose in his arms easily, felt smaller than she was, and Morgan carried her like that to the bed. Before he put the girl down he stood for a moment holding her. He had the most wonderful feeling he'd ever had.

Then he laid her down and took off her shoes. After that he pulled a blanket over her and sat down on the edge of the bed.

"Give me your hand, Lindy," he said.

She moved her hand over and he took it in both of his, holding it there and stroking her hand. "There, Lindy, there—" he kept saying.

She was exhausted, and with Morgan there she became calmer.

"Now tell me," he said.

She looked up at the ceiling and kept her hand in Morgan's. "I haven't cried like this, but once."

"I know when," he said.

"And I remember what happened then."

"Lindy, please. Don't get that way again."

"What?" she said. "What do you mean—"

"You know. Like a zombie."

"Ah, yes." She looked at him and said, "I don't know if I could. Yes I know I could. I can feel it coming again—"

"What happened, Lindy?"

She took her hand out of his and rubbed her eyes. Then she put her hand back in his and kept it there. Morgan thought it felt like a small bird in his hand.

"John," she said. "You know why he's here?"

"I thought— I guess not."

"You know who he is?"

"Who is he?"

"There was a girl who got shot on the street, remember? The time you and Tarpin and..."

"I remember. She caught a stray."

"She was his. His girl, Morgan."

"Christ!"

"Yes. He's here, killing everything in sight and in reach, till he finds the killer."

"Christ."

They said nothing for a while. Linda thought about what she had said, because it was the first time she had put it so clearly, to anyone and to herself. Bunting was killing everything within sight, and when everything was dead, he would have rest. He had found no other way—

Morgan was rubbing the hand absently. He felt worried, and was shaking his head without knowing it.

"Who did it, Morgan? Did you?"

"How could I have—" he said and kept shaking his head.

"It was an accident, wasn't it?"

"Oh," he groaned, "a bad one—"

"I'm so worried, so worried, Morgan."

It brought him back to the present and Morgan sighed. He smiled at Linda. "I know, honey. I know. That's why I'm talking. Why I'm here."

"You know what he's doing, Morgan? A party! He's giving a party!" Unaccountably, it made her laugh, and very quickly the laugh moved into hysteria.

"Lindy!"

She stopped and seemed to sink further into the bed. She closed her eyes and just paid attention to Morgan, to the way he was holding her hand.

"Tonight?" he asked.

"Yes. For all of us."

"Okay, Lindy. I'll watch him. You go there and you just know that I'm watching him."

"Thank you, Morgan. Dear Morgan," she said.

"You know I like you, Lindy, that's why."

"Yes, Morgan. I can't thank you—"

"And John too. If he'd let me. You know?"

"Give me a kiss, Morgan. I want to sleep."

Morgan bent over her face and then he closed his eyes. He kissed her. Then he went out of the room and out of the house.

Outside he squinted under the sun and stood on the gravel a moment. He saw the blank street, which was no street really, just a bare space between the two rows of small houses, and he looked at the washing machine nearby. He went over to it, put his hands into his pockets and gave the machine a hard kick. Then he walked away.

Chapter 20

For a small party, it couldn't have been worse. The room was actually a house-length porch, a sunny place in the daytime, with chairs and tables for the lunch and supper crowd.

They had taken out the tables and stacked the chairs against one wall. Two bulbs hung from the porch roof, making a dusty light. The screens along the lakeside kept out the bugs but let the moisture in. The bugs would hang their legs into the screens and show their bellies.

Bunting had spent most of the money he had left. In order to get the room or porch at Freddy's Landing, he also had to buy the liquor there. It cost more and Bunting bought a lot. Then there was extra for the "party decorations." There had to be party decorations, or no rental. This meant paper streamers hanging in a line along the ceiling and one cluster of balloons with faces on them. There was Mickey Mouse, Minnie Mouse, and the two Katzenjammer Kids. Then, for an extra price, a case of soda and a case of ginger ale. And, for nothing, they had given him a phonograph together with a pile of records. There was a further charge, called a deposit, for broken glasses, records, and balloons. In addition, Bunting bought food in the town supermarket. He bought one bologna, several breads, a jar of mustard and five packages of potato salad.

Bunting was ready at nine o'clock. He put matchbooks under two of the table legs because the floor of the porch slanted toward the lake. He looked at all the bottles and the glasses and hung the bologna on the refrigerator door. Then he sat down.

There was a smaller porch, just big enough for one couch, a table and a swing, which might have been better for his party, but that porch wasn't screened. It had a door connecting with Bunting's party room. They stored outboard motors there, and Bunting could smell the gasoline.

Bunting took out a cigarette and sat close to the railing with the screen. He blew some smoke at a bug that hung there, but the bug didn't leave. It had a yellow belly with dark striped joints. Bunting watched how the belly seemed to pump, first getting flat, then taut. Bunting dropped his cigarette and put his head between his hands. Maybe a drink. Or anyway, maybe he should break the seals on all the bottles. And olives. There should have been some olives.

Something hit one of the bulbs, bumping it several times, so that vague patterns made a movement on the empty floor. It made Bunting feel dizzy and he closed his eyes. He sat there on the long and empty porch with chairs stacked up against one wall, with brand new bottles on the wooden table, and felt the wet draft come through the screens. If it were light outside, at least they could have seen the lake. At least the place wouldn't look so cheap. He felt tired and for a while he didn't think of anything.

They should be here. And if they were, they wouldn't fill the place. They wouldn't change a thing for Bunting.

He got up in such a way that the chair fell down behind him. It startled him, but he didn't pick it up. Maybe some records— Later. He tried to look out of the screen and see the lake, but all he saw was blackness. And then the refrigerator kicked on, making a whine, shaking the floor. The sound made the night an empty night.

He was so tired, he sat down on the floor, next to the upturned chair, and picked up the cigarette he had dropped. He sat like that, his back against the screen, and pulled pieces of tobacco out of the paper cylinder.

"Man! A party!"

Bunting's head jerked up and he saw their faces at the door. Just the four faces through the screen, looking at him.

"I'll go first and try to wake up the host," said Jesse.

By the time he was in, Bunting was on his feet and grinning hard. He walked toward them, swinging his long arms, and grinning at each one in turn. When nobody said anything else he started talking fast, chattering about the weather, about the servants not being there because it was their night off, about the party decorations being almost new, being like new, because the last Fourth of July had been rained out so that the decorations had been hanging there without actually having been put to any use, chattering and talking, with his face stretched painfully into a grin that moved his ears.

"This is it?" said Tarpin.

They all seemed to wait for Bunting to answer, say something clever perhaps, and the silence was thick.

"I would like a drink," said Linda. "Would you..."

Bunting felt almost grateful. He laughed and ran to the table, but Jesse was there already. Bunting laughed again and let Jesse make the drink. He kept laughing about nothing, and didn't look at Linda.

They turned on the music, they all had drinks, and Bunting went around with the bottle. They all exchanged words when they had to and Jesse had a few dances with Linda. In a while it was almost a party, and

Jesse and Tarpin took off their coats.

Morgan kept on his jacket, because he carried his gun. He watched Bunting from across the room, and Bunting had his jacket on too. Morgan didn't let Bunting get out of his sight.

"More, Tarpin? Lemme see you drink up around here." Bunting came up with the bottle.

"I'm drinking the Scotch."

"Oh. Pardon me." Bunting changed bottles and pulled up a chair. He poured for Tarpin and looked around the room. Morgan, his arms folded and holding a drink; Jesse, changing a record and tapping his foot. And Linda. She held her glass and Jesse's.

Bunting turned back to Tarpin. He looked into the man's face and studied his eyes.

"I ain't drunk yet," said Tarpin. "If that's what you're looking for."

Better laugh now. Even make it sound foolish for the suspicious bastard.

"You really having a whale of a time, aren't you, Bunting?"

"Sure. Free liquor—ha ha—free conversation, you know—"

"Got a cigarette?"

"No filter, though. I been watching you, Tarpin, how you chew on those filter ends."

"Is that right?"

"Drink up, man. Drink up." Bunting gulped down the liquor in his own glass.

"You got a cigarette?" Tarpin asked again.

Bunting made a lengthy apology, sounding drunk, and gave his pack to Tarpin. "Morgan," he yelled, "bring our boy here—"

Morgan was there with a light. Didn't even have to finished the cockeyed sentence, Bunting thought.

"A drink, Morgan, you hear? Come on, boy, I'll do the proportioning."

"Sure, John." Morgan stood by while Bunting mixed it strong. He watched Bunting sit down again opposite Tarpin, and then he walked across the room to his own corner. Jesse was explaining about orchestrations and Linda was listening. When it looked right, Morgan sloshed his drink through the screen.

"And then there's another trick you got," Bunting kept on. "You got the ability to jerk your scalp, right, Tarpin?"

"I guess so."

"Come on. Lemme see you do it."

"Later. Too early."

"Too early? Here, let's make it later." Bunting tilted the bottle into Tarpin's glass.

Unless Tarpin wanted the liquor all over his pants, he had to hold still. He held his glass steady and decided that Bunting was drunk.

"I never seen you so happy," he said to Bunting.

"I rarely am this happy," said Bunting. "You wanna know why I'm happy? Listen to this." He leaned over and talked from close. "A surprise."

"I don't like surprises."

"Except this one. You know what I done?"

"Yeah. You decided to have a party."

"You know why, Tarpin?"

"Not so close, huh? I'm getting crosseyes."

"I got it arranged for some entertainment in a while. Real entertainment," he said.

The vicious streak in the voice, Tarpin decided, was because the man was drunk. And he didn't want to hear about the entertainment. "Tell it to Jesse. He'll flip."

"Who just vented my name?" said Jesse.

Bunting grinned, with feeling this time, because Jesse sounded thick.

"Entertainment," said Bunting. "A while later."

"Who needs women?" Jesse reached out and yanked Linda over. "Huh? Who needs 'em."

Linda, Bunting decided, was her old self. She was under one of the bulbs and the light made her eyes look swollen and sluggish. He felt free to look up at her and laugh in her face.

"Change the record," said Morgan. "Come on, Jesse."

For a brief moment it looked as if Jesse were going to resent the remark, but then he put his glass on the table and got busy with records. When he was done and had picked up his glass, it was full again.

"Go away, everybody," said Bunting. "I'm talking conversation with the boss here."

"Your glass is empty," said Tarpin. "Like a real good host."

Bunting had to fill up. Bunting had to make talk and play the clown. Bunting had to keep his eyes on everybody and his mind on everything and most of all he had to keep building up to a harsh pitch inside, which was the hardest of all. In the middle of all the strain he suddenly found that he didn't hate anybody! He suddenly found that he wasn't relating to a single soul in the small party, that they were flat and inanimate to him, and he had no feelings.

"You look a little sick," said Tarpin. "How come?"

"I do? Christ, do I?"

"Like I said."

"The cheap liquor. Whoever got this cheap liquor here..."

"I got to take a leak," said Tarpin and he got up.

Bunting giggled about it and watched Tarpin go out the door. He almost decided to go too, but then went to the screened side of the porch, the side where he thought Tarpin might go. He stood there and stared out into the black, whistling the beat that came out of the phonograph.

"Like that tune?" Morgan said.

"Oh, yeah. Like that tune, Morgan?"

"Just fine, John."

"Look, Morgan, I'm sorry. I haven't been talking to you, but you know how it is, host and all that, buttering up to the boss and all that—"

"That's all right, John." Morgan came closer. "I'll tell you what. You being so busy, I'll tell you what. Just relax there, with Tarpin, and I'll handle the bar, huh? I'll keep an eye on the liquor so..."

"Wait, wait! You sound like you're trying to guard it, man! Don't guard it, man. I want you..."

"Here's Tarpin."

"Excuse me," said Bunting and crossed the room like a host. He looked Tarpin up and down and watched him sit. "Christ," he said. "What you do out there, Tarpin? You're wet all the way up past the ankles!"

"I walked inna stinking lake."

Bunting said nothing.

"Black out there, lemme tell you." Tarpin was pushing his shoes off.

Bunting started to smile, but covered it. He went to the table, picked up a bottle and sat down opposite Tarpin. Then he filled Tarpin's glass.

"So you don't catch a cold."

Tarpin took the glass and threw down a large swallow. Tarpin was drunk.

"Work hard, play hard. You're my kind of boss," said Bunting. He talked much more quietly now.

"Stop soaping me, you creep."

"I mean it, Tarpin. I couldn't handle the kind of thing you must be going through."

"What am I going through, mental pause?"

"You're handling a big venture. You really..."

"Big what?"

"Big deal, I mean. Hell, a million details, a million worries, and everytime something goes wrong nobody to handle it. Just you."

"Nothing goes wrong, Bunting. Get that."

"Watch your glass, you're..."

"Thank you."

"Everytime something goes wrong, I meant by that all those little things, see what I mean? I don't mean big planned stuff, I mean—you know, like that little scrape there before you left town."

"What was that?"

"The scrape. Truesdell Square."

"Oh. Yeah. Never got my hands on those books. No matter though."

"You see, Tarpin? *That's* what I mean. The way you can shrug it off." Bunting looked into his glass and fished for the ice there. He looked very absorbed. "If I'd shot that girl, I wouldn't be calm. I just couldn't be, you know that?"

"A man can get used to anything."

The music stopped and there was just the sound of the needle hissing. Bunting sat very straight, very stiff. The ice was rattling in his glass.

"Somebody play that again, will you, somebody?" he said, without turning. He said it so loud they all looked at him. "Will somebody play that crazy song once more, now, please?"

Somebody did. Bunting didn't know who it had been, but he heard Morgan laughing and Linda was making a remark of some kind. The foot tapping must have been Jesse's—

"Tarpin," said Bunting. He leaned close again, feeling that his spine was now a smooth, flexible curve. "Tarpin, you just underestimate what you can do. Not everybody can do that."

"You got a cigarette?"

"Not everybody can say to himself: me, I can..."

"You got a cigarette, Bunting? Whatsamatter, you got plugged ears?"

"Here's your damn cigarette, Tarpin." Bunting could have been saying, "Here's your morning mail, sir."

"Don't light it. I'll just hold it like this."

"Yes."

Bunting watched Tarpin hold the cigarette in his teeth and a wide, stone calm came over him now. As if all of him had gone to sleep except one thing: his eyes, looking straight at the killer. This now was flesh and blood. This was now no longer an idea in his head, a decision made in his head, but a real live object to feel and to deal with. Right now, for a small moment, wait just another moment, and feel Tarpin all over, with the eyes.

"Did you aim for the forehead, Tarpin? Or was that a fluke?"

"Who, me?"

"Yes. You, Tarpin."

"Aim at the forehead, you say?"

"The girl you shot."

"Hell, I was at the wheel of the car already. I shot in the leg. The guy come outa the building and I got him in the leg. Remember reading one guy ended up in the hospital—or was it two guys—"

"The girl, Tarpin!"

"Oh, yeah. The girl. I seen her drop from where I was behind the wheel. They were still shooting when I was at the wheel. Man, somebody sure got her bad. I'll take a match now—"

Chapter 21

Tarpin had to ask twice for the match, and when Bunting finally lit the cigarette, he saw only a mouth and a face. Everything was flat again. Tarpin was no longer flesh and blood, and he, Bunting, was a puppet.

He got up, went outside, stood by the edge of the lake. The black air was all around him and cold throughout him.

If I don't move now I'll never move again. If I don't feel it now, the way I'm supposed to feel it, then it's like nothing has ever happened. I can walk into the lake and feel that, I can cough and hear that, I can see as far back as the night where Linda—when Linda was real.

He held on to the only thing he wanted to be real, the loss of a long time ago, and in a moment it wasn't so hard.

They were laughing inside. Bunting turned and saw Morgan up on the porch, like a black target. When the angle of vision was right, he could see Jesse and Linda dancing by. Two black targets. They didn't miss him, they didn't look. Bunting, in the dark, felt big as the lake and as inhuman.

"There he is!" yelled Jesse. Bunting had slammed the screen door into the couple as they danced by. "Captains, you know, never leave the sinking ship. Just rats do. Right, Captain Bunting?"

"Right. Right you are, Jesse. Right!" He stopped the couple by putting his hands on their shoulders. He smiled at them. "I got to tell you this, Jesse, how grateful I am you're keeping this girl here sober. She's a terror when she gets drunk, huh, Linda? Remember the time you and me got drunk, back in town?" She didn't follow him, so he reminded her, clear and cruel. "That night in Joyce's room. We spent only one night in Joyce's room."

Linda took a deep breath; otherwise she would have started to cry.

"I wasn't trying to keep her down," said Jesse. "I was trying to work her up." He laughed.

"I don't like you to talk vulgar to me. I don't like it," said Linda.

She said it sharp and irritated. She felt the irritation and tried not to let it get bigger. She looked at Bunting, she looked and hoped he would see her now, but Bunting was watching Morgan.

"Hey, he's coming on just like a cop," said Bunting. "You're coming on just like a cop who's coming to break it up."

"Well, no," Morgan said. "I didn't mean anything like that—"

"Yes, you did. Break it up, you looked like, break it up here." With busy gestures and harsh voice, Bunting now pushed his scheme. "We will, honest. Right now, as a matter of fact. I myself am going over there, where Tarpin is resting, and you, Morgan, can come the same way, where the bologna is resting. With everybody resting up for the rest of the brawl, you two go rest some place, too. Jesse, see that door over there?"

"What door? That door?"

"Screen door, to the porch there. Go rest it, Jesse. I'm gonna be busy with Morgan and no time for you, so just rest with the rest, okay, Jesse?"

"I don't get thrown out, if that's what you're planning. Only rats leave the ship before sinking time. I'll make two drinks," he said. "One for me..."

"Sure, Jesse, sure. Linda is dead on her feet." Bunting watched Jesse run to the table, where he started to make two fresh drinks.

"John," said Linda. She put her hand out, but Bunting had taken a step. "Don't worry," he said. "Jesse's fixing the drink."

"You mean this, John?"

He leaned close and grinned, but didn't see her. "You said I was sick and all that. Didn't you, Linda?" He paused for breath. "You want me to get sicker?"

"No."

"You don't want me to get sicker? Then tell me, Linda, why don't you make me well?" He stood up straight then and yelled, "Here she comes, Jesse!"

Morgan didn't know what to do—none of this was clear or simple. He touched Linda's arm and looked at her for an answer.

Her face was blank, but she seemed ready to say something warm. She just patted Morgan's arm. "It's all right," she said, and turned so that neither Morgan nor Bunting could see her face.

"Here she comes," Bunting yelled.

She walked to the door of the small porch and knew she was very close to giving up. She could feel the safe stupor creep into her bones. Perhaps that was best—

"You see Tarpin over there?" said Bunting, and turned Morgan around by the arm. Tarpin was on the floor by the table, sleeping loudly.

"He's out," said Morgan.

"That's right. He's out of it."

Bunting grinned to himself and held on to the plan. It was close now, and simple. Just two now. Here was Morgan, there went Jesse. Either one would do and nothing else mattered. Bunting saw to it that nothing else mattered.

"I'm now gonna get drunk. Come on, Morgan."

"I don't know. I don't think..."

"Right." They walked to the table.

"I think, John—" Morgan frowned painfully. "I'm worried, John. I'm worried about something."

"Them? Ha!"

"No. Lemme say something, John."

"I gotta take a leak. Just a minute."

Bunting rushed to the other door, just to make the movement. He had to, suddenly. Move and rattle that door.

"No, hell no. First a drink." He ran back to the table. Like a chicken without a head, it went through his mind. It was too quiet. Tarpin had stopped the snoring. Did the swing creak back there, did something rustle?

"Morgan, make music! Come on, you're right next to the damn box!"

Morgan obeyed. He would do this quickly and get it out of the way, and if Lindy needed him she would let him know. Make the music and pay attention to Bunting. The man was a frazzle, didn't know what he was doing—like that bit with Jesse. No more drinks for that sick bastard.

"Put it down," said Morgan, but Bunting couldn't have heard. The music was on much too loud.

"Put what down? This?"

Morgan took the drink out of his hand, pushed Bunting's arms down by his side. The man was like wire—

"Listen, John. I got to straighten out something in my mind. And yours, maybe."

"Quiet—"

"John, you talked to Tarpin, I think you talked to Kuntz that time, and once..."

"Quiet, and turn down that blare, that box there—"

Thick drops of sweat were running down Bunting's face. Morgan had never seen sweat run like that.

"Can't you hear?" Bunting said. "You hear it? God, my head! It can't be in my head—"

Morgan flipped the switch of the machine and the needle swerved with a whine. Then Morgan heard the two voices, harsh, fast voices. And Bunting heard them.

A silence. Then the scream ripped out.

And Bunting, fast as a beast, had a gun in his hand, tore at the door to the porch, had it open.

Morgan never tried for his gun then. With one movement he snatched the bottle, the nearest bottle, and let it arc high and slam down on Bunting's wrist.

The gun clattered down with a noise, there was noise in the dark porch, frantic noise.

How Bunting got Jesse nobody but Linda could see. Morgan could hear his big grunts, three, four times, and then Jesse fell into the light, bleeding and numb.

Freddy of Freddy's Landing thought he'd better have a look at what was going on, but he never got into the lit porch and he didn't see anything but two drunks, Tarpin and Jesse, and one man, Morgan, who was stone sober and told him to beat it, the party was private. Freddy left.

And it was very quiet right after that. The sober man left in a short while and somehow carried the two drunks, both at the same time. He drove them away. That left two others, probably on the dark porch. Just as well.

Bunting had gone down to the lake. He didn't know how he'd got down there. He kept his mind on one thing, admiring his clear-cut ability to concentrate on one thing only: a talk with Linda. He didn't even think the name Linda, which was also an admirable trick of the mind. He thought: the one who had talked to Jesse, Jesse who was one of Bunting's remaining two choices.

"I'm up here," she said.

He turned away from the lake and dimly saw the girl standing by the parking lot. When he got to the parking lot she was walking up to the highway. He caught up with her and walked by her side, down the dark highway.

"What did he say? He talk?"

He couldn't see her nod because he was looking straight ahead. All he saw was a black band, the road, a wall of mangrove on both sides of the road, and the sky.

Then she said, "Yes, he talked."

She was holding her dress in front where it was torn, and one hand was placed gently over the place where she hurt.

"Ah. Getting somewhere," he said. He walked faster and faster so that Linda had to run.

"What did he say? Did he say who killed that girl?"

Linda stopped and wouldn't walk any more. The way he had said that girl was frightening to her—it was so impersonal. The only thing that made Bunting act, made him alive with rage and purpose, was something that no longer struck him as alive.

"Well? Who shot that hole through her head?"

And once she told him it would all be up to him. "It's worse than you think." she said. "Because Jesse saw it clearer than any of them. And later, they even talked about it, all of them who had been there."

"Who? *Who's the killer!*"

"None of them know."

Chapter 22

He sank down on the ground. He hunched on his knees in the middle of the straight road, and after a while he put his hands on his thighs, as if he were used to squatting like that.

It was still night, but dawn would soon be coming up, and she could see him much better. She wondered what he would do if a car came down the highway.

"That's it," said Bunting.

She didn't know how he meant it. She had to wait quite a while before he did anything else.

"Help me. I'm stiff. I hurt something."

She held out her hand and he took it to make getting up easier.

"Walk with me?" he asked her.

"Yes."

They walked and in a short while they could see each other much better. She saw that his face was lined with wrinkles, but they weren't those of a frown, or lines of tension. The gray light made it worse. He moved his mouth sometimes or squinted his eyes—nothing more.

When he looked at her and finally became aware of the scratches and the torn clothes, he closed his eyes, held his lip in his teeth, and slowly moved his head from side to side. Like the rhythm of an animal in a cage.

"I can't ask you," he said. "I only wish I were someone else and could ask you to forgive what I did. It's all gone," he said.

"It is bad," she said.

They walked and he kept his eyes closed. Once he stumbled into her.

"It's bad," he said, "because I think that I'll never be through."

"It isn't over for you?"

"Set like cement," he mumbled.

"I'm sorry, if that's—your way."

"I don't know. I don't know flesh and blood. Just a scheme I made and the scheme isn't finished."

"You feel nothing else?"

"The scheme says it's over when I kill the killer."

She looked at him and wanted to say something to him, but she couldn't talk. He wasn't there. Talk to what?

"John." She stopped on the road and he stopped. "If you can feel anything, John, do!"

"Out of character," he said. "Out of the scheme." He even smiled at the awkward words.

"I know what you did," she said, "to yourself and to everything. Listen to me, John."

"I'm listening. I'm not being polite, Linda. I'm listening." He smiled again.

"A long time ago you had your loss. You know what a loss means? It means you want something back."

"I know. Then comes revenge."

"Your scheme. Your revenge."

"Yes."

"It was easy at first, wasn't it? Revenge."

"Oh, yes. Live revenge."

"How alive is it now?"

He moved his head again the way he had done before, back and forth. "It's a scheme. A flat black-and-white blueprint. Blue and white."

"Now you know why it got harder and harder for you. The scheme doesn't fit any more and it hurts."

"Oh, yes. That's a fair picture. It certainly is."

"John," she said, and put her hand on his chest. "In there, revenge doesn't mean a thing to you any more. It's dead."

"That's why I got a scheme, instead."

"You don't know why it's dead?"

He looked at the sky, seeing how light it was now. "I can't think now," he said. "Let me take you back. There's liable to be a change back there."

She didn't know that he was thinking about Saltenberg's change in plans. He had to keep track of the men back there. They might leave today, after the first mail.

The walk back was quite long, seemed longer because they had nothing to say to each other. Bunting, the way he had arranged things for himself, didn't have to think. And Linda didn't think about anything because she wanted to wait. She had seen Bunting alive only twice when he had cried and when he had beaten Jesse. And both times he had wanted her.

They picked up her car at the Landing and drove back to town. They went through the town and out to the motel. There was traffic on the streets. It was nine in the morning.

Bunting didn't get tense until they swung into the motor court. Then, when he drove up to the back row where they lived, he suddenly gunned the motor, wheeled around hard, and stopped. He rammed his door open and jumped out, cursing hard. He stood there and cursed vile and long. He repeated himself because no new words came to him.

Linda watched him and her face became pinched. "You want me to leave?" she said.

"Leave?" But he hadn't heard anything but the word. "Leave? They left! Those rats left! The cars—"

He saw Linda walk to the row and it made him stop shouting. He went after her.

The door to Tarpin's place was open. Linda and Bunting could see inside, where Morgan was sitting. He got up and came out of the door. Morgan looked bland, as he always looked, but his voice was different. It was worried and frail, and he made no effort to change it. "You came back— Why did you come back?" he asked. He was looking at Bunting.

"They hightailed out of here, didn't they?" Bunting shouted.

"Yes. There was some mail and some phoning. Saltenberg clamped on the lid."

"And they're gone? They're not coming back?"

"No." And now Morgan talked without the half tones and without the worried sound in his voice. He was serious and even cold. "I don't have a car," he said. "They took both of them. Will you give me a lift?"

"You're damn right I'll give you a lift. Where to?"

"I want Linda to come,' said Morgan. "Never mind your things, we won't go far."

They just followed him. They went to the car and sat in the front.

"Turn right when you get out of the gate," said Morgan.

Neither Bunting nor Linda wanted to talk to him. They, didn't recognize Morgan.

"Left at the depot."

"There's nothing to the left of the depot. A lane—"

"Just take it." Morgan hitched himself around in the small space and reached into his pocket. "Here's your gun," he said. "You left it."

"Oh—thanks."

The car rocked and waddled in the overgrown lane.

"Here's good. Pull off."

"Here? Where?"

"Just stop."

Bunting angled out of the lane as best he could and turned off the motor.

He looked around fast, saw nothing but brush.

"Linda comes too," said Morgan. He had never said Linda before.

Bunting was holding his gun. He felt keen and ready.

"In here," said Morgan. He took Linda's arm and helped her across the low ditch and over the wild growth on the other side. Bunting followed with his gun. For a crazy moment he saw himself playing cowboys and Indians.

"Stay here," Morgan said to Linda and then, waving at Bunting, he said, "You stand over there. That's good, by the bush."

He himself took a few more steps and then turned around. They now stood in a triangle, far enough apart so that Bunting had to raise his voice. "What, Morgan? By the way, you have a gun?"

"Yes. Here." He tapped his chest.

"Now what?"

"Now listen," said Morgan. "Just listen."

They all looked at him. He looked small and out of place in the overgrown terrain. He looked softer in the face than Bunting remembered and the black dots in his light eyes seemed very prominent.

"I've worried about this for hours," he said, as if he had rehearsed the words. "I never worry, but I did on this. Linda talked to me, and you, you talked to me. That's how come."

"How come what, man?"

"Because I like Lindy and I have a feeling for you." He rushed over that but talked clearly again. "You found out about the girl getting killed, didn't you? From Jesse."

"Yeah. First straight answer," said Bunting.

"Here's another one."

"About what Jesse said?"

"Yeah. Jesse was wrong. Because I shot that girl."

Bunting was afraid. He didn't know where it came from or why, and in a short moment it would go away. But he was afraid to draw a deep breath.

"I worried about this because I knew something," said Morgan, "except I never thought about it before. When I did, it all came back. Simple. You want to know how it went?"

"Talk..." Bunting was no longer afraid. He was back on the square where the girl lay in the snow with a hole in her forehead.

"I'm a good shot. Trained. I was aiming right for this fellow's arm, and I also saw this girl sort of in line. But I didn't worry about that. Right then

Tarpin comes rushing by, for the car, and Jesse squeezes one off too close to my ear, like so—this direction—and Tarpin bumps me a little." He paused, rubbing his hands. "You get the picture? Okay. That's when I squeezed, and she gets it." He shrugged. "Accident."

"Accident— You—"

"Yes. And I'm sorry, but that's nothing to you." Morgan straightened up and talked very clearly. "Lindy ?" He kept looking at Bunting. "Lindy, this man, he's come far. He had all this planned a long time and I can tell— now that I know why he's here and how it makes him sick—I can tell nothing will do for him but the finish."

He lowered his voice, directing it straight at Bunting, "Kill your killer."

Nothing happened at first. Morgan said, "I have a gun. We start even, John."

Linda made a sharp movement and Morgan said, "No! Don't move, Lindy."

Morgan wasn't half through when Bunting started to raise his arm. He had his scheme, and he had his end for it, and Truesdell Square was as real as the present. He remembered, he tried to remember, but it became harder. He could hear Linda breathing, trying not to cry. He couldn't see the girl Ann on the square but only a corpse with a hole in the forehead. There was a pain, but the sight wasn't real.

Bunting could see Linda crying— He swiveled his head fast to see Morgan. The man hadn't moved, except for his arms which were away from the body a little.

Bunting kept his gun arm the way he had raised it, turned his hand, and the gun fell out.

He watched it drop. The weeds hid the gun and he didn't look where it had fallen. He sucked in his breath and let it out with a deep groan. He looked straight at Morgan and spread his arms.

"I can't," he said, and then turned toward Linda. "I can't... It's over."

He walked to her and held her head close to his face. "I know why it's over," he said to her. "The waiting is over."

Morgan rubbed his hands and looked at the two from where he stood. He watched them walk back to the road, stand there, and look at him. Morgan coughed and walked over. While he walked he watched how the weeds caught at his pants.

He stopped close by and looked at Linda and then at Bunting. But they didn't say anything. Morgan put his hands in his pockets and gave a slight nod. "Good-by," he said and turned up the road.

They didn't answer. He thought Linda had nodded at him, but he wasn't sure.

THE END

PETER RABE
by Donald E. Westlake

Peter Rabe wrote the best books with the worst titles of anybody I can think of. *Murder Me for Nickels. Kill the Boss Goodbye.* Why would anybody ever want to read a book called *Kill the Boss Goodbye?* And yet, *Kill the Boss Goodbye is* one of the most purely *interesting* crime novels ever written.

Here's the setup: Tom Fell runs the gambling in San Pietro, a California town of three hundred thousand people. He's been away on "vacation" for a while, and an assistant, Pander, is scheming to take over. The big bosses in Los Angeles have decided to let nature take its course; if Pander's good enough to beat Fell, the territory is his. Only Fell's trusted assistant, Cripp (for "cripple"), knows the truth, that Fell is in a sanitarium recovering from a nervous breakdown. Cripp warns Fell that he must come back or lose everything. The psychiatrist, Dr. Emilson, tells him he isn't ready to return to his normal life. Fell suffers from a manic neurosis, and if he allows himself to become overly emotional, he could snap into true psychosis. But Fell has no choice; he goes back to San Pietro to fight Pander.

This is a wonderful variant on a story as old as the Bible: Fell gains the world, and loses his mind. And Rabe follows through on his basic idea; the tension in the story just builds and builds, and we're not even surprised to find ourselves worried about, scared for, empathizing with, a gangster. The story of Fell's gradually deepening psychosis is beautifully done. The entire book is spare and clean and amazingly unornamented. Here, for instance, is the moment when Pander, having challenged Fell to a fistfight, first senses the true extent of his danger:

> Pander leaned up on the balls of his feet, arms swinging free, face mean, but nothing followed. He stared at Fell and all he saw were his eyes, mild lashes and the lids without movement, and what happened to them. He suddenly saw the hardest, craziest eyes he had ever seen.
>
> Pander lost the moment and then Fell smiled. He said so long and walked out the door (page 47).

Kill the Boss Goodbye was published by Gold Medal in August of 1956. It was the fifth Peter Rabe novel they'd published, the first having come out in May of 1955, just fifteen months before. That's a heck of a pace, and Rabe didn't stop there. In the five years between May 1955 and May 1960, he published sixteen novels with Gold Medal and two elsewhere.

Eighteen novels in five years would be a lot for even a cookie-cutter hack doing essentially the same story and characters over and over again, which was never true of Rabe. He wrote in third person and in first; he wrote emotionless hardboiled prose and tongue-in-check comedy, gangster stories, exotic adventure stories set in Europe and Mexico and North Africa, psychological studies. No two consecutive books used the same voice or setting. In fact, the weakest Peter Rabe novels are the ones written in his two different attempts to create a series character.

What sustains a writer at the beginning of his career is the enjoyment of the work itself, the fun of putting the words through hoops, inventing the worlds, peopling them with fresh-minted characters. That enjoyment in the *doing* of the job is very evident in Rabe's best work. But it can't sustain a career forever; the writing history of Peter Rabe is a not entirely happy one. He spent his active writing career working for a sausage factory. What he wrote was often pate but it was packed as sausage—those titles!—and soon, I think, his own attitude toward his work lowered to match that of the people—agent, editors—most closely associated with the reception and publishing of the work. Rabe, whose first book had a quote on the cover from Erskine Caldwell ("I couldn't put this book down!"), whose fourth book had a quote on the cover from Mickey Spillane ("This guy is *good.*"), whose books were consistently and lavishly praised by Anthony Boucher in the *New York Times* ("harsh objectivity" and "powerful understatement" and "tight and nerve-straining"), was soon churning novels out in as little as ten days, writing carelessly and sloppily, mutilating his talent.

The result is, some of Rabe's books are quite bad, awkwardly plotted and with poorly developed characters. Others are like the curate's egg: parts of them are wonderful. But when he was on track, with his own distinctive style, his own cold clear eye unblinking, there wasn't another writer in the world of the paperback who could touch him.

The first novel, *Stop This Man*, showed only glimpses of what Rabe would become. It begins as a nice variant on the Typhoid Mary story; the disease carrier who leaves a trail of illness in his wake. The story is that Otto Schumacher learns of an ingot of gold loaned to an atomic research facility at a university in Detroit. He and his slatternly girlfriend Selma meet with his old friend Catell, just out of prison, and arrange for Catell to steal the gold. But they don't know that the gold is irradiated, and will make people sick who are near it. The police nearly catch Catell early on, but he escapes, Schumacher dying. Catell goes to Los Angeles to find Smith, the man who might buy the gold ingot.

Once Catell hides the ingot near Los Angeles, the Typhoid Mary story stops, to be replaced by a variant on *High Sierra.* Catell now becomes a burglar-for-hire, employed by Smith, beginning with the robbery of a loan office. There's a double-cross, the police arrive, Catell escapes. The next job is absolutely *High Sierra,* involving a gambling resort up in the mountains, but just before the job Selma (Schumacher's girlfriend) reappears and precipitates the finish. With the police hot on his trail, Catell retrieves his gold and drives aimlessly around the Imperial Valley, becoming increasingly sick with radiation disease. Eventually he dies in a ditch, hugging his gold.

The elements of *Stop This Man* just don't mesh. There are odd little scenes of attempted humor that don't really come off and are vaguely reminiscent of Thorne Smith, possibly because one character is called Smith and one Topper. A character called the Turtle does tiresome malapropisms. Very pulp-level violence and sex are stuck onto the story like lumps of clay onto an already finished statue. Lily, the girl Catell picks up along the way only to make some pulp sex scenes possible, is no character at all, hasn't a shred of believability. Selma, the harridan drunk who pesters Catell, is on the other hand real and believable and just about runs away with the book.

An inability to stay with the story he started to tell plagued Rabe from time to time, and showed up again in his second book, *Benny Muscles In,* which begins as though it's going to be a rise-of-the-punk history, *a Little Caesar,* but then becomes a much more narrowly focused story. Benny Tapkow works for a businesslike new-style mob boss named Pendleton. When Pendleton demotes Benny back to chauffeur, Benny switches allegiance to Big Al Alverato, an old-style Capone type, for whom Benny plans to kidnap Pendleton's college-age daughter, Pat. She knows Benny as her father's chauffeur, and so will leave school with him unsuspectingly. However, with one of Rabe's odd bits of off-the-wall humor (this one works), Pat brings along a thirtyish woman named Nancy Driscoll, who works at the college and is a flirty spinster. At the pre-arranged kidnap spot, Pat unexpectedly gets out of the car with Benny, so it's Nancy who's spirited away to Alverato's yacht, where she seduces Alverato, and for much of the book Nancy and Alverato are off cruising the Caribbean together.

The foreground story, however, remains Benny and the problem he has with Pat. Benny doesn't know Pat well, and doesn't know she's experimented with heroin and just recently stopped taking it because she was getting hooked. To keep Pat tractable, Benny feeds her heroin in her drinks. The movement of the story is that Benny gradually falls in love with Pat and gradually (unknowingly) addicts her to heroin. The characters of Benny and Pat are fully developed and very touchingly real. The hopeless love story never becomes mawkish, and the gradual drugged deterioration of Pat is beautifully and tensely handled (as Fell's deterioration will be in *Kill The Boss Goodbye*). The leap forward from *Stop This Man* is doubly astonishing when we consider they were published four months apart.

One month later, *A Shroud for Jesso* was published, in the second half of which Rabe finally came fully into his own. The book begins in a New York underworld similar to that in *Benny Muscles In*, with similar characters and relationships and even a similar symbolic job demotion for the title character, but soon the mobster Jesso becomes involved with international intrigue, is nearly murdered on a tramp steamer on the North Atlantic, and eventually makes his way to a strange household in Hannover, Germany, the home of Johannes Kator, an arrogant bastard and spy. In the house also are Kator's sister, Renette, and her husband, a homosexual baron named Helmut. Helmut provides the social cover, Kator provides the money. Renette has no choice but to live with her overpowering brother and her nominal husband.

Jesso changes all that. He and Renette run off together, and the cold precise Rabe style reaches its maturity:

> They had a compartment, and when the chauffeur was gone they locked the door, pushed the suitcases out of the way, and sat down. When the train was moving they looked out of the window. At first the landscape looked flat, industrial; even the small fields had a square mechanical look. Later the fields rolled and there were more trees. Renette sat close, with her legs tucked under her. She had the rest of her twisted around so that she leaned against him. They smoked and didn't talk. There was nothing to talk about. They looked almost indifferent, but their indifference was the certainty of knowing what they had (page 93).

The characters in *A Shroud for Jesso* are rich and subtle, their relationships ambiguous, their story endlessly fascinating. When Jesso has to return for a while to New York, Renette prefigures the ending in the manner of her refusal to go with him:

Over here Jesso, I know you, I want you, we are what I know now. You and
I. But over there you must be somebody else. I've never known you over there
and your life is perhaps quite different. Perhaps not, Jesso, but I don't know.
I want you now, here, and not later and somewhere else. You must not start
to think of me as something you own, keep around wherever you happen to
be. It would not be the same. What we have between us is just the opposite
of that. It is the very thing you have given me, Jesso, and it is freedom (page
131).

And this opposition between love and freedom is what then goes on to
give the novel its fine but bitter finish.

Rabe kept a European setting for his next book, *A House in Naples*, the
story about two American Army deserters who've been black market oper-
ators in Italy in the ten years since the end of World War II. Charlie, the
hero, is a drifter, romantic and adventurous. Joe Lenken, his partner, is a
sullen but shrewd pig, and when police trouble looms, Joe's the one with
solid papers and a clear identity, while Charlie's the one who has to flee to
Rome to try (and fail) to find adequate forged papers. In a bar he meets a
useless old expatriate American drunk who then wanders off, gets into a
brawl, and is knifed to death. Charlie steals the dead man's ID for himself,
puts the body into the Tiber under a bridge, then looks up and sees a girl
looking down. How much did she see?

In essence, *A House in Naples* is a love story in which the love is poisoned
at the very beginning by doubt. The girl, Martha, is simple and clear, but
her clarity looks like ambiguity to Charlie. Since he can never be sure of
her, he can never be sure of himself. Once he brings Martha back to
Naples and the vicious Joe is added to the equation, the story can be nothing but a slow and hard unraveling. The writing is cold and limpid and
alive with understated emotion, from first sentence ("The warm palm of
land cupped the water to make a bay, and that's where Naples was"-page
7) to last ("He went to the place where he had seen her last"--page 144).

A House in Naples was followed by *Kill the Boss Goodbye*, and that was the
peak of Rabe's first period, five books, each one better than the one before.
In those books, Rabe combined bits and pieces of his own history and
education with the necessary stock elements of the form to make books in
which tension and obsession and an inevitable downward slide toward disaster all combine with a style of increasing cold objectivity not only to
make the scenes seem brand new but even to make the (rarely stated) emotions glitter with an unfamiliar sheen.

Born in Germany in 1921, Rabe already spoke English when he arrived in America at seventeen. With a Ph.D. in psychology, he taught for a while at Western Reserve University and did research at Jackson Laboratory, where he wrote several papers on frustration. (No surprise.) Becoming a writer, he moved to various parts of America and lived a while in Germany, Sicily and Spain. His first published work he has described as "a funny pregnancy story (with drawings) to *McCall's.*" The second was *Stop This Man.* In the next four books, he made the paperback world his own.

But then he seemed not to know what to do with it. Was it bad advice? Was it living too far away from the publishers and the action? Was it simply the speed at which he worked?

Fortunately, with his twelfth book, *Blood on the Desert,* Rabe gets his second wind, goes for a complete change of pace, and produces his first fully satisfying work since *Kill the Boss Goodbye.* It's a foreign intrigue tale set in the Tunisian desert, spy versus spy in a story filled with psychological nuance. The characters are alive and subtle, the story exciting, the setting very clearly realized.

My Lovely Executioner, is another total change of pace, and a fine absorbing novel. Rabe's first book told completely in the first-person, it is also his first true *mystery,* a story in which the hero is being manipulated and has no idea why.

The hero-narrator, Jimmy Gallivan, is a glum fellow in jail, with three weeks to go on a seven-year term for attempted murder (wife's boyfriend, shot but didn't kill) when he's caught up in a massive jailbreak. He doesn't want to leave, but another con, a tough professional criminal named Rand, forces him to come along, and then he can't get back. Gallivan gradually realizes the whole jailbreak was meant to get *him* out, but he doesn't know why. Why him? Why couldn't they wait three weeks until he'd be released anyway? The mystery is a fine one, the explanation is believable and fair, the action along the way is credible and exciting, and the Jim Thompsonesque gloom of the narration is wonderfully maintained.

And next, published in May of 1960, Rabe's sixteenth Gold Medal novel in exactly five years, was *Murder Me for Nickels,* yet another change of pace, absolutely unlike anything that he had done before. Told in first person by Jack St. Louis, righthand man of Walter Lippit, the local jukebox king, *Murder Me for Nickels* is as sprightly and glib as *My Lovely Executioner* was depressed and glum. It has a lovely opening sentence, "Walter Lippit makes music all over town" (page 5), and is chipper and funny all the way through. At one point, for instance, St. Louis is drunk when he suddenly has to defend himself in a fight: "I whipped the bottle at him so he stunk from liquor. I kicked out my foot and missed. I swung out with the glass club and missed. I stepped out of the way and missed. When you're drunk everything is sure and nothing works" (page 164).

Nineteen-sixty was also when a penny-ante outfit called Abelard-Schuman published in hardcover *Anatomy of a Killer,* a novel Gold Medal had rejected, I can't think why. It's third person, as cold and as clean as a knife, and this time the ghostly unemotional killer, Loma and Mound, is brought center stage and made the focus of the story. This time he's called Jordan (as in the river?) and Rabe stays in very tight on him. The book begins,

When he was done in the room he stepped away quickly because the other man was falling his way. He moved fast and well and when he was out in the corridor he pulled the door shut behind him. Sam Jordan's speed had nothing to do with haste but came from perfection.

The door went so far and then held back with a slight give. It did not close. On the floor, between the door and the frame, was the arm.

... he looked down at the arm, but then did nothing else. He stood with his hand on the door knob and did nothing.

He stood still and looked down at the fingernails and thought they were changing color. And the sleeve was too long at the wrist. He was not worried about the job being done, because it was done and he knew it. He felt the muscles around the mouth and then the rest of the face, stiff like bone. He did not want to touch the arm.

... After he had not looked at the arm for a while, he kicked at it and it flayed out of the way. He closed the door without slamming it and walked away. A few hours later he got on the night train for the nine-hour trip back to New York.

... But the tedium of the long ride did not come. He felt the thick odor of clothes and felt the dim light in the carriage like a film over everything, but the nine-hour dullness he wanted did not come. I've got to unwind, he thought. This is like the shakes. After all this time with all the habits always more sure and perfect, this.

He sat still, so that nothing showed, but the irritation was eating at him. Everything should get better, doing it time after time, and not worse. Then it struck him that he had never before had to touch a man when the job was done. Naturally. Here was a good reason. He now knew this in his head but nothing else changed. The hook wasn't out and the night-ride dullness did not come (pages 7-9).

It is from that small beginning, having to touch a victim for the first time, that Rabe methodically and tautly describes the slow unraveling of Jordan. It's a terrific book.

There was one other novel from this period, a Daniel Port which was rejected by Gold Medal and published as half of an Ace double-book in 1958, under the title *The Cut of the Whip*. Which brings to eighteen the books published between *1955* and *1960*. Eighteen books, five years, and they add up to almost the complete story of Peter Rabe's career as a fine and innovative writer.

Almost. There was one more, in December of 1962, called *The Box* (the only Rabe novel published with a Rabe title). *The Box* may be Rabe's finest work, a novel of character and of place, and in it Rabe managed to use and integrate more of his skills and techniques than anywhere else. "This is a pink and gray town," it begins, "which sits very small on the North edge of Africa. The coast is bone white and the sirocco comes through any time it wants to blow through. The town is dry with heat and sand" (page 5).

A tramp steamer is at the pier. In the hold is a large wooden box, a corner of which was crushed in an accident. A bad smell is coming out. The bill of lading very oddly shows that the box was taken aboard in New York and is to be delivered to New York. Contents: "PERISHABLES. NOTE: IMPERATIVE, KEEP VENTILATED." The captain asks the English clerk of the company that owns the pier permission to unload and open the box. The box is swung out and onto the pier.

They stood a moment longer while the captain said again that he had to be out of here by this night, but mostly there was the silence by this night, but mostly there was the silence of heat everywhere on the pier. And whatever spoiled in the box there, spoiled a little bit more.

'Open it!' said the captain (page 11).

They open it, and look in.

'Shoes?' said the clerk after a moment. 'You see the shoes?' as if nothing on earth could be more puzzling.

'Why shoes on?' said the captain, sounding stupid.

What was spoiling there spoiled for one moment more, shrunk together in all that rottenness, and then must have hit bottom.

The box shook with the scramble inside, with the cramp muscled pain, with the white sun like steel hitting into the eyes there so they screwed up like sphincters, and then the man inside screamed himself out of his box (page 12).

The man is Quinn, a smartass New York mob lawyer who is being given a mob punishment: shipped around the world inside the box, with nothing in there but barely enough food and water to let him survive the trip. What happens to him in Okar, and what happens to Okar as a result of Quinn, live up to the promise of that beginning.

But for Rabe, it was effectively the end. It was another three years before he published another book, and then it was a flippant James Bond imitation called *Girl in a Big Brass Bed,* introducing Manny deWitt, an arch and cutesy narrator who does arch and cutesy dirty work for an international industrialist named Hans Lobbe. Manny deWitt appeared twice more, in *The Spy Who Was 3 Feet Tall* (1966) and *Code Name Gadget* (1967), to no effect, all for Gold Medal. And Gold Medal published Rabe's last two books as well: *War of the Dons* (1972) and *Black Mafia* (1974).

Except for those who hit it big early, the only writers who tend to stay with writing over the long haul are those who can't find a viable alternative. Speaking personally, three times in my career the wolf has been so slaveringly at the door that I tried to find an alternative livelihood, but lacking college degrees, craft training or any kind of useful work history I was forced to go on writing instead, hoping the wolf would grow tired and slink away. The livelihood of writing is iffy at best, which is why so many writing careers simply stop when they hit a lean time. Peter Rabe had a doctorate in psychology; when things went to hell on the writing front, it was possible for him to take what he calls a bread-and-butter job teaching undergraduate psychology in the University of California.

It is never either entirely right or entirely wrong to identify a writer with his or her heroes. The people who carry our stories may be us, or our fears about ourselves, or our dreams about ourselves. The typical Peter Rabe hero is a smart outsider, working out his destiny in a hostile world. Unlike Elmore Leonard's scruffy heroes, for instance, who are always ironically aware that they're better than their milieu, Rabe's heroes are better than their milieu but are never entirely confident of that. They're as tough and grubby as their circumstances make necessary, but they are also capable from time to time of the grand gesture. Several of Peter Rabe's novels, despite the ill-fitting wino garb of their titles, are very grand gestures indeed.

If you enjoyed this title, you might enjoy the following from

Stark House Press

Storm Constantine

0-9667848-1-2
CALENTURE
by Storm Constantine
$17.95
Fantasy novel set in a
world of floating cities.

0-9667848-0-4
THE ORACLE LIPS
by Storm Constantine
$45.00
Signed/Numbered/Limited
Edition hardback collection
of the author's stories.

0-9667848-3-9
**SIGN FOR
THE SACRED**
by Storm Constantine
$19.95
Novel about the search
for an elusive messiah.

0-9667848-4-7
**THE THORN BOY
& OTHER DREAMS
OF DARK DESIRE**
by Storm Constantine
$19.95
Nine voluptuous, erotic fantasies.

Elisabeth Sanxay Holding

0-9667848-7-1
LADY KILLER / MIASMA
by Elisabeth Sanxay Holding $19.95
Two classic novels of suspense from the
author of *The Blank Wall.*

Algernon Blackwood

0-9667848-2-0
INCREDIBLE ADVENTURES
by Algernon Blackwood $16.95
Fantasy stories that
defy categorization.

0-9667848-5-5
PAN'S GARDEN
by Algernon
Blackwood $17.95
Fifteen stories of
fantasy and horror.

0-9667848-6-3
**THE LOST VALLEY
& OTHER STORIES**
by Algernon Blackwood $16.95
Ten stories for a long, dark night—includes
"The Wendigo."

■ ■ ■ ■ ■ ■ ■ ■ ■ ■